A novel inspired by a true story about the Repatriation of a Mexican American Family by United States government economic and political policies which urged the family to take the Repatriation train to Mexico during the economic depression of the 1930s.

The family, all third and fourth generation United States citizens, survived destitution in rural Mexico where they lived from 1932 to 1937. They challenged the policies of Mexico's political revolution of 1910. They managed to return home despite problems with United States agents at the border.

In this story, symbolism is used to give outward things or actions an inner meaning to express religious insights. The story attempts to answer the question: where was God in the life of Antonia, Fortunato, and their family during the time when they made life changing decisions, suffered ordeals, and sought God's deliverance from their bondage?

Antonia carried in her arms her six month old baby boy, probably the youngest refugee on the Repatriation train. After many years, he tells his family's story.

Santos C. Vega

To Everette Fusthorne,

Hope you enjoy the
story, Best wishes,
Santos C. Vega
1-27-08

Introduction

Political and economic adversity has often challenged the survival of migrant families and workers caught up in immigration across national borders throughout the world. In the United States of America, in particular, the economic downturn in 1929 called the Great Depression coupled with the national and state political policies of Repatriation had a direct impact on its citizens and non-citizens of Mexican descent.

The Repatriation compelled Mexican workers in the United States to return to Mexico and in this way removed them and their families from federal, state, and county sponsored work, food, and health support services reserved only for United States citizens. The Repatriation's social and political net, however, included both Mexican and United States citizens. The estimated 500,000 repatriated comprised not only Mexican citizens, who had lived and worked in the country for many years, but also included members of the Repatriates' families who were citizens of the United States, of two or three generations, and their children, who were citizens by birth. Families decided to stay together and were forced to join the Repatriates to Mexico in the 1930s. The majority of the United States citizens sent to Mexico on Repatriation trains were school children who underwent traumatic experiences in being forced to leave the United States, the only country they had known, and go to a foreign country, in this story Mexico, wherein they had never resided.

This novel is a story of how one family prevailed over lack of rain for their crops; how it survived a plague of locusts; how it suffered from on-going but belated political revolution policies in a rural area of Mexico. How the family survived the ordeals and finally overcame all their social and political problems, including being stranded in the border town of Nogales, unable to cross the border into their own country. In the story, Lorena, through her intrepid role in the scheme of events, during those five years, finally helped her family return home. This unique story is based from the memory of the family that survived the ordeals of both the Great Depression and the political policy of the Repatriation of Mexican citizens in the United States during the 1930s. The story is a creative work; it is not a report on the Great Depression or the Repatriation. This composition is based on a true experience and inspired by a true story based on oral history, memory, and theological insight. Through an act of imagination the story emerged from that experience and given life.

The family crossed geographical, cultural, and political borders from the United States to survive in Mexico. Fortunato, the repatriated father and husband, with his wife Antonia, challenged harsh conditions in rural Sinaloa, and with their children: Lorena, elder daughter; teenage sons Samuel and Jose; seven year old daughter Catalina; and six-month old baby son Santos strived for survival in a rural agricultural area.

Fortunato had been born in the *municipio* of El Fuerte in the state of Sinaloa. At age nineteen, he had left his home; when he returned thirty-eight years later, he found it as it had always been: a primitive area, along the El Fuerte River, in a rural arid valley comprised of several hamlets called Aliso, Bacori, Mezquital, Mezquitalito, a native Indian village, and surrounding *rancherias*. It seemed this isolated area had been forgotten in time and bypassed by Mexico's federal and state government efforts to improve economic, educational, and social life in the nation. It was from such isolated areas that thousands of Mexican citizens, for years had escaped destitution and migrated north to the United States to seek better economic opportunities. Until Mexico turns its attention to its rural and indigenous areas, immigration will continue. Ironically, Fortunato, who feared the loss of his untilled lands to Mexico's federal policies of land distribution, brought his family to this impoverished environment.

Antonia, a third generation United States citizen and her children, fourth generation Americans from Arizona, encountered cultural and linguistic differences that made their life difficult. The rural area where the family went to live lacked a school, a church, and all the amenities of their Arizona home town.

Lorena, an almost ten year old girl, failed in her attempt to stay in her hometown, Miami, Arizona. She and her family, all American citizens except her father were taken in the Repatriation Train. Lorena planned her return home to continue her education in Bullion Plaza School, but she was always confronted with situations that prevented

The Worm in my Tomato

her escape. She did not lose heart, and the story tells how she learned life survival skills; how and what she learned from nature; how and what religious lessons she learned from ants and other creatures.

Samuel and Jose as young adolescents left their high school classes. They struggled to find a place in the economic and social life of the valley. They took advantage of whatever the valley offered and made the best of it, and from their experience they learned valuable lessons. The younger children Catalina and Santos learned from their own experiences of life in the valley, and from their lack of proper food, education, and health care.

The experience of the other thousands of Mexican Repatriates of the 1930s, who have their own story, no doubt, can relate to the suffering and hardship endured by the Vega family. All these stories in turn share some common ground with the true story and experience of other immigrant families in the world, of thousands of immigrant and migrant workers and refugees throughout the world. The experience of human immigration has been repeated in the past and will be repeated in the future. Thus, with sincere appreciation for suffering, pain, and triumphs, and with sympathy for the loss, at some times and in some situations, of basic human rights to inept political governments in the world: this story is offered in unity with all immigrants in thanksgiving, appreciation, and with love to God.

Santos C. Vega

The Worm in my Tomato

The Worm in my Tomato

Dedication

In sincere appreciation, this book is dedicated to my sisters Lorena Marie V. Reade of Phoenix and Catalina V. Valenzuela of Miami, Arizona. With love, my sisters and I, in turn dedicate this book to our family members now deceased: our mother Antonia Carbajal Vega; our father Fortunato Vega; our brothers Samuel C. Gutierrez, and Jose C. Gutierrez.

Community Documentation Press
Braun Sacred Heart Center, Inc., Tempe, Arizona
sanvega@aol.com

Acknowledgments

My sisters Lorena and Catalina told me the story about their experiences and those of our family in Mexico after their repatriation from the United States in 1932. Our brothers, Samuel and Jose, in our collective memory, added unique dimensions to our life chronicle. Memories of our parents endeared our remembrance and appreciation of our life in exile.

In gratitude to my family, friends, and teachers: Special thanks to Josephine R. Vega, Monica Minjarez, Vikki Cervantes for reading early drafts of my manuscript; to Vivian Rivera, Carlos Vega, and all my children for their encouragement; to Hector Ricardo Rodriguez from Choix, Sinaloa for gift of photos of the Rio Fuerte valley; to David Martinez and José Muñoz, photographers, for photos of Miami, Arizona; both sets of photos are now in my personal collection. With much appreciation, I thank Andrew Mullarky, photographer of Kelley's Studio in Miami, Arizona who at one time made available to the public at large his photographs, and my brother-in-law, Vicente Valenzuela, selected and took the photos of the Repatriation train and depot in Miami. His wife, Catalina, my sister, gave me copies of the pictures which are now in my personal collection. Thanks to Blanca Gutierrez Wikstrom for photos related to her father Samuel C. Gutierrez. Thanks to Avelardo Moulinet, graphic artist, who designed and formatted my book. Thanks to Christine Hanson, Gary and Blanca R. Traywick, Arturo Villaseñor, Rosy Vega, and Rita M. Esquer for their sharing information on the huizache tree and its Aztec mythology. Thanks to my friends at Braun Sacred Heart Center: Pete R. Dimas, Abe Arvizu, and David Almendarez for their encouragement. Thanks to Ida Ann Pedregó, Julian Reveles, Frank Barrios, Christine Marin, and Doña Rosita.

Santos C. Vega

Contents

PART ONE Page 11

Year One 1932-1933
How the Repatriation Prompted Personal, Cultural, Psychological, and Theological Decisions

PART TWO Page 134

End of Year One and Years Two and Three 1933 – 1934 – 1935
The Municipio El Fuerte, Sinaloa, Mexico
A Second Repatriation to a native Indian Pueblo

The Worm in my Tomato

PART THREE Page 282

Year Two, Three, Four, and Five: 1933 – 1937

The Theme of the Story

The theme of the story is: "We give thanks to God whose power is revealed in nature and whose providence is revealed in history."

Christian Prayer: The Liturgy of the Hours.
(New York: Catholic Book Publishing Co., 1976), p.866.

The Old Testament gives an account of God of nature and of God of history. Bernhard W. Anderson in his book, Understanding the Old Testament (1998), pages 173-175, wrote: "…Canaanite view, divine power was disclosed in the sphere of nature — specifically in the mystery of fertility." "In Israel's faith, on the other hand, divine power was disclosed in nonrecurring *historical* events.

For Antonia, this story has a theological theme because Antonia lived her Christian faith in a sacred manner: she held marriage and family in holy esteem. For Antonia it was God's Will for all things that happened; God wrote their life story and was intimately involved in their everyday events. For this reason, she petitioned the saints in heaven to join her in obtaining God's intervention in her family's daily needs. Thus, she believed in a God of history.

Lorena learned her spiritual faith from nature in a rural area without a church: for her, God expressed his love in all his creation.

Fortunato prayed for a successful harvest. In this regard, God's helping power was called upon to reveal itself in nature.

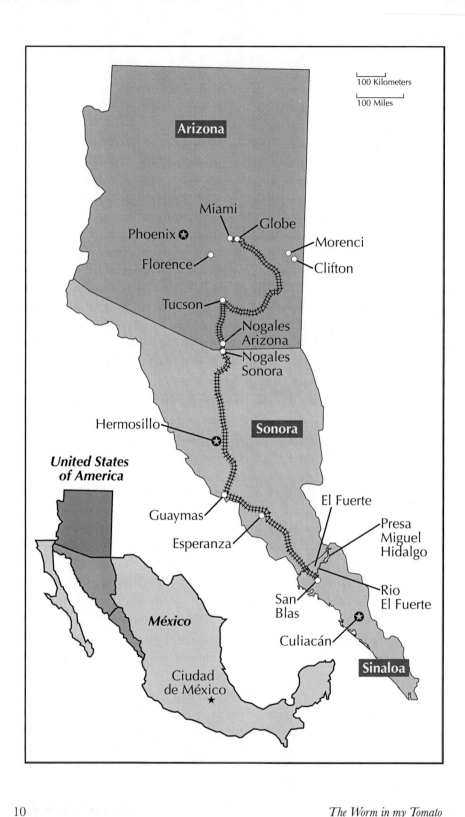

Part One

Year One 1932 ⁓ 1933

*How the Repatriation Prompted Personal,
Cultural, Psychological, and Theological Decisions*

One

Isabel Luna
Antonia seeks advice on the Repatriation

Isabel Luna waited for Antonia, her grand-daughter, who a week before had written a letter in which she informed her that the politics of the Repatriation threatened her family to board a train to Mexico. Antonia and her husband Fortunato would come to visit her today and to seek advice: Their future depended on what they decided to do. Isabel sat by her front room window of her home in Florence, Arizona. She was a short woman of about four feet eleven inches tall, firm of body, strong for her ninety-two years of age, and with her eyes, she could still see far. She was pretty with dark thin Indian features. She waited; watched the early morning light creep up along the blue wall of the sky, from the horizon in the east across the wet fields nearer to town. Isabel looked out the window and with her eyes followed the straight dirt road as far as she could see. She thought to herself, the fifty-three miles from Miami, Arizona was not far, Antonia should be here soon.

Isabel sipped her hot coffee to warm up; she remembered that Antonia told her that Fortunato intended to leave Miami for Mexico because he was not a citizen of the United States, and that the United States government's policy of Repatriation encouraged Mexicans to return to Mexico on a train provided by the political Repatriation program. Antonia had said that she wanted to keep her family together, and she did not want to go to Mexico. In her letter, Antonia asked her grandmother, whom Antonia called by the endearing term, *Nanita*, what to do. Isabel worried that she may not know what to say; she thought about what her neighbors informed each other: the sign of the times in the United States where an economic downturn called the

Great Depression covered the country like a blanket of deprivation and caused poverty everywhere. Isabel had prayed for the hungry people, standing in long lines, who begged for a cup of soup; for the thousands of homeless people who lived under bridges and beside roads and in the woods. Isabel knew that in Arizona, also, there were no jobs, especially in mining towns like Miami. Isabel prayed for Antonia after the mines shut down and citizens sought government support.

It was then in February, 1932 when Antonia planned to come to Isabel's house and ask for her advice. She thought to herself that perhaps Antonia wanted her to take a position against Fortunato and urge him to stay. Thus, Isabel worried and hoped Antonia would not ask her to decide what to do. She slowly puffed at a cigarette and quietly smoked. She waited for Antonia, Fortunato, and Lorena, their young ten year old daughter, to arrive.

Nanita felt satisfied; she had coffee and sweet bread waiting, and soup on the stove. She looked out the window, again, and saw the car entering the road which led to her house. It is a pain to stand up, she thought, as she slowly stood up and continued her work about her kitchen. In her mind, she had annoying thoughts. Anxiety about what would happen filled her heart. She silently prayed to God for a solution that would keep Antonia home.

"Sit here at the table Antonia," Isabel began to pour cups of hot coffee, "Little Lorena, my great-granddaughter, my, she has grown so fast," Isabel busied herself about the kitchen; "Fortunato can sit on this other side of the table. We will have hot coffee and Mexican *pan dulce*, *pan de huevo*, *cochitos*, *empanaditas*, you will see Lorena."

"Oh, Nanita, I just love Mexican sweet breads," Lorena exclaimed; she hopped about the kitchen with an energy only a ten year could have, with a smile on her ruddy face, and her brown straight hair bouncing on her skinny shoulders.

"Thank you Nanita," Antonia, a more subdued adult of thirty-seven years, sat down and stirred her coffee and reached for a *pan de huevo* dusted with cinnamon and sprinkled with sugar, "Umm, Nanita, this bread is so fresh and soft," Antonia chewed a piece of bread; her emotions in her mind and heart, however, prompted her to voice what she had come to see her Nanita, "But I am so frightened about what

The Worm in my Tomato

might happen to us because Fortunato plans to return to Mexico," Antonia said, addressing her concerns at hand; her face cinnamon in color flushed crimson with emotion. She smoothed back her dark black wavy hair, long and silky, flowing over her shoulders.

Fortunato, an older man, age fifty-seven, of medium build and average height, with pale white complexion and light brown hair, promptly defended his decision, "Nanita, there is no work except for the government work program. But I am refused any kind of work because I am not a citizen of this country," Fortunato said, and then drank coffee from his cup. Antonia gave Lorena a piece of Mexican sweet bread. "I have felt the pressure," Fortunato continued, "from the Repatriation political policy of this country for Mexican citizens to return to Mexico."

The wind outside the house whipped the rain drizzle against the window pane. "It is a cold February, this year," Isabel said. "Antonia wrote me a letter, which I received yesterday, explaining how the Repatriation policy of the United States will provide train passage to Mexico for you and your family, Fortunato."

"I feel a draft of air from the outside, Nanita," Antonia edged herself closer toward the wood stove.

Isabel got up to put another small piece of wood in the iron stove and opened the oven door to let out some heat. She thought to herself about how much she had suffered in Mexico. "I want you to know how I feel about Mexico, Fortunato," she said.

The cold air, seeping through underneath the front door, brought in the scent of wet earth and moldy hay from the fields. Isabel secured some rolled newspaper underneath the door to keep out the draft. Lorena, who was reading her school book, *On the Road*, arose from the table to help Nanita push the rolled paper under the foot of the door. "Thank you, *mija*," said Nanita, and continued speaking, "I, myself, would never return to Mexico," Isabel said and she looked at Antonia, sipping her coffee, "I hope my story of my experience in Mexico helps you and Fortunato to make the right choice."

"I know, Nanita, as my mother Manuela told me," Antonia recalled, "that our family's story in Arizona begins when you escaped in a wagon pulled by two oxen from your native Chihuahua, Mexico in 1872."

The Worm in my Tomato

Isabel, who loved company and liked to talk, now told her story:

The rich landowners governed their haciendas in Mexico with strict and demanding ways, at that time, when the rich and powerful *patrónes* were dictators within the boundaries of their own vast ranching domains. Landowners took advantage of their power for their own personal gains. The patrones worked their poor peons in their ranches, sun up to sun down. The workers lacked proper housing, food, and health care. There were no schools for children to attend.

Antonia slapped her right knee and asked, "Why didn't the government or the church change that situation?"

"My daughter," Isabel answered, "If the powerful patrón took a fancy for a particular beautiful woman, single or married, young or mature, who lived in his hacienda; he would sexually abuse her." Then Isabel looked at Fortunato, "Well, who could change that situation?" Isabel raised her voice, "It was true, men with economic and political control, who have abused others, can be found in the haciendas and in governments. At one time or another, these institutions were only for the advantage of the land owners, the rich, the generals on horseback, and the powerful politicians."

The dark clouds outside darkened the kitchen; Isabel lit a second kerosene lamp. "I suspect that in our family conversations, among my own children, there may have been a rumor or two about me, how their Nanita, escaped from such a situation in the hacienda of some powerful hacendado."

Fortunato smiled, and said, emphatically, "That was in 1872, Nanita; Mexico today is different; it is safe, progressive." He glanced at Antonia, "I must go to Mexico and farm the lands my father bequeathed me," Fortunato drank his coffee. "If I don't cultivate *El Potrero*, the federal government may either claim them as uncultivated lands or assign the lands to a native Indian pueblo." He stood up and walked about the small kitchen. " My sister Tila in her letter told me that the federal soldiers, just last month in January of this year, shot my brother Oton when he protested their fencing in of his property.

I should go to Mexico and help preserve our family lands," Fortunato wiped his eyes with his handkerchief. "Land laws in Mexico may cause our family great loss; besides, cultivation of my lands is the only way Antonia and our children can survive the Great Depression." Fortunato sipped his coffee and added, "I and my family, without a doubt, must make a sacrifice to survive by escaping known dangers and seeking opportunities for success and a better life: we must not fear the unknown, but work in faith, hope, and love for our family.

"I, too, have grieved the death of Oton with you, Fortunato, but I am not so sure farming is what you should do,"Antonia said firmly, "You have never farmed. You have provided for our family from your managing the card games at Limonada's Pool Hall and from your winnings from gambling."

Isabel said, "I am sorry to hear about the death of your brother Oton," and she put another pot of coffee on the wood stove. She intended to complete her story, and she said:

> In the dark of night and in the least of time that it took to wake my two young sons, Jose Maria and Stanislao, and hitch a team of oxen to a wagon, we escaped from the agricultural hacienda in northern Chihuahua. We made our way to Clifton and Morenci, Arizona.

Lorena showed interest in the story. She asked, "How did you escape, Nanita?"

Isabel smiled at Lorena, and continued her story:

> We scurried across the border in Juarez, Mexico. Stanislao poked the oxen's rump with a long stick; the oxen quickened their pace, kicked up the dust and pulled our wagon across the border into the United States.

Lorena giggled and coughed as she almost gagged with the bread in her mouth. "Lorena, be careful and don't choke with your bread," Antonia commanded.

Isabel continued her story:

The Worm in my Tomato

The night was black, indeed. The moon must have died that night and buried itself into the Gulf of California. Heavy heat of summer clung to us all, and the oxen's backs glistened wet in the dim starlight. We stumbled past the dry fields. The blackness as a blindfold constrained our eyes, the taste of wet grass soured our mouths, the heavy odor of death gagged our throats, and aborted harvest's odor of decay suffocated our breathing: we struggled along the path over the rough rutted road. My two sons prodded the oxen as they pulled the wagon over the winding dirt road's heavy stones and clutching sand for the nine-hundred miles of numbing chill by night and scorching heat by day. With our teeth full of sand grit, our mouth dry, our ears tortured by the never ending drone of squeaking wheels, and our skin itching from mosquito bites: we pushed on to Arizona; the wind was not at our back.

"Nanita, you were a real pioneer that crossed the deserts and skirted the mountains," Antonia said and smiled joyfully.

"Yes, that is correct, Antonia," Isabel added, "But not only me, all Mexicans that settled the southwest since the late 1500s were pioneers."

They all drank coffee with milk and they enjoyed the Mexican sweet bread. The kitchen was warmer, now. "My family and neighbors always described me as tough as an ox and smart as a fox, but I was, as you know, a petite Mexican Indian woman with a heart shaped face," Isabel said.

"Her friends always remarked about Nanita's tight smooth cinnamon colored skin, without wrinkles, and Nanita's small twinkling dark almond slanted eyes." Antonia said to Fortunato, and then to Isabel, "You have not changed a bit over the years, Nanita."

"Thank you, Antonia."

Fortunato, sitting on the edge of his chair, his right leg crossed over his left knee, with his right foot shaking up and down, with forced respect and patience had listened to Isabel, but anxious to explain his desire to return to Mexico, said "That reminded me of when I ran away from home, from my father who wanted me to be a farmer. I was nineteen years old, then, anything but hard work in the fields. Now I want to return and farm my lands that my father left for me, to honor my father in a way," Fortunato said, and then seeking to justify himself asked, "What was your tribe, your people, Nanita?"

The Worm in my Tomato

"Where my tribal ancestors came from to Mexico during the dawn of some forty thousand years ago, only God knows for certain," Isabel answered.

"Nanita, we your grandchildren, in later years, considered you and your sons and daughters, a pioneer family that came from Chihuahua to the Morenci copper mining area in Arizona," Antonia said.

"We came to an area called 'Las Carpas' because there were no houses, only tents, and we all lived under the tents; before it was named Morenci." Isabel wiped the top of the table with a dish towel. "My sons Stanislao and Jose Maria, young rough miners, came to labor in the mines of Clifton and Morenci." Isabel offered Fortunato more coffee, "The soup will be done and ready to eat for lunch," Isabel continued her story, "We did not consider ourselves pioneers or whatever; we knew we were hungry and we were willing to work. I set up a boarding kitchen iron wood stove and cooking utensils under a canvas tent. I, in less time than two sunsets, was in business making lunches for thirty hungry, tough miners. One thing, in truth, to help earn a living: men did not like to cook their meals, or wash their clothes for themselves. So in less time than it takes to milk a cow twice, I was in business. I kept the miners working. I also washed dirty clothes and ironed shirts," Isabel said.

"I am not cold now, Nanita, it's nice and warm in your kitchen," Antonia said.

"Yes, Antonia, the thick adobe walls of these houses in Florence keep the rooms comfortable all year around."

"What happened to your sons, Nanita?" Fortunato wanted to know.

"They worked in the mines," Isabel said; her eyes welled up with tears, "They left the area; Mexican miners worked hard but were paid less than other workers. They only brought home $2.96 per day or about $30.00 paycheck every two weeks."

"What happened over the years before I was born, Nanita?" Antonia asked.

"Well, Antonia, that is another part of my story that I will tell you, briefly."

Isabel told her story:

The Worm in my Tomato

During these years of hard work and settling in, I met Mr. Sylvestre Granado, your grandfather. He was slight in stature, prim, cordial man with a serious demeanor. I never knew for sure where he worked, but he never lacked for money, and provided for himself, quite well. He courted me; in a short time we married. Then, Manuela your mother was born; she was a beautiful baby born in 1880 in Clifton, Arizona. Manuela quickly grew up into a strong willed and hardworking young lady. She helped me with the boarding house, the kitchen, and the washing.

"Tell me more about my grandmother please, Nanita," Lorena asked.

Oh, Lorena, your grandmother, Manuela, was a strong girl, with long dark braids, and flashing black eyes. Manuela did not stay single for long. She met a miner named Jose Carbajal and within a year or so they married. Jose was a quiet prayerful man. He practiced Christianity. During some times, when he and Manuela stayed in my house, I observed that he prayed the rosary after work in the silence of night. But at other times, he conversed with other prayerful men, friends of his who came to visit, who appeared to do a type of singing prayer. I wondered if he was also of the Jewish faith and if those men were Sephardi Jews by way of Spain.

"Sephardi Jews from Spain came to Chihuahua, Mexico," Fortunato said.

"Tell me about my mama, now, Nanita, please," Lorena requested.

All right, Lorena, your grandmother Manuela's first child, Antonia, was a ruddy girl with light reddish brown hair, born on June 13, 1895, in Morenci. Two years later, Manuela brought into light a second child; he was a cute chubby brown boy with thick black hair; Jose and Manuela named him, Tomas. In later years, Antonia lived with me, I helped raise her; she helped me in our boarding house kitchen in Morenci, until she married and went to live in Miami.

"You see, Nanita?" Antonia said, "That is why I don't want to

The Worm in my Tomato

leave Arizona and go live in Mexico; I will lose my heritage."

"That's why we must go to Mexico," Fortunato emphasized, "The heritage of Arizona came from Mexico. Besides, we have lands there and my father's big house in which we can all live."

"Through hard work, Nanita, you and my mother helped numerous miners to contribute to the copper industry of Arizona: by keeping them well-fed. I felt that with your family, during your long life, in combination with thousands of other Mexican pioneering families: you contributed to the growth and development of the state of Arizona," Antonia said. But glancing toward Fortunato, she said, "That is why, Fortunato, we must remain in Arizona and continue our contributions and build a future here for our children."

"Did your sons stay in Morenci?" Fortunato asked Isabel, and ignored Antonia for the time being. He thought that perhaps they had returned to Mexico.

"My two sons, God bless them, were so handsome, with dark Mexican Indian features." Isabel got up slowly with much difficulty to stir the soup. "Jose Maria and Stanislao, however, went on to live their own life. I lost contact with them, and I don't know what finally happened to them." Isabel sat down, "I decided to come live in Florence, an agricultural community, as you see, far different from the copper mining towns. But, I am happy here, not far from you, Antonia."

"That is why I want to stay in Miami, Nanita, to come visit you now and then," Antonia said.

"We don't come too often," Fortunato said and added, "Wish we could, but most important, we have to live where we can make a living and support our family."

"You are correct, Fortunato, you live where you can support your family and where you can keep your family together." Isabel agreed with Fortunato, but then added, "Florence has a wonderful church, Our Lady of the Assumption. In a short time, I made many prayer friends, with whom to visit. We pray novenas for the souls of deceased family members and friends, just like I did in the past, with other women, in Morenci."

"It is so important to live in a place that has a church to attend religious services," Antonia said, and added, "A town also needs social places like where we can go to dances and movies, and a town needs schools for our children." Antonia looked at Fortunato and said, "I wonder if there are churches, theaters and schools in rural El Aliso where you want to take us, Fortunato."

"You are correct, my daughter," Isabel agreed with Antonia. "Florence, even if it is such a small town, provides all that families need; Florence is a community where people help each other," Isabel said.

With tearful eyes, Antonia sat quiet, thinking; she wished she could ask Nanita for advice; Antonia again wanted to ask Nanita: what should she do? How to convince her husband to stay; she wished her Nanita would tell them outright what to do. Antonia wrung her hands in frustration; she needed to decide if either she should stay here and let Fortunato go by himself or should she make the journey with her family to Mexico: most important to her was to keep her family together.

Fortunato rubbed the back of his neck, perplexed, he was thinking whether he should either abandon his children in Miami and go to Mexico by himself, or take his own three children to Mexico and leave Antonia in Miami with her two boys.

Isabel calmly set the table ware, "Serve yourselves and let your hot soup cool down some." She sat down and again told her story, "We are Arizonans; this is our land. Why should we cross borders? Mexico has not changed from the time when I escaped the hunger and misery." Isabel sipped her coffee. She softly blew over her soup to cool it. "Antonia," Isabel looked her straight in the eye; Isabel then also looked at Fortunato with a penetrating look, as well, "If my sons and I survived poverty and hunger, why shouldn't you both do the same, here in Arizona?"

Isabel felt she had gone too far in telling Antonia and Fortunato what to do, but she thought that she had only advised Antonia and Fortunato from her Christian cultural beliefs. She knew that the decision of whether to stay or cross the border into Mexico and of how to survive the Great Depression and the Repatriation would have to be made by them. "If you, Antonia and Fortunato stay, I will help you all I can; even if I am ninety-two years old. Now, there must be something I can do. If you leave, my heart will be broken because I probably will never see my Antonia, again. How long will you be

The Worm in my Tomato

gone? Will you be gone forever? No, no, Arizona is your home." Isabel was beside herself, having trouble believing what she had said; she had done what she at first had intended not to do. She cried softly and tears ran down her dark cheeks.

"This is a difficult decision, Nanita," Fortunato said.

"You know, Fortunato, when I was born in 1839 all of Arizona was Mexico." Nanita dried her eyes with her dish towel. "The United States took the land by force of arms in the war of 1846; but it was the government of Mexico that lost the war and the land, but not us, the people, there is a difference." Isabel dried her eyes, again, this time with her handkerchief, "I tell you, Antonia, this is yet our land because we live here. We are Mexican and my ancestors have been here in America since forty thousand years ago." Isabel stood up and looked out the window at the long shadows stretching down the road and over the fields. "Antonia and Fortunato, I only suggest that you stay here and fight the Great Depression and the Repatriation." Isabel sat down and spooned up some hot soup.

"But, Nanita," Fortunato responded, "I am not a citizen and the laws will make it difficult for me to work here; that is why I want to leave. Also, the United States federal and state governments are pressuring Mexican citizens to return to Mexico, that is the purpose of the Repatriation."

"I do not know much about this Repatriation law, Fortunato, but I do know Christian faith. A family must always stay together, no separation and no divorce." Isabel looked at Antonia and said, "A Christian wife must support her husband that is, carry her cross, by keeping the family together; remember what Saint Paul said, Antonia."

Fortunato squirmed and massaged his left arm. Lorena chewed on a piece of meat. Antonia took a piece of tortilla, and Isabel continued speaking, "A husband loves and protects his wife, no separation." She turned to look at Antonia and held her hand in her's, "You pray and decide what to do, you and Fortunato." Isabel regarded both of them with tenderness, "But, both of you, think it over carefully. What will happen to your children? How will your family survive?"

Both Fortunato and Antonia sat in silence with a determined look in their face; their eyes stared over empty soup bowls. Antonia's eyes welled with tears and Fortunato lowered his head for a time. Both seemed to want to keep the family together and respect and love each other.

Isabel began to clear the table of dishes, "Does anyone want more soup?"

"The soup was delicious, Nanita," Lorena said.

Fortunato and Antonia both nodded their heads in ascent, "Yes, very good soup, Nanita," Fortunato agreed. "What about my mother-in-law Manuela, when she lived with you in Florence, Nanita?" Fortunato asked.

"Manuela worked hard in helping me with the boarding house in Morenci and she worked very hard with her own boarding house in Miami. But Manuela became ill, however, when she came to live with me in Florence," Nanita answered.

Antonia said, almost crying, "I hate to leave all my family history buried here in Arizona, Nanita," Antonia whispered and moved her head from side to side as if saying 'no'.

"Well, Antonia, again, I will lose my family." Isabel said, "I will miss you if you take that journey to Mexico, but the decision can only be yours and Fortunato's. I only hope that what ever you do, that in the end, you, Antonia, and Fortunato and your children will be together, all of you, with God in your hearts."

"It's the terrible economic situation, Nanita, and the racist Repatriation government policies, Nanita, that forced my decision. Already, all over this country, families of Mexicans can no longer survive, there is no work; they have returned to Mexico. My hope and prayer is to be successful in raising crops in my land, Nanita, and support my family," Fortunato said.

"Don't worry, Nanita, Fortunato and I will work together, but we need to decide yet, what is the best decision." Antonia's eyes implored again from Isabel for an answer, "What do you think we should do?" She asked again, "Tell us what to do."

"No, you must make your own decision; think about your situation carefully, Antonia. Remember my story." Nanita ambled to the stove and served herself another cup of coffee, "I believe, in my time, that God called me to escape the abusive hands of the hacendado. It may be, now, that God has come to our immigrant community and is calling

　　　　　　　　　　　　　　　The Worm in my Tomato

it to return across the border; to escape an abusive situation; its work has been done, and like waves of the ocean that come and go for the good of all, the Mexican worker must leave." Nanita sat down at the table, too tired to stand up on her feet for too long. "God is the author of our life story," Nanita said, "I have told my story to you again, it should help your heart find the right answer to your questions." Isabel sipped her coffe, and then she stood up slowly and walked to Antonia and hugged her, and she said, "Please, Antonia, you should not depend on me to make the decision for you; please don't ask me again; you must trust in God, have faith, and do not fear the unknown in the future, perhaps now, it is your turn; God may be calling you on this journey; carry your cross with faith."

Standing:
Antonia Carbajal Vega
Born June13, 1895 in Morenci, Arizona.
Daughter of Manuela
G. Carbajal and Jose Carbajal.
Married Fortunato Vega, 1920 in
Miami, Arizona.

Manuela Granado Carbajal
Born 1880 in Clifton, Arizona;
Daughter of Isabel Luna Granado
and Sylvestre Granado;
Married Jose Carbajal; Mother of
Antonia and Tomas Carbajal.

The Worm in my Tomato

Antonia
How could I leave my deceased family members in Arizona?

Antonia, Fortunato, and Lorena left Isabel after she blessed them for a safe return to Miami. When they left Isabel's house, Antonia felt emotionally drained and in a confused state of mind. What was she to do? She wondered: many thoughts raced through her mind because she knew that she and Fortunato must decide to go or to stay or who would go and who would stay? Fortunato had not said that he might leave without her and take their two girls, Lorena and Catalina, and Santos, their baby, with him to Mexico, but that possibility, Antonia knew, was not impossible. Her mind swirled in worry; she tried to shake the chills from her cold body, and her sweating hands felt cold. Antonia's emotions were at a high fever pitch. She thought that Fortunato must explain what he meant to do; she certainly intended to keep her family together, including her two boys, Samuel and Jose, from her previous marriage.

Fortunato married Antonia shortly after she became a widow, and Antonia knew that Fortunato, at the time, had accepted her children as his own. She remembered how Fortunato loved her and accepted her children, she felt certain that Fortunato had no intention of separating their family into groups. But if Fortunato tried to separate the family, she was determined not to allow that to happen. Isabel, herself, had pleaded with both of them that no matter what they did, to keep the family together. Antonia wanted to think out her decision carefully; she thought of how to plan with care; and at once she was determined to have a serious talk with Fortunato. She wanted to convince Fortunato not to return to Mexico and not to take their family to live and possibly die in a faraway place. But most of concern to her was that she did not want Isabel to die during the time she would be living in Mexico. No, Antonia felt that she simply could not bear the role of being *La Llorona* in a foreign soil, and she all the more desired with all her heart to convince Fortunato to stay.

The next day after they visited Nanita, Fortunato and Antonia sat around the kitchen table; they slowly drank a cup of coffee. The day, bleak and dreary, cast a dark reflection through the kitchen glass window. Outside, a chilly wind blew loudly, and the scent of wet earth from a distant rain permeated the house whenever the children opened the front or back door.

"Fortunato, I can not bear losing my family, if you were to take them to Mexico." Fortunato leaned toward Antonia as if he wanted to hear her every word. "There is a reason for my worry; my family has lived in a shadow of death; four of my children have died. To me life is a mysterious joy mixed with tragedy," Antonia said.

"I know Antonia, and this is why you have fear of moving to Mexico." Fortunato drank from his cup of coffee. "You find it hard to think about it, the death of our children, what with your mother being a healer, a *curandera*, and your grandmother being a mid-wife, a *partera*, and both being prayerful women, who prayed day and night their novenas and their rosaries for our children, but it did not help keep your daughter Toni from dying. She could not be healed from typhoid fever; no amount of prayer helped. Both of us found it hard to accept Toni's death in the Gila County hospital in Globe."

"What makes it so bad for me, is that Toni died barely last year, only a year ago, can you understand that?" Antonia turned aside and yelled at Lorena, "Lorena, tell the boys to keep the door closed, the cold air is coming in, and to keep quiet, Santos is sleeping."

"Yes, I know. That year in Miami, the typhoid fever epidemic caused many deaths, but we must get past our sorrows and go on with our life, Antonia."

"But, again, I have had to relive a similar incident in my past. It was the same, as when my other daughter, Catalina Gutierrez, my first Catalina, daughter of my first husband, Samuel, died. She also died young, in 1920. I had to overcome my sorrow and go on with life, so I know I can do it, but I hate to leave all my family buried here," Antonia said.

"I am sorry that you have suffered so much, with so many deaths in your family, over a few years. But I have grieved with you, as well, after the death of our own children, and I have also mourned the death of our parents, yours and mine. I yet cry when I think of my brother Oton, shot last month by federal soldiers for protecting his lands against government take over; but we must plan for our future, Antonia, and Mexico at this time offers me more opportunity to support our family."

"So it was with my other children who died, the mysterious invisible events of death silently sneaked in again, cold and miserable, through the cracks of our dusty house, along with the smelter smoke, and took our baby twin daughters, Maria Socorro and Maria de Jesus, to become little angels in heaven. They, your heart and soul, Fortunato, remember, yet, neither you with your poetic lamentations, nor Nanita with her prayers, saved them. They died as babies. I could cry no more, there were no more tears left in my eyes to be pressed out by sorrow," Antonia said. She walked toward the window to look outside. "It is so cold, today, and our neighbor down the street, Mrs. Cota, is ill with a cold. I should take her some soup." Antonia returned to the table, "I can not help it, Fortunato, but I remember each of my babies who died, now gone forever, and wonder what may have been; I dream of them at times."

"I remember them, too, but what is the point of continuing to grieve? We must let go, and place them in the hands of God; remember that according to the Christian teaching, and you should know, Antonia, those who die continue to live in a spirit world with God, and yet remain with us." Fortunato spoke louder and pronounced each of his words in a more definite tone, "What does this have to do with our making the decision of staying in Miami or going to Mexico?" Fortunato, like a stallion, considered the Repatriation's portending danger and was eager to escape.

"For me, it is very important to keep our personal family history; I don't want to leave our heritage buried here in Miami," Antonia responded.

"I understand, Antonia, but you must see that because of the economic situation in this country, Mexicans who are not citizens are coerced to return to Mexico; yes, compelled to climb aboard Repatriation trains and taken to Mexico. I myself have not been able to find work; my card games at Limonada's have ended, no one has any money." Fortunato continued talking as he walked to the stove and poured himself another cup of coffee. "The laws of the United States refuse me government unemployment services. The Repatriation policies of the federal and state governments make it difficult for Mexicans to make a living here, don't you see them shuffling about the empty streets." Fortunato looked at Antonia. "I think you have two choices, Antonia, you can choose to go with me to Mexico, or you can choose to stay here in Arizona. You and our children are United States citizens, you can go or stay, and if you stay, you will be eligible for government help."

"I want to stay here for the benefit of our children, our family history, our legacy, and for the conveniences offered by the church, schools, stores, and for other reasons like that," Antonia said.

"I have no choice, I must go; I have lands in El Aliso, Sinaloa, bequeathed to me by my father, Eudoro. We have a place to live in my father's big house, and there I can grow and market agricultural crops, in this way support my family. What future do we have here in this country with its Great Depression, the mines closed, and there are no jobs." Fortunato stood up and paced about the kitchen like a caged tiger.

"How can I leave, Fortunato, when part of me is buried here in the cemetery, I will not be able to visit my family, especially not during All Souls Day, *El Dia de Los Muertos*." She began to wash some lettuce and tomatoes.

"Antonia, please, don't play the role of the *Llorona*, the crying woman of the Mexican legend; the *Llorona* who went about crying for her lost children, searching for them in canals, rivers, and seas, wherever they may be, after the Spanish invasion had destroyed their villages. Our children and other family members who have died will be safely buried here in Miami. We must let go and place them in the hands of God." Fortunato, feeling anxiety, pleaded, and again like a caged tiger paced back and forth about the kitchen.

Antonia, while cutting lettuce and slicing tomatoes, looked out the window at the drizzle peppering the kitchen window.
"Death should not be the focus on which we base our decisions, Antonia, but rather we must concentrate on keeping life and finding a better future for our children," Fortunato said as he sat down again.

"I agree, but the reality of death was a central focus of our life in 1931. Last year nine members of our family died. Even my mother

The Worm in my Tomato

Manuela, a *curandera*, a healer, who had healed many sick and poor women, died. My father, Jose, also died in the same year. It was like if my mother Manuela did not want to cross the great divide alone. How can I just up and leave my family behind so recently departed from my life? Antonia said, raising her voice. "What if Nanita dies and we are not here, think of that," she continued, "In addition, Fortunato, I don't want to die in Mexico; I don't want to be left alone, buried in Mexico. Our children will surely return to their country of birth. I really think they will return and leave us in Mexico, dead and buried." She glanced at Samuel and Jose, who were entering the house from playing in the front porch, and said, "Please, boys, keep that door shut."

"Let's talk about life, Antonia, remember that there was, however, one light of joy that came into our hearts. Our baby boy Santos was born on September of last year, yes, 1931, when so many of our family members died. It was, also, the year of the typhoid fever when Santos was born, and against all odds, survived. The typhoid fever still raged in Miami. I will always remember when Dr. Brayton came to our house to deliver our baby Santos. Remember, Antonia, the first thing the doctor did when Santos came out into his new world, was to submerge the baby into a small tub of cold water; he shrieked, shook, and squealed: This warded off the fever, it worked, Santos is still alive," Fortunato laughed.

"Of course, I remember, but now, I fear for his life if I take him to Mexico. I am not sure how life will be there," Antonia said. She began to gather vegetables, potatoes, and filled a large pot with water from the faucet.

"Well, we know how life is here; let's be realistic, Antonia, this is the year of endings. The copper mines are closed. Now we fear for our very life's survival. But the year can be, as well, a year of new beginnings." Fortunato walked about the kitchen.

Antonia said nothing; she washed potatoes and diced them, but she listened.

"We must face our new life reality, a taxing reality that we never dreamed would come. Antonia, our family now seems, against our will, to be embroiled in and sharing with the social and political life experience of two nations, something we had nothing to do with initially. But now here are the social and political realities: a danger of ravenous monsters seeking to devour us." He walked to the front door, left open by the boys and closed it.

It seemed to Antonia that she had lived twice in one life. Because of copper mine strikes and labor issues, she left Morenci with her parents, and arrived in Miami in 1910. Antonia met Samuel Gutierrez in Miami and they married in 1912. They lived in a small two-room house of a number of small houses in Inspiration Hill to the north of Claypool, a small community east of Miami. The houses were one-half wood on the bottom with the upper one-half including the roof made of canvas, like tents. During the few years with her first husband, Antonia had five children: Samuel called '*Lito*' born in 1913, Antonia called '*Toni*' or '*Chata*' 1915, Jose called '*Guero*' 1917, Catalina 1918, but died in 1920, and Francisco 1919 who lived only one day. The last two children were born in Florence, Arizona where Antonia and Samuel had moved to live in 1918 to be near her grandmother Isabel, 'Nanita'. Samuel had become ill with miners' lung consumption called Silicosis and he died in 1919. Francisco, the baby, who had died a day apart from his father, shared the same casket, asleep in his father's arms. Yet, Antonia survived this first part of her life, and so, Antonia, in that frame of mind, said to Fortunato, "I believe we can survive the Great Depression and the Repatriation, now in the present time of our life, here in Miami."

"I have no doubt, Antonia, that we can survive better in Mexico, yes, quite well," Fortunato persisted, "we must seek the opportunity."

Antonia's second life, it seemed, began with her being a young widow. She returned to Miami to work with her mother Manuela '*Yela*' in the *cocina* where they made lunches for miners; they also cooked dinner for them. In those times, Mexican men came alone from Mexico to work in the copper mines of Arizona. They did not have a wife to cook for them so they paid a boarding house for their food. Manuela and Antonia operated such a boarding house; they made lunches for 30 miners. Antonia was content being with her mother and keeping her family together. Antonia was a young widow of twenty-five years of age with three children, supporting herself and her children. Fortunato, who had gambled profitably in large cities in California, had sought a small mining town with miners eager to gamble, had settled in Miami where he met Antonia. He considered her beautiful, intelligent, and hardworking: he courted her and they married in 1921.

Fortunato's and Antonia's first child, Lorena, was born in July 18, 1922. Their second child, Catalina, was born on November 25, 1924. In 1927, Antonia gave birth to their twin girls, Maria Socorro and Maria de Jesus. Twenty-eight days later the twins died. In 1929, Antonia gave birth to Maria Guadalupe "Lupita" and she died on July 4, 1931. She was two years old. The day was cold, and the doctor came to treat Lupita; he did all he could, but baby Lupita died. The loss of her children grieved Antonia and she suffered at times from deep sorrows, remembering her children, and she cried during such occasions.

"Fortunato, my heart broke in two, as well, at times, and in my mind I left this world. Who can explain the mystery of death and its persistence? Death was not done with us; my lovely girl of sixteen years, Antonia 'Toni' died too: few could withstand the Typhoid Fever epidemic that raged through Arizona in 1931. We have too much of our family and life history here, we must stay." Antonia beseeched Fortunato, "I could open a boarding house to support ourselves," she offered.

"You won't have to work in Mexico, Antonia; I will cultivate our lands and support our family," Fortunato answered and added, "On the contrary, Antonia, we must leave. This is too much to comprehend. Like we Christians have learned to say, God has given and God has taken away; Blessed be the Lord," Fortunato, who was versed in the Holy Bible, countered.

"Upon reflection of my life experience these last twelve years, Fortunato, I concluded that the only human certainty is death. This certainty caused me great alarm when I thought that I may die in Mexico. I would not like to die away from Nanita, away from my loved ones, all buried in Arizona. No, bury me in my homeland under Arizona sunsets. I will do my best to convince you, Fortunato, not to return to Mexico, not to take our family to live and possibly die in a faraway place. I could not bear the role of La Llorona in foreign soil."

"That is the truth, Antonia, no one can dispute that death is universal. But death can happen anytime, any place, to anyone. Death stalked our family not only in Miami but even in Mexico; that same year 1931." Fortunato served himself a cup of coffee. "Now, the Great Depression has caused hundreds of suicidal deaths, and the Repatriation can lead desperate families to end their way of life in the quest for survival, yes, these two economic and political snakes are dangerous."

In 1931, Fortunato received a letter from Sinaloa which informed him that his mother Lorenza Ruiz Vega had died. He grieved his mother and lamented that she had died so soon after his father had died. Three years before, Fortunato had sorrowed over his father Eudoro Vega, who died in 1928. Eudoro died as a vaquero, a rancher, at the age of 83 years. "Don't you think that I have a legacy to pursue?" Fortunato asked Antonia, "Now, I want to be a vaquero, a rancher like my father; I must cultivate my lands, El Potrero," Fortunato drank his coffee and continued speaking, "I will raise cattle; my sister Tila told me by letter that she will give Lorena and Catalina each a calf, and I also want to help preserve our lands from the federal government. I want to help my sister Tila and my brother Jorge who both will help us, Antonia. We must go to Mexico because here there is nothing for me, no work and no help from the government." Fortunato, the tiger, nervously paced the kitchen floor.

"Fortunato, you must admit that in Mexico, death covers the land like an invisible fog of pestilence. People may begin to think the country is bewitched. Mexico's historical culture has always given belief to there being witches or brujas. There are always persons who believe someone makes an evil eye to an innocent child and so the child then is constantly ill from the hex. There are always revolutions for no cause; remember what the religious sisters, for whom we provided a home here, said about the federal war on the Catholic Church."

Fortunato said nothing and remained silent. The overcast outside was complete. The kitchen glass window continued in its punishment under the steady drizzle. The wind howled outside. Antonia began to prepare lunch. The smell of distant wet earth had given way to a heavy smell of muddy earth. A storm seemed to be on its way. Both Antonia and Fortunato continued to discuss their critical issue.

"You, perhaps, Fortunato, may have a legacy to pursue, but is Mexico safe? Could our children really have a future there? If the truth be accepted, the majority of people in Mexico have always been killed by one of many never ending feuds between warring generals with their armies. Bullets; not words, is what settles the argument."

Antonia had a point. The Mexican revolution of 1910 spewed out a million refugees to the United States. The Cristero-federal government war of 1926-29 forced out of Mexico numerous priests and religious sisters that sought asylum in the north. Antonia's son Samuel, an eighteen year old freckled face red headed senior in high school, a researcher and writer for a periodical, had told Antonia all about this history of Mexico.

"I know, Antonia, we gave shelter to two religious sisters in our backyard one room guest house, and it sure served a noble cause." Fortunato said and added, "The sisters escaped Mexico from a government that was in conflict with the church. But now, the Mexican government covets uncultivated lands and will take Church lands and lands from hacendados who leave their lands unproductive to sell for raising government funds and to endow other lands to native pueblos as Ejidos or communal land. Tila told me all about this in her letter in January. This is why I must help keep our family's lands and my own El Potrero." Fortunato said and emphasized, "We must go to Mexico."

"I worry about my children's safety and for their future. For example, Lorena desires to continue her education, and so do Jose and Catalina." Antonia said and busied herself with preparing lunch.

In Mexico, since the beginning of the 1900s there was much violence over land holdings. Emiliano Zapata from the state of Michoacan, in 1908, had struggled in his futile efforts to recover the common lands lost by native Indian pueblos to corrupt hacendados since colonial times. This political concept of land recovery for the Indian pueblos had been passed along as a desired goal of national government administrations over the years, but never fully realized. Yet, after the revolution of 1910 and the subsequent new constitution of February 5, 1917, President Plutarco Elías Calles (1924-1928) began land distribution. Calles' presidential influence would continue with three presidents that followed him, Emilio Portes Gill (1928- 1929), Pascual Ortiz Rubio (1930-1932), and Abelardo Rodriguez elected in 1932. Fortunato and his brother Jorge and sister Domitila had reasons to be on guard as the federal government, they thought, in the fashion of social radicals may take from the large land holders land to create ejidos or pueblo communal land plots for the indigenous tribes. Then too, the land laws had provoked much controversy and blood-shed in the past.

Antonia chopped onions. She wiped away the tears making their way over her cheeks. She sliced tomatoes, and began to cube tender round steak into ground meat mixed with onions and potatoes in preparation for meat *burros*. In the meantime, Fortunato inspected some federal forms he had received in the mail. The children argued noisily in their rooms.

In some parts of Mexico, where land was taken out of cultivation, in those rural areas, people were dying of hunger, or in some cases, shot dead for their land. Former land holders predicted that those who received parceled out *ejidos* or plots of land from the federal government would not cultivate the land because the government would fail to provide farming equipment and seed for crops. Also, there was lack of rain in some places where there were no water irrigation systems. Then there was always the problem with harmful insects to the plants. Already, Fortunato's brother Jorge told him in a letter, that the lack of food crops caused hunger in many parts of Mexico; these conditions were worse in poor countries: Mexico's poverty made the Great Depression in the United States seem like a cornucopia of plenty.

Antonia turned to Fortunato; she held high the meat cutting knife in her hand and said, "What really concerns me Fortunato is that El Aliso, Sinaloa, like other rural areas in Mexico, may not have a church. We need a church and a priest. I would not want our children to grow up without religion."

Fortunato responded, "My extended family, the Vega's, unlike myself, who learned religion in California, seemed cold to the Catholic Church. Even to me, they seemed not to be Catholic like the majority of the Mexican people in Mexico. They seemed to have no religion. In Mexico there are many anti-Catholic Church sentiments by many of its citizens; the federal government has waged an extensive war against the Church in Mexico. Perhaps the Vega's in Mexico did not want to bring trouble upon themselves by practicing the Catholic religion." Fortunato got up and walked to the front room window to look out at

The Worm in my Tomato

the dark clouds bringing with them an early night. He returned back into the kitchen, "Looks like heavy rain this afternoon," Fortunato sat down at the table again, "The war waged by the government against the Catholic Church was known as the Cristero Rebellion, and it turned out to be a bloody tragedy whose recrimination has lasted beyond its years of violence and bloodshed." Fortunato got up and served himself another cup of coffee. He continued his conversation, "There is more at stake in Mexico than destitution; the complex cultural conflicts are the source of much violence, but so much of this is out of our control. My main concern is that I must seek ways to protect our family's lands." Fortunato studied the papers pertaining to the state and federal Repatriation policies.

"Fortunato, ask yourself, honestly, if rural El Aliso, Sinaloa is the environment in which you want our children to grow up, and if this is the place where you wish to live yourself in danger of getting shot." Antonia looked at him tenderly, with a knife on her right hand and a lettuce in her left hand. "It seems so unsafe, that I would not approve for you to go alone without us."

"I admit, Antonia, the environment is hostile from time to time, but I would not have invited you and our children unless I sincerely believe it is best for us. We can not let others' misfortunes keep us from seeking our own good fortune. Remember, I left Mexico at age 19 to seek a better life in the United States for which I have given my loyalty and good work for thirty-eight years, but the United States proves ungrateful by its Repatriation policies, you know, in forcing economically and politically thousands of Mexicans like me to return to Mexico." Fortunato sipped his coffee, "Now, however, I think Mexico offers me the only place I can live and work."

Antonia placed the ground meat in a frying pan on the stove and seemed not to really hear what Fortunato said. She said, "Another thing, Fortunato, you know that Mexico, through its land and religious laws, created problems for the Catholic Church, forcing it at one time to go on strike for three years, completely shutting down, you understand me, no baptisms, no weddings, no confessions, no celebrations of the Holy Mass. Will we have a Church in Mexico, in El Aliso, Sinaloa, for our family; again I ask you to think about it."

"I fear that you, Antonia, will have to content yourself with the seasonal celebrations of feast-days in the native village and a periodic visit by a priest from Los Mochis or Culiacan. I remember that during *Cuaresma*, the forty days of Lent, Indian runners ran from village to village re-enacting a Christian chase of other villagers acting the part of being Jewish Pharisees; at a village an Indian wearing a headdress with antlers performed the deer-dance. Both the native runners, those who played the part of being Pharisees who chased other natives acting the role of Christians, when they reached a village, they all got fed food by the village families. But this was thirty-eight years ago, Antonia; I don't know for certain how this village Christian custom is faring today in the rural areas."

"Well, that is interesting; it seems that the faithful do live out their faith by re-enacting parts of the Christian story. But all that you have said, Fortunato, convinces me the more to stay."

"But I can't stay. Even, if I take into account all the problems with Mexico; the problems which I told you about; I think it is better for me to go. Here in this country, I would be a useless shadow of a man, yes, a shadow hiding in dark corners, from the law, and perhaps even in hiding from vigilante groups, hunting me down like a dog with rabies." Fortunato stood up from the table and paced about the kitchen. He said, "Yes, like a dog, to prevent me from federal government work programs. Perhaps even deny welfare commodities to my children, notwithstanding the fact that you and our children are citizens. Yes, my children, fourth generation Arizonans, punished because of me; that would be unjust, don't you think, Antonia?" Fortunato poured himself another cup of coffee. "No, I will not stay and furthermore, you can stay here with your two boys, Samuel and Jose, and I will take my two girls, Lorena and Catalina."

"And the baby, Santos, he's yours, too?"

"He's a baby, how can I take care of a baby?"

"How can you take care of Samuel and Jose, my two boys, for whom you became responsible, when you married me, if you are not where they are?"

"I must admit, I am desperate, trying to help my brother Jorge and my sister Tila and myself to protect our lands from probable takeover by the Mexican federal government. Then too, my children will not be beggars in this country."

"Does that include my two boys?"

"Yes."

"Well, I don't think Mexico is safe for you to go alone, and Nanita did say for us to keep the family together and that I must carry my Christian cross in our marriage."

"But I repeat, I just can't stay; I can't stay, Antonia, I must go to Mexico, even if I leave you here with the children. You are all United States citizens."

"If we go, on condition that our children agree to go as well, promise me that we will return home to Arizona in five years, after you have stabilized your lands and safely leave them with your family, promise me."

"All right, woman, this is my home, too, I suppose, after having lived in this country for thirty-eight years."

"Good, this way we will keep our family together, like Nanita wants us to, and we will return home for the children's sake, but they should voluntarily agree to go." Antonia felt a sense of relief from the stress, and she placed food from the pans into serving plates. "Fortunato, furthermore, we will return home after five years."

"Only God knows, Antonia, our reality is that our Mexican community lies uprooted from the country we had adopted, in which we had made our contributions in labor for many years." Fortunato sat at the table and began to serve himself a plate of food, and he said, "My countrymen, I know, are too proud to accept charity and they will return to Mexico. As for those who are United States citizens, when will they return, if ever, only God knows?"

Lorenza Ruiz Vega, Fortunato's mother, died in 1931 in El Aliso Sinaloa, Mexico.

The Worm in my Tomato

Three

Family
Conversation and Decisions

The children, anxious and hungry, had been waiting in the hall, and Antonia invited them into the kitchen, "Let's eat our lunch." The children came in, subdued, and took their seats around the table. Fortunato said grace, giving thanks for the family's meal, and all ate in silence. The hungry children ate with gusto. There was plenty of meat *burros* wrapped in warm *tortillas*.

Fortunato assumed the children had heard his and Antonia's discussion and said, "The Great Depression has closed the mines in Miami." Fortunato continued to speak slowly and emphatically, as he put chile over his meat and tortillas, "The Repatriation policy of the federal and state government has threatened my future as a working man and as a provider for my family: In all reality, I have no choice but to move to Mexico."

Fortunato looked sad and forlorn.

Tears welled in Antonia's eyes and she felt discouraged in trying to convince Fortunato to stay in Miami, or if he insisted on going to Mexico, to let him go by himself and leave all the children here. But Antonia had no idea at this time about what the children would decide to do for themselves. She knew how each one of her children was so independent in thought and character. Who would decide to stay or go, and how would each one who decided to stay convince Fortunato to stay? Santos was of course only a baby, a brown baby with a head full of black hair. Catalina was seven years old, fair complexioned with brown wavy hair and light brown eyes. Jose, aged sixteen, sturdy built, with a ruddy jovial face, enjoyed the outdoors. Samuel, eighteen years old, in his last year of high school, tall for his age, sturdy, red-headed and freckled face, quiet, thoughtful, studious young man, was the intellectual of the family. Lorena, almost ten years old, a sinewy and fair complexioned girl, with long straight brown hair, was a bundle of curiosity

The Worm in my Tomato

and nervous energy, and always reading, studying, and wanting to learn about everything, and more independent than the other children.

Outside, the March wind blew harder. Now the family could hear the heavy pitter-patter of large rain drops striking the house roof and pelting the kitchen glass window. The late dark afternoon was illuminated, from time to time by distant lightning bolts, like light bulbs that switched on and off. Thunder boomed and lightning flashed, and their sound and light invaded the house. Catalina ran and hid under her bed. Antonia lit a candle and placed it on the kitchen table and she and Lorena prayed a Hail Mary. After the prayer, Antonia told Lorena, "Hurry Lorena and go comfort Catalina who is under her bed."

Antonia said a silent prayer within her heart for God to take over their life and for God's Will, be done. Antonia could not help but think that leaving for Mexico might be an easy way out. No, she thought, we must struggle against the social, economic, and political powers of the United States and of Mexico, if need be. She became a mother eagle protecting her nest and urging her young to fly. Nevertheless, Antonia began to doubt that Isabel's novenas could avert Fortunato from leaving Miami. She felt terrible, but kept all her emotions to herself, but she considered various possibilities in her mind. She could not help but wonder if Fortunato would change his mind and not return after five years and furthermore that he would keep her girls in Mexico? Or would he say no, that he would not stay and furthermore that she would have to stay here in Miami, by herself with all her children, without Fortunato present to provide a father's protection and love?

Antonia decided to be logical about the situation; the children yet had to be persuaded. She knew that her children would have to make a great effort to adapt in the rural setting. Antonia wondered how the family would do against the challenge of government and economic depression in Mexico, but she knew Fortunato still believed that their family would be better provided for in a rural setting with an agricultural way of life. We'll see about that, Antonia thought.

The aroma of the meat stew in the kitchen mixed with the smell of a heavy rained wet earth, trees, and wood, that sneaked into the house through under the front door. Antonia knew their sacrifice as a family would be great; she was not certain, but what if there was no church building or Christian practicing community like the faithful Christian body in Miami? But Antonia planned to carry in her large tin trunk her altar statues of her saints' icons. Antonia would take along her devout faith and practice, being positive, expecting to find a church as a place of worship. Antonia's head swam in dizziness and she felt sick to her stomach. She worried about losing her children and had decided that their children must stay with her. Wherever I am, there should my children be; the mother, after all, is the nest builder, the comforter, and provider of the care that keeps a family together, she thought.

Antonia felt certain that the children needed to know what was going on and what she and Fortunato planned to do. She knew that the children would be involved in the consequences from whatever decisions were made. Their children Samuel, Jose, Lorena, and Catalina sat around the table after dinner waiting for the family meeting. Antonia made some Kool-Aid for them. The children were all ears and eager to participate in the talks. Lorena, being more inquisitive, curious, and proactive in nature seemed eager to begin. Samuel, pensive and studious, would listen carefully, and patiently make up his mind.

Outside the rain increased with the loudness of hail. Lightning struck with more frequency, and Antonia promptly lit three candles and placed one on the kitchen counter, one on top of the stove and one on top of the kitchen table. Lorena held tight onto Catalina's hand to keep her from bolting to hide under her bed. Antonia began the conversation: "Children, according to our Mexican customs our culture includes our extended families; I would have consulted with my mother Manuela, if only she were alive. I will talk with my brother Tomas; it is necessary to talk with all our interested family and relatives because each will be concerned by what we do."

"Is that why a family gets mad, momma?" Catalina asked. She drank her Kool-Aid and then said, "Like you and papa, in talking?"

"Oh, no, we were not mad at each other, but we became excited because each insisted for what each wanted," Antonia explained.

"What does the talk between you and father mean to you, mother?" Samuel asked.

"Well, I am thinking that we could stay here in Miami and face the Great Depression, quite well. If I, for example, was more like

The Worm in my Tomato

my mother Manuela and Nanita, I see how both my mother and my grandmother can help me with this problem of staying or going to Mexico. What I mean is that perhaps I can be a *curandera* and a *partera*," responded Antonia.

"Just why would you do that for, Antonia?" Fortunato wondered out loud, "My mother-in-law Manuela did her work in a natural way to help the sick women and children who were too poor to afford doctors."

"Well, yes, but women are always having babies. The poor women and children are always sick, and need help, why not?" Antonia said and added, "And we could get paid some money and food."

"But what does this have to do with staying in Miami or going to Mexico?" Fortunato said and stood up from the table and paced up and down in front of the wood stove.

"Well, we need to live in a place where we can make a contribution to where we live. This is an important reason to help me make the right decision. You, see, Nanita was an experienced woman of prayer. She led novenas and rosaries during wakes, church holy-days, or when the community faced a storm, a crisis, or the miners were involved in a strike against the mine owners," Antonia said. She continued in trying to make her point: "During the first world war of 1917, Nanita led many prayer services for peace and the safe return of my brother Tomas and other soldiers from the war." She took a drink of Kool-Aid and said, "Both my mother, in her life-time, and my grandmother, as cultural Catholics, practiced home religion by praying novenas and saying the rosary in front of home altars. Nanita, especially, always prayed for the souls of deceased persons and prayed at wakes and funerals. It was customary to pray novenas or nine days of prayer for the souls of deceased persons following the wake in their home." Antonia waited to see if there were any questions, and seeing there were none, she continued, "In this way we prayed not only with our family but with families in our community; in this way we built a community of faith and prayer. It is important, for religious and spiritual reasons, always to belong to a community of worship and prayer with other like-minded persons."

"I like to hear about my family, especially my grandmother 'Yela' and my great-grandmother, Nanita," Lorena exclaimed.

The Worm in my Tomato

"My mother Manuela for years was a *curandera* or healer. She healed many people with the use of herbs and prayer. Grandmother Isabel, Nanita, was a midwife, and as a *partera* when called to homes of Mexican pregnant women, delivered many babies. When pregnant women knew the baby was ready to be born, they summoned Nanita to help them bring their babies into the light," Antonia said.

"We pray at home, now, and at Church, don't we, mother," Catalina offered.

"Yes, Catalina, our family problem of staying here or going to Mexico, now, to me merits prayer; if not as much, maybe more than all of these other problems of the Great Depression and the Repatriation. Can't you all see, our family's future is at a cross roads." Antonia stood up and walked over to the front room and looked out the large window, trying hard to make sense of what she felt. She walked back into the kitchen; she studied the faces of her children; they were listening, but Antonia was not sure if they understood the gravity of the situation. She thought this was the time to be like Nanita, strong as an ox and smart like a fox.

The kitchen became hot and muggy; the day's rain and wind passed on and the earth, trees, and houses were soggy wet. The sun seemed to chase the storm clouds away and followed with its rays that blazed through the window glass; there were no clouds to help protect the land and homes from the late afternoon burning heat rays. Antonia walked to the kitchen counter and began making lemonade. Samuel chipped ice from the ice box upper chamber; Jose set the glasses. Lorena and Catalina smiled in anticipation. Santos slept blissfully in his baby crib, unconcerned with his future. Antonia could see that Fortunato was thinking hard, in his position that he took when deep in thought, with his head bent low as if studying the kitchen floor boards. The cold touch of reality, however, energized Antonia's numbness and motivated her back into some semblance of common sense. In her mind, she reminded herself that Nanita was ninety-two years old now. She may very well die before their return from Mexico in five years.

"Want lemonade with ice chips, mama?" Samuel served Antonia lemonade, as she, brought back from her own deep thoughts, nodded yes.

Lorena and Catalina, with young girls' exuberance of age ten and seven, both hugged Antonia and kissed her cheek. The family sat around the kitchen table again to talk; they drank their cold lemonade.

"I like lemonade, I could drink a whole pitcher by myself," commented Jose.

Lorena asked Antonia, "Mother, tell us about yourself and father."

"Yes, please," begged Catalina, as she snuggled close to her mother.

Nanita had told Antonia her story; Antonia always felt better when she remembered it. So Antonia began to tell her story. "Fortunato and I met at an Alianza Hispano Americana dance in 1920; I was a young widow at the time. My first husband Samuel Gutierrez had died one year before from miner's consumption or Silicosis. My life required much sacrifice as a widow with three children, two boys, Samuel, the oldest, Jose, and Antonia called Toni, my daughter."

"That's my sister Toni that died when she was sixteen years old from typhoid fever, huh, momma." Catalina glanced at her mother and then at Lorena.

"Tell now, about my father," Lorena wanted to know.

"Well, your father, Fortunato, did not work in the mines but earned a living from gambling and running the card games at Limonada's Pool Hall. But when necessary, he did work with his hands as a laborer. He had worked on the winding highway between Miami and Superior and also on the construction of the Arizona Roosevelt Dam. He enjoyed his work with cement."

"Then what happened," Catalina chuckled.

"We fell in love and we married. He was twenty years older than me, a mature man forty-five years old, with smooth hands adorned with diamond rings. He usually wore blue suits. He had a gold chain attached to his large round watch he kept in a vest pocket," Antonia said.

"Tell us the part where grandmother Manuela didn't like him," Lorena asked.

"Well, Lorena, your grandmother, at first, had not approved of Fortunato because she thought him as being too old for me, her only one daughter. My mother would say, "He will die sooner than you, Antonia, and leave you a widow with more children." "Besides," she added, "he is a gambler, taking away paychecks from hardworking

The Worm in my Tomato

miners and food from their children's mouths." She would point at me and shake her index finger, "Someday, he will lose all he has, too."

"Oh, momma, what grandmother Manuela told you; now tell us about what Nanita said to you." Catalina laughed in amusement.

"My grandmother Isabel, also, had not approved of Fortunato, because he did not appear to be a practicing Catholic and probably, she said, did not attend Mass on Sunday." Your grandfather Jose Carbajal, my dad, did not approve of your father, either, because when they shook hands at their first meeting, father had noticed Fortunato's smooth hands. Your grandfather Jose thought for certain that your father was not an honest working man, who worked with pick and shovel. "My father said, 'He is not a working man with his hands and does not earn his life by the sweat of his brow, thus, you will have a hard life with him, my daughter.'"

Fortunato and the boys, Samuel and Jose, could not help themselves and broke out laughing. "Oh, this is so funny," cried out Jose.

Antonia laughed, too, but continued her story:

"I heard all the reasons why I should not marry Fortunato, but I loved him, and I married him, anyway, and I had no doubt that I had made the right decision. I was a young widow, after all, aged twenty-five years, with my three young children. Samuel was the oldest of the boys, he was five years of age, red-haired and freckled face; Jose, aged three, with dark brown hair and with long eye-lashes that shielded his drooping brown eyes; Antonia, 'Toni', my daughter, creamy white like a china doll with smooth dark hair and large brown eyes, was only six years old at the time. Fortunato accepted my children; he demonstrated his love and kindness for them, to me, this was most important, smooth hands or rough hands, if he loved my children, we would be a happy family. We married and lived on happily ever after, like in stories," Antonia said and smiled.

"Tell us about us, now," Lorena insisted.

"You, Lorena, were my first child of my second marriage, and you had a crown of brown hair on top of your potato white face," Antonia said.

Lorena and Catalina broke out in laughter at this part of the story.

The Worm in my Tomato

They held themselves with their folded arms tight over their stomachs. "Oh, it's so funny, Lorena with a potato face," Catalina said and expressed amusement.

"Mama, tell her to stop," demanded Lorena. "What Mama said, means white face, like a potato, dumb." Lorena scowled at Catalina.

"Behave yourselves, or I won't continue," Antonia said, "In a few years, God blessed us with three children and a set of twins, but only two lived, you, Lorena, and Catalina, and of course, baby Santos, who was born last year."

"This makes our family," Samuel said.

"Yes, and we hope to keep it together, no matter what," Antonia said.

"But now," Samuel asked, "Tell us what happened when you and father visited Nanita."

"Yes, mother, since Samuel and I stayed home," Jose agreed, "Tell us what happened, what did Nanita say?"

"In Florence, we talked with Nanita. I told her about Fortunato's wanting to leave to Mexico on account of the Repatriation."

"What did Nanita say about the Repatriation?" Jose asked.

"Yes, mother, what did she say?" Catalina beamed with her big smile.

"Nanita listened, we prayed for holy guidance, and after we drank our coffee and ate Mexican sweet bread, we talked." Antonia paused and looked at Fortunato and said, "Nanita wanted to know, 'What is this *Repatriación*,' and I explained as best I could and Fortunato filled in the spaces and made clarifications," Antonia said.

Fortunato motioned for Antonia to let him speak now, "The Repatriation is," Fortunato, took a drink of lemonade from his glass, and said, "I told Nanita, 'Nanita, as you know, the poverty of our country is real bad. The Great Depression like a blanket on fire has burned up all jobs and economic opportunities across the land. Those Anglo-Americanos who quickly must blame someone else for the problem, as usual, have accused the Mexican and passed laws to force us back to Mexico.'"

"Then, Nanita said, 'But, Fortunato, how can this be, when for centuries we have worked in sweat and pain in this part of our country?'" Fortunato quoted Nanita and said, "I simply informed Nanita that, nevertheless, these Anglo-Americanos have organized into campaign groups and incited their politicians to enact laws against Mexican immigrants."

Fortunato continued quoting Nanita, "Nanita asked me: 'What? Then not all immigrants are exposed to these laws.' "But, I told Nanita: No, no, the anger, hatred, and fight are against Mexican immigrants from Mexico." Fortunato took a drink of Kool-Aid from his half-empty glass, and said, "Nanita, then asked your mother if it was not true, that there were many immigrants from other countries living in Miami, as well." Fortunato looked at Antonia, as if wanting her to complete the answer to the question.

"Yes, I answered Nanita," Antonia told the children, and she continued speaking, "I said: 'It is true, Nanita, but Repatriation is not against the Chinese, the Serbs, the Greeks, and the Lebanese that lived in Mexico for years and emigrated to the United States during the 1910 Mexican Revolution, or against the English, French, and German that have come across the Atlantic and from Canada into our country,' I told Nanita." "Nanita then said, 'Well, it goes to show you, daughter, that laws benefit some groups but hurt others.'" Antonia used a tone of disgust, "Nanita said, 'It all depends who has political power to rule and make the laws.'"

Fortunato stood up from the table, wiped his face with his white pocket handkerchief; he looked out the window at the long shadows stretching down the street from west to east, and he said, "I told Nanita, frankly, that I want to return to Mexico and farm the land my father left for me to farm." He stared at the long shadows, "I am Mexican and my country needs me, too."

Then, Antonia told the children that Fortunato had asked Nanita: "'Why didn't you ever go back to Mexico, Nanita?'" Antonia paused, "Nanita answered Fortunato: 'Nato, mi hijo, as you know I am Indian or called Indian by the Spanish conquerors and the Mexican army that came later when we lost our tribal lands. Anyway, in Mexico, all of us indigenous people are Indios, and at one time in the distant past, the Mexicans were only the Aztec and Mechica peoples. Each Indian tribal group had its own name, its own lands, spoke their own language, and each of us had our own culture and heritage. But, only the large tribal groups have survived to this day, the rest of the smaller tribes were lost. My tribe, for instance, disappeared. Who am I, what is my tribal group? Thus, what is there in Mexico that I should return to?'" Antonia continued speaking, "Remember Fortunato how Nanita gently wiped her tears from her eyes with the corner of her apron, when she had said that about herself?" Antonia walked to the stove and began preparations to start the fire for cooking supper. "My poor grandmother, how she has suffered, but she survived, and yet she struggles by herself." Antonia said, and added, "To Nanita, I attribute the words from Psalm 92, 'To me you give the wild-ox's strength; you anoint me with the purest oil.' She is as smart as a fox, too."

"Actually, the part that I really enjoyed learning about," Fortunato said, "was her story when she escaped from Mexico in the dark with her two sons, escaped into the night, as Nanita and her sons fled to Morenci and Clifton, Arizona."

"The part I enjoyed," Antonia said, "was when Nanita said, 'This is my land, now, this should be your land, too, Nato,'" Antonia laughed lightly, "And remember when Nanita rolled up a cigarette and handed it to me; I lighted up a match for Nanita's and my cigarette."

"That was a precious moment with your Nanita," Fortunato agreed.

"We smoked in silence, watching the light blue smoke curl up above our heads," Antonia whispered, "Each one of us embraced in our own private memories and thoughts, and do you remember, Fortunato, how Nanita puffed smoke in doughnut shaped circles?"

"I do, mama," Lorena said.

Finally, Fortunato freed his thoughts from the confines of his mind and expressed an emotion from his heart, and shared with Antonia and his children, his own thoughts and feelings: "I agree with every word Nanita said." Fortunato carefully selected his words, "I don't have a tribal group, and my family came to Mexico from Spain hundreds of years ago. We have no home in Spain. All I have to call home, now, is Mexico. I, too, am a Mexican, even if I am of the Spanish people, but I am of the Mexican culture and heritage by birth. That makes me Mexican. Perhaps in the future I could become a citizen of the United States and then I would be American like my children. But for now, I am Mexican, and given the Repatriation push, I must return to Mexico."

"That is what all this time and talk together is about," Antonia said.

She turned to the children, "Your Father wants to return to Mexico. He told me that he might take you two girls with him to Mexico." Antonia looked at Lorena and Catalina.

Lorena began to cry softly, "No, no, mama, I will not go. I will talk to papa." She ran out of the kitchen to her bedroom and slammed the door.

"I don't want to go, momma," Catalina cried softly. She looked frightened.

Samuel and Jose, who had been attentive to all that was said, did not speak much in today's family conversation. They excused themselves and retreated to their rooms.

Antonia said to Fortunato, "I did not want our children to feel threatened; they are like poor little chicks in need of the warmth and protection under their mother hen's wings." She placed potatoes in a pan with some water in it on top of the stove's fire. "This is why I carefully included them in our conversation. Somehow, I wanted to encourage, in a gentle way, our children to tell us what they think and agree on their own to go to Mexico. But at the same time I do not want you, Fortunato, to go to Mexico alone, by yourself."

"I have told you many times, now, Antonia, that I am leaving for Mexico and very soon. I want Lorena and Catalina to go with me, as well, and you should, too. I am threatened by government policies; I must go to Mexico, even if you don't, Antonia. It is not a question of love, I love you, but I have no choice. I want to earn my own living and support my family."

"I can not forget what Nanita said to me, 'Antonia, daughter, you must carry your Christian cross and support your husband,'" but Antonia, now deeply moved, said, " I do not want to go to Mexico to live; I was born in Morenci in 1895, that is thirty-seven years in Arizona; Arizona is the only home I have ever known: Miami, Arizona is my home." Fortunato was silent, so Antonia continued speaking. "That is why tonight I included our children in our conversation, to find out what they wanted to do, but once they realize that Arizona is their home, too, they may not want to go with you Fortunato. Their heritage, history, and cultural roots will motivate them to want to stay here and not go to Mexico."

The Worm in my Tomato

"Antonia," Fortunato's face reddened and his voice sounded angry and despondent, "Did you try to convince the girls with stories about our life to choose to stay? If you did, that was not right."

"It was the only fair way to prepare them to make their own choice. The journey to Mexico will involve their memories and emotions. We don't want them to become ill, don't you think, Fortunato?"

"I will go to Mexico and I will convince Lorena and Catalina, too, to choose to come to Mexico, and furthermore, Antonia, I will also convince Samuel and Jose to come along, as well."

The family conversation at the table ended. The children had returned to their rooms. The backyard was too wet for Samuel and Jose to play a game of washers. But Fortunato went out into the yet wet and muddy yard to sit down under the china berry tree and think about the differences in staying here in Miami or going to Mexico. Fortunato knew that Antonia remembered what Nanita had said: that Antonia must keep the family together. He was certain that she knew that she must carry her cross as a Christian wife.

Antonia sat down at her kitchen table and drank some coffee, while thinking about what to do. The question was: who is expected to go? She thought. Antonia really did not want Fortunato to go by himself. After careful reflection on Nanita's different perspectives and Fortunato's obligations, Antonia decided to make the journey to Mexico. But how could she and Fortunato convince their children to agree and to come with them to Mexico, willingly? Antonia planned to talk with Fortunato about convincing their children on making their own choice to go to Mexico. Antonia did not see any other way out of these problems. Antonia felt that Lorena would be the one to object the most to leaving Miami for Mexico. Antonia decided to call Lorena and involve her in some housework and in this way talk with her. Antonia called Lorena, "Please help me prepare for dinner, Lorena."

Both Antonia and Lorena prepared dinner in the kitchen "My memory of Miami will always remain in my mind and heart, Lorena," Antonia said. "My life here with my mother and our work in the boarding house can never be forgotten. All my family and friends have a space in my heart. Especially fond for me is my love for those that now sleep in our hometown cemetery, down in Central Heights. But life, however, brings changes and one must be ready to accept them. You understand, Lorena, and we must support your father in his going to Mexico."

"I know mama," Lorena said softly, "But I don't want to go to Mexico."

Miami, Arizona, 1932

Life in Miami in the early 1930s resembled an extended family celebration on a daily basis. People who lived in the canyon or mountain-side neighborhoods knew each other, depended on each other for survival and supported one another.

Outside the house a truck horn blowing away in repeated beeps startled Antonia and Lorena. "Oh, there is the meat truck, mama," Lorena yelled.

From the outside came the cries, "Meat, fresh meat."

Almost every other day, Antonia and Lorena rushed outside their front door to the sidewalk, when they heard the yells, "Meat, fresh meat." Today, Antonia and Lorena dashed outside. Antonia's blue apron flapping at her side, with her right arm flailing in the air, she said, "Hurry, Lorena, before the truck passes us by."

Lorena ran outside the front porch and hailed the meat truck to stop. After a firm stop of his meat truck, Mr. Suárez, the butcher and storekeeper, jumped out from his 1928 Ford black truck's front door and opened the large panel doors in the back. Don José Suárez wore his usual white apron. He was a Spaniard, in his late fifties, short in stature, with a pale face adorned by a long gray mustache. He showed his straight white teeth by his ever present smile, and he said, "Sorry, I am late, the rain kept me indoors for some hours."

Inside the truck were large 100 lb. blocks of ice in a meat chest, covered over with white paper wrapped meat packages. Other chunks of ice, heaped over with wrapped pieces of meat, filled up the meat chest. In other boxes were chicken, separated from the fish boxes. "What do you want to buy today, Mrs. Vega, the usual?"

Antonia, with her long black hair combed straight back, wiped her hands on her blue kitchen apron, looked over the produce of meats: "Yes, *don* Suárez; give me a large meat bone for the *cocido*." The cocido, Antonia's Mexican-style stew, made with small diced pieces of beef steak, a large meat bone, mixed with a variety of vegetables such as potatoes, carrots, celery, white onions, and chile peppers, was a favorite of Fortunato and the children. Antonia cooked a huge pot of *cocido* at least two times a week.

Antonia watched carefully as Mr. Suárez deftly sawed off a piece of meat bone with all its chunk of meat attached around it from a larger leg of beef, plump with red meat around the bone. Mr. Suárez trimmed off the white protective layers of fat, like adhesive covering, sticking to the red, thick, meat. He then weighed the roast hunk of meat on a scale that hung from the ceiling slat inside the truck near the open panel door. He turned to Antonia and said, "One dollar fifty, please"; he smiled.

He took the money Antonia had pulled out from her dress pocket. "Something else, for you, today, Mrs. Vega, that you wish to buy," He pointed to the white slabs of tripe for menudo, jars of pigs-feet on top of chopped ice in a tub, cut bacon strips, T-bone steaks, thick bacon strips and ham hocks to cook with a pot of pinto beans, and rainbow trout and catfish on ice. All meat products carefully kept preserved on ice and sold fresh the same day after Mr. Suárez picked up the meat from the Alabama truck depot that delivered produce overnight from the slaughter houses in the valley near Phoenix.

"Not today, thank you Mr. Suárez." Antonia and Lorena walked back into their house; they stood momentarily at the door to watch Mr. Suárez close the panel door and climb back into his truck and drive away to the next waiting customer.

Inside her large kitchen, Antonia started a fire in her huge wood stove. The stove stood on four strong iron pedestals, one on each corner of the square base of the stove, and had four round iron plates on top of its surface, on which Antonia placed her cooking pots, frying pans, and other pans for boiling her cocido. Antonia placed a large stew pan on top of the stove plate. Lorena put water into the stew pot. Antonia cooked the meat stew because Fortunato and her boys, Samuel and Jose, especially, loved to eat the soup with vegetables. Antonia used the hot surface of the four iron plates to cook tortillas, or sometimes, she cooked them on a flat-iron heated over the hot iron plates.

"You know, mama, I don't like the idea that many of the women in Miami are in the custom of rising at five in the morning to make tortillas in their outside yard stove." Lorena said as she washed potatoes.

"It's cooler then, but I don't do that, Lorena, and I use my cooking stove, in my kitchen, with these fine large round flat irons, on which to stretch the tortillas." Antonia preferred her kitchen wood stove. Above the cooking stove iron plates, as part of the front panel of the stove, was a warmer space in which Antonia placed food to keep it warm, during the cold months.

"Mama, besides wondering about where I will go to school, I worry about simple things, mama, like where will we cook, get the meat and vegetables. Here we keep, near the stove, a stack of rough fire wood. If we move to Mexico, who will bring us wood to cook with, like the woodman Mr. Galvan does here in Miami?" Lorena busied herself slicing tomatoes and celery.

Mr. Galvan, one of several woodmen in town, sold wood for the stove to Fortunato and Antonia. "I know, Lorena, here Mr. Galvan sells us truck loads of old mine leftover lumber, cleaned up as firewood suitable for burning in our home wood stove." Antonia had trimmed and cubed the beef and placed it in the pot to cook.

There were several other woodmen in Miami who gathered wood from mezquite and other types of trees in the surrounding mountains and sold the wood for the home woodstoves.

"Even vegetables and fresh fruit are easy to get, mama. Just think of the variety of truck produce that we purchase some days according to our need."

Mr. Julian, the vegetable peddler, drove through the Mexican neighborhoods to peddle his fresh garden produce in season. He had his regular sales routes and his customary customers. Mr. Julian drove a light blue colored half-ton pick-up truck. The truck bed held wooden racks holding wooden boxes leaning backwards obliquely toward the middle of the truck, and facing outward to the sides of the truck. The boxes held the fresh produce for the customer to easily see, choose, and purchase.

"You know, Lorena, I enjoy looking at the green lettuce, red tomatoes, green chile bell peppers, long red and green chile, fully ripe persimmons, green cabbage, and other vegetables in season such as sweet potatoes, squash, green onion, and red potatoes."

"That is not all, mama; I have seen at the back part of the truck in the bottom of the bed the gunny sacks of fresh yellow or white corn on the husk. Remember, how other times, the truck was full of watermelons, sweet cantaloupes, and yellow melons. Before the end of October Mr. Julian drives around the neighborhoods selling large orange pumpkins. I really like that, because we used the pumpkin to make a Halloween lantern goblin," Lorena laughed.

"I know, Lorena, if we move to Mexico, I will miss Mr. Julian's vegetables and fruits. I appreciate it, when at other times he specializes in oranges, grapefruit, bananas, or pears and peaches, depending on what fruit is in season."

"I don't think we will be happy if we move to Mexico and find out all these services are missing, mama." Lorena said as she sliced large white potatoes.

"That is certain, Lorena, but these peddlers selling their goods throughout the streets and canyons of Miami may soon stop; a lack of sales, you know, as more and more families move away; many times families move because the man of the house has to work elsewhere: your father, also, has no work here," Antonia said.

"I know, but my main interest is continuing my education. I enjoy my school classes at Bullion Plaza, and my favorite teacher Miss Yoakum is helping me learn so much with her vocabulary drills." Lorena finished the potatoes and sliced the celery.

"I know Lorena, you will miss your school, and I will miss my church, and all that Miami offers us. You know that the other house-to-house peddlers include my *compadre* Matias. I asked him and his wife Chonita to be godparents for the baby's baptism. My *compadres* Matias and Chonita, in my opinion, are the best bakers of Mexican bread in Miami."

Mr. Matias Rodriguez delivered bread in card-board boxes in which he transported his bread on a push-cart that he pushed around the near-by neighborhoods for years, because he did not own a car or truck. In time, however, he saved enough money to purchase a car, and now, with his family car, modified in the inside to hold bread boxes, he delivered his bread throughout many of the canyons and streets. He carried large cardboard boxes full of fresh-day bread that he baked each week.

"I am so happy for my *compadres*," Antonia said.

"Mama, my favorite sweet bread with a glass of milk is the egg-bread, although I also enjoy the pig- shaped brown ginger bread and cinnamon buns." Lorena, looked at her mother, smiled and added, "Mama, we better stay here; you convince father to stay, all right."

In her kitchen, Antonia had a large tan-colored wooden ice box. At the bottom of the ice-box, she placed a pan to collect the dripping water from the melting block of ice. A fifty pound block of ice had been placed inside the top compartment of the ice-box. Under the ice holding compartment were the three tiers for placing the food items and quart glass bottles of milk. The iceman in his ice delivery truck delivered blocks of ice for the icebox throughout all the neighborhoods. Or the ice could be purchased at the icehouse located on Live Oak Street across the street from the Silver Front Pool Hall.

"In my kitchen, Lorena," Antonia placed the cubed meat into the pot of soup, "The food, ice, and wood peddlers play an important part of our life. I am happy with my life; you know we have grocery stores near our house that we can walk to like Portillo's Market, Becerril's Market, and Don Jose Suárez grocery store. We can go downtown shopping in stores like J.C. Penney's, Miami Commercial Store, Ryan Drugs, La Paloma Café, and other places downtown. All stores are close enough for our family to walk to and shop. I would miss the stores, if we move. I would yearn for Our Lady of the Blessed Sacrament Catholic Church. I would surely wish for Doctor Brayton's downtown office. I would miss Miami with all its important places in our life being so close, within walking distance." Antonia sprinkled salt and spices into the large stew pot over the diced meat which slowly cooked before she placed the vegetables in the pot.

"Then why do we move, let's stay, mama," Lorena wanted to know.

"I don't know, really, why we do things, Lorena. After we visited Nanita to talk with her and seek her advice about going to Mexico," Antonia checked on the fire, "I still don't know." All the diced meat was cooking, and the vegetables would go in last after the meat was well done. Antonia had to watch the fire and keep the pot from getting too hot; she knew that the heat and duration of time for each kind of food were so important in cooking a pot of cocido. She gazed at Lorena with tenderness and said, "I think Lorena that just like we make this cocido, God makes our life, you know, I think God wrote our life story, and our learning of God is in our life's journey."

"Yes, mama, something like Nanita's story, God wrote up her story, too. I enjoyed the trip; really happy to see Nanita."

"Well, what she told us was very important, Lorena." Antonia moved the pot a little bit to one side, to prevent it from getting the direct heat, for now, "your father and I are yet in full discussion about his returning to Mexico. I do not want to go. I am comfortable here in Miami and we have all we need. I think that all of you children have expressed yourselves in favor of staying here in Miami. Your father, on the other hand, thinks and feels that he must leave. He thinks it is necessary for our survival as a family, given the Great Depression that now rages in our country, and given the Repatriation policy with all its uproar that is pushing him out and into a train to return Mexicans to Mexico."

Fortunato and Antonia did not really know what would happen to them in Miami because of the lack of jobs, after the copper mines closed, and general destitution rampant throughout the states. The Repatriation policy of the national and state governments, however, pushed non-citizens like Fortunato to return to Mexico. Fortunato believed the country had failed his family, being that they were all United States citizens of many, many years. Antonia understood the great pressure Fortunato was under to make the right decision; what should they do, Antonia asked her self, over and over again. But Antonia was not alone in not knowing; unknown to her, there were hundreds of thousands Mexican families in the United States suffering the same question: how to keep the family together when many of the children in each family were United States citizens.

Antonia wanted Lorena to try to understand her father's position and see if she could accept the change in their lives and decide with Antonia to keep the family together. "We can keep the family together through making this journey to Sinaloa together," Antonia said.

Lorena was silent for a long moment, she checked the meat by sticking a fork into a piece of meat to see if it was done; next, she added the vegetables; she knew that heat and timing were important ingredients for a good *cocido*.

Antonia could not help but think that they in their life were all in some kind of a similar pot, so to speak, like in a family stew, cooking up a decision to stay in Arizona or go to Mexico, and their voices like the steam from the stew pot floated up and out the kitchen and both became an aroma of vitality mixed with the outside world and then vanished.

"How will all this turn out, mama?"

"I really don't know." Antonia served herself a cup of coffee, sat down at the table and slowly sipped her black coffee.

"I don't want to go, mama. No, I won't go, and more than that, mama, I plan to convince my father to stay. If he won't, I will beg to be allowed to stay with another family, you know, like my friend Mary Cota's family, or my Uncle Tomas and Nellie."

Antonia knew by the sound of Lorena's voice that she was determined to stay in Miami. Antonia just sat there at the kitchen table and stared into her coffee cup as if hoping for an answer about what to do to appear in the coffee grounds. "Why us?" she said out loud to herself. She cried softly her warm tears into her cup, "Will you come with us, Lord?"

Tomas Carbajal, born 1896 in Morenci, Arizona, served in U.S. Army during 1918 First World War. He was 22 years old.

During the first world war of 1917, Isabel and Manuela led many prayer services for peace and the safe return of Manuela's son Tomas Carbajal and other soldiers from the war.

The Worm in my Tomato

Four

Fortunato
To Return to Mexico or Stay in the United States?

Fortunato had spent a sleepless night after having heard Antonia's and the children's conversation around the kitchen table. Fortunato, tired and not ready to get up and face another day, groped his way out of his bed. This was another day. He looked out his bedroom window; there were few house lights on outside in the neighborhood; no person can afford to pay the electricity, he thought.

Later in the morning, Fortunato went down to visit Limonada's Pool Hall to retrieve personal items from his desk and to see what was going on. He wanted to know what other Mexican families in town were going to do about the Repatriation policies of the United States. Fortunato took Lorena with him to help him carry his personal items home; he hoped this walk downtown, however, would give him an opportunity to talk with Lorena; he planned to convince her to go with the family to Mexico.

Lorena and Fortunato, when they walked along the main street, saw the homeless keeping warm around their wood fires under the bridges, and he remarked to Lorena, "Soon, if we stay here, we'll be sleeping under a bridge, you know Lorena." He knew that he wanted to take his family with him to Mexico, and he preferred to convince them to go on a voluntary basis. He did not want to force any one of them to go, but he felt that it would be easier to convince the Monarch Butterfly not to migrate to Mexico from Canada and back each year.

Inside Limonada's Pool Hall several fresh air fans hung from the ceiling and turned the air in the cave- like game room; the wide spacious room contained pool tables on one side and a wet bar on the other. In the front of the large miners' cave were chairs facing a long wooden table beside a waiting room, chairs, and shelves for magazines, where some women and children waited, read a magazine, or participated in conversations with other women. The women waited for the weekly rations parceled out by the union charity auxiliary. Opposite the pool tables and the bar, down a long hall, were the card game rooms, but now that part of the cave housing gambling rooms was quiet and dark. Fortunato felt crushed in disappointment with the loss of his job, gone with the lack of a poker game, black jack, or even table dice to manage.

Limonada's Hall seemed to have a full house; everyday, a number of unemployed miners gathered to talk in Limonada's Pool Hall. Fortunato and Lorena looked around at the crowd of some wives and mostly miners, large muscular miners, rough miners dressed in light blue Levis pants and work shirts, tough miners who in the past, like untrained horses, which didn't easily accept their bridle and metal bit, but now, the miners were dejected, nodded in agreement, listened like school children to *Caballón* "Big Horse" Hernandez. *Caballón* Hernandez, a former miner's union organizer, captivated the miners' attention by speaking about what miners should do. He hollered out in a loud voice, as was his custom; his voice carried loud with some resonance, "Some southwestern states in our country, including Arizona, deny the feeding of hungry families of Mexican nationals. Agencies obstruct welfare through political legal ways, even though we pay taxes, too!" Miners in agreement, like horses moved their heads up and down. Fortunato and Lorena sat nearby at a table and observed.

Above the drone of the fans, hopeful miners heard the strident voice of *Caballón* Hernandez, "Politicians, frightened by an uproar of organized hate mongers, sought federal and state legal means," Hernandez paused to emphasize his next point, "To deprive Mexican families from welfare assistance reserved, in their eyes, for American citizens."

"Yes, yes," heads ascended up and down.

"To prevent Mexican nationals from draining the welfare programs, the United States Congress passed the Repatriation law." Hernandez slapped his thigh, and said, "Several county governments took immediate action under provisions of the 1917 Immigration Act's Section 23, and repatriated Mexican nationals and their families by train to Mexico." He paused, looked about the hall, and moved his own large head with a long dark black mane, up and down, and appraised the other "horse heads", nodding in approval, and he

The Worm in my Tomato

continued speaking, "Numerous Families, as my family and your family, have family members who are American citizens." He slapped his thigh, again. "Hell, no, it's not right," he gazed out into the dim hall, "Thousands of Mexican nationals and their families like tramps piled high, ride trains back to Mexico." Caballón raised both his long arms up toward the roof ceiling, "But, don't you do it, this is where you belong, where our people have mined the copper, got gassed in the world war in 1917, raised our families, this is where we belong." He paused, "The Mexican vaquero, the miner, the rancher, the explorer, and the settler have lived in the Southwest since the late 1500s. We belong here."

Miners cheered "Yea, yea, *es verdad*, that's the truth." A miner named Manuel Garcia said, "Hell yes, man; hell yes, this is our country, too. Our people began the ranching, the mining, and the trade here in the Southwest, man, and we've fought in every war to defend this land, man; our people live on both sides of the border, man."

"That is why I am going to buck those copper and other labor unions that for years have worked against immigration because of fears of lost jobs and lower wages. Hell, yes, I am going to fight it in my own union, too." Caballón "Big Horse" Hernandez sat down amid the hand clapping and yea, yea cheers of all the want-to-be big horse heads. Caballón looked at Fortunato and asked, "What about you, Vega, what do you plan to do, stay here or hop on the Repatriation train?"

Caught by surprise, Fortunato, who planned to leave for Mexico on the Repatriation train, blushed, his blood rushed up into his face, red faced, singled out and vulnerable, he became a frightened bull in the arena, seeking escape, tongue-tied, in his mind, he asked himself, whose business is it, anyway, what I do? With emotion clouding his thinking and slurring his speech, Fortunato said, "I am thinking about it. Uh, Uh, my brother Jorge wants me to go to Mexico and cultivate lands given to me by my father in Sinaloa." He did not know what else to say at the moment.

"Stay here, Fortunato," a miner named Cuco Estrada said, "Even if you're not a citizen, you'll get by."

"Yes, Yes," the horse heads ascended up and down, led vigorously by Caballón, his black mane bouncing up and down.

Fortunato regained his composure; he told Caballón, "We'll see,

The Worm in my Tomato

my family is thinking about it." Fortunato turned to leave, "Have to go, maybe tomorrow we'll have card games?"

"I doubt it, Vega," Cuco Estrada yelled back, "We're all broke, maybe play poker for beans."

"Fortunato, remember, don't be threatened by Immigration armed forces, weak minded politicians that enacted the Repatriation laws, which pandered to dull-witted and unauthorized vigilantes, and political organizations that voiced petulant anti-Mexican tirades: Yes, what all pushed Mexican workers into trains to return them to Mexico." Hernandez yelled.

Fortunato only nodded his head and felt like a confused bird that struck a glass pane, as he hurried out the door into the street. Fortunato walked home through the empty streets, thinking about what Hernandez had said. Lorena trudged beside him; he looked at Lorena, carrying a small box with some of his personal papers, and said to her, "I can't put my trust on the "Big Horse," maybe he belongs here, but not me, I am not a citizen, and my situation is different." Fortunato thought to himself that he had to confront the destitution of the Great Depression, for the sake of his family. Fortunato thought seriously about his eviction from the United States after his thirty-eight year residence. He wondered if there could have been a better solution to this problem of people whose extended families lived in two adjacent countries separated by a political border where for centuries there had been no borders. Now, his children, all United States citizens would have to cross the political border and encounter problems and issues caused by culture, society and language differences: try to survive like sheep in a rocky desert. Could not an agreement have been made by Mexico and the United States to create a dual citizenship for people living in states along the border separating the two countries? If not, perhaps grant a permission passage card allowing free entrance and exit and right to work and reside on either side of the border, he thought. Fortunato thought about what effect the Repatriation would have on his family; he felt repulsed by the fact that the Repatriation aimed to break-up his family, even if his wife and children were all native Arizonans and American citizens. "I know for a fact, Lorena," Fortunato said, "that the political laws in the United States will not

The Worm in my Tomato

feed my children; the country's relief programs will not help them. I am not a citizen. Well, hell, it's true that the closing of the copper mines, like a mule, kicked me down, but my wife's family, especially our children, should be spared, they are all born in the United States and their heritage and roots go back to Nanita who has lived here for years since the 1870s."

"I know, father, Nanita came over in her wagon pulled by oxen, that her sons made them go faster by poking their rumps with sticks, and she did not fear the dark or the hot desert, and we must not fear the Repatriation, we will be fine, I don't want to go to Mexico."

"Well, I know, my daughter; the roots of the Mexican people go back before the United States- Mexico war, and well-beyond the 1600s. But the United States and its people either do not know or do not honor our history. But I know in my heart that I, personally, do not have options, if I want my family to survive. I must leave so they can get help from the government and ride out the Great Depression."

"Father," Lorena began tentatively, "Couldn't we stay, father, and you could go and later come back, after you farm the lands?"

"Yes, my daughter, I can return to Mexico and my family can stay here, in this way all of you can survive. You can not survive, unless I leave, and your mother becomes the head of the family." Fortunato explained his position to Lorena and he glanced at her, who was silent and deep in thought. "In reality," Fortunato continued speaking, "This lack of work for our towns' people, the absence of card games at Limonada's and the general poverty in Miami will obligate my departure to Mexico."

When Fortunato and Lorena arrived home, Antonia greeted them with a hug and a kiss, and she poured a glass of milk for Lorena and a cup of coffee for Fortunato. They sat down at the kitchen table to eat some bologna sandwiches. "What do you plan to do, Fortunato?" Antonia asked, in an urgent tone, "What are the other men and their families going to do? What did they say down at Limonada's Pool Hall?"

Fortunato looked at Antonia, took a cautious drink of his hot coffee, and like a snail backing upon its own shadow, finally spoke, trying to make some sense of the situation, "Your family is all American born; your grandmother, Nanita, pioneered settlement in Arizona." He sipped his coffee. "My children are all American born citizens; all your family are American citizens, except me. I am a pure Mexican, without a doubt, and I am proud of it. I will accept the government policy of Repatriation and the government's policy of denying government assistance and jobs to me because I am not a citizen, although I've worked here for years." Fortunato said. He rose to his feet and paced about the kitchen and then sat down again. He looked at Antonia, and with compassion, like a doctor informing a patient of a needed surgical procedure, gazed directly into her eyes, and whispered "I will leave for Mexico so my family will receive the help they need, that is the best solution."

Antonia reached out and held his hand, peered into his eyes in return, and gently pleaded, "We can survive, I will do whatever work I can and you can work at odd jobs," she entreated, "You'll see."

"Antonia, there is no money in this town, the mines are shut down, there are no paydays." Fortunato held his hands out, palms up, hoping for understanding on her part, "There were no card games at Limonada's today for me to deal, even fun games are gone; players just have no money." Thoughts formed in Fortunato's mind, but he was not able to speak, yes, Fortunato thought that he must make sure that his family would be all right: "Yes, I will make the arrangements and leave for Mexico on the Repatriation train," he said. He needed to make his intention clear: "I am leaving on the train, Antonia; you will become the head of the family, so the family can survive." He stood up and walked to the kitchen window and he paced back and forth, like a caged tiger. He looked out the window in amazement and surprise to see how fast the day had ended, and dusk, with a dark blanket, had crept over a mute town to cover it with darkness: there were no flowers for the dead mines, the dead miners, the dead place and for those subsisting under the bridges. Fortunato turned to Antonia and said, "I am sorry for all our family members buried in the cemetery, but I will make the arrangement tomorrow at the county court house with those government officials administering the Repatriation train departures." Fortunato felt like crying.

"Remember our visit with Nanita in Florence and recall her advice, Fortunato," Antonia whispered, "Please, we might perhaps go live in Florence."

"Antonia, you know, as I have told you before, my father left some land for me to farm." Fortunato felt in his very own bones that farming those lands would be the best solution, "My brother Jorge wrote to me that letter I showed you, remember," Fortunato stated his case slowly, "Jorge said that he and my sister Domitila will help me." He paused, and then he said, "The federales shot dead my brother Oton at his ranch in La Noria. The government enclosed his home with barb-wire fence, in January, of this year, mind you, and Tila says in her letter that the government will be confiscating lands like my lands of El Potrero, if I don't cultivate them."

"Let's talk with Nanita, again, and see what she says now, before we make a decision, Fortunato," Antonia pleaded.

"I have to make a decision, Antonia, whether to go or to stay, but do whatever I think is best for the family." Fortunato poured himself a second cup of coffee. "My pocket is pinched by the Great Depression and the Repatriation threatens to push me out of the country." Their home, a hushed mortuary, began the requiem for their departure. Lorena had left the kitchen table and gone to bed, long before this part of the conversation. The children were asleep, it seemed, but Antonia thought that they were all ears to their conversation this night. Fortunato continued speaking, "Yes, I have decided to go by myself and if things work out, you and the children can come later to live with me in El Aliso, Sinaloa."

"Fortunato, let's talk with my brother, Tomas, with some of our friends, with Father Westhoff, please," Antonia urged.

"It is too late," Fortunato concluded. Outside the town was dark and quiet; Fortunato got up from the kitchen table, he walked out into the porch: he wished a moon and stars but there were none.

Antonia stood up and went to look out the window. Outside in the early night, the streets were quiet, people were not walking anywhere in a somber downtown. She did not think the thoughts of Fortunato; otherwise she would have known the town had died.

Fortunato turned back into the kitchen, he drank a glass of water and then continued talking, "Down at Limonada's Pool Hall, Caballón Hernandez asked me today about what I was going to do: Caballón said, 'What about you, Vega, what do you plan to do, stay here or hop on the Repatriation train?'" Fortunato remembered about himself, now, a bull with lowered horns close to the ground and scraping the dirt with his right leg's hoof, at that time, he had seen a red flag waved by Caballón, "I became emotional and asked myself what business was that of him." he looked at Antonia, "But, now I see that this is a problem for all our Mexican people." He continued speaking, "This is not only my problem; all over the country Mexican families are facing the same problem as we are. All I know is that this political reality has forced me to seriously consider returning to my native state. I considered it and I am leaving." Fortunato said with a definite tone of voice, and he added, "I will not speak to Tomas, Nanita, or the priest."

"Remember what Nanita said, she said that we must keep the family together," Antonia answered in a loud enough tone to make sure a departing Fortunato could hear. There were no dogs barking outside in the neighborhood. Antonia felt hungry and decided to make herself some scrambled eggs. The aroma of fried eggs, raised fluffy because Antonia usually mixed in a bit of milk or some yellow cheese, pleasantly filled the kitchen; Antonia served herself her scrambled eggs with a buttered toast. She wondered how it would be like, living alone without Fortunato, but she thought in her mind that he should not go alone. In her heart she knew that life, no matter how tangled, held a better promise for a united family. Antonia's silent tears mixed with her scrambled eggs.

She knew in her heart that every human must suffer, but she wondered if she would be able to do all that would be demanded of her. She thought in her mind that God would be with her and her family and their road would be prepared by his love.

Fortunato Vega, born in the year 1875 in El Aliso, Sinaloa, Mexico to his parents Lorenza Ruiz Vega and Eudoro Vega, journeyed to the United States, at age nineteen, where he worked for thirty-eight years until 1932 when he was repatriated to Mexico. His wife and children, all United States citizens, accompanied him to keep the family together.

The Worm in my Tomato

Five

Lorena
Confronting our enemy with hope

There seemed to be a general agreement among Lorena's brothers and sister with her mother and father to go to Mexico. Not Lorena. She had hurried out of the kitchen to her room, where she cried and made plans to convince her father to stay in Miami. Lorena had told her mother that she did not want to go, and Lorena planned to do her best, yet, to convince her father and mother to stay. There must be another way to solve father's problems with the United States, Lorena thought. Lorena wondered why she should have to suffer the consequences of the conflicts between her father and the government of the United States.

Lorena planned to find out all about the words that crashed through her ears into her head and were causing her problems. She conceived the words in her mind, but she had not known of them before. She hated the very thought of "Crate Deprashon" and the "Repatreeashon" as she had heard the words spoken out loud enough times by her father, mother, and even heard them used by señor "Caballón" Hernandez, but Lorena had not seen them in print and really did not know their significance. Lorena planned to ask her teacher, Miss Yoakum, in her class, to explain these words and what they meant. Monday, when Lorena went to class at Bullion Plaza Elementary School, she was determined to have Miss Yoakum explain to her about the Great Depression and the Repatriation.

Lorena asked Miss Yoakum, "What is a *Crate Deprashon*," Lorena needed to know.

Miss Yoakum said, "Most citizens of the greatest country on earth and most rich of all nations could not believe that it could happen in the United States of America, but it did." She looked sad. "Our country lost all its money," she paused to look at her students, "And that is an economic collapse called the Great Depression." She went on to tell her class that numerous rich men, who had lost all their wealth because of the Great Depression, had killed themselves, "They committed suicide," she said.

Lorena worried that the same thing might happen here in Miami. Already, the mines had died in a way, too, she thought. In Lorena's mind, the Great Depression was mean; it had killed the mines. In a strange way, Lorena did not worry about her father; Lorena was sure her father would not kill himself: he was not rich. But Lorena wondered what would her father do to fight this so- called killer; she wondered how would her family challenge the Great Depression; what could her father do, she thought; what with her father, not even a citizen of the greatest and richest country on earth. Lorena asked herself over and over again, what would her father do against the Great Depression? "Miss Yoakum," Lorena raised her hand, "My father is worried about the 'repattreeashon,' what is that really?" Lorena waited in anticipation for that knowledge.

Lorena's favorite teacher, Miss Yoakum, was very patient with her students; she thought for a while before answering Lorena's question. "The Repatriation is, Lorena, a government policy that seeks to urge Mexican citizens to return to Mexico because there is fear that Mexican people without work, food, or health protection will burden the government relief systems and also there is fear Mexican people will compete for jobs that should be reserved for Americans, especially white European-Americans. These fears caused groups of people to influence and advocate state and federal legislatures to pass laws to bring these policies about." Miss Yoakum looked at Lorena, and Lorena could see that Miss Yoakum's look in her eyes wondered if Lorena had understood. "Repatriation is a government program to help Mexican citizens return to their country, Mexico," Miss Yoakum said, "because their work contribution to our economy is now not necessary."

"I understand, Miss Yoakum," Lorena said. She really did, for that is what her father had told her. "But, Miss Yoakum, can the government force a person who is not a citizen to return to Mexico?"

"Yes, that is called deportation. But searching for, arresting, and convicting in court suspected non-citizens is expensive, thus the

The Worm in my Tomato

government finds it easier and less costly to force by different ways Mexican non-citizens to leave voluntarily on trains provided by the government. This latter political process is called the Repatriation." Miss Yoakum carefully explained.

"Is it painful?" Lorena asked, "Can my father die from it?"

"No, Lorena, it is not painful and you don't die from it directly, but indirectly and in time, it is possible that political realities like the Repatriation policies can cause pain, poverty, death, or any number of dire situations," Miss Yoakum explained.

"Then, Miss Yoakum, my father should have nothing to worry about right away, I mean, like during now."

"Well, that is not altogether true, Lorena, there are always present time difficulties that may happen," Miss Yoakum said and added, "The government at first has made it difficult for non-citizens to survive by denying them government sponsored assistance. Vigilante groups, citizens who take the law into their own hands, may threaten non-citizens, through a variety of means, to leave on a voluntary basis. Do you understand Lorena?" Miss Yoakum studied Lorena carefully and continued speaking, "If non-citizens don't leave voluntarily, the government can deport them. If they leave voluntarily, the non-citizens may get transportation assistance on American trains to the border cities."

"Thank you, Miss Yoakum." Lorena appreciated what she had learned but sensed by looking at the other students in the class that they wished she would ask no more questions. The students knew that Miss Yoakum as usual would ask students to follow-up with a word drill on all words she had used in her sentences and expected her class students to use the words in their own sentences.

"Lorena, are you worried about the Repatriation, as well?" Miss Yoakum was one teacher, among all the other teachers in Bullion Plaza, who showed sincere concern for a number of students, including Lorena, who showed signs of worry, over what they heard and saw in their homes, about the Great Depression and the Repatriation.

She sensed that Lorena may not really know the words Miss Yoakum was using, thus she then spelled out the words of what she had talked about. "Children, write these words down in your word drill notebooks. She spelled out the words with white chalk on the blackboard: *G R E A T D E P R E S S I O N* and the *R E P A T R I A T I O N*. Lorena wrote down the words and repeated them softly to herself, as Miss Yoakum had pronounced them. Lorena was glad that Miss Yoakum always conducted vocabulary drills in class. Miss Yoakum was her favorite teacher and vocabulary class was her favorite, after reading time. Lorena had already finished reading "On the Road," a book about going on a trip to visit grandfather in his farm in the country where all was fresh, green, and the rooster crowed while standing on a white fence.

"Lorena, where were you born?" Miss Yoakum asked after sitting at her desk.

"I was born in the blue house on Live Oak Street, here in 'Mayahma', Arizona, the house number is 922 and it is blue and it has a porch out front by the sidewalk," Lorena answered.

"Well, you are an American, and you should not have to worry about the Repatriation. But if your family takes you to Mexico, for one reason or another, remember that you are an American and that you have every right to be here, in Miami, Arizona," Miss Yoakum asserted, and added, "Just tell anybody who asks, that you are an American and have every right to be here."

"Yes, mam, I won't forget," Lorena answered, and she meant it, too, with all her heart.

Later, at home, all Lorena heard her father talk about with her mother was about the, as he called it, "dammed *Repartition*." He often said, "The political policies of this country threaten thousands of Mexican citizens with a return to Mexico," he hissed, "Dammed." He shook his fists, but Fortunato had already packed his bags. He knew the land distribution policies of Mexico as well threatened his inherited El Potrero lands.

Now, what Lorena wondered about was why the Repatriation worried her father so much? Lorena knew that the Repatriation did not kill, like the Great Depression. She felt some real concern for her father, however, when she remembered what Miss Yoakum had said: 'Indirectly and in time, it is possible that political realities like the Repatriation policies can cause pain, poverty, death, or any number of dire situations.' Lorena thought how important time must be and how

The Worm in my Tomato

time held hidden within it what would happen in the future, but for now it was unknown. She wondered about all this and the unknown gave her grave concern. In truth, not the least of all, Lorena wondered how all this would change her life. She, at the same time resented the Repatriation, what with all going so nice and dandy for her in school and movies and her friends, she thought. Lorena thought about how her father had lamented, "This town is dead." She recognized that it was true: the mines were not breathing; Lorena had noticed *that*; for months now, there had been no smelter smoke in the air. Lorena herself realized that on her way to school, the canyon valleys looked green, fresh and wet with clean dewdrops. Everyone knew that the mines' machinery gears and what not were shut down; silence covered their grounds. The sky was clear and blue except when it stormed, but now the plants and flowers stood straight, full of color, and danced with the breeze every morning: the air, crisp and clean, kissed the flowers hello.

Lorena had heard her father complain to her mother that the gambling games, down at Limonada's Pool Hall, were not happening; She worried about her father who lacked gambling games to earn his money. Lorena had heard her father exclaim: 'It is true, many miners spend most of their time at home wringing their hands or they spend their time in the bars and pool halls, not drinking, doing nothing, no one has any money to play card games.' Lorena remembered that her father had the sad face look on him, at those times. But she kept reminding herself that her father was not rich and this helped her sleep at night, although she worried about the unknown that the day might bring.

The night fell over the town like a heavy dark cloud, not even the moon showed up. Lorena could hear her father all night, pacing up and down in his bedroom; she thought that her father spent a great amount of time thinking how to challenge the Great Depression and the Repatriation. Lorena looked at the words in her school notebook; she slowly pronounced them carefully over and over again and again, until she fell asleep.

Saturday, Lorena's mother sent her on the usual errand: to take her father his sack lunch and a thermos of coffee downtown to Limonada's

The Worm in my Tomato

Pool Hall. And as usual, Lorena was ordered to wait until he finished his lunch and return to her mother the utensils, the cup and thermos bottle. That was all right for Lorena; she rested on a small sofa, and read some comic books scattered among other books, left over from better days. Mr. Limonada, during the time when the mines were open and the miners were working, had provided new up-to-date magazines and books for women and children when they came and waited for a husband or a father to hand over the check or whatever money was left over, after the husbands and fathers had gambled for hours. But now that the mines had died, only old left over copies of books, magazines and comic books, which women and children could read, were available. The women and children sometimes used the newspapers with stories about the Great Depression, to swat flies. Lorena remembered when the mines were alive, her father, then, had been in charge of the gambling tables. Those were the "good old days" she remembered her father had said. 'Better days,' he had said, 'when the mines were alive and running.' There were many women and children, then, Lorena remembered. Today, Lorena was the only one, and she was certainly not a woman waiting for a husband's pay check. No, not at all, Lorena thought to herself, I am a student of Bullion Plaza School, here studying my word drill book. Lorena did not think of herself being a child, either. Lorena was almost ten and in the fourth grade, already. By July 18th, her birthday, she would be ten years old, by September, she would be a fifth grader, and fifth graders were considered by Lorena as being as big and smart as the students in the sixth, seventh, and eighth grade: nobody pushed fifth graders around at Bullion Plaza, Lorena smiled. She remembered when Miss Yoakum had told her mother Antonia during an open house at school that Lorena was a very *precocious* girl, a student that should plan to attend college after high school graduation. Antonia had said nothing, but Lorena knew that, by her mother's facial expression, she was in trouble and may get a scolding at home. Indeed, Antonia had told Lorena in no uncertain terms to pay attention in class and to be quiet and quit being "*loquacious*."

A few men sat around tables playing dominos, checkers, or black-jack, using beans. Lorena could hear them talking and smell their awful smoking stink of cigarettes and cigars. She noticed that they did not smile; she saw that their table ash trays were full of gray ashes and cigarette butts and a few old cigars smoked to the very end. Lorena thought to herself that the old cigar butts were probably Caballón's. One of the men talked loud in a rough scratchy voice. "This shit of a Great Depression, even now going strong in 1932, is the worst ever in the United States, and it has ruined us all and messed up the life of our family." He slammed a newspaper hard on the pool table.

A man without a left arm and hand, called "El Mocho" by his friends around the table, responded: "Sure, you're right, there's no work. It's worse than a strike, at least with a strike, there is hope; the copper union would help us."

How true, Lorena thought, she remembered how her mother had said the same thing, her mother had told her children that mine workers had no jobs, food, and had lost their houses, 'So be prepared for hard times ahead,' her mother had said. Lorena's father worked at Limonada's Pool Hall and he did not have a miner's job to lose. But still his games had ended. Lorena's girl friends at school had told her that their parents had said that it was all like a "domino's effect", you know, that many people had lost their jobs in stores, car dealers, restaurants, and the city dump, and so on. My father had lost his card games in the same way, Lorena thought, and here I am: watching the Dominos games; the men playing on their green flannel covered table did not even care, she told herself.

Lorena also tried hard to understand the comparison between the Great Depression and the Influenza plague. She thought that better this economic depression situation, and not a disease like last year's Influenza plague; the Great Depression had only killed the mines and the "economy", like mother had said. Besides I know Typhoid fever killed my sister Toni, Lorena said to herself. Lorena had seen this morning how the downtown hotels, restaurants, stores, and other places of past employment were boarded up tight and dead for sure. She remembered that in the past, all of the school kids in the families had lacked money, but never seemed to really know it. Now, large numbers of the mothers and fathers of her friends lacked money, but were scared by it. Lorena's friends like Maria Cota, told horrible stories, like when they asked for a nickel for a candy bar or a soda, they didn't get it, not even a penny. It was bad for our teachers, too, Lorena thought. School teachers like Miss Yoakum and Miss Jackson at Bullion Plaza Elementary were paid, as they told Lorena's class, with credit coupons which could be exchanged for food at the stores, Lorena knew all about that. But the Repatriation must be worse than the Great Depression, Lorena concluded, because the Repatriation made families get on trains and leave all behind, family, friends, and even her sister Toni in the cemetery. Lorena knew her father was correct; it was a *"Repartition,"* after all.

After returning home with her father's lunch utensils and coffee thermos bottle, Lorena greeted her mother and her brother Samuel, who were in the kitchen. Antonia was washing dishes in the sink, and she said to Samuel and Lorena, "It is all over the radio and the newspapers, especially La Prensa Mexicana," Mother looked at Samuel because he worked at La Prensa, "People talking everywhere, that the time of the Great Depression in the United States, a time of hunger and homelessness, may also be the end of the world," Antonia said, and added, "Say your prayers to the saints and behave yourselves, especially these days, children should obey their parents."

"Everybody can see that many families lack a home, food, and health care," Samuel responded, as he drank a cup of warm mint leaves tea: "Radio voices scream it out every day."

Lorena, while drying the dishes with a dish towel, listened and she said, "I know. Miss Yoakum talked about it all in our library class. She said that millions of people on the streets formed long lines; persons hungry for soup." Lorena imagined long lines like the Conga, she thought, waiting for food at almost empty soup kitchens. "When I walked to Limonada's Pool Hall this morning, I saw many homeless men under the bridge that is over our town wash."

"Where they came from, who knows," Samuel said and added, "I saw homeless men, making coffee over a stick fire under the bridge, they pushed and pulled at each other, I guess, fighting with each other for space, around the fire. This was a month ago, in February, especially cold this year." Samuel sipped his mint tea.

Antonia told Lorena and Samuel that she heard stories of homeless persons who died under bridges; many men in search of work became hobos who hitched rides on railroad cars to somewhere, that they thought would offer a job. "Everyone knows, the radio voices, teachers, lonely men down at the pool hall, the priest at our church, Mr. Julian, the fruit and vegetable seller, Mrs. Cota, our neighbor, they all know: a bad economy caused hunger, homelessness, and illness," Antonia said.

"Yes, mama, my friend Maria Cota and my other classmates, all know, that the same conditions are all over our richest country, where millions of people lack employment, like Miss Yoakum says; babies are hungry, and men came to live under our town's bridges, but worst of all, the mines died," Lorena told her mother and Samuel, "There mama, I finished drying all the dishes, can I study my word drill book, now?"

Since Antonia and Samuel remained silent, Lorena continued speaking. "Our neighbors, the families of my classmates, and I guess the rich men that had lost their million dollars, but who had not killed themselves, and all the miners in our own town, became dependent on government help."

"All are on social welfare programs, except your father, Lorena," Antonia said. "This is why your father wants to leave for Mexico and work the lands that will give us food and a home." Antonia began to wash the soup pan.

Fortunato walked into the kitchen and helped himself to a cup of coffee, "It is a time when the Mexican workers are pushed out instead of a time when they are pulled in to do the work." He sat down at the table to drink his coffee, "It is a time when the political policy of *Repartition* has raised its ugly claws in the form of national and state laws to push out Mexican workers back to Mexico." Fortunato stood up and paced around the table, and then again sat down at the kitchen table. "There is no way out, we will have to go to Mexico," Fortunato exclaimed.

"I don't want to go, father, please let me stay with my Uncle Tomas," Lorena pleaded, putting down her word drill book she had been studying.

"No, Lorena, we must keep the family together, as Nanita said," Antonia addressed Lorena directly. "Your Uncle Tomas and his wife Nellie can not care for you in their home."

The Worm in my Tomato

"I will then ask Maria Cota if I can stay with her family, I don't want to go to Mexico. I want to continue my education here at Bullion, *Mayahma* is my home," Lorena insisted, "Why don't you convince father to stay, mama?"

"Your father will not be able to get government help here, there is no work, and no one knows how long this bad economy will last. Your father needs to go work the lands his father left him."

"Let's talk it over as a family, again, mother," Lorena insisted, "and see if this is what we should do."

"No, Lorena, we have discussed this already over and over again. No, you will not stay with anyone's family, and furthermore, Lorena, you will go to Mexico. We will take this journey as a family," Antonia emphasized.

Lorena did not respond, and she hurried away from the kitchen and went to her room. She sat on her bed to ponder her 'dilemma,' as Lorena remembered Miss Yoakum had used that word many times and Lorena had written up her own sentences using the word *dilemma*. She thought about the problem which she felt her family should see, but it seemed that they could not see it. Maybe, she thought, that perhaps she was selfish as Samuel had told her. Lorena thought that it would not be to her advantage to stay with Nanita and Aunt Josie in Florence; in her mind, the town was simply a small rural farming town. Lorena wanted to stay in Miami, she thought again about staying here in Miami with her Uncle Tomas and his wife Nellie. Uncle Tomas was her mother's only brother, and *that* was it in Lorena's mind: he would take care of his only older niece, she thought. Lorena decided to try again to convince her mother and her father that she could protect her mother's only brother from the "Domino's game." But first Lorena planned to convince Samuel and Jose to help her with her plan. This time Lorena intended to involve her brothers in her plan to her advantage. She knew that Uncle Tomas was her last chance.

Lorena did not want to move away with her mother and father to Mexico, Lorena called going to Mexico: "My Mother's Journey to Egypt," Lorena saw no reason for it. Lorena thought about how her father called it "Repartition" and in her mind Lorena saw that her parents were *repartitioning* the family. She thought how both her mother and father had talked about nothing but the Repatriation for weeks. She remembered how her mother blamed the 'Poverty of the wicked Great Depression' that had closed the copper mines in Miami and in other mining towns in the state. Now, Lorena had observed how people were leaving for California and other states to be near families. Many of her classmates had left and her class was only half in size. Lorena thought about how a girl named Jodie, who she met at the Real Market, had come from Oklahoma, but her daddy had told her it was no use going back. People stood in soup lines and begged for food. Lorena wondered if that soup was like the 'cocido' her mother cooked for her family with the meat bone she bought from Mr. José Suárez, the store keeper and meat seller, and she thought of perhaps standing in line to find out.

Lorena thought about the homeless who lived under the bridges that crossed over the big wash in her town. She wondered if her father, along with many other Mexican men, non-United States citizens, was being forced to be a hobo. Lorena knew that many other men, like her father, who were fathers of some of her classmates who had left school, were offered train rides by the United States government Repatriation office and had returned to Mexico. In most cases, the family members of these men encouraged to participate in the Repatriation had never been to Mexico. Lorena remembered how scared her school friends, who knew nothing about Mexico, had been. She thought about how she had never been to Mexico, but, she was sure, that the government did not care.

Mexican citizens were sent back, even if their wives and children were American citizens. Lorena had not slept that night and in the morning she could not bear to think anymore of any of this Repatriation and she ran to Mary Cota's house to talk things over with her friend. Lorena and Mary sat on a bench outside in Mary's backyard under the Chinaberry tree. Lorena told Mary all she knew: "My father has planned to return to join his family in Mexico where he has 'inherited'," and Lorena thought to herself, thank you Miss Yoakum, "some land from his father, now dead and gone."

"What has he planned to do in Mexico?" Mary Cota wrinkled her nose in her customary way, "My father says that Mexico has the Great Depression, too."

"He has planned to grow tomatoes, other food crops and cotton. We would all do just fine," Lorena gestured with an emphatic downturn of her head, "he'd be helped by Aunt Tila and Uncle Jorge, my father's family." Lorena felt odd, like if she was trying to make a good thing out of what her father planned to do. Lorena continued with making the good thing: "My mother and my family would live in grandfather's big house in El Aliso, now taken care by my father's sister, our Aunt Domitila, called 'Tila' for short," Lorena felt uncomfortable not knowing why she was trying to impress Mary Cota.

"But what does your mother say about this?" Mary Cota stretched her arms out with palms up, "My mother told my father that if he wanted to return to Aguascalientes, she would pack his bags, and he'd go by himself."

"Then your mother would not carry her Christian cross; doesn't she have a Nanita?" Lorena was surprised and added, "Mother has been won over by my father after their many talking times in the kitchen as they drank their morning, afternoon and evening coffee." Lorena peeled some bark off the Chinaberry tree, for no reason, and said, "Mother has been convinced to go to Mexico even after she had tried so hard to keep the family and my father in Miami." She threw the bark pieces away, "My brothers Samuel and Jose are in agreement with mother, too," Lorena's straight brown hair flipped side to side as she shook her head, "they were already packed from the first day and my little sister and baby brother had nothing to say at all," Lorena, annoyed, sat down on the bench. Lorena looked at Mary Cota straight in the eye and without blinking, asked her: "Could I stay at your house?"

"That would be fun," Mary smiled, then, she puckered her lips and her face wrinkled in sadness, "I already have asked mother if you could stay with me, but my mother said no, because dad is not working." She wriggled on the bench, "My dad, too, may have to take the train to Aguascalientes, Mexico where his family lives, and look for work."

Lorena nodded, understanding, and scattered her collection of yellow chinaberries off the bench. In the same movement, she scurried out and said, "Good-bye, Mary." Lorena's thoughts were swirling again as she tried to sort things out and make sense of what was happening. My mother should stay in Miami, where she has lived forever, like umpteen generations in Arizona. She should let my father return to Mexico alone, like Mary Cota's father, at least for awhile, on his own, Lorena thought. But Lorena remembered how her mother had made up her mind to accompany her father on his Repatriation: Nanita told my mother that she was obligated to follow her husband because she was my father's wife and that at any cost she must carry her cross as a Christian wife. Lorena knew that where the Christian wife and mother

went, the family was sure to go. Lorena found it hard to admit that she herself was included as part of the family. Lorena found it difficult to plan her talk with her Uncle Tomas; she wondered what she would say, but she made up her mind to visit Our Lady of the Blessed Sacrament Church to pray and talk with the priest.

The town wash ran from west to east through the middle of town and divided the town into two north and south sides. During rain storms it carried torrential flood waters from the Pinal Mountains on the southwest. Flood waters overflowed the cement paved sides of the wash and flooded homes.

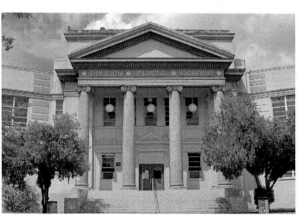

Bullion Plaza School, constructed in 1923, served Mexican-American and Apache children. Lorena attended the school until the Repatriation policy of the United States ended her education in March, 1932. This is where her teacher Miss Yoakum taught for many years.

The Worm in my Tomato

Six
Lorena
An ordeal to overcome

When Lorena hurried into her house after visiting Mary Cota, she overheard her father telling her mother, over their coffee in the kitchen, "We are moving away to Mexico within a week." A terrifying emotion gripped Lorena, her hands became cold and sweaty, and she could not stop trembling.

Lorena just knew it, that her life would become a series of torments. Lorena's throat immediately went dry; her eyes became dams of held-up tears threatening to gush down the gullies of her cheeks. Her natural self-interest, like a dormant volcano, came back to life, erupting questions: "Will I ever return to my hometown?" "What will happen to my education?" "Can I stay here with my Uncle Tomas?" Weakness in Lorena's knees almost toppled her under. A queasy sensation upset her stomach, threatening at any moment to cause her to throw-up, sick with worry. Lorena kept telling herself, out loud: "I am not rich, I am not rich; the Great Depression can not kill me."

Lorena's father paced around the kitchen table, again like a small tiger, a medium tall man, husky of frame like Antonia's brother, Tomas, his high- pitched voice, at the moment, betrayed an unwanted nervousness, but unexpectedly, Fortunato laughed a joyous low sound. From Lorena's vantage point, seated to one side of a large wooden cupboard standing up-right near the entrance to the kitchen from a hallway, she studied her father's face: Pale white smooth skin, soft brown eyes, prominent jaw and forehead; his face, although recently shaved in the morning, yet showed a shaded dark blue hued shadow around his cheeks and jaw.

Hidden, out of sight and un-obtrusive, but determined to shout her protest to her father's crazy ideas, Lorena shouted: "No, father, I will not go, I can't go and leave my school, my friends behind forever, no, I will not go," Lorena gasped out of breath; tears poured out of her eyes.

"Your father returned from a visit, this morning, to the government

The Worm in my Tomato

office that promotes and administers the Repatriation policy of the United States." Antonia said, and she sternly fixed Lorena with her eyes, but her eyes betrayed a tenderness for Lorena, and Antonia added softly, "Listen Lorena, listen, your father has promised we will go only for five years and then return to Miami, just give him a chance to farm his lands and help his family keep them safe from the federal government, please daughter." Antonia kissed Lorena on the cheek.

Antonia, twenty years younger than Fortunato, always defended him, protected him, and loved him. She was not too tall, rather a robust five feet, two inches, with her long black hair rolled in waves short below her neck at her back. She looked formidable and beautiful. Light glistened in her large round brown eyes. "He can't find work, he can't force the government to undo the Repatriation law, do you want to stay here and starve?"

Fortunato stopped pacing in front of the kitchen breakfast table. He sat down. With a shaky hand he held up his coffee cup and sipped black coffee. He preferred black coffee, no sugar and cream. He would always say, "Why destroy the natural taste of coffee." He wore one of several usual blue suits that he had considered lucky in his work as a card dealer at Limonada's pool hall's back room gambling sessions that some times had lasted late into the night. Fortunato had taught himself to read, learned the ways of people and wisdom in the manner of life. He was well-versed in the Holy Bible and liked to write poetry.

"What exactly did you find out?" Antonia asked Fortunato, with an urgent tone in her voice.

Lorena had picked up the baby from his crib when she heard him cry, and held her baby brother in her arms, she kept him content with a rubber pacifier nipple in his mouth; Lorena moved closer to hear what her father had to say.

"One week to pack. The government train will transport us and our home furniture to Nogales. From there the Mexican train will take us and our belongings to San Blas Sinaloa, and it should not cost us much, maybe nothing, it's all the government's Repatriation business." He sipped. He stood up. He sat down. Lorena's neck began to hurt from just following all her father's nervous erratic movements. Lorena continued thinking, still determined to stop *this* moving to Mexico madness, and she wondered about what to do.

"What about money?" Habitually practical Antonia asked.

"My brother Jorge will telegram me a check tomorrow. We'll buy the children clothes and buy Lorena a new pair of shoes," he sipped, he stood, and he sat. Lorena did not move her neck, but only concentrated on his words.

"What about my education?" Lorena squeaked, loud enough to startle Santos into crying.

"You'll have a new dress and a pair of shiny black leather shoes." Lorena's father answered her as he turned to leave.

"Father, we need to talk, really, my school teacher said..." But Fortunato had sipped, stood, and hurried out of the house with Lorena tagging behind him to the front door.

"Lorena, let your father go. He's going to see Mr. José Suárez about taking over our house for money we owe." Antonia "sh, shushed" the baby and rocked his cradle; Antonia began to busy herself about the kitchen.

With some temerity, Lorena approached her mother in the kitchen while her mother prepared a bottle of milk for her baby brother. "Mother, could we please stay here and just let my father go by himself to Mexico; Mary Cota's mother is not carrying any Christian cross for her husband and she packed his bags," Lorena said.

Antonia's dark black wavy hair glistened in the light from the open window as she turned to face Lorena. Antonia smiled, and her large brown eyes twinkled. "Lorena, please understand that the copper mines have closed," Antonia gave Santos the bottle and he greedily began to suck the nipple and guzzle up the milk, "your father has no work here," and she continued, "Here, hold Santos; burp him afterwards," She turned to wash more potatoes, "Our family has to stay together."

"Well, then, could I stay by myself so I can stay in school," Lorena pleaded.

"Who could you stay with?" Antonia asked, drying the potatoes.

"I could stay with my friend Mary Cota and her family," Lorena blurted out, fully knowing that Mary Cota had already told her that she could not stay with her family.

"No, Mr. Cota lost his job at the mine, too, and Mrs. Cota told me that they may have to leave for Aguascalientes." Antonia set the

The Worm in my Tomato

potatoes down on the counter by the sink, preparing to peel and dice them, and she said, "Burp the baby and go place him in his crib, and then come back to help me prepare lunch."

"What about Nanita?" Lorena asked, looking back over her right shoulder while taking her baby brother to his crib in his room. "She could come live in our house." Lorena could hear her mother bang a skillet and rattle a pan. Lorena hurried back into the kitchen.

"No, Nanita is ninety-two years old, Lorena; didn't you see how frail she looked when we visited her last week?" Antonia stopped cutting onions for a moment, "And your Aunt Josie already has enough worries to have you add to her problems; cut the tomatoes and the lettuce." Antonia washed the potatoes, "Hurry, your father and the boys will be here soon," Antonia said with finality, indicating the conversation was over.

In silence, Lorena went through the motions of helping her mother in preparing lunch; she fought back her tears. Lorena felt like screaming out her frustration. Lorena thought about how she had approached her mother with her request and she planned to talk with her again. But for now, Lorena wondered how she could convince her parents to allow her to stay in Miami. The family would still keep together, except for Lorena. Lorena hurriedly chopped potatoes to fry with ground beef and onions. Her eyes were blurred with tears. She needed mother's support. But next, Lorena decided to approach her father, again.

After lunch, Lorena sought out her father in his room where he was sorting out suits and shirts. "Father," Lorena began in a soft voice, "You know how much I have always loved school." Fortunato stopped folding a shirt for a moment. He looked at Lorena with his soft brown eyes. But Lorena swallowed hard and pressed on, "My desire is to continue my education. I just started fourth grade last September and don't want to drop before May," Lorena studied him as he patiently folded his shirt. "We have an exciting new reader titled "On the Road" and I want to read the stories over again about visiting grandfather in the country farm," why didn't he say something, Lorena thought; her father just began slowly to fold another shirt. "Well, I want to go to high school and later attend college here in Arizona." Lorena felt like screaming, but controlled her emotion and simply said, "Could I stay here in Miami?" There, she had said it.

The thought had a life of its own as it swirled inside her father's head and exploded out his ears. "Lorena," he responded in his quiet way, "you are so young yet." He looked at her with gentleness in his eyes and smiled, "You have a life-time to get an education."

"My teacher told us in class to start planning now," Lorena persisted. "My friend Mary Cota and I were making plans on how we would go to college." Lorena walked over to a straight-back wooden chair and sat down. "I could stay with Mary Cota's family."

"The Cota family and all the other families we know are being *repartitioned*." He said firmly, "You can't stay here with a family."

"What about Nanita and Aunt Josie," Lorena beseeched, "Both could come live here in our house."

"Nanita is old now and your Aunt Josie must care for her and Josie would not have time to care for you, too," he pointed this out with both his palms facing up, gesturing up and down, "Can't you see?"

"I am really big for my age and can take care of myself," Lorena stood up from her chair. "I help mother with the housework and cooking and take care of Catalina and Santos," Lorena stood up on her tip-toes, stretching herself tall as she could, "I will be eleven in July, too."

"No, you will be ten years old, and yes, you are tall for your age and strong; that is why you should go with us, because Catalina is too young and Santos is a baby." He reached for another shirt and said, "Your mother, he explained, "will need you to help her care for them in Mexico." He sat down at the edge of the bed, and just gazed at Lorena while holding up his shirt to fold.

"Samuel and Jose, they are eighteen and sixteen years old," Lorena explained, "and they can help mother care for Santos." Lorena supposed that her brothers Samuel and Jose desired to go to Mexico, anyway.

"They are boys," her father said with some exasperation in his voice, "They must work to help the family."

"They are older than me, and mother can care for Catalina and Santos," Lorena determined to try again, "can I stay, and Aunt Josie look after me?" That was the only solution she could think of at this moment.

"Never," he said impatiently, "you would have to stay in Florence

The Worm in my Tomato

with Nanita and your Aunt Josie, not in Miami," he placed an opened suitcase on the bed and began to neatly fit his shirts into it, and added, "We have to vacate this house immediately and turn it over to Don Jose Suárez." He looked grieved and in a state of agitation. Lorena felt that he almost wanted to yell at her; Lorena thanked him and walked out his room, quickly.

Later in the day Lorena found her father in the kitchen having his afternoon glass of tea. Unlike her Uncle Tomas, Fortunato did not drink beer or whiskey and he did not smoke, what he did was gamble. Lorena said to her father, "Can I stay…"

"Lorena," Fortunato said sternly and startled her back to reality, "you have strained my patience past the breaking point." Lorena could hear Santos wailing in his crib; she could hear muffled sounds from mother, "shs, shs, shs, there you are," and she imagined Santos in her mind taking his bottle and again greedily sucking out the milk. "You have worried your mother with your ideas of staying behind and you have argued with your brothers," her father quickly slurped up his tea, "I don't like it." His tone of voice rose up louder, "I don't like it when children nag and nag and try to make the decisions," he looked anxious, "I have made all the arrangements with the government office here, the train will take us to Mexico, your mother will have all her furniture that she plans to take with us packed and loaded on the train," he gulped another mouth full of tea and drained the glass empty, "for the final time, the answer to your staying is no, no, no and no, again; furthermore, you will be the first to get on the train," he drew up air from his empty glass, "you are going, and that's final," he shouted.

Again, Lorena thanked her father, and like a little dog, just having been brushed out side the door, with a broom, that shuffles out with his tail between his hind legs, Lorena shuffled out, too, tears streaming down her face. Lorena, again, went to the church to pray, and she knelt at the foot of the altar and said, "Please, God and Our Mother Virgin Mary help me somehow to stay in *Mayahma*." Lorena, a gentle dove, then told Father Westhoff, who at the moment had stepped into the church to arrange the altar, "I don't want to go to Mexico." The priest said: "Our Blessed Mother's home is in Mexico; she is Our Virgin Mary of Guadalupe, Mother of the true God." But Lorena did not

The Worm in my Tomato

understand what he meant, and she ran home.

When Lorena entered her house, she said, "What about my education?"

Lorena heard her father's loud voice in her left ear, "Your education is my business; I make all decisions regarding your education, now go pack."

"My cardboard shoes are torn," Lorena blurted.

"Today, I will be receiving the money telegram from my brother Jorge and my sister Domitila. I will give your mother some money so she will purchase clothes for you children; I will purchase a new pair of shoes for you, Lorena, now leave." Fortunato hurried out, no doubt on his way downtown for his last day at Limonada's, Lorena thought.

Lorena was on the verge of tears and red faced and unhappy as she bolted out from the kitchen to her room for a long silent cry. She thought that perhaps there was still someway to stay; suddenly, Lorena had an idea, she needed to talk with Samuel and Jose.

The following morning, after her talk with her father the day before, Lorena took direct action. She quickly searched for Samuel and Jose, and found them in the backyard playing their game of washers. They stood behind a line scratched on the ground and then each in turn tossed small iron washers into a narrow round hole in the ground that was twelve feet distance away from the line.

"What a silly game," Lorena said, "and a waste of time." Both boys ignored her. Lorena said again, louder, "Why don't both you boys look for work; you know that father lost his gambling dealer's job at Limonada's Pool Hall."

"Go away, Lorena," Samuel scowled, while he took careful aim at the hole in the ground and carefully, underhand, threw his washer, trying to get it to fall into the hole.

"Yeah, go play hop-scotch or jacks with Mary," Jose blurted out, taking his turn at the line and carefully aiming his toss to cause his washer to slide into the hole.

"I have a plan," Lorena persisted, "let's strike, you know, like the miners did at the mine that time, last year." She paused to see their reaction on their face. Lorena saw the blood slowly creep up their necks and into their red face. "Well, our parents would not be able to

The Worm in my Tomato

find other kids as strikebreakers, right?"

"Wish, mom would find someone else to take your place in this family," quipped Jose.

"Now, Lorena," Samuel stood with his hands on his hips, "We are going, see?"

"What about your education, your work with Mr. Mendoza in getting out La Prensa Mexicana to Limonada's," Lorena inquired, "don't you want to finish high school?" She did not wait for an answer, "I do, and I want *you* to talk to mother and father," Lorena stood straight and tall as she could, "and help me convince them to let me stay here with Uncle Tomas and Nellie."

"We are packed, already," Samuel answered, "it's an adventure I am looking forward to," and he looked at Lorena contemptuously. "Anyhow, I can get a job writing in Mexico, don't forget, I took two years of Spanish in high school."

"Yeah, I can get a job anywhere, besides I want to live in the "Big House," Jose commented. "We're not interested in helping you, Lorena," Jose stated firmly, "mother needs you to help her with the baby, who else would help her with the housework?"

"Don't be so selfish," Samuel remarked, "Lorena, don't you know, family comes first?" Samuel flung the washer at the hole instead of carefully sliding the washer toward the hole and said, "You can't stay with Uncle Tomas and live in his house with Nellie, both spend too much time celebrating with beer and other alcohol stuff." Samuel stared at Lorena for some time, "No, you can't stay; we will not help you, and another thing, don't talk to us again about your not wanting to go to Mexico and about your education."

"Yeah," blurted Jose, "besides, mother said that we all go so that father does not go alone, and that we keep the family together."

Lorena felt devastated and tears welled in her eyes. She turned and ran away back into the house, to be by herself. She was in a quandary, what else can I do, Lorena asked herself. With the back of her right hand, she felt her right check to see if she was running a fever. Lorena had already tried to convince her parents and failed. But, somehow, she made up her mind to stay; she planned to go talk with her Uncle Tomas; somehow, Uncle Tomas would save her from this terrible ordeal, she hoped. Somehow, Lorena believed, Uncle Tomas would help convince her family to stay here, to keep together in Miami, or say to them that he and Nellie would welcome her in their home. Lorena prayed, "Help me baby Jesus; you were an immigrant, remember, and you crossed a border; help me not to go to Mexico but stay here in my home."

Antonia did not want to leave behind her many family members buried in the Miami Cemetery.

Lorena saw homeless men under the bridge that is over the town wash.

The Worm in my Tomato

Seven

Jose and Samuel
One last look at the town they loved

Next day, Jose told Samuel that they must run away, Jose didn't know if he was serious, but he knew that he was getting desperate, "We need to make a plan," Jose told Samuel.

"What," Samuel stared at Jose, "did Lorena get to you, too?"

Jose felt sorry for Lorena; he thought to himself that she had no sense of what was possible and what was not possible; he said to Samuel, "She should know that it is not possible to convince our father of anything, once his mind is made up." Jose added, "As for us, don't you think Samuel, that we should understand what Miami is like, and then compare our town later to Aliso, Mexico, where we are going: we can then decide if we want to stay or come back home?"

Although Jose was sixteen years old, he considered himself too young to run away from his family. One deterrent was that Jose had seen too many hobos under the bridges downtown, and even though he enjoyed his classes at Miami High School, Jose needed to reflect on the problem facing his family and consider what it meant, either staying in Miami or leaving his birthplace for Mexico. Jose knew that he and Samuel did not really want to go to Mexico, but Jose thought that they felt like orphans, always dependent on mother. "We are sheep, not knowing if we are led to a greener pasture or to something worse," Jose said.

"We will help mother keep our family together, Jose, we both will, but you and I, well, we hope to leave our family and be on our own, sometime, right?" Samuel said.

"Yeah, Samuel," Jose answered and added, "Why don't we invite Lorena for a last walk through town?" Both Samuel and Jose thought it a good idea to invite Lorena to walk with them. In this way they hoped they could help each other carry memories of their hometown in their hearts; also in this way their going away to a strange land would not

The Worm in my Tomato

be so bad; especially, they were concerned about their sister Lorena. They hoped to convince her to accept gracefully to go to Mexico to support their mother and father.

Lorena agreed, and they walked on one of the two long streets which stretched east and west, Sullivan Street, the town's main street; they walked east to the end of town, and then across a bridge spanning the town wash, and then walked west on Live Oak Street which doubled as a state highway. They walked around in front of Bullion Plaza School on the far west end whose grounds and building connected both streets, they walked in silence observing and thinking about their home town.

"*My-ah-ma*" as Mexican American natives enunciated the town's name, sprawled itself over hill-tops; a large wash or cement lined canal that flowed from west to east and carried flood waters during the storm season of July and August, split the town down the middle. Houses perched on top of hills with definitive names such as Church Hill because there had been a red-house church at the top of it, and Depot Hill because there was the train depot at the bottom of the hill. Between and at the base of the hills snaked dirt roads from the entrance up to the end where the hills came together. These were called "Canyons." There were, among others, Davis Canyon, Live Oak Canyon, Mexican Canyon, and Turkey Shoot Canyon. Canyon roads were usually dirt. Red Springs Street was the only canyon that had a paved road leading up the hill, and perhaps for that reason was called a street. Among the few streets of the town, other than Sullivan and Live Oak, were Gibson Street, and Frederick Street.

Along the sides of the big wash that ran through the middle of town, facing away from the wash and toward Sullivan and Live Oak Streets, were houses and stores that lined beside and fronting the sidewalks of the two paved streets.

"You see, here, Jose and Lorena," Samuel pointed out, "The whole town rests outside of and along the big wash and the rest of the houses sit on top of hills. Larger and higher mountains encircle and surround the town; these mountains are rich in copper ore."

"Yeah, I know, the Miami Copper Company and the Inspiration Copper Company," Jose pointed in the direction of the Mines, "are located on the north and east end of town up the mountains."

"What I didn't like was the smoke we used to have when the mines were operated," Lorena pointed with her hands above her head and gestured a circle around her, "Miss Yoakum told us, and I have written it down in my notebook that smelter smoke is bad for us, and bad for animals and plants; you remember mother's garden," Lorena glanced at Jose, "remember how the Smelter belched out constant smoke from the tall emission chimney; smelter smoke containing high content in sulfur dioxide," thank you Miss Yoakum, Lorena thought to herself, "and other acids that settled over the town?"

"Yeah, heck, the plants wilted and people were made sick. That is why I always hiked up to Cherry Flats," Jose pointed up toward the Cherry Flats to the west and south end of town, high up in the Pinal Mountains. There the mountains were covered with *manzanita* bushes, spruce and pine trees; white billowy clouds crowned these green-blue mountains and flowed on into the light blue sky.

"Well, Jose, one thing we can compare is our seasons, you know, how during the rain season, in July and August, the wash carries flood waters. The flood torrents scream as they dash downstream and scrape the sides of the wash walls and leap over the walls. Homes on both streets, during summer storms, get drenched and flooded and their rooms packed in mud." Samuel surveyed the streets with his eyes, as they walked along the streets.

"Yeah, Samuel, I wonder if the river in El Aliso floods the streets," Jose said.

"It would be *precarious*, thank you Miss Yoakum," Lorena said.

"Lorena, you may know the meaning of a large number of words which your teacher Miss Yoakum taught you, but you have to be careful to use them in the correct context," Samuel said.

"For sure, Samuel, I compose sentences with them in my notebook, what contest?" Lorena asked.

"*Context* Lorena, not contest," Samuel corrected Lorena, "context is how the words interrelate with each other depending on the situation or contextual environment." Samuel answered Lorena, smiling, and he said, "The better word would be *lamentable*."

"Well, whatever, you got the point because you responded, Samuel."

Lorena looked combative, "Anyhow, for sure, what I hate the most is dust. The dust here covers furniture like a thin transparent silk sheet. I always help mother clean house; I sure hope that there is no dust in Mexico for poor mama to clean."

"Oh, heck, Lorena, there is dust all over the world. But what I hated the most was to go outside to play washers and to be choked by smelter smoke. The stinking smoke irritated my eyes, choked the life out of mother's green plants, and contaminated the lungs of our neighbor Don *Chonito*, up the street, who conked out, and his wife Doña Pamphila took him to the mortuary in the middle of the day, no kidding, you knew about that, right, Samuel?" Jose added, "At least, it seems, we won't have smoke over in Mexico."

"I wonder what *El Aliso* looks like and how the houses there are made," Lorena said.

"Mr. Mendoza told me that the population in *El Aliso* is a few hundred, mostly Laborers who work in rural ranches. *El Aliso* is adjacent to a native Indian pueblo called *El Mezquitalito*. He said for us not to expect a town with paved streets, large stores, or a theater, anything like we have here," Samuel said.

Jose was deep in thought and said nothing, but he looked saddened; Samuel knew that Jose liked dances, parties, and festivals. "During the time when the mines were working, there were town festivals," Samuel told Jose and Lorena, " there were booths selling all kinds of knickknacks, foods, and arts and crafts, at times there were contests for the miners to engage in feats of skill or tests of strength in mine work: tasks like shoveling, hauling ore in a wheelbarrow, drilling or chiseling holes in huge boulders with a large hammer and a chisel, and there were individual or team contests of performing mining skilled tasks. These events happened during Miami's Boomtown Spree."

"Those were the 'good old days when the mines were open and working,' like father says," Jose said.

"I know that Miami also provided areas along the Salt River a few miles from town where families could enjoy a picnic, there were hiking trails up into the mountains where people stood in quiet reverence and contemplated the silent mountainous beauty: the expanse of never ending mountain ranges." Samuel continued talking, "When

The Worm in my Tomato

the mines were in operation, miners labored during day, swing and graveyard or night shifts. Many times I have seen miners walking down the canyons carrying their lunch box; they climbed up the trails at Mexican Canyon or up the cement stairs at Keystone Avenue."

"Heck, I saw lots of them," Jose exclaimed, "The majority took rides in cars and trucks that took them up to the mines or to the smelter." Jose took out an apple from his pant's front pocket and said, "The miners worked at the Miami Copper Company, the Inspiration Copper Company or the Smelter." Jose took a bite from his apple.

"The Smelter continually, like a giant cobra snake, standing tall into the sky, exhaled its poisonous chemical smoke into the atmosphere above the town," Samuel explained, "but because Miami sits inside the hole of a doughnut of mountains, the smoke had a way of settling down into the hole like a heavy blanket and contaminated the homes, gardens, trees, and of course infected the lungs of residents when they breathed."

"How do you know all that?" Jose asked.

"I wrote all about the dangers to our people's health in La Prensa," Samuel took a minute to write some notes in his small notebook, "I researched all that and more with Mr. Mendoza." Samuel assumed that Jose was not ready to talk, so he continued speaking, "Along our town streets live many residents who spend nights coughing, allergic to smelter smoke. Many miners also suffered and died from Silicosis, a lung disease caused from working underground in the mines and breathing the chemical polluted air."

"Well, Samuel, that is a good reason why we should get the hell out," Jose remarked, "I am happy that our father Fortunato is not a miner, he worked with cement at the building of the Roosevelt Dam, he worked in highway construction; he did this kind of work, however, only when he really had to do it, for money, when he was lacking in paychecks."

"Yes, but mostly he gambled and ran the card games down at Limonada's Pool Hall," Samuel said and added, "I think that is why he probably did not get silicosis." He looked at Jose and said, "You are right, we should leave Miami for the good of our health; I don't want to work in the copper mines, never, not if I may die from an

The Worm in my Tomato

accident or from silicosis."

"Heck, Samuel, what I like about Miami, is that the copper companies in Miami provide company stores, a health clinic, and a hospital," Jose flung away the apple core across the street.

In Miami, like in other mining towns, every family lived an existence from paycheck to paycheck, from week-end to week-end, many of the mine workers continued in debt to the company store during the duration of their employment. There were two mining companies and each had its own company store. The Inspiration Consolidated Company Store was located up on Inspiration Hill north of town; miners drove up there, people even walked up to the mine, store and homes, the store served miners who worked in the Inspiration Consolidated Copper Mine Company. Both mine stores served the general public as well. Fortunato and Antonia always bought their children's school clothes, shoes and other needed items at the Miami Commercial located in town at the east end of Sullivan Street. They also shopped for clothing and shoes at J.C. Penney.

Samuel blew his breath out, "Whew, we will lose all that kind of life when we go live in rural Mexico. Mr. Mendoza said that we would lose all this way of life, and he should know, always researching and writing articles for La Prensa Mexicana."

Samuel, Jose and Lorena talked about Miami, as they walked together along the streets as if taking their last sight of their town before departing for Mexico. "You know, Samuel, there are some things we can't do in Miami, because we are Mexican kids, you know that," Jose said.

"Well, Jose, we can't go swimming in the YMCA because Mexican kids are not allowed to go swimming during the week days, only when the water is being dumped out on Saturdays. Our town has these weird customs or *gringo* regulations as I call them," Samuel pushed back his red hair and straightened his cap, "We can go into the movie theater but only if we sit in the balcony, and no Mexican customer is allowed in the main floor."

"Heck, Samuel, even our Catholic Church is funny, when we go to Mass with our mother, we always sit on the left side pews because that is the Mexican side," Jose laughed, "Mother says," Jose shook his head

The Worm in my Tomato

backward and rolled his eyes, " 'Never mind, God loves us, anyway, we are all children of God our Father, and besides,'" "She said," " 'It is the evil people in the Church, not the Church, who do the bad things to us.'" Jose thought for a while and said, "That is a third good reason why we should leave Miami."

"Yes, for our health and for the good of our soul, right?" Samuel also laughed, "Well, Jose, don't think that all that will not exist in Mexico. You would think Mexicans can live there in freedom and go where they please, but that is not the case." Samuel looked at Jose, smiling, "If you think so, well, wrong, Mr. Mendoza told me that in Mexico, the native Indian populations are mistreated, and that the Catholic Church was persecuted for its lands," Samuel stopped and looked at Jose, "even president Obregon invited the Young Men's Christian Association, the so called YMCA, to come to Mexico. The federal government allowed all religions to come to Mexico and in that way its laws promoted the Protestant Church and other religions. Can you believe that; this happened at a time when the Catholic Church and the federal government opposed each other; can you believe that, Jose?" Samuel turned away from Jose and Lorena and resumed walking.

"Yeah, I can believe that; heck, remember that mother took in those two religious sisters to have a place to stay; heck, they were kicked out of Mexico during that war with the Church and the federal Mexican government; what was the war called, Samuel?" Jose asked.

"The Cristero War of 1926 to 1929; Mr. Mendoza told me that in the aftermath of the war, persecution continued and is still going on today." Samuel answered.

Behind the Vega main house stood a small apartment, with one bedroom and a kitchen that served as a rental but hardly ever rented. The "little house," as the family called it, usually was occupied with homeless persons whom Antonia took in from time to time, depending on who needed help at the moment. At this time in the little house were staying two Mexican religious sisters, refugees from the religious wars in Mexico, who had escaped and sought protection in the Vega family's home town. Antonia provided for the religious sisters' room and board in the little house. At that same time, hundreds of priests and religious sisters had escaped Mexico. The government soldiers fought the Catholic faithful in the Cristero war of 1926-1929; there had been numerous pitched battles and many had been killed. When Antonia invited the religious sisters into her home kitchen for some *cocido*, the religious sisters told their stories of persecution to Antonia and her family.

Samuel looked serious, "What do you think, Jose, our father is taking us right into a country yet in conflict with the Catholic Church. Also, we are going right into a Mexico that, Mr. Mendoza says, 'is yet promoting the policies of the Reform Constitution of 1857; talks about the ideals of its revolution of 1910 and land reforms of Article 27 land acquisitions in its 1917 Constitution,' *that* is what Mr. Mendoza says." Samuel gazed up at the blue bright sky, then looked down at the ground and said, " All that may just somehow take away the very lands father will be cultivating," Samuel grimaced.

To Samuel, Mr. Mendoza became a living encyclopedia from which he learned much of his needed information in his immediate world outside his home, his classes at school, work for Mr. Mendoza's periodical La Prensa Mexicana, friends, and Church. He particularly liked his job for Mr. Mendoza because Samuel loved to read, think, research and write. He learned, in conversations with Mr. Mendoza, much history of Mexico and the United States not normally taught in schools.

"Heck, Samuel, I lost track of all the reasons why it is good to go to Mexico to get away from the bad in Miami, and why it is good to stay in Miami to protect us from what is bad in Mexico," Jose said, "but do you think it makes a difference, being that our family is so darn independent?"

"Mother is like that," Samuel affirmed, "Mother is very independent and never seems to need anyone else, what I mean is that she knows what to do, "She says, 'we have our own movie theatre,' " Samuel said.

Miami had its own Spanish language theater; sometimes, Jose and Samuel went with their mother to see silent movies shown in a large barn like structure on Live Oak Street. Spanish speaking patrons of the theater enjoyed a wide variety of movies produced in Mexico, such as *"Semilla de Mis Amores,"* a silent movie with Ramon Novarro of 1930, *"Santa,"* the 1931 silent movie with Lupita Tovar and co-star Feliciano Rueda, and the 1929 film *"Sombras Habaneras."*

"Mother told me that she really liked seeing the movies with her favorite movie actors and actresses," Jose said.

"I know," Samuel interjected, "She has talked with me about Raquel Torres, Rene Cardona and Dolores del Rio."

"Yeah, heck, mother needs nothing or nobody as long as she has her church, the Mexican theater, and the Alianza Hispano Americana, gee whiz," Jose exclaimed.

"Even so, regardless of mother's independent attitude, I find it hard to understand these customs of the *gringo* political ruling class imposed on us by regulations, political policies, or laws." Samuel looked at Jose and asked, "Got another apple in your pocket?" Samuel took the apple from Jose, "But Mr. Mendoza said that this makes us a stronger people: 'forged in the fire of struggle, beaten into a shape of being a people of God, in resistance, patience and hard work,' " Samuel quoted Mr. Mendoza from reading his pocket notebook.

Samuel and Jose, like many Mexican American youth, had experienced the tension of living in a society controlled by many unfriendly ignorant prejudiced European-American citizens on the one hand and succored by many friendly and enlightened European-American citizens on the other. This situation confused them: they had suffered for it; but they and their people, the Mexican American citizens, had never grieved their pain out of their personal system, individually or collectively. The boys, like the majority of their people, only licked their wounds, so to speak, and went on their way, living life as best they could.

"Heck, Samuel, damn that Mexican president who invited the Young Men's Christian Association to Mexico, what was his name?" Jose asked.

"President Obregon, but I am sure he did not know how Mexicans were treated here; maybe he never heard of Miami, Arizona; this is our own land, too; land Mexico lost to the United States by force of arms by the war of 1846-1848, according to Mr. Mendoza," Samuel said.

So, thanks to the Young Men's Christian Association, Samuel and Jose, and all the Mexican boys in Miami, continued to hike three miles west of town to an area in the mountains called Bloody Tanks, where Mexican kids went swimming in a clear cold water pool nestled among huge boulders. It was free and they could sun tan, as well, and return home, a brown fried potato.

In such a situation, if there was a choice, Jose couldn't see one, it was hell to stay and it was hell to go. Jose told Samuel, "Heck, both of us prefer to stay if at all possible. We need to stay here and work against the *gringo* prejudice and customs that keep us out of the YMCA, the Grand Theater, and the right side of the Catholic Church." Jose watched Samuel eat his apple. Then he added, "I personally think that three mile hikes to go swimming is getting to be too much."

"Residents here in Miami have a subdued cough, no doubt caused by years of breathing smelter smoke," Samuel said as the three walked on Main Street, and then he asked Lorena "Would you miss Miami's mountains?"

Lorena said, "If I go to Mexico, for sure; whenever Mary Cota and I hiked up into the mountains, with her parents, the fresh breeze cooled my face as I stood and contemplated the *transcending* experience," thank you Miss Yoakum, she thought to herself, "of silent mountains into its own world of beauty."

Samuel told Lorena, "There in the Cherry Flats, I accompanied my friends to harvest the little apples of the *manzanita* bushes which gave small green apples, the size of marbles."

Further away to the west, toward the town of Superior, the vegetation gave way to the Palo Verde trees, the Mezquite trees, the formidable Saguaros, and everywhere the yellow flowers of the Palo Verde showered their beauty and aroma in the valleys intertwined with the mountain breeze that constantly swept through the canyon brush. The white flowers of the Saguaro cactus tree decorated the landscape. Samuel wondered why so many desert flowers were colored yellow and why was there such a variety of cacti?

"Lorena," Jose exclaimed, "Heck, gee whiz, the desert will be just as pretty in Mexico as here."

"I wonder if there will be winter snow, like here in Mayahma," Lorena said.

"Probably not, but who knows, Mr. Mendoza told me that as we travel south into Mexico the elevation of the land increases until you reach parts of Mexico about seven thousand feet elevation where it

The Worm in my Tomato

snows," Samuel said, "For the time being, the natural beauty of the mountains has escaped the mining operations of companies that have destroyed so much of other parts of the mountains to get at the copper in them. But for now, there are not enough eyes of Miami's citizens to discover all that exists in the desert, in the mountains, in the low hills, and within the deep canyons," Samuel said.

"Heck, man, the smelter smoke did not penetrate the heights but sank with its poison down over the town. Probably for this reason, many people of Miami take time to hike in the mountains and breathe the fresh air well above the sulfur smoke that sought to settle below in the canyons," Jose said.

"Well, Lorena, now that we have walked about town and discovered it all over again in our conversation, pointed to the mountains and discussed them, are you ready to take it all with you in your mind and heart, and go to Mexico with us and our parents?" Samuel asked Lorena, holding his breath.

"Oh, no, for sure, I am going to stay here. I will convince father and mother to leave me here with my Uncle Tomas," Lorena did not hesitate in responding. She gave Jose and Samuel a quick look, "Miami is a town of night, with lights and neon signs. Mexican citizens are a festive," thank you Miss Yoakum, Lorena thought to herself, "People, and that is why I want to stay here, and I thought you, too, Jose."

Samuel agreed with what he thought Lorena meant: *Mayahma* was a Mexican cultural town, the streets, mines, homes and mountains were only the superficial skin of a live breathing home town that had deep roots in Mexican culture. In the early evenings on top of the hills surrounding the town, in back yards of houses perched on top slopes of canyons, and in backyard *tardeadas* could be heard the music of guitars and singing; neighbors dancing in their afternoon Sunday home fiestas could be seen.

"Mr. Mendoza says that the singers of *Corridos* tell our history and heritage of many events of our people," Samuel said.

Lorena was correct in her observation. Few people owned radios. The pleasures of life were found and shared with families in their celebrations of birthdays, baptisms, weddings, and in an evening get together in backyard parties called *tardeadas* where musicians played popular Mexican songs, and dance music. Families and friends danced in their home backyards, the dirt having been sprinkled with water, swept clean of dust and pressed down hard. Samuel realized that it was not going to be easy to convince Lorena to accept leaving Miami.

There were other ways in which Miami exemplified Mexican culture: there were a few stores owned by Mexican merchants, small family owned stores that catered to its Mexican clientele; these stores supplied the spiced ground beef called *chorizo* purchased by clients to fry with eggs into a scrambled egg and *chorizo* breakfast. In these stores could be found the tripe meat for the family's specialty soup called *menudo,* the corn *masa,* maize dough for the making of their festive *tamales.* Some of these Mexican owned shops also provided many faithful clients with the Mexican cultural goods. The herbal stores selling herbs, candles, saints' pictures, pictures of Mexican movie stars, and Mexican music records.

Miami was a mythical place. The Miami area had plenty of stories and many were myths or oral histories told and retold until they were a story, perhaps believed or not, with human interest in the past. Miami was a place of sorrow where miners lost their lives in mine accidents or when old miners choked to death from lung disease. Miami mixed cultures from all over the world. Slavic languages like Spanish could be heard spoken in the canyons and streets. Slavics like the Spaniards made home wine from truck loads of large purple grapes. Miami was a spiritual town with churches representing a variety of religious faiths located throughout town. Catholics led processions up the "M" mountain during Holy Cross Day to pray at the foot of three white painted wooden crosses standing tall at the top of the mountain. Miami was a town of joy where on week-ends its sons and daughters danced at the Plaza dance hall, one night for Anglos and one night for Mexicans; partied at homes and private clubs, and drank beer at saloons found at various corners of Sullivan and Live Oak Streets. Miami nurtured tough miners, beautiful women, pious parents, obedient but boisterous children; they fought each other but during the First World War they all joined together to defend their country.

Silicosis not withstanding, Samuel felt strongly confident that they should not go to Mexico; there seemed to be no future for the family,

The Worm in my Tomato

and like Lorena, Samuel himself felt that he should do the same and try to stay. Samuel began to think of what he could do to prevent his family from going to Mexico. Samuel felt certain that he could stay in Miami with Mr. and Mrs. Mendoza. He wanted to complete his last year of high school, and he hoped to continue work at publishing *La Prensa Mexicana*. One thing in particular that Samuel determined: he would not try again to convince Lorena to go to Mexico.

"Bloody Tanks" swimming hole, located at the bottom of the north side of state highway 60, west of Miami; it provided an alternative to the Y.M.C.A. at the time. In the story, Jose said, "I personally think that three mile hikes to go swimming is too much."

Our Lady of the Blessed Sacrament Catholic Church, built on its present location on Sullivan Street in 1915, served the faithful in Miami, Arizona; among them, Fortunato and Antonia and their family. Mexican faithful were ushered to sit on the left side pews as recorded in the story.

Eight

Samuel
Samuel's efforts to stay in Miami

The day was bright and clear as Antonia could see it through the window in the kitchen. An aroma of frying eggs and cinnamon on cereal welcomed Jose and Samuel to breakfast. Samuel told Antonia during breakfast that he and Jose had invited Lorena, the day before, for a walk through town. "We wanted her to be glad," he scooped hot oat cereal into his bowl, "about the sights of the town, enjoy looking at the mountains."

Lorena, Catalina, and Mary Cota played a game of hop-scotch outside in the backyard, and their yells and laughter could be heard in the house. "What did she say," Antonia asked and poured a glass of milk for Jose.

"Thanks, mama," said Jose, and added, "We wanted for her to take in her mind how the town looks, so that she would not feel lonely and homesick, you know." He looked at Antonia, "Heck, you know, take in her mind and heart some good memories of Miami."

"But it did not work out that way," Samuel said. He chewed on his egg and chorizo burrito and said, "Lorena told us that she did not intend to take any memories in her heart or mind, because, she said, 'I am not going.'" Samuel saw Miami with a new interest, a new appreciation, and a new fondness for his hometown. Now, Samuel's goal was to point out the Mexican American history and heritage in Arizona to Fortunato. Samuel hoped to help his father see the importance of Samuel's staying in Miami so that he could continue making contributions in Mexican American history by writing articles in *La Prensa Mexicana*.

After breakfast, Samuel sought out his father and began a conversation with him. "I want to share what I have learned from doing research for an article for our paper *La Prensa Mexicana* with you father," Samuel said.

"That is fine, Samuel, what did you research and write about?"

"My article will be mostly on a Mexican American entrepreneur in the business of transporting goods, called freighting."

"Who is that person?"

"Esteban Ochoa is his name and he lived in Tucson, the dates of when he was born and died are 17 March 1831 to October 1888," Samuel said, smiling at his father and then he added, "That was the time during which Nanita drove her wagon pulled by oxen through Tucson on her way to Morenci or Las Carpas as Mexican pioneers called the area."

"Mr. Ochoa owned a freighting business with another Mexican American named Tully, and they named their company Tully & Ochoa and Company," Samuel said.

Fortunato and Samuel fastened with cord some large cardboard boxes into which Antonia had packed her kitchen utensils. "That is fine, owning your own business," Fortunato said.

"His business made him an important man in his community, helped him to make some money, and allowed him time to take part in civic affairs," Samuel said.

"I have heard that it is in Tucson where the Mexican people have made great contributions, right?" Fortunato showed an interest in Samuel's topic of his article.

"Yes, father, Tucson started, way back in 1774. A hundred years later, Ochoa donated a parcel of land in Tucson for Arizona's first modern public school in 1875, and at the same time he also served as president of the Tucson School Board and also as mayor of Tucson." Samuel and Fortunato tied the boxes, one after the other, with heavy cord.

"Oh, I think that is wonderful, a most remarkable man, no doubt," Fortunato said.

"Mr. Ochoa created an extensive freighting business by taking advantage of the early Arizona mining activities to haul ore and equipment and goods for the mines and smelters. His business became the leading Freight Company in the Southwest after the time of the Civil War." Samuel helped his father carry the boxes to the porch.

"The officials of the Repatriation will send out a truck tomorrow to take our furniture and boxes to the train depot to be loaded," Fortunato said.

The Worm in my Tomato

"Mr. Ochoa was a real patriot, too," Samuel said as both walked back into the house, "I wish I could do something like that," and added, "If I could stay here in Arizona, I would have a better chance to help our town or our state, don't you think so, father?" Samuel hoped his father would be convinced how important it was for Mexican Americans to involve themselves and make a public contribution.

"You can have opportunities to make social contributions that are helpful to society in Mexico, too, Samuel, you'll see, it is just a matter of wanting to be of service, but really now, I did not know about what Mr. Esteban Ochoa had done."

"Father, there are many other examples of hard-working immigrants from Mexico who as citizens of the Arizona Territory and later of the United States made various kinds of contributions." Samuel pointed out, and continued his conversation, "As entrepreneurs, in Arizona, I mention a few in my article." He and Fortunato fastened a cord around the tin trunk, already packed since the night before, and Samuel said, "Contemporary with Esteban Ochoa was Mariano Guadalupe Samaniego 1844-1907, a graduate of Saint Louis University in 1862, who after his arrival in Tucson in 1864 became a successful freighter, cattle rancher, and public official." Samuel saw that his dad became very interested, so Samuel continued speaking, "Samaniego, as did Ochoa, served several terms in the territorial legislature, promoted the public school system, served in the Tucson School Board, also served on the State University board of regents." Samuel and Fortunato carried the trunk to the front room.

"He certainly was a great man, but what about Mr. Jacomé, the store keeper in Tucson; I visited his store to purchase a suit, once," Fortunato said.

"Oh, yes, I write about him, as well: Carlos Corella Jacomé, born in Ures, Sonora, Mexico, on April 8, 1870. Later he moved to Tucson with his mother and family in 1876. He served in the Arizona Constitutional Convention of 1910," Samuel said with pride in his voice, and he continued speaking: "Mr. Jacomé managed his dry goods store into one of Tucson's leading stores."

"There is no doubt that, as your research proves, the facts of contributions made for Arizona by Mexican American citizens, motivates a business spirit that has lived on in countless business oriented Mexican American citizens who owned and operated successful businesses in Arizona," Fortunato said, seating himself down in the kitchen. "Want a cup of coffee, Samuel?"

"I will have a glass of water, thanks," Samuel slumped into a chair, rubbing the back of his neck with his right hand; a look of frustration crossed his face.

"You have done well, Samuel," Fortunato expressed a sincere affirmation of Samuel.

Samuel felt dejected; he realized that he had failed to convince his father on the idea that he wanted to stay in Miami and work toward making a contribution to Arizona. Samuel had researched Arizona history and reflected on the accomplishments of many Mexican Americans. Samuel knew that although the majority of Mexican immigrants came to work in the mines, the agricultural fields, the railroad, construction, numerous other service type of work, there had always been an active entrepreneurial class. Samuel thought about several historical points: that not only has this spirit of hard work existed in the trades but also has been expressed in entrepreneurial endeavors. There were those, fewer yet, who dedicated a good portion of their life to professional, public service, and business and trade. For example, in the spirit of Esteban Ochoa, who, while serving in the territory legislature, introduced Arizona Governor Safford's bill for the establishment of Arizona's public schools, many others followed who made needed contributions. Samuel felt sad that he would not have an opportunity to contribute for the social good and add to the legacy of this history and heritage of the Mexican American people.

Samuel asked his father if he had ever heard of Mr. Ignacio Bonillas, and he replied that he had not. Samuel then told him, "During pre-state times, a pioneer teacher in Tucson was Ignacio Bonillas, a graduate of Massachusetts Institute of Technology. I really think that many young Mexicans have been inspired and motivated to participate in academic and professional pursuits," Samuel said.

Fortunato listened and then commented, "Actually, our work, however, has been in the trades, in the mines, and in the fields, don't you think so, Samuel?"

The Worm in my Tomato

"Oh, yes, I agree, labor oriented Mexican American workers have also made great contributions, too. They have played an important part in the economic development of Arizona."

Samuel included in his conversation a story of his grandfather. "My grandfather Jose Carbajal worked in the copper mines in Morenci. The Mexican miners there in Morenci found it necessary to organize a miner's union and be active to improve their work conditions. My grandfather Jose was an active participant in union affairs."

Jose Carbajal

Lorena and Catalina entered the house laughing and pushing each other and came into the kitchen to get a drink of water.

Samuel continued speaking, "Thus, agricultural field workers have not been alone in suffering from hard work, unsanitary conditions, low wages, and discriminatory treatment. Arizona's mining history abounds in work strikes by Mexican American union copper miners seeking benefits, safe working conditions, and equal wages as paid other non-Mexican miners for equal work." Samuel took a drink of water from his glass. "Did mother tell you that during the 1903 strike, my grandfather, Jose Carbajal, was helping enforce a work stoppage up on the hill in Morenci?" Samuel asked.

"I think she mentioned it to me, once," Fortunato said.

"This story has been around in our family for a long time. From the other side of the hill, a government armed force approached the union miners to arrest them and perhaps cause much violence and death to miners. The women, mothers, wives, and daughters were down below the hill in the residential area, in their homes, praying, saying the rosary on their knees, petitioning God to protect their men," Samuel said.

"Oh, yes, I seem to remember your mother telling the story about

The Worm in my Tomato

a storm," Fortunato said.

"That is right, dark storm clouds gathered around Morenci and an ensuing downpour drenched both clusters of men: the state armed government forces and the civil lawmen, had marched up the hill to arrest the miners who were determined to win safety in the work place conditions and other benefits," Samuel took another drink of water from his glass, "but soaking wet, both groups retreated and a catastrophe was avoided by the prayers of the women, no doubt, who knelt praying in their homes." Samuel finished his glass of water, "Women like my Grandmother Manuela and 'Nanita' were good at organizing prayer brigades," Samuel said proudly.

"Now, that is interesting," Fortunato said.

Would you like for me to read part of my article for you, father?

"Yes, let me hear it." Fortunato served himself another cup of coffee.

Samuel read part of his article:

Mexican American population became a minority in the late 1800s and after 1877 the political, economic, and social power shifted from southern Arizona to the central and northern half. Two important factors causing population shifts in favor of Anglo-Americans and other Europeans were the Gold Rush of 1849 in California and the arrival of the railroads in 1877. Anglo-European-Americans, especially those that were cultured in the slave-holding states practiced prejudice and discrimination in the workplace and in social life.

By the time my mother was born in June 13, 1895 in Morenci, the white Anglo-European-Americans were more numerous in population, and they controlled the local, state, and federal governments which enacted laws for their own gain and benefit. Through laws, the majority controlled others. English speaking European citizens imposed discriminatory practices on Mexican citizens and other minorities. Minorities for many years were segregated into separate housing areas, places in movie theatres and churches, and segregated schools. These discriminatory practices caused responses by Mexican Americans for survival and public participation by creating their own living areas called barrios, organizing their own business operations, their own self-help organizations and social clubs.

The Worm in my Tomato

While the young Mexican children were legally and systematically segregated in school, the movie theatre and prohibited from swimming in the YMCA pool, the adults were segregated in church services, discriminated in many lawful ways made legal by the majority who promoted or supported the legislation of discriminatory laws. Mexican miners earned less than Anglo miners for equal or more hazardous work. That is the way the social, political, and economic way of life was in Miami and other towns throughout Arizona for many years before 1932.

"Thank you, Samuel, that is a good article and I know it is well researched," Fortunato said. He beamed with pride for Samuel's effort in writing his article, and Fortunato excused himself from the kitchen and left to do other work.

Samuel knew for certain, however, that his father, a proud man, with family in Mexico and lands his late father had bequeathed him, and being a gambler at heart, had made up his mind to return to Mexico. His father had decided, Samuel was certain, to take all his family to Sinaloa and farm there. Samuel decided to quit his effort in interesting his father in heritage and history of the Mexican American people in Arizona. Samuel had hoped his father would have allowed him to stay and continue his work with social issues history.

Unknown to his sister Lorena, Samuel had seriously thought about what she had said to Jose and himself in their conversation when they had walked through town. Lorena had voiced a good point or two, Samuel admitted to himself, and agreed that education and their way of life in Miami had certain values. Perhaps, Samuel thought to himself, that he should try and lend support to Lorena.

With this in mind Samuel approached his mother, who had entered the kitchen and had begun her work. "Mother, not every one in our street is leaving," Samuel sat down at the table, again, and looked at his mother, standing by the sink and rinsing a cup and saucer, "can't you help convince father to stay?" Antonia just stood by the kitchen sink and looked pensive; she did not respond. Samuel wondered that perhaps he was too late, and that getting mother to agree in convincing father to stay would not be possible. If only Lorena, Jose, and I could convince her to argue the point with father, for our sake, he thought to himself.

The Worm in my Tomato

In truth, Samuel knew that they would all hate leaving their hometown, it meant so much to them: this was home; in his research, Samuel had learned much about Miami and the state. In fact, Samuel had written of this history in some of his articles.

Samuel knew that his hometown of Miami in Gila County was located seventy-five miles East of Phoenix, in Maricopa County; and Miami was 105 miles northeast from Tucson, Pima County. Miami had started in 1907, became a copper mining boomtown, home to ten thousand residents of miners and their families in its peak days before the Great Depression closed its copper mines.

What Samuel liked about Miami was that his family history was so much a part of the history of his town and state, as well. Miami was an international town where many different nationalities from various parts of the world had come to work in the mines or establish a business. The majority of miners were Mexicans from different parts of Mexico, but primarily from Sonora and Chihuahua. From other parts of the world had emigrated a large contingent of Welsh, English, German, Irish, and Slavic; with fewer members of Lebanese, Syrian, Arab, Greek, and Spaniard. The majority were European Americans from other parts of the United States.

If people from any place in the world had known his hometown, Samuel thought, he was certain that they would have loved it. If anyone had lived part of their life in his hometown's time in the 1930s, they would never have forgotten it. Samuel took pleasure in thinking about his hometown and in the special vibrancy in the air, and in the boomtown spirit of his *Mayahma*, that he remembered with love.

"Mother," Samuel tried again to stir his daydreaming mother to start a conversation about convincing his father to stay: "Lorena loves Miami; she enjoys her school and her friends; she never suspected that her world as she knew it would end overnight. In my opinion, she is not ready to be taken away on a journey that, for her, has implications of ending her way of life, don't you think so, mother?"

Poor Antonia; she looked sad, pale, tired and sick. Samuel knew that for his mother and father it was a means for survival from the economic disaster that at this time had closed down the mines and ended employment for thousands: Fortunato wanted to use the

Repatriation to an advantage, seek survival in the cultivation of his lands, and at the same time help Antonia keep the family together.

Because his mother remained silent, Samuel continued speaking, "I know it for a fact, from conversations with Lorena, that she will never forget Miami. Her journey on the train will be hell; I suspect that her life in El Aliso, Sinaloa, Mexico will be intolerable for a person who knows nothing of Mexico and can speak Spanish in a limited way. At least, I can speak Spanish, and read and write it, too, after having taken two years of Spanish in high school," Samuel shivered because the kitchen had become cold. He waited for his mother to say something, but she was deep in thought. Samuel continued speaking, "I have read about Mexico and have discussed the country with Mr. Mendoza. I personally think our life in Mexico will be one of much suffering; I have held long conversations with Mr. Mendoza. He should know, having been educated in Mexico where he worked in the newspaper and magazine business all his life."

Antonia finally came out of her coma and sat down at the table with her cup of coffee. She carefully poured tobacco from a small tobacco bag on a thin white piece of cigarette paper and rolled it up into a cigarette and sealed it by licking the side of the paper; she lit her cigarette by striking a stick match on the side of the table and held her cigarette between her right hand's index finger and her thumb, and she slowly smoked it, softly blowing out gray smoke that spiraled up in circles into the kitchen air. She slowly spoke, "All that is true, Samuel, but there are more urgent and immediate concerns that trouble your father at this time: your father has already signed papers and made arrangements, the date set for our departure on the Repatriation train is March 15, three days from now," Antonia poured Samuel a cup of coffee, "Warm up, Samuel," she said, her voice shredded the smoke doughnut shaped trail formed when smoke escaped from her round mouth. Samuel felt the kitchen air cold and he gladly sipped his hot steaming coffee.

It would be, Samuel presumed, a wrenching moment when they would be physically torn apart from their extended family members: their way of life and culture; their family roots of almost a hundred years in the state of their birth, in the United States of America. Samuel thought of how all members of his family were United States citizens with the exception of his father. Samuel felt that if his people held majority political power, they could have legislated laws for keeping families intact, that if any one member of a family was a United States citizen, the whole family could exercise equal rights as citizens. But Samuel knew this could not be because the European-American majority who held political power would not experience the menace of the Repatriation.

Samuel knew that his father had lost his opportunity to make a living for his family because of the Great Depression; he also knew that his father was motivated by outside pressures of the Repatriation to leave the country. It was a moment of contending social and political forces across the United States that preyed upon thousands of Mexican American families, forcing thousands to leave the country, either mandatory or voluntary. For the Mexican, the Repatriation train was their bridge under which to take protection, their fire by which to keep warm, their journey to find a new hope: their American wives and children would pay the cost in suffering and pain.

Samuel had thought of all these things in his mind, as he sat next to the kitchen table. Antonia had not known with what words to reply to Samuel's question asking if she could convince Fortunato to stay in Miami. She simply sat by the table across from Samuel, to drink her cup of coffee and smoke her rolled tobacco cigarette. Antonia wanted to be gracious to Samuel, and she placed a piece of Mexican sweet bread for her son to eat with his coffee. They both cherished the moment in silence, likely a last time for them in peace and love of mother and son in their home kitchen: they were two birds in a pet shop cage before the sale that would take them away to a strange place.

In the context of the reality of the repatriation mother and son sat powerless as if waiting for execution. The family was naked now of all material possessions and would take with them only their clothes and Antonia's household utensils and furniture. The weight of poverty covered them as with a heavy blanket under which they could not find fresh air. Yet they held on to hope for a better day. The words of the prophet Habakkuk "…yet will I rejoice in the Lord and exult in my saving God," held out hope when all else had failed and they had nothing. Habakkuk: 3:2-4, 13a, 15-19.

The exiles in Babylon, From Psalm 137: as
Interpreted to relate to the exiles in Miami, Arizona of 1932.

By the railroad tracks of the Miami Depot,
There we stood marked for departure: We wept;
sad to leave Miami.

There on the platform
others wished us well:
"Be happy and sing."

The Mariachi band and singers tried and failed;
they played for a wake.
The authorities, the police; the train conductor;
the European Americans: all were festive.

We took our life on the train:
humiliated in our present;
we lost our heritage of our past;
what would be our future?

If I forget you Miami,
let me forget my loved ones
buried in our town cemetery.

Let me die as well,
If I do not remember you,
if I do not hold you in my heart: my joy.

The Worm in my Tomato

Nine

Antonia
On the Repatriation train to Mexico

It was too late for Samuel to have helped Lorena in her efforts to convince their father not to leave for Mexico. The boxes with the kitchen appliances and the household furniture were already on the train by the time Samuel had talked to his mother to try and convince Fortunato to stay in Miami. There was no turning back: the papers were signed, the forms completed; Fortunato only thought of going to Mexico; Antonia was determined to say goodbye to family and friends with a smile and in joy. Antonia intended to depart from Miami with inner strength and dignity; she was steadfast not to allow tears in her eyes, if that was possible, until the train pulled out of the depot, when at last it departed from Miami.

Antonia's heart held fervent emotions of sadness at leaving and of hate for her fate. She resented her situation in which she found herself being forced out of her own country, a country which accepted other immigrants from around the world, but a country which rejected Mexicans and Mexican Americans who were North Americans. It was a crossroads in Antonia's life that threatened her with her having envy for her neighbors and others staying behind in her hometown, in their homes.

Antonia stood waiting near the train, waiting to go on board. She held her baby tightly in her arms and she wondered what was to become of him in a strange country. Well, here we were, my family, after our soul searching decision over the last two months, Antonia thought. In contrast to her sadness and the frightened appearance of those departing, standing nearby the train, she saw that the crowds on

The Worm in my Tomato

the platform bidding them goodbye were almost festive. There was an undercurrent of sound of hundreds of people murmuring that reached her ears, the mumble of numerous voices meant nothing to her and easily mingled with the sound of the leaves vibrating from the strong breeze passing through the ash trees which surrounded the margin of the property. To Antonia the shaking leaves were like hundreds of babbling tongues demanding her family's repatriation to Mexico.

Throughout the country there had been hundreds of unthinking nonsense talkers and millions of acquiescing silent accomplices demanding the Repatriates Babylonian exile. The Repatriation political policies like a Roman Empire rule had won over a reasoned alternative and forced thousands of Mexican citizen families and including their United States citizen children to an exile in Mexico.

Antonia's eyes squinted in the brightness of the day. The sun had no impediment from the clear blue colored sky filled with yellow white light. It was not really windy, but enough movement of a slight stirring air that played with women's long cotton skirts; the men did not have to hold on to their fedora caps, but there was enough air to bring to Antonia's nostrils the acrid smell of the burnt oil emitting from the train engine; the acrid odor reminded Antonia of Miami's smelter sulfur smelling smoke, sour and deadly; she smiled and admitted to herself that she was leaving behind something she never cared for, and she covered her baby's face with his light blanket.

At the railroad station, Antonia was impressed with many groups of families crowded in the lines formed to board the train. The huge engine at the head of the train cars hissed out steam in big gray clouds. Antonia waved to the parents of Lorena's young friend, Mary Cota: they were there, among the blur of blue, gray, and white colored dresses and pants and coats of the throng of people standing on the depot platform. Maria and Mary Cota were not to board the train to Aguascalientes, but present to see Antonia and her family off and wish them a safe trip. Mr. Manuel Cota shook Fortunato's hand; Maria hugged Antonia and kissed her baby on the cheek. "Oh, Antonia, we will miss you so much," Mrs. Cota dabbed her eyes dry of her many tears, "now who will bring me hot soup when I am sick with a head cold, or worse yet, the flu?"

Antonia saw Lorena and Mary hug each other and Antonia heard Lorena tell Mary, "I will return soon to Bullion Plaza; Mary, you save me a seat in Miss Yoakum's class." Seeing Lorena and Mary hug each other, and hearing what Lorena said to Mary, caused Antonia to break her resolve and she cried softly, her tears freely streaming down her cheeks; she dried her eyes with her white handkerchief, but her tears and emotions against her will demanded to be expressed.

Antonia turned to search around for her brother Tomas, she saw him on the train depot platform, Tomas and Nellie hooked together in each other's arms, and both looked sad. Tomas walked over to Antonia, "I am sorry to see you go sister, you and your family," he said. Antonia rejoiced when she saw Tomas and Nellie well dressed and sober. Tomas hugged his sister and her baby in her arms.

Antonia searched the crowds: she knew that Nanita and Antonia's first cousin, Josie, would not be present because Nanita had been ill the last few days. Antonia was glad that Fortunato and she had already said their goodbyes to Nanita when they had visited her in Florence, three weeks before. Antonia's heart filled with more sadness, when she remembered Nanita telling her to go to Mexico because Antonia had to carry her cross until she buried it.

Antonia knew well that to carry one's cross was the Christian way. She noticed, however, that many men and some women were going to Mexico alone; she wondered how many families had been forced to break up. She noticed that single persons looked more troubled then those with families. She saw that young adults hugged and kissed on the platform and later some of the young adults got on board and those with which they had been hugging and kissing stayed behind on the platform.

Antonia's friend, Lucita Guzman, a fellow member with Antonia of the mutual assistance organization, the Alianza Hispano Americana, came over to where Antonia was standing and talked with her for a while. "You come back, Antonia," Lucita too was crying. Lucita expressed to Antonia that her wish was that she would return some day. "Please, Tonia," she whispered, "come back to us your friends and family."

"I pray to God that someday we will see each other again, Lucita,"

Antonia managed to answer in spite of her being emotionally choked up.

Just then, the two religious sisters, dark attractive Mayan women from southern Mexico, dressed in long black skirts and dark shawls, came up to Antonia and hugged her and baby Santos; the religious sisters, with their eyes filled with tears, spoke with Antonia. Sister Teresa said, "Antonia, Mexico is not a place for you." Sister Consuelo said, "This is not a good time for our Church, Antonia. Your children will grow-up in a pagan country: Yes, Mexico, the first country in America to become Christian, where the mother of God appeared in December 1531, yes, may our Lady of Guadalupe, Mother of God, pray for you Antonia."

"That country has now gone pagan and crazy," Sister Teresa said. She spoke her statements rapidly, then cleared her nose and dried her eyes with her white handkerchief.

A dust devil swept through the crowd on the platform and caused many to cover their heads with shawls and men to quickly hold on to their hats or caps. "Tell your husband that you must remain in this country for your family's sake," Sister Consuelo advised, her bright black eyes twinkled.

"Antonia, may God bless you, daughter," Sister Teresa said. Both sisters hugged Antonia and blessed her. "You were kind to us, when we arrived in Miami, when no one else cared to help us. Remember, we will always pray for you," Sister Consuelo said.

"And be careful daughter; the Mexican federal government is still making our faithful brothers and sisters suffer because of their Catholic religion," Sister Teresa exclaimed. "Remember," Sister Teresa held her forefinger up in the air in front of Antonia's face, "the Cristero conflict is still raging underground, especially in the rural areas, be careful," she whispered and she held Antonia's hand, "Ask your husband Fortunato to go alone and come back to you later, Antonia, keep your family together, here in your own homeland."

"All right, Mother Teresa, I will talk about it with Fortunato," Antonia promised.

Then the huge black iron animal let out a loud roar. The animal's trainer and conductor yelled out "All aboard." Fortunato led the way toward a train car. Antonia followed and carried baby Santos in her arms. Samuel and Jose stayed together and both held Catalina's hands. Lorena reluctantly followed behind at the rear. Suddenly, Fortunato turned and motioned to Lorena to hurry and move ahead of him. Lorena bravely ran forward first in line and her father helped her climb first into the train car.

"All aboard," yelled the stationmaster. Antonia and her family quickly followed Lorena, one by one they climbed aboard. Antonia could see over her shoulder that numerous other families trooped aboard. The train was full to capacity with Repatriated families on the railroad to Mexico. Antonia cried inwardly, as she sat next to Lorena, crying softly. Lorena looked at her mother and said, "You know, mama, I am thinking about being 'On the Road' to visit my grandfather's big house."

On the station platform, it seemed was the other half of the population of Miami, all waving goodbye. The men looked stern, dressed in denim work pants and wearing felt hats. The women wore dark dresses and black shoes and they wiped their eyes with white handkerchiefs. After those families leaving Miami had climbed on the train, gray clouds came up, the sun hid its face, the wind picked up, it was a windy day in March, after all, and dust devils swirled about the platform. Fine dust had a way of getting into one's eyes. Those on the platform, as well as those aboard the train, had tear- filled eyes. All those departing and all those on the platform cried unashamed and dabbed their eyes and blew their noses.

Antonia could make out her fellow members from the Alianza Hispano Americana and she saw her friends Juanita Bozovich with her sisters Belen and Rumalda with her husband Augustine; all who were still there. Antonia was happy that she had conversed with them and hugged them. They were her long time dear friends. Fortunato and Antonia had also said their goodbyes to Mr. Mora, the owner of the La Paloma Café. He had catered coffee and bean burritos for people to eat.

Mr. Mora had said, "So you will not leave hungry," his voice shook and his lips quivered, as he handed out bean burros and cups of coffee.

Antonia waved goodbye through the glass window to Mr. Jesus Vega and his mother Juanita Vega who waved back with their white handkerchiefs. Antonia remembered with fondness how Eliza and her husband Emilio Cook had hugged her and many others that were departing. Antonia had said goodbye to Mr. Vigil; he was from New Mexico, and Antonia smiled when she thought about how he had claimed to all in hearing distance that he was descended from one of the founders of Santa Fe in the late 1500s, "This was years before the Pilgrims landed and arrived in New England," he had pointed out. Today, on the platform, he had told Fortunato, "They can't Repatriate me to New Mexico, if they did that, then all Europeans would have to go back to England, France and Germany, too," he laughed.

Antonia's *compadres* Matias and Concepcion, "Chonita," stood to one side of the platform. They looked so sad, Antonia thought, and she knew that she would miss them dearly and miss their tasty warm Mexican bread on Thursdays. Antonia had hugged them earlier. Antonia also saw Mr. Julian the vegetable peddler, Mr. Galvan, the woodcutter, and Mr. Suárez the meat seller on the platform. She waved to them. They had all been there watching and saying goodbye to the Repatriates boarding the train.

Antonia saw, too, many of her acquaintances the store keepers: Lebanese, Serbs, Greeks, Arabs, as well as Slavic, German, Irish, English and Welch miners with their families, standing there on the platform. She thought about how they had asked her and many other Repatriates to be happy as they waived goodbye, but how could we be happy, Antonia thought, when we are forced to leave our homeland.

In spite of the fact that a Mariachi group had been there and played a few Mexican classic songs with their guitars, violin, and trumpets, the families who were leaving were not cheered up. The musical group mournfully sounded out sad music as they sang *Cielito Lindo* and played other festive songs about Mexico; Antonia thought sadly: never mind that our family was being repatriated to Sinaloa.

But Antonia saw grown people crying like babies because their families were being separated. Antonia personally was glad that Nanita had told her that she had to carry her cross because she had never wanted Fortunato to have gone to Mexico by himself. Antonia was glad to carry her cross like a faithful Christian wife; she believed her doing so had kept her family together. But Antonia, nevertheless, cried in her inner self because she did not want Fortunato and her children to see her in tears. Actually, Antonia worried more about her family

The Worm in my Tomato

being inside this iron machine that snorted and puffed and huffed, like a black bull, anxious to be on its way to Mexico. But she thought about what Sister Teresa had asked her to do: to talk with Fortunato. Antonia wondered if God was talking to her through Sister Teresa; she intended to talk with Fortunato, when the time was appropriate.

The iron black bull hissed and huffed loudly as it sped away through the flat desert. Dust devils rose up as if to tease the speeding bull. Antonia even placed her hope for a quick return to Miami on the swirling winds, but to her disappointment the engine pulled all the passenger cars right through long clouds of dust. Antonia noticed that when they came to a dark cloud fairly low in the sky or large dust devils that dashed dust against the window, that Jose would duck his head as he played a head ducking game with Catalina. She would also duck her head. Catalina's dark curls flayed the air and she raised her skinny arms to protect herself.

Out of her window Antonia saw the desert landscape which looked like a brown blanket with dull green patches of prickly pear and tall Saguaro cactus. Huge tall giant saguaros interspersed among the Cholla, Palo Verde trees and prickly pear cacti, stood tall and silent. The grease wood bushes dared to border the rail tracks, which split the flat desert, and like toreros harassed the steam huffing bull charging along the iron tracks.

"Look mama, the many Saguaros with their white and yellow flowers," Lorena pointed out the glass window. "The Saguaro tree flower is the Arizona state flower, Miss Yoakum taught us that, thank you Miss Yoakum," Lorena wiped away tears from her eyes with the palm of her right hand. Antonia knew that Lorena's smile masked her breaking heart; she understood what Lorena was experiencing.

Overhead the speeding train, the windy day of March began to fill up the clear sky with rain clouds. Antonia prayed that the rain would not develop into a thunderous storm because Catalina feared to death the lightning and thunder. When at home, Catalina would run and hide under the bed to protect herself from thunder and lightning. But inside the fast moving train, Antonia could not see anything which could help lessen the fear for Catalina.

Antonia turned to Fortunato sitting across the aisle from her,

"Fortunato, Sister Teresa warned me that it is now a terrible time to raise our family in a pagan Mexico," she said. Antonia studied his face for some sign, but he seemed undisturbed and willing to hear what she had to say. "She wondered if you would go by yourself for now and return to us later. If you agree, we could get off the train in Tucson and take the bus back to Florence. We could live with Nanita, what do you think?"

Fortunato's face whitened, as if all his blood had drained from his face. "Absolutely not, Antonia, we have talked for weeks about going to Mexico and starting over. We have decided, already. No, and further more, I refuse to reconsider.

After two hours the black iron bull slowed to a halt in a train station that had a large sign: Tucson Train Station. A greater number of Repatriates, more than at Miami, crowded the Tucson's station platform. Hundreds of families climbed on board, the children shuffled dutifully, holding on to their parents, many more persons stood on the station platform and waved goodbye. Soon the black iron bull with great power and strength pulled out hissing and puffing and sped away punctuating the silence with loud shrill wails across the desert on its way to the town of Nogales, Arizona.

In Nogales all the families were escorted across the United States boundary to Nogales, Sonora, Mexico. Both towns were adjacent to each other. The Repatriates were herded into Mexican trains. Various Mexican train routes were destined for southern Sonora, Chihuahua, Sinaloa, and Coahuilla. The Vega family with many other families boarded the train destined to Sinaloa. At the train station vendors yelled out *"tacos,"* *"empanadas,"* and *"dulces de bisnaga."* Antonia explained to Lorena that the *empanadas* were turnovers made with pumpkin, apple, or some other kind of fruit filling. The *dulces* were sugared candy made from round barrel cactus.

Antonia sat numb and quiet after her conversation with Fortunato, when she had suggested she and her family could get off the train in Tucson and take the bus back to Florence. For his part, he did not say another word. Antonia thought that after all, Fortunato should not go by himself. She knew that he was helping her live out her responsibility as a Christian wife.

The Worm in my Tomato

Antonia knew that the children wanted some *empanadas* and some Mexican cactus candy, but Fortunato did not buy any treats. Antonia fed the children *burritos* from her lunch basket, the baby only wanted his milk and had slept during most of the way, enjoying the swaying of the train and the swish of its wheels.

Antonia sat quiet and thinking of what she knew of Fortunato's family in El Aliso. The black hungry iron monster ate mile after mile as it sped to whatever fate awaited her family, Antonia thought.

Fortunato's family lived in Sinaloa, Mexico. They were agricultural folks who raised crops for local consumption and export sales; they followed the signs of the moon and the stars in the heavens and the seasons on earth for their cycles for planting and harvesting. They hated drought, cotton worms, insects, tomato larvae, and the plague of grasshoppers. Fortunato had told Antonia that against all odds, they followed the European farming methods learned in the climates of Spain's dry regions, and combined them with the farming methods of local indigenous Indian peoples who had farmed corn, beans, chili, and squash for thousands of years in their Indian pueblo communal lands.

El Aliso was located in a rural area of Sinaloa, as Fortunato had told Antonia, and the agriculture there depended on seasonal rain. Irrigation systems were almost none existent, although El Fuerte River passed adjacent to a greater part of the Vega lands. Antonia's worry about Fortunato's agricultural skills and knowledge now heightened as they approached the time and place for his new farming endeavor. He had mainly worked on construction and in cement, but only when necessary, as his main passion and means for supporting his family had been gambling and managing card games. Antonia could not help but think how much of a gamble his agricultural pursuits would now be, but Antonia had brought her household saints in her tin trunk, and she intended to pray long and hard for her husband to succeed as a farmer and rancher in El Aliso; Antonia could not help but worry about the unforeseen problems that may arise. They would have to wait and see, she closed her eyes, but her mind raced on in thoughts faster than the train as it sped on toward Sinaloa and on to their new way of life: she could not find tranquility of mind.

The Worm in my Tomato

Ten

Catalina
Family perceptions and delusions

It was a picnic on wheels.

On the train *Ferrocarril del Pacifico* from Nogales, Sonora that now sped south to San Blas, Sinaloa, Antonia and her children gathered closer together in their seats, as if seeking comfort, protection, and courage from each other. Seven year old Catalina told Fortunato, Antonia, Lorena, Jose, and Samuel: "I liked to think that this was all a picnic on wheels. All I wanted was to be a good girl. At first I cry; but later I had fun playing games with Jose and the clouds passing outside my window. It was so much fun; father took us on a train ride. It was a special train called the 'flying *Repartition* train', as father called it." Catalina smiled in nervous enjoyment.

Lorena said, "It was at the Miami train-depot, when our friends cried and yelled goodbye that was most difficult for me; I cried, too, for sure, believe me Catalina, it was no picnic." But Lorena hugged Catalina as if to protect her from unseen dangers.

Samuel said, "The departure of our going away made our town weekly newspaper, *The Silver Belt*, of that week, March 15, 1932. I was disappointed that Mr. Mendoza did not write about the event in our paper *La Prensa Mexicana*, but he had told me before that he thought the story too tragic and shameful to report on." Samuel lowered his head in dejection.

Catalina spoke, "Mother and father were so busy packing all our clothes and the house furniture last week because Mother took her ice-box, her radio, her wood stove, and her cupboard with four doors and a bin for the flour. She loved her house furniture," and Catalina added, "She told us that she must have her wood stove and her ice-box." Catalina smiled, "She said that she wanted to keep her stove and icebox at any cost. We took our clothes, Lorena and me. That day in

March, we all dressed like when we visited God in church."

It seemed Catalina felt like talking, so her family complied by listening to her. "Lorena wore her new shiny black leather shoes with gold colored buckles," Catalina said, "Father bought these new shoes for Lorena at the Miami Commercial Store. Lorena liked her new shoes, especially for her going on vacation to Mexico. Father did not buy me any shoes, not even second hand new ones. Father had hoped that these new shoes would cheer up Lorena and help Lorena to have a happy going away to see her grandfather's big house."

Lorena yawned in Catalina's face, "All right, jealous, you talk on and on."

"It's the truth, you wore your shoes during the train ride, and sometimes you would put out your legs into the isle to admire your shoes. You just wanted to show off your new shoes, I think," Catalina said.

Jose had laughed and teased Lorena as being a show-off, all the way to Mexico.

"But mother make Jose be quiet with one of her looks with her eyes," Catalina said.

Antonia began to feed her family from her lunch basket. Catalina said, "I liked it when it was lunch time. Mother gave us some bean and potato tortilla burros to eat and I thought it was a nice picnic all the way to Mexico, on our vacation. I was happy and I wanted to have fun at the picnic train ride."

"Children, remember that this is really not a vacation and that we must work hard to make a living here in Mexico." Antonia said and added, "We must help your father succeed and keep our family together."

Samuel agreed with what his mother Antonia had said, and he planned to do his best in helping his father succeed in farming, but in truth, he wondered how; he worried that he had no knowledge of farming. In fact, for now, he was thinking about his being a *repatriate*; as Samuel sat in the train, he reflected on his experience of being a repatriate.

Samuel remembered that at the Miami Train Depot, he had observed the crowds, as he waited to depart; he had already said his goodbyes to his friends and to Mr. and Mrs. Mendoza. Samuel and all other repatriates had been scheduled to leave within the hour, after all the passengers had been accounted for by the government officials; he thought about all the large crowds mingled together on the platform and around the buildings, and he thought that the whole event seemed like a celebration of sorts but that it also resembled a funeral gathering at the cemetery, what with the many people crying. Samuel remembered that some of the young people who were staying were laughing and whooping it up; they were hugging those leaving, the ones who were crying; young girls mostly, those with their boy friends and loved ones, were bawling out loud. Samuel could not really understand why they were so loud and he contrasted them with the adults who acted more subdued.

Samuel thought about the mariachi group of musicians on the platform playing all those favorite classic Mexican songs. It reminded him of when Mexicans celebrated special days like *Cinco de Mayo* commemorating the victory of Mexican troops led by General Ignacio Zaragosa against the French forces in the battle of Puebla, Mexico in May, 1862. The occasion tried to be festive like a *Fiestas Patrias* day, like when Mexicans celebrate the 16th of September Independence Day, which commemorates Mexico's independence from Spain in 1821. Samuel thought that in this occasion of the departure of Repatriates, the Mariachi had sounded mournful like in a funeral burial and not a farewell party. Samuel had written in his articles for *La Prensa Mexicana* about how the high percentage of Mexican population had turned Arizona into a multicultural state. There were many Mexican fiestas highlighting Mariachi bands and folkloric dances. The folkloric dances and music displayed Mexico's regional indigenous cultural heritage. Evenings, up on hill-sides of the canyons in Miami, there always had been Mexican youth singing songs and playing the guitar. But Samuel became annoyed when he remembered how town police scrutinized in a menacing way the singing group and commented with rude remarks such as 'Here they go again, howling at the moon,' while always the police had directed a blind eye on the Keystone Hotel, Miami's infamous place of prostitution managed by "Tex."

Therefore, to Samuel, the occasion of the departure at the train-depot had been a mixture of feelings: the day evolved into a sad, somber, tearful, and simultaneously festive, joyous day. He particularly recalled the Mexican Americans' European-American friends, themselves recent immigrants or descendants from immigrants to the United States, who among them were English, Czech, Lebanese, German, Yugoslavians, Serbs, Irish, Anglos, Celtic and other nationalities; he recalled how there *they* were standing, smiling and intermixed with the Mexican crowds; they had wished us well, Samuel thought: shook hands all around, and told us to 'cheer up' and 'have a nice trip.' Samuel began to understand that *they* were from among the same types of citizens in the state, in the nation, who had done nothing to stop the injustices in the treatment of Mexicans in unfair employment practices or loss of lands. Samuel's resentment built up in his heart, but he resolved not to tell his mother: she would only tell him to forgive as a Christian.

Samuel remembered how Lorena, with tearful red eyes, cried outwardly while, he was convinced, his mother cried inwardly. But there was hope expressed by the people in the crowds, there was faith in their heart; they hoped that family members and friends would soon meet again. But, many who were crying felt that they were saying good-bye to Arizona for ever; the majority of those leaving feared that they would never be seen again; in fact, Samuel thought that the repatriates would probably never return to Miami: The Repatriates along with their work and contributions to the economic life of the town, the state, and the nation would be buried in the passage of time.

Samuel considered in his mind the experience of the Mexican Americans; he was certain that few people knew that the Mexicans residing in the Southwest were granted citizenship in 1848 through the *Treaty of Guadalupe Hidalgo*. Therefore, the Mexicans were the first United States citizens in the Southwest, as the native tribal people were not granted citizenship until 1924. Yet, here we are, Mexican American citizens thrown out among the Repatriates, he thought.

Many of the Mexicans on the Repatriation train who were departing and many of those staying were descendants of Mexicans who had shared in the history of building the Southwest from the days of the Spanish explorers and the *Provincias Internas*, 1541, to the present times 1932. In addition, the *Treaty of Guadalupe Hidalgo* had guaranteed freedom of language, religion, culture, and protection for their lands under the Constitution of the United States. Samuel reflected on the meaning of this history.

Samuel knew all this history and he thought that perhaps now, he would live Mexican history and be part of that history as well. What issues and problems awaited us in our new home in Mexico, he wondered. If my brother Santos did not care, at the moment, because he is a baby and does not know, someday he will, he thought. Samuel was certain, too, that the thousands of Repatriates would gain new perspectives of themselves and the United States and that this experience would shape their reality in the future. Samuel said out loud, his voice merging with the sound of many other voices and many other concerns in the train and voices of the past, uniting with the present, and carrying the same message into the unknown yet to come: "We are God's children born of the Virgin de Guadalupe, called to share the message of Christianity with all in the Americas; to live with love, respect, and compassion for others." Samuel in his mind and heart, thanked Mr. Mendoza for having taught him all this knowledge and perspective; we are as Mr. Mendoza said: '*La Gente Puente*, building bridges from the known to the unknown, from the past to the present and to the future, from the wants to the realization of needs, crossing borders to conquer evil with good and love.' Samuel recalled what Mr. Mendoza had talked about.

Samuel looked at his brother Jose sitting by his side and said, "It is heaven and hell, brother: railroading us to the unknown."

Now, on the train, click-clacking its way to Sinaloa, Jose answered, "Gee-whiz, Samuel, heck, you are going to do all right here in Mexico I am sure." Jose said, and he added, "but I could not help but wonder about how my baby brother, you know, being a border crosser at six months of age, and he is an American citizen, you know, he is being railroaded the wrong way, don't you think, Samuel?" Jose laughed, "Is he breaking Mexico's Immigration Laws?" He looked out the window at the desert and mountains flying by like runaway quail.

Samuel turned to Jose and said, "You know, I myself did not understand what it meant at the time we boarded the train, but I quickly became aware of its consequences, especially after I thought on what I had learned from my conversations with Mr. Mendoza about our emigrating to Mexico."

"Heck, man, actually, our sister Lorena did her best to stay in Miami; I think now that she was right all along trying to convince father to stay," Jose said.

"I hate to admit it, myself, but I finally realized that the United States policy of Repatriation pressured our family across the border into Mexico. As Mr. Mendoza, himself, told me, here let me read it to you, I wrote it down in my pocket notebook, this is what he said: 'Your family, like many Mexican families in the United States, is not only figuratively, not only in a vague reality, but conceptually and literally robbed of a future, when forced to begin anew in another country.'" Samuel put his notebook in his pants back pocket. "That is what he said, Jose, in Limonada's Pool Hall. He spoke there to a group of men, father, and myself. I still see him in my mind's eye, when Mr. Mendoza took time to wipe his high forehead with his large red bandana, the day being hot; the overhead fans not blowing cold air. We sat and listened to him; I admired his great wealth of knowledge," Samuel said.

"Wow, gee whiz, why did Mr. Mendoza tell you that?" Jose asked, "Can someone be robbed of a future?"

"Yes, of course, when your potential is limited in its opportunity to grow and develop." Samuel said, and he continued speaking, "I knew that Mr. Mendoza would periodically visit Limonada's Pool Hall to talk with *Caballón* Hernandez, whom he called the 'Black Mane,' and all the rest of the copper union members, he called '*La Caballada*' or herd of horses, who followed the 'Black Mane,' in thought and emotions,' he said." "I think Mr. Mendoza wanted Caballón and the horses to comprehend the complexity of the situation; to think at liberty, to throw off bridle and bit." Samuel paused and looked at Jose, and Samuel added, "I quote Mr. Mendoza: 'I wanted Caballón and the horses to comprehend the complexity of the situation: How the Repatriation deserved a comprehensive study by both the United States and Mexico to limit the human deprivations of United States families made up of citizens of both countries." Samuel read the quotes from his notebook, and he added, "Youth, once robbed of their future, their potential: they may never recuperate its fruits.' That's what Mr. Mendoza said."

Jose quietly thought about what Samuel had said, and remained silent. Samuel continued to talk and read his notebook quotes: "Mr. Mendoza had continued to tell me, 'I can't understand why Mexico and the United States don't work together on all these issues that influence the ordinary citizens and especially families, of both countries, who actually live out their lives on one side of the border or the other; these are man-made artificial borders, you know,'" Samuel looked at Jose, and said, "That's what Mr. Mendoza said, Jose." Samuel continued to speak, "You see, Jose, the land or geography is one; the political agreement between the two governments, based on coercion by victory in a war between them, to divide the land is an artificial compliance based on political, economic, and social motivations, but the Mexican people living on both sides of the borderline remain one; there are extended families living on both sides of the border." Samuel paused, flushed, he looked at Jose, and said, "Jose, Mr. Mendoza is so intelligent, to have thought it all out."

"Gosh, yeah, the ones I feel sorry for are the little children like Catalina and babies, heck, what do they know," Jose exclaimed, "like our baby brother, personally, he embraced no argument and expressed no complaints, gee whiz; don't you think so, Samuel, that our baby brother has a one-vision outlook on life: his milk bottle to guzzle on?" Jose laughed. "He is perfectly content. As long as he has his mother's breast in his toothless mouth, his tongue wrapped around her nipple, clucking away and drawing milk, in a swallowing motion into his baby stomach, he has no complaints, gee whiz."

"Again, from what I learned from Mr. Mendoza," Samuel remarked, "Our baby brother has no idea of what is going on. He has no notion, non-whatsoever, of any kind of event, that is far off in time and that may probably rob him of a good life. He may suffer future hunger and deprivation; then watch his wailing. What awaits our family in El Aliso, Sinaloa, Mexico, God only knows; don't you think so, Jose?"

"You are absolutely right, Samuel," Jose said and stretched his arms out above his head from his train seat.

"As for me, I am the complete opposite of our baby brother Santos, just like you are Jose, no doubt. Personally, I worry like hell with every turn of the wheels and every whoo, whoo, of the damn train," Samuel said.

Once Fortunato entered Sinaloa on the train, with his family,

The Worm in my Tomato

he lightened up, and he talked and talked to Antonia, Lorena, and Catalina about his native state; he pointed out the mountains and the deserts and told his family historical facts and stories about long-ago revolutionary battles fought on signified spots.

Samuel and Jose moved closer to Fortunato to hear what he was saying and to look out the train window. Samuel was impressed with Sinaloa's landscape, but more so, he felt that he would be impressed with its historical past.

The bridge each member of the family had personally created for his or her own crossing the border would determine the achievement of heaven on the one hand or hell on the other or both mixed in joy and sorrow. This is like what Miguel de Cervantes once said: "It seldom happens that any felicity comes so pure as not to be tempered and allayed by some mixture of sorrow." There was now no turning back regardless of how each thought or felt, and furthermore, the family would have to bridge their differences between them to keep the family together. How each member of the family thought and what they did would determine their mix of joy and sorrow.

San Blas, Sinaloa

The *Ferrocarril del Pacifico* train arrived at San Blas, Sinaloa railroad station. San Blas was a small town not far from El Fuerte River. The *Ferrocarril Chihuahua-Pacifico* crossed over from Los Mochis to the state of Chihuahua and would carry the repatriates going to Chihuahua. Early in the morning, Fortunato and his family disembarked onto the station platform. A stout dark Indian man waited for them on the dirt road nearby. He stood in front of a wooden wagon hitched to two mules. Fortunato and his family from San Blas would have to cross to the west side of El Fuerte River to reach El Aliso, where Fortunato's sister Tila lived in the "Big House."

"Welcome to San Blas," the solid dark Indian man was dressed in white pants and shirt smudged with sweat and dirt. He took off his straw ranch-hand hat and flourished it above his head, "My name is

The Worm in my Tomato

Chapo and *Tila* sent me to take you to El Aliso," he said.

"Oh, thank you, Chapo," Fortunato shook his hand, "I am glad that my sister Domitila sent you."

Samuel helped his mother up into the wagon and she sat on a wooden plank bench. She held Santos in her arms. Samuel, Jose, Lorena and Catalina were helped up by Fortunato, and then he stretched out his hand for Samuel to give him a hand-up and help him climb on the wagon. Samuel noticed that Lorena, after she had taken a look at the wagon with its dirty and rough board planks, promptly took off her new shiny patent leather shoes, "I don't want my shoes to get scratched," Lorena said as her father helped her board the wagon.

The wagon rolled on down the road, and after some time, Lorena said, "Samuel," as she peered left and right, "All along the dirt and dusty road to El Aliso, I have looked for school buildings, and I did not see any school building, only flat fields." Lorena had looked all around the country side.

The Road with no school or church to be seen.

Samuel noticed that his poor little sister looked as if she wanted to cry. She said, "I feel betrayed; there are no school buildings anywhere for my going to school; it's all flat desert, fields, and distant mountains all around."

Samuel did not know what to say to Lorena and instead turned to his mother, sitting beside him, "Mother, I wanted to get involved in some public work, but there seems to be nothing here." Samuel said, and continued speaking with her, "I planned to learn about social issues that affect the ordinary citizen and do something about the problems in Mexico, maybe write for a newspaper, like Mr. Mendoza, but this looks like one huge empty desert in this area, don't you think?"

"No, Samuel, perhaps you better not involve yourself in any public issues in Mexico, it is very dangerous here," Antonia said.

"You are probably right, mother." Samuel decided to plead his case for himself in another way, "But could I do some research and some writing, at least, so I can contribute to the well-being of the people, like Mr. Mendoza taught me?"

"No, Samuel, no, no, and furthermore, don't confront the federal government; don't you remember the poor religious sisters that we helped in Miami, who were forced out of Mexico because of the religious conflicts of the church with the government?" Antonia said, and she added, "Writers that are considered as promoting dangerous ideas for defending the poor, the hungry, the homeless, and the sick get sent out of the country; remember what happened to Mr. Mendoza."

Samuel felt sick to his stomach, and he wondered what actually he would do in Mexico, and the more Samuel thought about it, the more he became devastated. He continued to wonder about his place in this Repatriation journey to Mexico. He decided to leave his concerns alone for the moment, but he definitely planned to find out later about what to do; he knew that he had to build his own bridge to cross into the future. Samuel remembered what Mr. Mendoza had told him, once, about how human beings stay only momentarily in the present but always have a hand in the future and with the other hand hold on to the past, like how grade school children in the playground move across the iron drops hand over hand.

The five or so miles along a dirt and dusty road to the big house were filled with the animated talk of Fortunato as he pointed out sights and told stories about events that happened to him in a time long ago. There was the chatter of Lorena and Jose responding to their father and asking more and more questions. The swaying and bumpity-bump of the wagon wheels over rocks and small ditches prompted Samuel and all members of the family into a more immediate survival: staying in the wagon by holding on tight.

Antonia thought that perhaps she had been too unsympathetic with Samuel in prohibiting him from doing research and writing about local issues, and about his involvement in local political affairs. She feared for his safety. As for herself, her intentions were to get along just fine with her husband's family, especially his sister Tila in whose home her family would be staying. But Antonia's goal in the near future was for her family to have their own home. Antonia's children would like

The Worm in my Tomato

that, she knew, and Fortunato and she would be much happier.

Fortunato had told Antonia his family's story. Fortunato's grandfather and three brothers had sailed to Vera Cruz, Mexico from Spain in the early 1800s. His family name, however, had been De La Vega. When the four brothers reached Mexico City, they had a disagreement. Two brothers stayed in Mexico City and two migrated north to Sinaloa. The two brothers who migrated to Sinaloa changed their name to simply 'Vega'. Fortunato's father's name was Eudoro Vega. Eudoro acquired land grants from the Mexican government to ranch and promote agriculture. During the time of Spain's rule, Spain had established an *encomienda* system which granted native populations of great numbers to encomenderos to educate the native peoples in Spanish culture for exchange for profits from their labor, but not land. In time, when the Spaniards acquired land, they ruled over vast estates or haciendas and became *hacendados*. These lands bordered Indian Pueblos and in many instances hacendados incorporated native communal lands. Mexico remained a colony after its conquest by Spain in 1521. Conquistadores, explorers and settlers who had been granted *encomiendas* had the responsibility to Christianize the native populations and to teach them the European ways of life. The natives had always struggled and suffered deprivations under Spanish rule. Even before its independence, Mexico through its Constitution of Apatzingan in 1813, and after Mexico gained its independence from Spain in 1821, through the Constitutions of 1857 and 1917, changed political methods of granting and administering lands. In subsequent social and political revolutions in the late 1850s as the *War of the Reform*, 1856 – 1861, and the Revolution of 1910, more explicit, Mexican governments sought to remedy injustices to the indigenous peoples and have lands returned to native pueblos. Some of these social, economic, and political changes had direct consequences on the Catholic Church in Mexico and led to conflicts between the Church and the federal government.

All this historical, social, and political debate led to a tendency to settle differences through violence and armed conflicts that never seemed to end. Thus, Antonia's fears about Samuel's involvement in public political issues.

The Worm in my Tomato

Eudoro's enterprises in cattle ranching and raising crops for local consumption and export had prospered. Eudoro built the 'Big House' now cared for by his daughter Domitila, since his death in 1928. Fortunato visited Mexico once when his father died. Fortunato's mother, Lorenza Ruiz Vega, also had died after his visit home and his return to Arizona.

Fortunato, unlike his brothers and sisters, had run away from home at age nineteen; he had emigrated north to the United States, where he roamed in California and Arizona, sightseeing and working in construction. His main passion, however, was card games in the gambling halls, where he pursued his trade as a card dealer. He kept his hands smooth and wore dark suits and bow ties; Antonia thought about how Fortunato reminded her of a penguin, she smiled about it when she remembered, at times she playfully called him *Senor Penguin*.

The Great Depression forced many gamblers out of Casinos. Fortunato had managed the card games for some years, and when the economic downturn closed the mines and dried up the card games, gamblers organized games in private homes to satisfy their itching addiction, Fortunato participated in home games for a time, but he

The San Blas, Sinaloa Train Depot

The Worm in my Tomato

never ventured into back allies to throw dice like the common imitators vying for small amounts of change.

Chapo snapped the whip over the mules' back and shouted "Heehaw, heehaw," and the wagon rolled on, pulled by the mules, their dark brown or black sweating backs glistening in the pale light of a day spent sun. The mules strained in pulling the wagon carrying Antonia and her family in a new journey in search of survival in an unknown country, in a strange culture, and among a people who may or may not appreciate them. Antonia found consolation in reminding herself that if her Nanita had traveled 900 miles from Chihuahua to Morenci, Arizona in a wagon pulled by oxen in 1870, she and her family could surely go five miles in a wagon pulled by mules, from the train station in San Blas to the "Big House" in El Aliso.

Fortunato's voice changed tempo and pitch depending on what he was expounding at any given moment. In a guttural tone he described how his brothers had supervised the digging of new irrigation canals to bring water to the fields watered at night by *Zanjeros*. In a high pitch he pointed out the land parcels divided by his father among his many children. "Over there," he pointed, "from that small knoll to the high butte to the river to the canal, the fields belong to your Uncle Jorge." His voice leveled, "Across the thicket desert, your Aunt Domitila manages the greater part of a *sitio*. In El Bacori, your Uncles Eugenio and Antonio farm 600 hectares and your Aunt Candida manages the second big house in Mezquital. At Estacion Vega your Aunt Guadalupe and her Russian husband have 200 hectares in citrus and another 300 hectares in garbanzo, pinto beans, and cotton, all for export by rail to Culiacan and Los Mochis and other parts of Mexico." He was elated, and he said, "I will help manage my sister Domitila's lands and plant cotton, tomatoes, and we'll see, raise some livestock near the Indian village El Mezquitalito. I also have twenty-seven hectares in El Potrero to raise tomatoes, beans and squash." The wagon swayed and buckled with Chapo urging the mules over the dirt road pitted with ruts.

"Look," Fortunato almost stood up but the wagon buckled and slammed him back on his wood plank seat, "there it is, the "Big House," he said.

Antonia's heart sank in disappointment. The "Big House" which she had imagined to be an elegant *Hacienda* with red adobe archways, looked smaller than what she had expected. Neither had Antonia seen other large houses nearby in the area, her desire to have her own house increased ever so much more, furthermore, she felt for certain that her relationship with her sister-in-law, Tila, would be one of dependency, and Antonia hoped that the time for her family sharing a home with Tila would be of short duration.

Part Two

End of Year One, 1932
and Years Two and Three 1933 ‿ 1934 ‿ 1935

A theological interpretation of the Vega family's immigration story based on Genesis 46: 1-4 (NRSV): When Antonia set out with her family and with all that she had and came to El Aliso, Sinaloa, Mexico, she prayed to God; she was not afraid to go down to Sinaloa, and she had faith that God would be with her family and that God would help keep her family together and bless them. She believed that God would be with them in Sinaloa and that God would bring them up again to return home. In reality, Antonia's daughter Lorena closed her father's eyes in Mexico and her mother's eyes in the United States.

Eleven

Lorena
Grandfather's Big House in El Aliso

In the wagon, during the bumpy ride to the Big House, Antonia wrestled with images in her mind of Fortunato as a vaquero and farmer, and she planned to build her bridges of friendship with his family, especially his sister Tila. Lorena searched in all directions for a school building. She also looked over the country side, through the fields, and under the trees for the *Big House*. Indeed, from the wagon, driven like mad by Chapo, Lorena had seen in the distance a huge house that like a mirror, glared bright white in the sunlight. Behind it were miles of a green canvas of fields marked out by dirt roads.

As the wagon neared the house, Lorena saw that there were several large mezquite trees scattered about the large front yard. Strangely, there were horses tied to horse hitching posts. But there were five automobiles, black colored, with dust covered fenders and hoods. There were horse-drawn wagons, painted green with elegant decorations; there were blue wagons, some yellow, and some simply gray. All were dusty. Some work wagons were parked under the shade of a large mezquite tree.

Chapo halted the mules under the shade of a tree; the mules nodded their heads, swished their tails, pawed at the ground, and neighed a sigh of relieve and in anticipation of water and hay. Three large barking dogs pranced about the wagon. The dogs wagged their tails to show their friendship and happiness at seeing visitors. The white one with black spots stayed out of reach, the black one ran in circles swishing its tail back and forth, but the chocolate colored one came over to Lorena and licked her hand.

"Heh, *Chocolate*, vamos," yelled Chapo, ordering Chocolate away from Lorena and the rest of the family. "Heh, *Dia*, heh *Noche*; vamos," yelled Chapo, and the white dog with black spots and the black dog sauntered away with Chocolate following after.

When Antonia dismounted from the wagon, she asked Fortunato, "Will we have our own house, soon?"

He quickly answered, "Yes, but not right away. I have to harvest and sell crops first, and get some money, and then we can build our own home."

"The Big House is not as large as I thought it would be; do you really think that we will all fit in the house?" Antonia asked Fortunato.

"Hope so; it's been years since I was here last, but houses in Arizona just appear larger."

"I don't want to be in a position of not having my own home; you must take us somewhere else, soon," Antonia said.

"No, not until after I prepare the land, plant the seed, nurture the crops in their growth, harvest and market the crops can we move, and furthermore, we have to stay here until I can pay for a house to be built; there are no houses in the area. Now, quiet, please Antonia, let's hurry, my sister Tila is waiting," Fortunato said.

From inside the big house emerged a group of young children, teenagers, young adults, and older men and women, all were smiling and their white teeth gleamed in the sunlight. All waved hello, "The North Americans have arrived," spoke out some teens, with gusto, "The *gringo Repatriados* are here," others yelled. Lorena had hurried and put on her new glossy black patent leather shoes. Antonia smoothed her new blue cotton and rayon dress. The smiling group approached Antonia and her family and hugged them; all family members doing the welcoming and those being welcomed were a long time hugging and staring at each other, and slowly the human mass in the midst of boisterous laughter, arm in arm, strolled into the big house. All were related: brothers, sisters, uncles, aunts, cousins; Fortunato glowed joy all over in being once again with his brothers, sisters, nephews and nieces.

Lorena followed into the house a little sad that no one had noticed her new shiny black leather shoes her father had bought for her at the Miami Commercial Store. Lorena studied her cousins carefully to select one to talk to about school. Lorena searched the girls' faces for a Mary Cota, whom she hoped would be her best friend and confidant. All Lorena's

The Worm in my Tomato

new found family chattered and laughed out-loud with one another.

Then one voice resounded with authority. Lorena quickly turned to face the owner of that authoritative voice; the owner of the voice was a not so tall, full-breasted plump woman; her short black hair hung straight over her ears and hugged her plump neck; she looked flushed crimson and had a serious appearance. "Time to eat lunch," she said.

Lorena sensed that the large woman was the boss in the big house. Just moments before all uncles, aunts, and cousins were so nice, but now the boss made them visibly tremble. "Yes, Tila, right away," some adults said in unison.

Lorena felt dislike for this woman and felt an instant fear, and she made up her mind at once never to cross her path in a wrong manner.

"All adults please sit at the table in the dining room; all children and teens sit around the kitchen table; dinner will be served immediately," Tila said.

All adults, including Fortunato, who pulled Antonia by the one arm that did not hold Santos, rushed into the dining room. Lorena's cousins hurried into the kitchen, and she did too. All the young teens stood around the large wooden plank table in the kitchen.

Lorena sat next to a girl cousin that she selected to be her adviser and answer all her questions. Lorena thought that the girl looked a little like Mary Cota with soft cinnamon colored skin, dark black wavy hair combed back and tied with a red ribbon. But unlike sturdy Mary Cota, this Mary was skinny and looked overworked, but her eyes sparkled like green turquoise.

For starters, Lorena asked her selected new friend who that large lady was. "That lady is our Aunt Domitila, called Tila for short," the girl blushed and slowly her cinnamon colored skin started to turn her face a golden-brown.

A tall tanned Indian lady, who undoubtedly was the cook, stood by the large cast iron stove. The kitchen stove was surrounded with adobe brick on both sides below the iron top. Without saying a word, the cook pointed to the chairs. The children sat down and carefully the lady served each one of the children food on a clay dish. Lorena, being hungry from a long trip, gobbled her dinner, and without asking permission, she sneaked over to the dining room doorway and peeked in. Loud and clear, Lorena heard Tila's voice, "Now that my dear brother Fortunato is here with us, I will share my home with him, half the house will be for him and his family. He will cultivate his twenty-seven hectares in *El Potrero* and supervise the migrant workers over my fields and his fields. I will also give a calf to each one of his little girls to help them get started with their herd of cattle," She said. Lorena heard her father stammer a "Thank you, Tila." Lorena saw that her father looked scared and she thought that tomorrow would be an opportune moment to talk to him about her going away to school.

Lorena returned to her place. "What is your name,"Lorena asked her new found Mary Cota; the girl looked shyly at Lorena and murmured, "Eligia."

Around the table, cousins began to introduce themselves; some were sons and daughters of deceased Oton Vega, from La Noria, Eugenio who lived in *El Bacori*; others belonged to the Antonio Vega family who lived in *El Mezquital* ranches, while other cousins were brothers and sisters who belonged to the Jorge Vega family of El Aliso, all together, Lorena counted twenty-two cousins.

"Where do you go to school," Lorena probed anxiously, loud enough to make herself heard above the noise coming in from the dining room.

"Keep quiet Lorena, let them talk," Samuel said, and he stared at Lorena. Jose looked embarrassed and irritated and he tried to give Lorena the intimidating eye, like mother sometimes did, but his eyes didn't have the control power.

"Oh, that's all right, we can tell you that," Eligia came to Lorena's defense.

"Where is your school," Lorena persisted, ignoring Samuel and Jose, "I did not see any buildings when we rode in on Chapo's wagon."

There was low laughter around the table, "That wagon does not belong to Chapo," a boy cousin glanced and jerked his head toward the dining area, "Aunt Tila owns everything in El Aliso," he said, and continued chewing his food.

"Chapo works for Aunt Tila," a young teenage girl called Fermina, voiced. Some girls giggled. Then another girl added, "There's a one room adobe school house nearby in El Mezquitalito about a mile

The Worm in my Tomato

down the road past the watering pond toward the desert," the girl cousin said and frowned.

"It's for the Indian kids who live in their pueblo *El Mezquitalito* closer to the El Fuerte River," a pretty girl with golden curls from the Oton Vega family group of cousins sneered and said, "If you want to go to school, you have to board out and stay in some school away from home Lorena, because you wouldn't want to attend school here with them."

Lorena's thoughts swirled again in her head and all of a sudden, Lorena realized why she had not seen any signs of a school. There was no school. Lorena's heart felt heavy with despair, as her stomach was full with beef, beans, spinach, and tortillas. Lorena was more determined than ever, however, and resolved to press her father for a boarding school education, if that's how it had to be.

"So then where do you go to school," Lorena insisted and looked all around the table waiting for her answer, just like Miss Yoakum back home would do when she asked a question from the class.

Lorena glanced quickly at Samuel, who probably would have pinched her on the arm as mama did sometimes, if he had been sitting next to her. She also noticed that Jose just shook his head and pressed together his lips in disgust. Both boys felt like edgy lizards scurrying to hide under a boulder. But Lorena's cousins ignored her brothers and it seemed to her that her cousins were eager to inform everyone and each other around the table of their education experiences. One by one and sometimes two or three at once told of where they attended school in the United States, in Mexico City, and one or two were studying in France. The Frei cousins said that they were attending a boarding school in Tucson.

"Oh, our train stopped in Tucson for a time to pick up repatriated families because of the Repatriation laws in the United States," Lorena said. Samuel and Jose, she noticed, just lowered their heads to their chests, and it seemed like they closed their eyes. The lizards, indeed, hid under their respective imaginary rock. The cousins just roared with laughter. Lorena wondered what was so funny. Eligia tugged Lorena at her arm. Lorena was glad Eligia was sitting by her side and not her brother Samuel.

Eligia whispered, "You've just opened the door to the self-importance of the Vega clan." Eligia gave Lorena a look of comprehension and confidentiality that told her that Eligia considered her different from the other Vegas. At the same time, a boy cousin who Lorena had not noticed because he had been very quiet and sat deep into his large chair, walked to her side, introduced himself by the name Gonzalo and said, "Not all your Vega cousins go to school, I don't; I live in the desert and the desert is my school." He quickly walked out the kitchen door.

The Vega cousins, after that, who were insistent and boisterous, dominated the conversation around the table and proceeded to try to impress each other about their experiences of where they attended school, their extracurricular activities, and their travels abroad in foreign countries.

Then all of a sudden, a voice boomed, "Good-bye now, have a safe trip, children," and cut through the commotion. Aunt Tila loomed in the doorway of the dining room. Tila looked magnificent to Lorena as she watched all her cousins hurry out along side their parents. The Vega clan gave those in the house and each other an until-we-meet-again embrace. The families jumped into their gasoline powered Ford sedans, they drove off, and the black cars, got powdered with more dust from a billowing dirt cloud clinging along beside each car as they sped down the road out of El Aliso. Somewhere, at the forks, each family took their particular roads to their haciendas.

Dust devils plagued the homeward bound cars on the dirt road, and Lorena's mind, like the dust devils, swirled with concerns, painful thoughts in her heart, and her eyes misted over. Lorena envied her cousins who would return to their boarding schools in Mexico City or some foreign country. Lorena's heart mixed with heavy envy and hurt was tied up like a ball of mud kneaded with vinegar. Their schools, Lorena knew, were no Bullion Plazas, for Mexican kids only, as in her hometown. "But that was not so bad," Lorena consoled herself. For certain her cousins, she thought, for sure, had never had a teacher as good as Miss Yoakum. Also, Lorena convinced herself, that her cousins, in spite of their education in boarding schools in faraway places, would not have known anything about the reader "On the Road," if she had had a chance to ask them the question. Lorena was determined, however, to convince her father to send her to a boarding school in Tucson, not far from Mary Cota.

After lunch, in the afternoon, Antonia, Samuel, and Jose were walking outside inspecting the grounds. Lorena noticed her father had returned inside with her Aunt Tila. Lorena sought an opportune time to speak with her father. Lorena looked about the large front yard and calculated it to be three times their previous backyard back home where Samuel and Jose had played the game of tossing washers into a hole in the ground. Now, here, Lorena thought, they had more room to play washers. There was a whole desert for a backyard for Catalina and Santos to romp, she smiled, and mama can grow a giant of a garden.

The backyard stretched back into a desert of cactus and mesquite, and beyond that stretched the fields for crops. Not far from the big house, a *huerta* could be seen; the large vegetable and fruit garden provided food for the big house. The air laden with the odor of the animal droppings drifted from the direction where there were cattle pens, hog pens, and horse corrals. The sweet smell of green vegetables, the aromatic aroma of flowers from the huizache trees, and the dry hot smell of desert cactus mixed with all the other odors to confound the nostrils of those who dared breathe in this life for the first time.

Lorena wondered if Dick's grandfather's farm would have also stunk. Of course the pictures in the "On the Road" reading book showed a red rooster crowing from the top of a neatly painted white wood picket fence. From Tila's front yard began the fields with the dirt road that stretched for a mile, on which Chapo drove the wagon and cracked the whip over the bobbing heads of the sweating mules. At the end of the road along the fields was a juncture where a road turned left to Mezquitalito and the other road turned right to Bacori. The straight road from Tila's front yard continued to El Fuerte, a small town across the El Fuerte River. Farther away facing the opposite side of the river was San Blas. The Repatriation train had brought Antonia's family to San Blas where Chapo, who had been sent by Tila, picked Fortunato and his family up to bring them home.

The huge adobe *Big House* was constructed with sun-dried adobe brick, plastered with clay and white-washed with lime. From a distance the house had looked white, but close up it was more of a light gray color.

The sun began to set in the low horizon past the fields opposite the right side of the house. As Lorena faced the sunset, she thought that way was west, where the sun sets, Miss Yoakum had taught her in class; to Lorena's left was south, toward Mezquitalito and the watering pond, the Indian pueblo, and the desert that her boy cousin, Gonzalo, had talked about. That was the direction the Indian school was located, she thought. Facing away from the yard, opposite the sunset was east and to her left, looking up the road, was north, the road to Arizona. Lorena thought that if she ran away from home some dark night, like Nanita, she must run north by the light of the moon all the way to San Blas and catch a train to Nogales. From there, she thought, that she would take a bus past Tucson to Miami. Lorena felt delighted that she had a route all planned out in her head. She was certain that what she wanted was to go to school somewhere, soon. But terrible thoughts filled her mind; a heavy feeling tugged at her heart: would she go to school? Where would she be able to attend school? Lorena planned to ask her father, and she even thought that she might ask her Aunt Tila, if she would help her go to school, but Lorena was not sure that her Aunt Tila would accept her. Aunt Tila did not look too friendly to Lorena, she had seen how her father had that look of submission when he was around Aunt Tila; everyone around here knew Tila was in charge, there was no doubt about that.

Lorena rushed inside the big house to search out her father. Darkness had prematurely filled the large adobe house because of few windows that let in the fading sunlight. She was surprised to see Eligia going about the house as she lighted what Lorena thought at first were candles, but after closer inspection, turned out to be small tin cans that were cut in half, and contained some oil, and held up a wick dipped in the oil and when lit gave light. The cans were held up by nails on the walls about the house. Several of these tin cans were soon lit in the kitchen and dining room areas and provided a dim light. Lorena, out of curiosity, examined the lighting apparatus that served as night lamps. She saw how the oil climbed up the wick to provide a source for fuel that when the oil in the wick burned, the oil provided the light. Lorena noticed the dancing silhouettes of shades on the lighted walls created by the bouncing flames of the burning oil wicks. Around and behind each tin can dark smudges left by soot and smoke dirtied

The Worm in my Tomato

the walls where the tin cans were nailed in place. Eligia going about lighting the lamps reminded Lorena of the old lamp-lighter in the song she sang in school. Lorena stopped Eligia and held her a moment by the shoulder, "What are you doing here?"

"I have to light the *cachimbas* before bed-time, for awhile."

"No, I mean *here* in this house," Lorena explained.

"I live here with my mother, why?

"Nothing, it's that I thought you were one of my cousins and had left."

"Well, I am one of your cousins but I live and work here," Eligia said.

"Who is your mother," asked Lorena.

Eligia pulled away toward the kitchen, and she motioned for Lorena to follow her. Lorena followed her into the kitchen where the Indian servant cook had finished cleaning up the table, put away the clay dishes, the pots and pans, and wiped the large kitchen table. Eligia stood by the tall dark handsome woman who served the house as cook, Eligia motioned to her, "She is my mother, Luisa."

Lorena was astonished and stared; she did not know what to say for a moment, but then blurted out, "Oh."

Just then, the authoritative voice said loud and clear, "Good night, I go to sleep with the roosters," said Aunt Tila and she looked at Lorena and ordered, "Go to bed Lorena, tomorrow look for Eligia here in the kitchen at 5:00 in the morning to begin your household chores; Eligia will show you what to do."

Lorena was speechless. Eligia guided her away gently toward the half of the big house where her family would live; Eligia whispered "Goodnight," and hurried away.

Lorena found her father showing the boys their room where they would sleep. Fortunato, Antonia, and the baby shared one room; Catalina and Lorena shared one room. Father explained to all that Chapo would bring the furniture from San Blas on the following day. Fortunato explained that tonight the family would sleep on the *catres* which were made with wooden cross-bars at each end with leather thongs threaded across a wood frame to make a cot. Fortunato and his family used borrowed blankets for cover. The legs of the *catres* stood in small cans filled with water. Lorena complained to her mother that there were no pillows, but Antonia had gone to do other chores.

Fortunato returned into the room and said, "The bathroom for tonight will be the buckets in our rooms until we learn where the outhouses are located, it's too dark outside anyway."

"Father," Lorena uttered, "I want to go to school somewhere, perhaps in Tucson."

"No, you can't just yet," Fortunato answered.
"But, father, you said that you would help me go to school in Mexico," Lorena persisted.

"I already asked Tila, and she said there are no schools here," Fortunato looked across the girls' bedroom through the open door and saw Antonia nursing the baby, and he said "Furthermore, you have to wait until I have a good harvest and I get a good price for my crops." He turned from Lorena and walked away.

Soon the tin can *cachimbas* were blown out, no doubt by Luisa on orders from Tila. The house was plunged into a heavy black darkness held down by a silent stillness, a heavy nothingness. Lorena felt humiliated and her eyes filled with tears. Lorena bit her lower lip and determined not to give up until she either went to school here or ran away on the north road. Lorena determined that tomorrow she would speak with her father, again, about her education. For some time during the night, Lorena heard tossing and turning sounds from dad's room. The boys' room, dark and quiet, had died. Only Catalina snored in bliss; probably dreaming of her 'Picnic on wheels,' thought Lorena. As usual, the baby sucked loudly on his milk bottle and let out an occasional "haw" of satisfaction, and Lorena hoped he would not grow up to be like his Uncle Tomas, the way he craved his bottle.

Lorena kept awake into the darkness, she worried about how to convince her father to send her to boarding school, or if not sent to school, she planned to run away. The only certain knowledge for Lorena tonight was that her family was the poor Vega family, the have nothing family, the ones blown in by the winds of the Great Depression, forced out from their native country, carried into Mexico by the politics of the Repatriation: Lorena was certain that her family was the unwanted one, railroaded out of their country, her country.

The Worm in my Tomato

With stark realization, she knew her family had become what they had tried so hard to escape: hoboes living under the bridge. Lorena cried softly into her flat pillow; she knew that she had to make some tough decisions and take drastic action. Lorena thought with out a doubt that her family was so poor and so out of place in Mexico, that she would go north, and in her fantasy she became an eagle flying north.

Mezquitalito

El Fuerte River

The Worm in my Tomato

Twelve

Lorena
Survival Education

The very first night after her arrival to the Big House, Lorena had cried herself to sleep after her father had given her no hope of going to school. Lorena wondered how she would ever go to school in this rural desert without schools. The night was black dark and quiet with no signs of life. Finally, Lorena fell asleep without hope and without dreams.

Lorena was shaken awake in the dark by a strange hand on her left shoulder. She sat up, startled. "Don't get scared, it's me, Eligia," Lorena heard the unseen speaker whisper as Eligia led Lorena out by the hand; Lorena stumbled out after Eligia.

Outside the house, Eligia could be discerned clearer. Lorena shivered and crossed her arms over her chest in an effort to keep out the cold, "What is it?"

Eligia explained rapidly that they must do their morning chores. Eligia said that Tila wanted her to show Lorena the chores today. "Tomorrow you will be on your own," Eligia said.

Confused and somewhat angry, Lorena followed Eligia about the hacienda, learning the chores that Lorena would have to do daily. Lorena felt that she would have revolted then and there, but she assumed it was a price to pay if she wanted to go to school. It was yet dark and the mist covered both girls like a cold ground cloud. In a way Lorena was excited, learning from Eligia would be like her first day of school, filled with expectations, Lorena thought.

"I am willing to do this work, Eligia, if somehow, and some day, it will help me go to school."

"Oh, Lorena, don't you know that the kind of school you want is only for the rich?" Eligia looked at Lorena with a stern look, "The only kind of school for you and me is the school of hard work, sun up to sun down, with a place to sleep and some food to live on and a peso or two for our pay, and hopefully a peaceful death, as my mother says."

"Oh, yourself Eligia, you quit that, talking about death, we are both young, and have many years to live yet, learn, and go to school."

"All right, true, but it is also true that those long years we live will be full of hard work," Eligia said.

"What about education?" Lorena asked.

"No, there is none here, and furthermore, Lorena, there may not be any government school in our area, so you should make up your mind to learn only what hard work has to teach and from nature and people around you."

Thus, with that final note from Eligia, Lorena's survival education began. Eligia told Lorena what she had to do first. The clay pots in the kitchen and two clay pots in the dining room had to be filled with water. Lorena asked, "Where's the faucet?"

Eligia stared at her, puzzled, "The what?" She carried a curved mesquite pole, about five feet long that was slender with a curve in its center, each end of the pole had a short rope with a bucket at its end, "This is a *palanca*," Eligia said, and she also carried a metal dipper with her. "The what?" she repeated.

"The faucet," Lorena gestured with her hands. "You turn the handle like this and a stream of water comes out," Lorena drew a faucet in the air with her hands.

"Oh, no, here you go like this," Eligia gestured pulling with both her hands alternately like pulling a rope, "You draw out the water from our ground well."

Eligia led Lorena around the house some fifty yards distance toward a clump of trees. She showed Lorena a high square mound made of adobe brick plastered with white lime clay. On four sides around the brick square and facing each other were large tree posts. The poles supported cross beams that formed a cross over the top and above of the center of the square. Hemp rope tied the cross beams. At the center of the crossed poles, tied together with rope, was a pulley, secured tight with leather strands, through the pulley ran a hemp rope with one end tied to a tin bucket. The remaining length of the rope was looped around an arm of a tree post buried beside and outside the well. On top of the well opening were four flat wide boards that served as the well covering.

"This is the best well in El Aliso," Eligia pointed to the well and ran her hand over the pulley, "Never let the rope touch the ground or the top of the well, always un-wrap the rope slowly as you let the bucket down, but first you must remove these two center boards."

She yanked one board out and then the other. She placed the boards carefully on top of the outer boards. "Now, lower the bucket down slowly until you feel it has touched water, and then pull on the rope sideways, like this, to allow water to fill into the bucket," Eligia demonstrated. "With the other hand hold to the end side of the rope and began to pull up with both hands one after the other, like this." Eligia pulled out the bucket full of crystal-clear water, gleaming and sparkling in the early dawn light. She tipped the water out from the well bucket, emptying the water into one of the two buckets tied to the mesquite curved light pole that she had carried with her from the kitchen.

She took the dipper and scooped out a dipper of water and carefully drank her fill, "Ahhh, the pleasure of drinking water before the sun comes up, try it Lorena."

Lorena scooped a dipper of sparkling water and drank deeply. It was cold, crisp, slippery and fresh, not like the water in the kitchen with the taste of clay they had drunk last night. "Wow, this is wonderful water, unlike the water in the kitchen," Lorena drank another dipper of God's pure mystery; she became a deer thirsting for liquid life.

Eligia laughed out loud, "You are right Lorena, both this water and the water in the kitchen came from the same well but water changes because of location and time. Place and time are everything. The water is marvelous when you first take it from its body below the well and it brings with it the sweetness from the ground. It also brings with it freshness in cool temperature of the dawn in the morning." Eligia's face shown in light, making her cinnamon skin ruddy, and in Lorena's mind, she looked like an angel, but without wings. "Now, hurry, Lorena, your turn to draw water, for practice, and fill the other bucket of the *palanca*."

Lorena lowered the bucket into the well, gave it a twist to tip the bucket in the well and help it fill with water. Then she drew the bucket out of the well by pulling the rope, hand over hand with great difficulty, through the turning wheel of the pulley. At times the well

The Worm in my Tomato

bucket bounced from one side of the well to the other.

"Keep it straight, Lorena, keep the rope straight or you will pull up an empty bucket," Eligia giggled.

Lorena strained with every ounce of her arm strength. Finally, she had the bucket out and carefully tipped the bucket from the top of the well to let water fill into the empty bucket, tied to the mezquite slender pole, standing on the ground. Lorena had to twice more draw water out from the well to completely fill the bucket.

Eligia pulled the two board planks back over the well to seal it. "Now," Eligia instructed: she lifted the curved mezquite light pole up with the extended hemp ropes from each bucket resting on the ground; she lowered herself down by bending her knees and placed the center of the pole over her shoulders across the back of her neck. Then, she straightened up. The buckets at each side of the pole, balanced across her back, hung straight and held the water. She walked away from the well toward the kitchen.

"Wow, this is a wonderful tool of wood, ropes and buckets to carry water," Lorena exclaimed. "What's this pole and buckets called, again?" Lorena walked beside Eligia.

"This pole is called a *Palanca*, now you try it," Eligia, in slow motion, lowered the buckets to the ground.

Lorena carefully with bent knees lowered herself underneath the palanca and with great effort lifted up and began to wobble on toward the house. Eligia laughed and held her sides with both arms, "Walk steady, Lorena, or you'll spill out the water and we'll have to repeat getting water again," she walked faster beside Lorena. "Hurry, this chore took too long, I hear the chickens cackling," Eligia said.

Lorena labored under the mezquite wood *palanca* walking as fast she could. She kept the buckets level and steady. Finally, they reached the kitchen and from the buckets Eligia ladled water into the clay pots in the kitchen and dining room area. Eligia then set the palanca with the buckets down beside the wall in the kitchen. Then Eligia grabbed a large clean tin pot. She pulled Lorena out from the kitchen, and they hurried down to the large barn-like building that stood away from the house on the opposite side of the well near the fields to where the chickens were kept. A rooster perched proudly on top of a fence post

The Worm in my Tomato

and began to crow, welcoming the rising sun in the east.

"He's late and we're late and Aunt Tila will be angry with us, Lorena," Eligia talked, "next you have to go into the barn and fetch the chicken feed," she led Lorena to a side barn door locked with wire twisted to hold two doors together. She untwisted the wire and showed her inside where the feed was kept inside a barrel covered with a tin tub. Eligia took an old clay pot and dipped it inside the barrel and filled the pot, "Only fill it up to this mark," she showed Lorena a black line drawn up about three-quarters of the pot, "or Tila will get angry." The chickens are turned loose on some days to forage for themselves, but never after the fields have been planted with seed, as the chickens would dig it up to eat."

Eligia hurried out and began to spread the feed even handed to the jumping, tumbling chickens that dashed after the seed corn. Eligia returned the pot and locked the barn doors by twisting the wire. She returned to the chicken coop yard, "Always check to see that their pans have water, plenty of water, so the chickens won't die in the heat during the afternoons, although the flock stays resting under the mesquite trees in the shade until evening."

Eligia scooted past Lorena to the other side of the barn where a different larger space kept the family cow waiting to be milked. Lorena noticed that the cow had only one eye. "We milk 'One Eye' the *Tuerta* every morning for the milk we use during the day for our meals and baking," Eligia said and took the large tin pot she had carried under her arm and began to deftly squeeze the cow's udders. The stream of milk splattered into the large pot and the white foam rose up. "Here," she got up from her kneeling position, "you milk her."

Lorena did as Eligia had done but no milk came out. 'One Eye' just turned her massive head and winked her one eye at Lorena. Eligia showed Lorena again how to do it. After a few tries, Lorena finally began to move out a puny dribble into the tin pot. "After some practice, you'll be a champion milker," Eligia smiled. "We'll practice tonight in the kitchen with a soaked towel, after I will show you how to light the *cachimbas*." She fed One Eye some hay. "We'll be back and let her loose for a while in the pasture," Eligia said.

The girls rushed back to the house. "We'll have breakfast, now, but

The Worm in my Tomato

afterwards we will go feed the pigs and haul water from the irrigation canal to fill their mud hole so the pigs can wriggle in the mud to survive the heat and the mites," Eligia said.

In the kitchen, Eligia's mother Luisa was waiting to feed the girls. Lorena was told that Aunt Tila, Catalina, her brothers Samuel and Jose, and her parents had earlier eaten breakfast. Santos had gone to sleep; he had not been assigned chores. Catalina was helping mother in their rooms. Father and the big boys had left for their chores in the fields. Lorena wondered if their chores were as exciting as hers.

In the sunlight streaming through the open window of the kitchen, as Lorena munched her potatoes, beans, white cheese and tortilla, she noticed how attractive Eligia's mother was. Lorena thought that Luisa was pretty. Luisa was tall, strong, with a heart shaped cinnamon colored face, and she had long black braids tied with a red ribbon. Lorena thought that Luisa looked young, yet, compared to her Aunt Tila who looked over fifty and stood not-so-tall when contrasted with Luisa. Lorena thought her Aunt Tila was a stout woman.

Lorena thought how fortunate Eligia was to have a young pretty mother. Luisa served the girls another egg, some fried chorizo, more fried beans, a boiled potato, a tortilla and a glass of milk, still warm and foamy, from 'One Eye'.

After breakfast, Lorena asked Eligia," what now?"

"We help in the kitchen unless Aunt Tila needs us to help in the cheese room," Eligia said.

Lorena asked, "What time is it?" There was no clock to be seen anywhere. "It's nine in the morning," Eligia said as if she had seen a clock. Lorena looked around but there was no clock.

"How do you know, if there is no clock?" Lorena asked.

"We go by instinct. I just know when it's five in the morning because I wake up at five. It takes until eight to complete the morning chores. At eight we eat breakfast and rest until nine. It's nine. We work until noon and then we feed the pigs and fill their mud hole. We will take two buckets from the small barn to haul water from the irrigation ditch or even from the river if necessary," Eligia spun out the words.

"You will know when it's noon because the sun will be directly above our heads. After that every hour the shadows of all things begin

151

The Worm in my Tomato

to face east and extend longer with each hour from one to five, then the shadows will flatten out and the sun sets at six in the west behind the *sierras*. This pattern changes depending on what season it is. For example, the sun sets earlier in the winter and later in the summer," Eligia explained.

Eligia began to wash the morning dirty clay, china, and tin dishes used for breakfast. Luisa had poured hot water from the adobe wooden stove into a small wooden tub for Eligia. Eligia used brown soap. "This is home-made soap made from hog's lard and lime boiled outback by Telesforo," Eligia said.

"We eat at noon, right?" Lorena remembered the tasty breakfast. Lorena was already hungry again after all that work from five to eight in the morning.

"No, we eat the day's main meal at two in the afternoon." Eat everything Aunt Tila gives you, because in the night around eight all you will get is coffee or chocolate and a piece of bread depending what my mother has baked," Eligia said.

Lorena had used her chore performing time to plan in her mind her encounter with her father to convince him to send her to a boarding school. Now, she planned to see him out in the fields when Eligia and she would go pay a visit to the hog enclosure.

Lorena really did not mind the hard work, if it did not go on day after day. She began to wonder what was going to happen to her. In her mind, Lorena thought, this is hard work, harder than the oxen's work that pulled Nanita in the wagon for 900 miles to Arizona. Will this work go on forever? Lorena wondered and she hoped not. Lorena inwardly prayed, God, please help me. Lorena planned to speak again with her father; she just had to go to school somewhere.

After helping her mother for a while and then sweeping some rooms for Luisa, Lorena hurried out with Eligia to take care of the hogs; to do the hog work. Luisa took a palanca leaning against the wall outside the house and placed two large old buckets, one each tied to a short hemp rope at each end of the palanca. Luisa handed the palanca to Eligia.

The girls hurried across the yard into the Cheese room. It was a huge long room inside a large barn, away and behind the house to the west side. The room was constructed of thick adobe walls plastered with cement and lime. Inside the long cool room, there were long rows of wood planks; on the top of the boards were placed large round thick cheeses covered with thin cheese cloth. Each cheese looked to be about twelve inches across the middle and four inches high. Eligia told Lorena that the white cheeses were *curing*.

Two vats held the sour milk that was fermenting and changing from a liquid cottage cheese like substance into a hardening fresh white cheese. Eligia with a large ladle scooped out the skimmed yellowish sweet liquid into the palanca buckets.

"We have to take this '*Suero*' to the hogs," she evenly distributed the suero into both buckets. "This will keep the buckets balanced," Eligia said.

The girls next returned to the kitchen door where Luisa handed to Lorena a food bucket with the left-overs from the kitchen. Eligia deftly carried the two buckets with the palanca resting over her neck and shoulders. "Chapo feeds the hogs in the morning. We just feed them the *suero* and kitchen left-overs at noon. Nothing must ever go to waste," Eligia explained to Lorena as she carefully balanced the palanca with the buckets full of *suero*. "Then we'll draw water from the near-by irrigation ditch and supply the pigs' mud holes so the pigs can play in the mud and refresh themselves during the hot part of the day," Eligia said.

Lorena followed Eligia like a lost and hungry puppy with one eye toward the fields searching for her father. Eligia and Lorena finished with the hogs in no time. There were only six hogs. One of the hogs was a large female hog, bulging and waiting to deliver a litter of piglets. According to Eligia, hogs were kept only to grow fat with corn, *suero*, and food scraps and then they were butchered. Eligia told Lorena that Aunt Tila has Chapo make '*Chicharones*', skin cracklings, lard, and turn the rest of the hog into a variety of pork chops, roasts, ribs, steaks, bacon, and even pickled pigs' feet.

Every part of the hog was used; Lorena thought, and bitterly added in her mind, Yeah, and every second of the day was used for work and nobody cared about her education. Somehow, Lorena felt sour, unlike the yellow sweet *suero*; she felt as tired and bent out of shape as that crooked mesquite pole called a *palanca*.

Lorena determined in her mind and heart that she would not do this hog work for long and furthermore, she would go to school or she would run away, soon. Lorena glanced toward a huge mesquite tree near the field and she saw her father standing his horse under it for shade, probably to escape the noon heat, Lorena thought, and said, "Eligia, please wait for me here by the fence, I'll run over to that mezquite tree and talk with my father, it won't take long." As Lorena spoke, she ran toward the tree and yelled for her father. Lorena saw him acknowledge that he had heard her as he waved back to her.

Fortunato stood under the big mezquite tree. He dismounted and stood beside Lorena, smiling. He pointed to the cotton fields where a group of Chinese field workers were at that moment hoeing the weeds along the rows of cotton. "Mi *niña*,my child, that cotton is going to make us rich and then you will be going to one of the best schools in Mexico," He said, the shadow of his body wrapped itself around the tree trunk and draped it in darkness. Lorena's stomach growled and in its own natural language told her it was hungry. Lorena thought that her stomach simply had to wait another half-hour until two o'clock in the afternoon. I must hurry, she thought, Eligia may grow impatient and leave without me. Her father looked at Lorena with his brown eyes sat deep under thick black eyebrows. He smoothed his black hair and rearranged his straw hat.

Lorena took a deep breath and blurted out, "Father, let me go to Bacori and live with Uncle Eugenio's family so I can attend school, please," Lorena's whole face expressions begged her case. This was a now or never situation.

His shadow shifted and became blurred with the rocky ground. "No, Catalina is going to Bacori. There is only a private kindergarten school run by one of your aunts for the children that live in that area. There is no school grade for your age," his voice, soft like feathers floating in the air but that actually to Lorena his words felt like stones pressing down on top of her head, and Lorena became a fence post driven into the ground with each word a blow.

The Worm in my Tomato

"Then send me away to a school in Mexico City or Tucson like some of my cousins," she pleaded, crying in the inside of her heart, "Please, Father, I just have to go to school."

"No, there is no money, that is why I am growing the fields of tomatoes over there," his shadow unwrapped from the tree and disappeared as he stepped to the east side of the tree and he cast his own shadow. He pointed to a nearby field, "When the tomatoes break ground, I'll show them to you. With those tomatoes and that field of cotton and those vegetables on the other side, and that field of beans beyond, we'll sell and be rich." He smiled at Lorena with his straight white teeth gleaming in the afternoon light, "We'll be rich and you will go to a fine school, I promise."

Fortunato saw that Lorena did not look too enthusiastic. Her heart was just not in it, for a future depending on desired images of tomatoes and cotton sold on the market.

"Tell you what; I will hire a tutor to come teach you at home, three times a week, how about that?" His shadow wrapped itself again across the front of the tree trunk, the shadow making a weird X on the rocky ground, as well.

"I want to go to school, if not to Bacori, someplace else," the satisfaction Lorena bargained for at this moment did not include a tutor. At a side glance, she saw Eligia coming across the open ground toward them.

"Now, don't nag, Lorena," Lorena thought that her father was his usual self-obstinate, "you will stay here for this year to help your mother care for Santos, and wait until I sell the tomatoes and cotton." He shifted and his shadow coiled around the tree, again, "We have no money just now."

"Borrow from my Aunt Tila," Lorena spoke as if her teeth were grinding sand in her mouth.

"She won't lend me anymore, it's enough that she loaned me the money for the seed to plant these fields, purchase the water and pay the Chinese workers," his shadow unwound itself straight, as Fortunato paced back and forth like a tiger. "Besides, she gives us room and board for the time being," his words were heavier stones that pelted her on the head. It was a mystery to Lorena how his soft words were actually stones that weighted down upon her.

"My mother and I work hard for our room and board for our family," Lorena spit out words that were grinding sand from her mouth, but she could not spit the dryness, out.

"There is nothing else to say, you will stay with us and furthermore, daughter, don't bring this school business up again until the tomatoes ripen and we harvest and sell them along with the cotton," Fortunato's shadow spun around and disappeared as he strode off toward his horse that was hungrily nibbling some dry grass.

Eligia joined Lorena. Lorena felt like a bucket of stones that Eligia could carry home with her palanca. Lorena knew that she had to run away, escape up north. She thought to herself that if her father did it when he was nineteen, she could do it, too. "But who would help mother and take care of baby Santos?" Lorena asked herself out loud.

"What?" Eligia asked.

"Nothing, I was just thinking out loud."

They walked in silence and their short shadows tended to grow longer in the direction of the big house and the main meal of the day. Lorena kept thinking over and over again that she had to run away. Yes, she said to herself, escape north, swim across the *El Fuerte River*, climb across the mountains, hike through the deserts, run to Bullion Plaza School in Miami, Arizona, she thought.

Lorena began to make plans about how to run away. Eligia might help me, she thought.

Eligia hurried ahead toward the big house and Lorena moped after. At the big house, Eligia headed for the kitchen and the main meal of the day. Lorena hurried on to her room with a hurting headache; she held her fancied bloody head in her right hand. In her room, she cried herself into the afternoon siesta.

Antonia came to Lorena's side of the bed and gently tried to console her. Lorena thought of telling her mother of her plans to go away to the north and seek her education in Arizona, but Lorena did not want to add worries to the many problems she knew her mother already had, especially with Aunt Tila.

It was a short night. Next morning at five in the dark of dawn, Eligia gently shook Lorena awake. The girls went to splash water on their sleepy faces and proceeded with their morning chores. Lorena pulled water from the well and filled the two buckets tied to the palanca which then she balanced precariously over her skinny shoulders and stumbled back to the house. The water pots in the kitchen and dining hall were half-filled that morning.

Lorena ran out and hurried to the chicken house and fed the chickens. Then she milked One Eye and fast stepped back to the house with half a pan of warm frothy milk. At last, to breakfast where Eligia and Lorena were fed by Luisa some hot *atole*, as Luisa called her grain meal porridge, and Lorena found out that it was brown-sugared porridge sprinkled with cinnamon. "Umm, this atole is tasty," Lorena said. Then Luisa gave each girl a scrambled egg mixed with chorizo sausage, hot fresh tortillas, which Luisa had made early in the morning, some milk, and white Mexican cheese. The kitchen swam in these delicious pungent aromas of eggs and chorizo. But, in her mind, Lorena thought that she had worked for it, and now she devoured her food.

Lorena knew that her mother and the rest of the family would come in later and enjoy the good breakfast that Luisa had cooked that morning. Lorena was certain that Catalina would just love the *atole*; Lorena knew how her little sister liked sweets and was especially fond of brown sugar.

Even if Lorena thought Luisa was the best cook in the whole world, all morning Lorena had thought about how to escape from El Aliso. Lorena figured that if a dozen or so Chinese could cross an ocean from China, cross the hot deserts, and arrive here to work for Aunt Tila, she could cross the Fuerte River, cross the border, so as not to work for Aunt Tila. Had we not survived the disgrace of the Repatriation policy of the United States? Lorena thought.

Lorena felt that she could survive the hot deserts, swim the deep rivers, and climb the high mountains to return to Miami, to Bullion Plaza, and to Miss Yoakum. She was a stray cat that must return home. Perhaps her friend Mary Cota was still there, Lorena hoped. Lorena felt that as sure as the clouds cry and the moon is not cheese that Mary Cota's mother would not have gone to Aguascalientes with her husband. Mary Cota's mother would not carry her Christian cross, whatever that means. "Only my mother carried her Christian cross,"

Lorena said out loud. Lorena would have liked to tell Mary Cota about the *atole* that Luisa cooked.

But how to tell Mary Cota about the *atole* and how to escape, Lorena mused on these questions, as she hand over hand pulled the rope through the pulley, punctuated by a bang or two of the bucket. Later, Lorena studied several options of escape as she milked One Eye. No matter how Lorena squeezed, One Eye smacked the back of Lorena's head with her tail, and Lorena winced each time. But, the milk squirted into the pot and some found its way onto the ground, but most of it or at least half of it ended in the pot. Well, Lorena thought, I did my best, but she said out loud, "Santos should not drink so much milk, anyhow."

Lorena planned her route north as she tossed plenty of chicken feed at the chickens and scattered the seed on the ground for the motley chickens to gobble up. Lorena mumbled to herself as she stumbled back to the house under the load of two buckets half filled with water. As Lorena satisfied her famished self, she decided to talk over her plans with Eligia, when they would go to water the hog mud holes. Lorena also wondered, indignantly, as she remembered Miss Yoakum had taught her the word *indignantly* in the class vocabulary drills: just why, she thought, Chapo didn't follow up with the mud holes.

After their morning chores at the big house, Eligia and Lorena walked slowly, carrying two buckets of sour milk to the hogs. Lorena was in deep thought wondering if she should or should not tell Eligia about her planned escape north to attend school in the United States. Lorena was thinking that after all the trouble of her escape, it would not be Bullion Plaza and Miss Yoakum but a better school in Tucson with several Miss Yoakums and a library filled with books like "On the Road" readers. Lorena decided to confide in Eligia because that was what friends were for and Eligia and she were buddies in working for Aunt Tila, like the Chinese.

Eligia deftly balanced the palanca over her shoulders behind her neck and gingerly quick step after quick step in a kind of running gait, hurried on and not a drop of swill or of *suero* spilled out of the buckets. Then Eligia would stop and allow Lorena to carry the palanca, "for practice," Eligia would say.

The Worm in my Tomato

However, to Lorena's dismay, during her turn to wrestle with the mesquite stick and two buckets of suero, the going was laboriously slow. As they snailed their way toward the hogs, Eligia yelled "Oops"after each spill of a drop of swill. She kept yelling "Oops" all the way to the hog pen cement troughs. There the hogs oinked and gruffed their complaint at getting only two half-buckets of swill and of *suero*.

Lorena in embarrassment, yelled at the sky, "I quit," and she told Eligia, "I am going to run away up north."

"Lorena," Eligia said, "But what about your family?"

"No, don't talk to me about anything, and furthermore I am leaving tonight, I will not work like this for another day."

The road north to San Blas past an Indigenous village near El Aliso; the hills of San Blas can be seen in the distance.

The Worm in my Tomato

Thirteen

Fortunato
The gamble, the risk, the choice in Mexico

The first night at his sister Tila's house Fortunato tossed and turned, unable to sleep, his mind raced on with questions begging answers and with problems seeking solutions. Through it all, Fortunato knew that he wanted to make a comfortable life for his family by farming his lands. In his heart, Fortunato lamented not being able to help Lorena attend school; he regretted his harsh answers to her last night. In his mind, he wondered how to escape the consequences of the Great Depression and the Repatriation that he thought yet pursued him to Mexico to destroy him and his family. In his mind he was yet that bull in the arena of economic and political life, threatened by dangers he could not perceive clearly and were yet unknown. How could this be possible? The blackness of the room at night engulfed him, no light entered the bleak house, no enlightening thoughts illumined his mind, and darkness grasped his mind, obscuring his past decisions and clouding those pending. He was a bull in the arena going in circles; not knowing where to thrust.

All was quiet outside the house: no traffic of cars could be heard like in Miami; no singers bathed in moonlight on top of a hill serenading; no revelers meandering on the sidewalk, returning home late at night; there was only one large window on one side wall of the Big House, through which no neon lights in red, yellow, and blue glints greeted Fortunato: there was only darkness and silence in this strange arena which engulfed him prisoner.

It was a strange and mysterious existence; its origin was unknown to him; his family being here at this time, an unknown fate integrated with the lives of his wife and children. Fortunato thought to himself: who would have thought that he would return in this way to his grandfather's Big House, to the land his father bequeathed to him. Not only the blackness, the absolute silence, but a stifled heaviness pressed

The Worm in my Tomato

upon Fortunato, as if to hold him down; like the Great Depression and the Repatriation, he thought.

Fortunato's brother Jorge and his sister Tila were the two persons he wanted to talk with, to find answers to his questions about his work in the family lands. First thing in the morning of that first night, Fortunato planned to seek them out, but then, Fortunato worried late into the night; he wondered how could a baby snore so loud, or was that Antonia?

Next morning, when the sun beams began to crawl over the pale blue horizon of the dark green eastern mountains, and with pink glowing fingers opened the sky curtains to let in the light of the first new day; Fortunato found his sister Tila and his brother Jorge, who had come by at the break of dawn, as was his custom, in the kitchen. "Come in Fortunato, sit down, join us for our morning coffee and some breakfast," Tila greeted him with a good-morning embrace, and she motioned for Luisa to serve Fortunato eggs and *chorizo*.

"Our extended Vega families, Fortunato, raise cattle on their ranches and work with the vaqueros who herd, pasture, brand, and de-horn cattle," Jorge said, then he added, "Tila uses the cow's fresh milk to make white round Mexican cheese to sell in her ranch market; she markets the cheese and beef for local consumption and for export; all of this ranch life is constant, hard backbreaking labor, with small profits on the margin. Agriculture, in this part of Sinaloa, depends on rain for watering of crops; an irrigation system of canals carrying water from the Fuerte River is limited, *acequias* are few and ditches deliver unsubstantial water to the fields." Jorge said while he chewed on a piece of tortilla he used to scoop up a bite of eggs and *chorizo*.

Jorge resembled Fortunato, but was taller and broad of shoulder. His hair and eyes were brown.

"How much land will be mine to plant my crops, Jorge?" Fortunato asked.

Outside in the yard could be heard the dogs Chocolate, Dia and Noche romping about, playing a game. Toward the east, streaks of pink tinted the underbelly of floating fluffy white clouds, a March warm desert breeze from the south flowed in and out of mesquite brush and trees, causing the leaves to flutter, and waves of air spread the aroma of blooming wild flowers.

Tila invited Fortunato and Jorge to sit on wood benches outside under the spreading *mezquite* tree that shaded Tila's house on the eastern side, "Our father, Eudoro, left you eleven hectares in what is known as *El Potrero*," Tila said.

Jorge nodded his head in ascent, as he enjoyed the aroma in the refreshing breeze; during the mornings the day was cool under the tree. "Mezquite gum runs loose down the bark at this time of year and glistens like caramel in the light," Jorge said, as he scraped some golden gum off the bark with his pocket knife.

"I remember chewing tree gum when I lived here as a kid," Fortunato said.

"Yeah, well I never stopped, want some," Jorge held out a large lump of soft golden colored mezquite gum at the tip of his pocket knife.

"No, thanks," Fortunato chewed on his last piece of hot tortilla wrapped around scrambled eggs and chorizo, "Um, that was good, Tila, thank you." He took out a small black leather pocket memorandum booklet and looked up metric measurement tables, "Eleven hectares at 2.47 acres per hectare gives me roughly 27 acres in which to grow my crops of tomatoes."

"That will keep you busy," Jorge chewed on his mezquite gum, "But remember El Potrero has no irrigation; you'll be at the mercy of the season climate of dry and less rainy weather." He looked at Fortunato, "But, I know you are a gambler, brother," Jorge smiled.

"Well, don't forget, Fortunato, you will be overseeing the Chinese field workers for me," said Tila.

"Will you allow me some of your land to plant crops of corn, cotton, and vegetables?" Fortunato asked Tila.

"No. You'll do fine with what acreage you have; I will sell to you the seed. My expenses in paying the native Indians and the migrant Chinese to work my fields will cost me a large amount of money. I also need to pay for the water from the *El Rio Fuerte* river irrigation *acequia association*," answered Tila, and she said, "Furthermore, if you put too much investment into your fields and you lose your harvest, your losses will be greater, keep your crop seeds to the minimum."

"You'll do fine with El Potrero," Jorge said to Fortunato, "Let's go walk around the fields so you will get a feel for the place." Jorge began to walk toward the fields west of the house.

"I myself will give you two calves, one for each one of your daughters, Lorena and Catalina, to get them started in their raising of cattle," Tila said to Fortunato.

"Thanks to both of you for all your help," Fortunato said; he and Jorge walked toward the fields. The morning had started to heat up, "I will meet up with you, later, Tila," said Fortunato. He and Jorge walked along the fields, "You know, Jorge, my memories of *El Aliso* are coming back. The sight of the desert, the high Sierras Occidental, hazy mountains in the distance, the mud smell of the Fuerte River carrying its caramel colored muddy waters to the west, reminds me of *El Aliso* as I remembered it in my mind when I lived in Arizona. I was always surprised as how much Sinaloa formed a part of me."

"I am happy you have returned, brother, and I hope you stay here in your own country, and cultivate your land as it may be in danger of being lost under the decree of 1915." Jorge said.

"I intend to stay here, now," Fortunato said, and added, "As a nineteen year old youth, you recall, I ran away from all this life of hard agricultural and ranch work. I roamed California and Arizona for years, where I worked at times in construction and cement work. But my real passion found its fulfillment in gambling, in card games. I cultivated my gambling habit as a means to make a living. I did quite well at Limonada's Pool Hall in Arizona. The Great Depression and the Repatriation of Mexican citizens, however, changed my life, and so here I am."

"The work is hard, indeed, and the responsibility of supervising the field workers is demanding, but you should do all right."

"Of course," answered Fortunato, "I will do my work with desire and confidence."

Jorge inspected the side of the irrigation ditch for overgrowth of grass, "You have to get some workers to clear all along the ditch, Fortunato, but in all truth, Fortunato, we must be realistic. If the lack of rain does not cause the seed, that you carefully planted, to burn up with the heat of the scorching sun, if the insects do not destroy your harvest, and if the international market price for your crops you sell does not bankrupt you, then you shall do well." He studied Fortunato's frown, "Just do your work with desire and confidence."

"Oh, yes, of course," Fortunato answered, "I must succeed, there is no where else to go, nothing else to do, and anyway, I am older, now, with slower reflexes, in addition my eyesight gradually started to fail, eventually I was forced to depend on eyeglasses, but I could still manage the card games at the gambling tables with ease and fast hands." Fortunato inspected the wire fence along the field, "I gave up gambling, promised Antonia I would stay away from card games, especially here in Mexico. So you see, I must get a good harvest."

"Well, I guess you know better than I that a good hand of cards depends on a great deal on chance and skill," Jorge walked along a wire fence and inspected the mezquite poles, "Some of these posts have rotted at the base and will need replacing," he said, "Yes, brother, here you can raise a harvest and do well or the weather and insects can choke you into deeper poverty, but just work hard and see what happens. All depends on good seed, earth, rain, sun, good behavior of insects, and on the crops you harvest and the market at the time you sell." Jorge added, "As I said before, it depends on chance, on what the unknown deals to you."

"Well, brother, with the coming of the Great Depression and loss of gambling revenues, at approximate the same time, at my age of fifty-six years old, I began to dream about Sinaloa and saw it in a vision. I became obsessed with Sinaloa. I was determined to return to Sinaloa for a fresh start as a farmer, to grow cotton, corn, beans, and chili, crops my father cultivated, remember," Fortunato said. "What else but fate disguised in a dream-like vision came to me during the dark winter nights of January in Miami, while trying to sleep, often I would have visions of a strange apparition of land near a sea, wrapped in mist, a land I presumed to be Sinaloa; its vision periodically beckoned me to come to it," he said.

Jorge and Fortunato had turned around the end of the fence at the far end of the field and had walked back to the house. They sat down to a cup of fresh coffee with their sister Tila, who had returned to the house from supervising the cheese makers in the cheese room. "I went over for a few minutes to see how the workers Lepo and Telesforo are coming along with the making of the cheese," Tila said.

Jorge stirred a cube of brown sugar in his cup, "Fortunato, Mexico has changed since you left it years ago," Jorge said.

"Oh, yes, it has changed for the worst," Tila chimed in, sitting down at table with her cup of coffee, "It's always the laws. Politicians have nothing better to do than legislate laws that destroy life for the people," she studied Fortunato carefully, "Nato," she said, "You have been gone a long time, so it won't be easy for you to adjust to a life as we live today," she blew softly over her cup to cool her black steaming coffee that she had poured for herself from the large coffee pot that Luisa always kept hot on the wood stove. "I have crops in my fields, Fortunato, you can supervise my Chinese field workers, and when we sell the harvest, of course, you can get paid and make money as well. Then you can begin to ready your own cultivation in El Potrero."

Outside in the yard under the shade of the mesquite, the dogs Chocolate, Dia and Noche slept stretched out on the ground. Tila continued speaking, "It will be even harder for Antonia to adjust," she cautiously took a sip from her cup, "Be sure and tell her to be very careful about whom she talks with and what she says. There are too many rancheros eager to please the *federales* by telling lies on each other to cause trouble and possibly even take over some land." Tila looked preoccupied, "You know Fortunato, these problems of land for the landless, and with the federal government appointing itself as the solution finder and land distributor will never go away."

Jorge stood up and stretched himself and said, "It was the constitution of 1857 with its Ley Lerdo that prohibited the Catholic Church and civil institutions from owning or administering real property not directly used in day-to-day operations. The federal government was after church lands, but it caught the native Indians in its net, because one of the civil corporations forced to sell its property was the *Ejido*, the institutionalized communal landholding of the Indian village. Many Indian villages were forced to turn over their uncultivated properties for sale at the various auctions. Our own neighbors here, the Indian village of Mezquitalito, lost much land. Only the very rich hacendados in this valley purchased the land at bargain prices. The politicians made out well, like they always do, you

The Worm in my Tomato

know, the government paid a few debts, paid the federal workers, paid the federal armed forces and of course rewarded the rich." He sat down again and crossed his legs, with one leather boot dangling out in front, sipped on his coffee, and then he rolled a paper cigarette, "But I keep myself involved in politics, too."

Fortunato agreed, and he said, "I know about the misery of so many people in Mexico throughout its history with no end in sight." Fortunato could see through the open kitchen door that outside the calm morning desert breeze picked up its tempo and whipped about the trees, like if shaking tree limbs in play, and making a few dust devils around the dirt front yard. In the yard the dogs, did not care for the wind, and were no where to be seen.

"Fortunato," Jorge addressed him directly, "We ourselves have experienced problems involving lands and Church from current governments of Mexico. President Calles, who served as president from 1924 to 1928, and then by Calles's outside influences by pulling puppet strings on the presidents that followed him, first Emilio Portes Gill, 1928 to 1929 and then Pasqual Ortiz Rubio, 1930 to this year 1932. I am only too glad you have returned to cultivate your land *El Potrero*, to protect it from the federal government." Jorge stood up and walked to the kitchen to get another cup of coffee, and looking back at Fortunato, he said, "The future does not look good for these rural areas for now." Jorge returned to his chair at the table. "Distribution of land began under President Plutarco Elias Calles, but there was too much history concerning acquisition, sale, and legal ownership of lands that distribution became a most difficult mandate to carry out by federal and state governments." Jorge drank from his cup and then continued talking. "Actually, state governments have sold idle lands or untilled lands to raise operating funds. So there is no doubt that politicians or military men in high command acquired communal lands from the native Indian pueblos."

"I am glad to be here, Jorge, and do what I can, but I need to catch up on my knowledge about Sinaloa and Mexico," Fortunato said. He drank his coffee. "But, let me ask you, Jorge, is this not an on-going land issue that never seems to go away?" Fortunato asked.

"Well, it seems that way because Mexico inherited a land heritage of who could own land from Spain, and those concepts met head on with native customs of land ownership. The natives owned land in common but lost lands during the many years of *encomiendas* and later other schemes which forced migratory native tribes of gatherers and hunters into communities. In more recent times, to restore lands to the villages, the federal government decreed in 1915 a plan of land restitution and endowment. Villages in states that could prove title to lost property could petition for its restitution. State governors and our own governor here in Sinaloa, of course, have been authorized to review these restitution petitions. Of our Vega lands, the most critical would be Eugenio's lands and yours Fortunato, El Potrero." Jorge said.

Tila arose and went to a cupboard from where she took out a folder, "I have taken the trouble to look for and find a good data report on Sinaloa, only to show you what a wonderful state we live in, and to have you understand that you have brought your family to a new start with a promising future in a state with much promise," Tila said and she handed a booklet to Jorge, "Here Jorge, you read it and explain the information about Sinaloa to Fortunato, I have to go now and work in the store," Tila went out the door.

"Let us go and take a look at El Potrero fields and see what work we have to do there," said Jorge, "and I will read and discuss the information about Sinaloa with you, Fortunato." Jorge and Fortunato walked up the road to the east side along dry, brown dirt fields.

"Well, Fortunato, the information on this booklet states that the land size of Sinaloa is 56, 496 square *Kilómetros*," Jorge said. "You will have to pick up the fence where it is fallen down, replace mezquite posts, and repair the wire; Chapo has not taken care of these fields in some years."

Fortunato straightened a post leaning almost to the ground, "Looks like all the fence will need to be replaced," Fortunato said.

"You are lucky you only own eleven *hectares* of Sinaloa's land mass, it's a fairly large state," Jorge said, "Anyway, it says here that two large mountain ribs run from north to south in Mexico. These mountain ranges are twins named *Sierra Madre Oriental* in the east and *Sierra Madre Occidental* in the west, of which Sinaloa is backed up against its ribs. " and Jorge added, " The best way to understand that is to visualize in your mind, Fortunato, the Sierra Madre range being a huge wrinkled mammal with numerous abundant breasts nursing the countless villages nestled in the valleys and low lands, in fact we have thirteen rivers."

"But of all the states, is not Sinaloa one with most economic potential?" asked Fortunato.

"Yes," Jorge helped Fortunato pick up a strand of wire and attached it to a post,

"Yes, indeed, it is naturally endowed. Sinaloa is snuggled like a puppy against the western twin, the Sierra Occidental of the west. The state drinks deeply from the life-giving mountain's thirteen breasts, Sinaloa's rivers, which run from east to west and empty into the Gulf of California."

"I can see that here in El Aliso, we are fortunate to have the Fuerte River," Fortunato said.

A whirlwind whipped across the field shaking brush and throwing dirt at the low bushes as Jorge started to read from the booklet, "The Pacific coastal plain runs north to south, and has gifted Sinaloa with some shipping ports. Around and about these rivers, plains, and harbor live and work a large number of its inhabitants."

"What I am interested in is the possibility of rain for my crops," said Fortunato.

"Well, the climate in Sinaloa according to this booklet runs from dry, warm, semi-humid, to very dry during the year in different parts of the state. Precipitation ranges from only 600 millimeters in the north desert like terrain and up to 1,400 millimeters in southern Sinaloa. I guess you know Fortunato, we live in the 600 mm if that much per year," Jorge said, and he continued reading, "Water is an important resource for Sinaloa superficial agriculture; a small amount is irrigation farming in most of Sinaloa north and south of Culiacan, the state's capital city."

"I can see there is little irrigation around here," Fortunato said, shielding his eyes from the sun in the west as he walked with Jorge toward the house.

"Yes, Fortunato, in the main our agricultural pursuits are seasonal, and at the reliance of uncontrolled rainfall in a dry warm area," Jorge said as he read the information in the booklet. The wind picked up,

The Worm in my Tomato

and both men turned their backs to the field and hurried on to the house. "We have always been seasonal farmers; we have depended on the rain from that annual 600-mm in northern Sinaloa. But now, we have started to build some small amount of irrigation. Many times we have lost our crops. It would probably have worked out except for the unknown and unexpected factors like insects, worms and hungry grasshoppers," Jorge yelled above the din of the wind.

"Given the high possibility of failure, is there some other alternative for making money to pay back Tila's investment for my loan for seed, water, and cost of field laborers that I will need to work my lands in *El Potrero*?" Fortunato asked.

"No, there is no other work here in the valley, and you don't have a herd of cattle, yet, to work and sell calves, meat or milk," Jorge said.

The two brothers reached the house and went in to have some coffee and talk with Tila who had just walked in from her store.

"Tila," Fortunato said, "I asked Jorge if there was some other way that I could make money to pay you on the loan, you know, in case my crops fail."

"My hacienda store barely sells its merchandise and my white cheese. Antonia and Lorena need to help with the work in the house, the store, and help with making the cheese. No, brother, there is no other way, but succeed with the cultivation of lands, harvest the crops, and furthermore, hopefully, get a fair price in the market," Tila said.

Fortunato did not know what to say to Tila, and he told Jorge and Tila that Sinaloa had changed from the 1895 through 1932-life journey of his in the United States. "Thirty-seven years is a long time to be away from making a life from agriculture. It is true I had returned to visit my family after our father and then my mother died, but I did not stay long and soon departed again for Arizona."

Fortunato poured himself a cup of coffee, "Now, I plan to stay, however, because, as my wife Antonia said, that we brought our family out of the famine of Arizona to Mexico where its agricultural plenty like that of ancient Egypt will provide for our life needs, that is what she said, and I hope it comes true."

Fortunato indulged himself and simply emptied himself of what had been pressing within his mind and heart for so long. "But in conjunction with all this, Sinaloa yet haunted me. Now, I have found her not only in my dreams. But I have discovered her in my reality. Sinaloa and I will dance to the music played out by the mythical phantom in my bones toward a finality of understanding and knowing about my family's homeland."

"I see you are still a poet, brother, since I remember you when you were young, you were a poet and a philosopher," smiled Tila, "It is a mystery, Nato, you had a reason to return and Antonia had a reason to make her own journey with her family to El Aliso," Tila drank from her cup, "We will see."

"We will start you on your work real soon, brother," Jorge patted Fortunato on his right arm as he stood up to leave, "but remember, you must work very hard to lessen the gamble, and another thing I do is prevent myself from antagonizing politicians at any level but especially federal government ones," Jorge smiled, "I have made friends with politicians at our state and municipal level; you just don't know when you'll need help."

Fortunato nodded yes in return and said nothing, the emotions that pervaded his entire being could not be explained, what was worse,

El Aliso, Old House, typical adobe block house.

The Worm in my Tomato

he had no thoughts to come to his defense. Fortunato thought now how a prison inmate must feel and think, when upon release, after his time is up, he has no place to go and nothing to do, he does not even know where his next meal will come from. The situation reminded Fortunato of the homeless warming themselves by their fire under the bridge in Miami. The Great Depression, Fortunato felt, did not exist only on the outside, somewhere out there, in the United States, but it had followed him to Mexico, and its economic poverty took over his whole being inside of him. Fortunato knew that he would not be surprised if some type of the destitution would take hold of his family here in Mexico. But he determined to work hard and began to plan in his mind on how he would work the lands. For now he was not the prisoner out of prison and he was not the hobo from under the bridge, but he could easily end up in either place.

Fourteen

Antonia
Arizona Furniture and homesickness and other issues

Antonia's great disappointment began the very next day after she arrived with her family in El Aliso from the United States. In a distressed way, she realized they had made a mistake and allowed the Repatriation policy to sentence her family to a desert prison of deprivation. Antonia searched with her eyes in all directions. She did not see one single church building. She discovered there was no church available in El Aliso or surrounding villages.

Already, boredom had come to set in and be Antonia's constant companion. She kept busy cleaning rooms, taking care of the baby, and sometimes helping Tila in the ranch store. When Antonia saw Luisa taking a break from her chores, Antonia sat in the kitchen and, over coffee, in conversation, Antonia learned about the valley villages and people. One day Luisa told Antonia about Julieta whom she described as a religious woman who conducted prayer services in her home, taught catechism, and periodically, with the help of the religious underground *Cristero* Movement, sneaked in a clandestine priest to her home to celebrate Mass for people of faith in the Indian village and other faithful nearby.

"Luisa is there a church somewhere near El Aliso?" Antonia asked, "Where can we attend Mass?"

"You can't attend Mass Mrs. Vega, there are none, and furthermore, there is no church, no priest, in this rural valley," Luisa said with finality.

"No priest," Antonia said, uncomprehending and unbelieving.

"No, a priest comes now and then to Julieta's house. Maybe, a priest will come sometime soon, you can ask Julieta," Luisa answered.

If there had been an itinerant priest in the past, there was none now. Antonia stared at Luisa with a blank daze in her eyes and a heavy dull feeling in her heart, and with conviction she knew she was a fish out of water.

The Worm in my Tomato

"Mrs. Vega, if you wish you and your children can join me and Eligia on Sunday for a prayer service at Miss Julieta Santander's ranch home. "She wiped her hands with her apron. "This is all that is available. There is no resident priest anywhere near," Luisa said, and added, "The Religious Laws in Mexico have a way of prohibiting the public service of the Holy Mass."

Antonia often thought about these religious issues and wondered how she should think and behave, but she determined to do whatever she could to help Fortunato, her boys Samuel and Jose, and her family to survive the malaise that now like an unexpected stiff wind blew dust in their face, but could very well at any time become a sand storm. Antonia planned to have Samuel walk with her to visit Julieta.

Antonia went to visit Julieta, who owned a nearby neighboring ranch which she supervised herself. Antonia wanted to find out from Julieta if and when a priest would come into their area to celebrate the holy Mass; she determined to celebrate it, accompanied with her children; she had always attended Mass together with her family in Miami. She wanted to see about catechism teaching and preparation of Catalina for first Holy Communion.

At another time, Antonia talked with Luisa over coffee, "I must ask Samuel to research these religious laws; it is too bad that people let their government do this, and Mexico being a Catholic country," Antonia commented.

"In Mexico," Luisa informed Antonia, "religious sisters and priests are not allowed by law to wear religious dress or be identified as being priests or religious sisters."

Antonia learned all of this from Luisa who had learned it from Miss Julieta. "The Religious Laws in Mexico prohibited the Church to carry out its responsibilities, years ago; this forced the Church to declare a strike for three years, and its doors were closed, and there was no public service of the Holy Mass or any way for providing the people with the sacraments," Luisa said.

Thereafter, on a Sunday, Antonia, Lorena, Luisa and Eligia walked north along the dirt road for two miles to visit Julieta and participate in a prayer service held in the large parlor in her house. The day was warm and sunny with a light breeze that made walking pleasant. The aroma of dryness and of green corn plants in the fields thirsty for water floated in the air.

"Julieta is a stout woman who seems to me to be between forty-five and fifty-five years of age," Luisa said.

"Here in Mexico, I have observed that the constant struggle and revolutions have robbed people from ten to fifteen years in age appearance, people seem to physically age more," Antonia said.

"Julieta rides her horse as she supervises her vast fields of cotton, corn, beans, and tomatoes for which she employs local village field labor, and she has vaqueros to manage her cattle herds. She pays fairly and does not believe in taking advantage of the Chinese immigrant cheap labor. She and Tila are not on speaking terms," Luisa told Antonia as they walked to Julieta's house to attend Sunday prayer service.

Antonia hoped that her going to prayer services on Sundays and days when novenas for the departed souls were prayed in Miss Julieta's house would not taint her sister-in-law Tila's attitude toward her and Lorena. She wanted Lorena always to accompany her to a liturgy of the word service or to a prayer service on days when Julieta led the prayer of the holy rosary.

As they walked along the road, Antonia recalled how her sister-in-law had warned her to be careful. She remembered Tila's words to her: 'You, Antonia, can be reported to government authorities for being a religious supporter, you could even be mistaken for being a *Cristero*, or at least a sympathizer, and in that way bring trouble upon Fortunato and myself. You should not attend prayer services at Julieta's house because you possibly may cause problems for Fortunato, and worse, put our lands in jeopardy,' Tila had said.

Antonia mentioned to Luisa what she had recalled about Tila. Luisa asked Antonia, "What did you say?"

Antonia replied that she doubted that attending services at Julieta's would bring trouble on Fortunato and Tila. "As you well know, Luisa, the Vegas are noted as being indifferent to the official Church and for that matter to all manner of anticlericals as well. I have observed that they have no interests except in their work, and Fortunato has told me, as well," Antonia said.

Tila had told Antonia: 'Anti-religious sentiments yet prevail in

The Worm in my Tomato

1932 here in El Aliso,' and Tila had looked preoccupied. 'Antonia,' she emphasized, 'It is best that everyone here go about their daily life tasks without discussions on political or religious matters, and you, especially, a stranger, a *Repatriate* that just came to Mexico: a wet hen with her soaking chicks, into our valley; keep quiet and out of sight, so as not to bring upon us the fury of the federal government and its armed troops,' Tila had urged.

Antonia had ignored Tila's request of not going to prayer services held in Julieta's house. She continued to attend. After one recent Sunday prayer service, attended by Antonia with her baby Santos, Luisa, Eligia, Samuel, and Lorena, Miss Julieta proved to be an exception to the general silence about church and religious matters. After she served coffee to Antonia and Luisa and lemonade to Lorena, Eligia, and Samuel, she freely discussed with her guests the issue of land laws and religious laws. In the privacy of her home, she talked against "those Communistic Liberals" that controlled Mexico at the time and that were meant on closing the Catholic Church. "The Liberals' Revolution government, since 1917, have controlled Mexican government plans, under force of arms if necessary, to redistribute agricultural lands comprised of small ejidos, or individual plots, to indigenous pueblos, at the point of federal guns, for individual indigenous farmers to cultivate their fields," Miss Julieta explained to Antonia, trying to control her emotions, "My lands have legal title and I can prove it, but enough of the Vega's lands may be at the risk of being lost to the state and federal government to be returned to the indigenous pueblos." Julieta drank coffee from her cup. "We will make something to eat, soon," she said.

"What about the Church, why is there not a church here and a priest to serve the residents of our area?" Antonia asked Julieta.

"There have always been enemies of the Church, Antonia," Julieta glanced at Samuel, "Samuel, do you want some more lemonade?" She looked at Luisa and said, "Want more coffee, Luisa?" She looked at Lorena studying a catechism book, "What about you, Lorena and

The Worm in my Tomato

Eligia?" Julieta served more lemonade to Samuel, Lorena and Eligia. "But despite Article number three of the Constitution of 1917, the church still operated schools." Julieta said.

"Do you mean that the federal government had prohibited Church involvement in education?" Antonia asked.

"Yes, the article banned church involvement, but the priests and nuns, who lived in monasteries and convents, although prohibited by law, operated schools." Julieta said, and she looked at Antonia, and added, "We have seen the results of removing the Church from education, have we not, Antonia, just consider our large city social school systems today, and the general life of populations in the cities, where pleasure and self-gratification is a way of life, don't you think, Antonia?"

"Yes, of course, but why is there not a church or a priest here?" Antonia asked again.

"The fact is, Antonia, that after years of persecution, the Catholic Church in Mexico has dwindled in the number of priests to serve the faithful. Article 130 of the Constitution of 1917, a most anticlerical law, declared priests as members of a profession and not allowed to wear religious dress." Julieta arose from table and said, "Come, let us make something to eat, and she walked to her kitchen."

Antonia, Luisa, Eligia and Lorena followed Julieta to the kitchen. Lorena told Julieta that her Uncle Jorge had already explained to her, after she had inquired about going to school, that the central liberal Mexican government intended to construct public schools to promote social public education; "But that the government would not support Catholic schools," Lorena said.

"It has been a terrible mistake; the Church had always been the first in the country to educate the masses," Julieta said. Eligia motioned her agreement with her head in an up-and-down movement to affirm all that Julieta said. "But the real problem has been the land laws," Julieta added. "The government wants to break up large hacendados and grant egidos to the pueblos for communal use."

"Is it possible that federal government troops may enter our valley to enforce land transfers?" Antonia wanted to know.

"There are dissatisfied groups in El Aliso rural village and in other villages of our agricultural valley that have protested; federal troops

The Worm in my Tomato

may have to come here. Actually, the whole country is inflamed in heated discussions, arguments. Most, if not all, ready to seek solutions to aged-old problems by turning into blows and armed conflicts," Julieta said. She took out some potatoes to wash, and she said, "State governors are of course authorized to review petitions from villages that can prove title to lost property and are seeking its restitution."

Lorena said that she had overheard her Aunt Tila and her Uncle Jorge discuss the danger of federal troops coming into the valley to take lands by force from landowners who can not show proper legal title.

"We are living in hard times," Julieta said, as she heated some tortillas, "even families are divided by differences of beliefs and interests about religion, education, land, and political interests."

Antonia could see herself that the Vega families in La Noria, El Aliso, Bacori, La Laguna, Mezquital, and El Mezquitalito were no exception to being divided in their perception about these problems. Antonia had listened to the heated discussions about these issues and differences of opinion that took place between Fortunato, his brothers Jorge, Eugenio, Antonio, his sister Tila, and other Vegas. They were one large extended family of frustrated members. For that reason Antonia, regardless of her differences of opinion with Tila on attending prayer service, could not blame Tila for being on edge, pensive, and difficult to communicate with at times.

Antonia had heard from Fortunato that the Vegas did not intend to stand still and let the state and federal governments take lands from their holdings to return to the indigenous pueblos. EugenioVega, in particular, along with other family members, felt that they had held the lands long enough and invested the cost of many improvements to the land holdings. Fortunato knew that his El Potrero land was in danger of being lost, but he could not claim long term investments or improvements, as he had been gone from the rural area during his long stay in the United States.

Julieta knew she held proper title for all her land holdings and had cultivated her lands for years, but her concern was the federal religious laws. "What really irritates me is why the federal government menaces the Church. The Catholic Church objected strongly to the hostile federal government religious laws instituting adverse conditions, such as prohibiting the Church from teaching religion in church schools, can you imagine that the Church was prohibited from teaching religion in its schools," Julieta complained, and she washed the potatoes and began to slice them.

"Oh, let me do that, Julieta," Eligia took the kitchen knife and sliced potatoes.

Lorena's world, on the other hand, revolved around her desire for a school and she said, "But there is no church here with schools, so what about public education here in Aliso, Julieta?" Lorena asked and added, "we want to go to school, Eligia and I really want to go to school, don't we Eligia," Lorena said.

Since their end of prayers, Julieta, Luisa, and Antonia had been busy mixing white flour dough for making tortillas, as Julieta knew that she did not have enough tortillas. They had shared coffee and lemonade at the table as well, but now they worked in the kitchen. As they conversed with one another, the women and the children rolled the dough into balls and then stretched the balls into round thin tortillas. These were placed over the hot skillet by Luisa. As the tortillas were cooked, Lorena and Eligia placed them into a bread basket.

"Public education has a goal to prepare the country's youth and young adults for being loyal Mexican citizens. The government schools emphasize arithmetic, reading, geography, Mexican history, and skills in a trade or profession," Julieta said as she stretched a tortilla and gave it to Luisa to place on the hot skillet, "but, our young people need religious and moral training by the church; yet, the federal government curtailed religious education and religious practice. President Venustiano Carranza of 1917 to 1920 left Article number three and number 130 uninforced, but the administrations of Presidents Alvaro Obregon, 1920 and President Plutarco Elias Calles, 1924 to 1928, were responsible for causing more recent problems with the Church."

"What bothers Tila is that the Mexican government enacted laws that promoted the repatriation of non-citizen Chinese immigrant labor and other immigrants from Mexico," Antonia said. "My sister-in-law Tila and my husband Fortunato agreed in keeping Chinese immigrants in field labor. They both did not agree with the repatriation of Chinese immigrants because they would lose affordable labor and risk agricultural ruin of crops, and loss of profits," Antonia pointed out, as she kneaded dough into a ball and began to stretch it out and flatten and round out a tortilla.

Luisa had prepared fried potatoes and beans. The tortillas were all cooked. Julieta and her guests sat down to eat. After lunch, her guests were ready to depart. "I would like to visit again and continue our conversations about Mexico." Samuel said.

"Yes, please come again on a Sunday and after prayer service we can continue our conversation, I would like to learn more about the United States as well." Julieta said, as she and Antonia, Luisa, Lorena and Eligia all hugged and wished each other well.

Antonia, Luisa, Samuel, Lorena and Eligia walked along the dirt road to return home after their Sunday prayer service.

Antonia did not experience any problems from her continued attendance at Sunday prayer services with Julieta, but trouble began for Antonia in another way, from her concern with the Chinese immigrants. Since the very beginning, after the first week or so of her arrival in El Aliso, Antonia took notice of the situation in El Aliso in regards to the labor situation of the Chinese field workers and also of the unfair treatment of the indigenous people from the Indian village. Antonia had noticed that the quantities of food, carried in large pans by Chapo on his wagon each day to the Chinese field camp, were meager. The workers labored in the field sun-up to sun-down, with short time breaks, with a light breakfast followed by the main meal of meat, beans, and vegetables at two in the afternoon. In the evening they would make their own field coffee or tea in their camps which they drank with a piece of bread. That had to suffice until the next day breakfast.

Tila's family and domestic workers in the big house had the same eating schedule and menu but they ate their fill under the careful generous eye of Luisa. In Antonia's mind, the amounts of food sent to the camp were woefully insufficient. The Chinese workers had complained to Fortunato of their hunger. Fortunato had told Antonia that he had told the Chinese workers that his hands were tied. "I lack the authority to augment food supplies," Fortunato said.

Some weeks after Antonia's visit with Julieta, again she found out from Fortunato about the workers suffering hunger, so she approached Luisa and asked her to increase the amount of food. But Luisa said, "I can not do it Mrs. Vega, unless Tila tells me."

Antonia then talked with Tila but learned from her, to Antonia's dismay that Tila refused to increase the food amounts, justifying her decision: "Antonia, the food is costly and the Chinese, unlike us, are used to eating less than we do." Red faced, Tila stared at Antonia, and said, "No, I will not increase their food amounts, but instead, to save on food costs some more, I will order Luisa to decrease their amounts of food in the food pails."

Antonia later noticed that the amounts of food taken by Chapo to the Chinese field workers had decreased and instead of some variety with vegetables, consisted now in the main of rice and beans. Antonia regretted having spoken up on their behalf, and worse, Fortunato had said to her, "Antonia, my sister Tila has more experience in these matters, and in her judgment, she must do all things necessary to survive in this difficult undeveloped rural life and keep her agricultural pursuits in a margin of profit."

Antonia, of course, felt displeased with what Fortunato had said. Another disagreement between Antonia and her sister-in-law involved Tila's small ranch store which was located in a large square one room adobe structure near the Big House and on the same grounds. The store contained food staples such as sugar, salt and home made lard, cheese, tortillas, sweet breads and *empanadas*. The store sold fresh meat when a beef was butchered; *chicharones* when Chapo butchered a hog and made boiled pig skin chips; sweet breads baked by Luisa, general house and work goods such as coils of hemp rope, woolen blankets, baskets, clay pots, straw hats, household goods such as stick matches, thread, needles, some cachimbas, tin buckets, and flat griddles for making tortillas. There were at times, available vegetables, corn on the husk, oranges, tomatoes, and mangos in season.

There was a continuous but small business trade because the potential indigenous customers from the village or others passing by lacked enough money. Consequently many purchased needed food on credit and ended in debt that remained a family inheritance from father to son. The aroma, in the close quarters of the shop, with food and greens on one side competed with the smell of dry blankets and hemp rope on the other. The stale air was mixed with pungent and sweet scents of dry goods and fruits and vegetables.

Antonia volunteered some of her time to work in the store, she helped clean, arrange items in order, and sometimes looked after and served customers. Antonia had noticed that when an Indian customer purchased a large spoon of lard, Tila would dip the large spoon into the lard can and bring out a spoonful of lard which she would then scrape it against the brown paper, careful to scrape off the top of the spoon and return the spoon into the lard can with lard remaining in the deep part of the spoon. Then Tila would roll the brown paper and fold its two ends, and charge the customer for a full large spoonful of lard.

Antonia in a private conversation with Tila argued for a full spoon of lard on behalf of the Indian village customers. This did not sit well with Tila, to say the least, and the conflict between Antonia and her sister-in-law escalated. Antonia had at times worked in Tila's store serving the customers, but she had always made sure that the customer received a total full large spoon of lard, including the lard in the deep part of the spoon. When Tila found out that Antonia was not cutting corners to beat the margin, she asked her not to work in the store at any time in the future.

Antonia and Fortunato began to argue after Tila had reproached her to him. Fortunato, of course, found himself in an awkward position between two quarreling women. Antonia's husband found it difficult to follow Tila's advice, after she told Fortunato, "Hitch up your pants in the house like a man and shut up that woman of yours or else." Tila, it seemed to Antonia, had never liked her because Antonia was from the United States where, Tila presumed, women considered themselves equal to men and not subservient to their husbands. This had perturbed Antonia because she knew in her heart that she had carried her cross in faithfulness to her matrimony and love of Fortunato, and to keep her family together.

To make matters worse, it seemed that Lorena's chores and Antonia's cleaning the house in addition to their family rooms was just

The Worm in my Tomato

simply not enough to pay for their family's room and board. Fortunato's cash crops of tomatoes and cotton would not be ready for some time to harvest and market for the badly needed money. It was then that Antonia wrote home to her brother Tomas and to her grandmother Isabel and begged for some money. Nanita promptly answered her letter and included a five dollar bill. Antonia's brother did not respond for several weeks and then she received a crumpled envelope with two dollar bills in it. It was then that Antonia was reminded again of the hardships caused by the Great Depression in Arizona.

While Fortunato busied himself out of the house in the fields, fixing field fences and preparing the soil at El Potrero, Antonia and Lorena worked inside the house. The day was a happy day for Antonia when Chapo delivered Antonia's furniture, which had been lost or misplaced when reloaded on the train Ferrocarril Chihuahua-Pacifico, in his wooden wagon from the railroad station in San Blass. Antonia stood in her three rooms and went about measuring and pacing distances, wondering where and how to place and use her furniture in Tila's house. Antonia asked Tila, "Tila, can I set up my furniture in our three rooms and my stove in the kitchen?" she asked.

"No, there is not sufficient room for your large American beds in your three rooms assigned to you, Fortunato and your children," Tila said.

"What about my wood stove, it is large and is good for cooking and Luisa can use it, as well?" Antonia asked.

"No, there is no room in the kitchen for your stove. Luisa already has a good wood stove to use," Tila said and then added, "Furthermore, you can't use your ice-box, which Chapo unloaded and brought into the house; there is no ice making plant, here, only in the large cities." Tila looked at Antonia's other furniture scattered about in her family's three rooms, "I suggest that you sell your furniture, our Vega families in the valley may be interested," Tila said.

Antonia felt sick to her stomach, "Excuse me, Tila, I have to go take care of Santos's meal, now," she walked away from Tila.

Antonia fed Santos; she did other chores, but continued to feel sick and in a daze. She thought about what to do. Antonia remembered that after her conversation with Fortunato, when they first arrived at the big house, and they had alighted from the wagon, she had asked that they find their own home. Fortunato had insisted that only after the harvest could they afford to have their own house built. Antonia felt miserable now as did then, but did not know what she could do; she wondered, and she began to think about her family; she remembered Arizona. Antonia needed to make some decisions and do something. A deep sensation of homesickness settled in her heart. Antonia's only remedy for her state of being was to sit down in a chair; just close her eyes to her present world and reflect on her past.

Antonia reflected how her relatives in Arizona had scratched deep in the tunnels of the earth to send up onto the surface the ore from which copper and other valuable metals were extracted. Her grandfather and other miners worked with pick and shovel. Her mother's family and neighbors had been industrious people who were accustomed to hard labor and they worked in dangerous underground environments. Antonia's family in their copper mining hometown had always dreaded the mine sirens that indicated a mine accident had occurred. Miners in time developed silicosis, a lung disease caused from their breathing the fine dust in the tunnels underground. She thought about all these events and tried to find consolation in them.

Antonia remembered how her mother Manuela and her grandmother Isabel, Nanita, had operated a boarding house for miners. They had worked long hours in the preparation of meals and lunches for single workers. Manuela and Isabel had taken in washing and had ironed clothes for boarders. Wherever the Mexican mining families congregated, there grew up a barrio or a colonia, usually named after the Mexican state or town from which they had immigrated. She remembered how at one time, the town where she was born, prior to being named 'Morenci,' had been called 'Las Carpas' because the early Mexican pioneers in the area lived in tents.

Now, Antonia regretted she had brought her family to a flat desert land full of cactus and thickets. It was evident that Fortunato's family had scratched, cleared, cut, and turned over the earth to make it grow crops of corn, tomatoes, peas, string beans, pinto beans, and other crops. Their acres of agricultural land had for many years grown crops for local consumption and export. She knew that both their

The Worm in my Tomato

people had been hard workers either as miners or as farmers and ranchers. This moment of reflection had made her feel better. Antonia knew, however, in her heart, that her children may not be farmers or ranchers. They may not even be miners, she thought. She felt certain that her children would leave and go search for a new life somewhere when they grew older and were able. But for now, after her family had arrived in El Aliso, Antonia had made it clear to her children that they must support Fortunato. Her children had not responded, so she didn't know for sure what was in their hearts: what they would do. Antonia had encouraged them to come along on this journey so her husband would not come alone: so they would keep their family together. Also, her nanita Isabel had urged her to carry her Christian cross of a married woman, if she wanted to live a Christian life.

Antonia worried, however, about what would happen, in a strange land, where there was no church, no school, no grocery stores, no Alianza Hispano Americana, no friends, no electricity, and to her horror: no ice making plant. Also, the day when her furniture arrived, she immediately realized that her furniture and household items she had insisted be placed on the train and brought to Sinaloa, were useless in El Aliso. Antonia hated the thought that Tila had suggested she sell her furniture, but Antonia realized Tila made good common sense: why hold on to furniture she could not use; but her heart ached at the thought and her eyes cried abundant tears.

Antonia also realized that as immigrants in a new place, not their home, she and her family would have to overcome everyday the ever new and strange. Antonia also worried about how they would survive as a family in this desert. She knew that El Aliso was a rural desert agricultural pinhead stuck near a muddy river called *El Fuerte*. Other pinhead size villages or smaller hamlets, stuck in a forsaken desert, were named Bacori, Mezquital, and El Mezquitalito, surrounded El Aliso and were not far from Tila's ranch, and a Mayo native indigenous pueblo was practically adjacent to El Aliso. Her realization about this reality helped Antonia finally agree with herself that there was no need for her icebox, her large high wood stove with four steel plates, her wooden cupboard with a bin for the storage of flour. There was hardly space in Tila's big house for Antonia's large bed, and her bureau with a mirror. In addition, she decided her dresses and high heel shoes would remain boxed and stored in a shed in the field nearby the chicken coop.

Antonia slumped outside the house as she sat on a wood bench under the mezquite tree, wishing that Fortunato would come by, soon. She held back her tears. She thought to herself, what did I do? She screamed to herself as she walked out into the dirt road leading no where but to *El Mezquitalito*, the Mayo native pueblo. Had she come to a dead end, she asked herself. What would happen tomorrow and tomorrow's tomorrow? She was angry with herself, and said out loud to no one in particular but to all the desert plants, "Why did I let the black iron monster haul us away from our home?" she kicked at the dirt in front of her. To keep from losing her mind, she had recalled her life in Arizona, and it had helped. Antonia again thought about Fortunato. Her husband had worked in Miami, his hobby was working with tombstones for family and friends; he sculptured the letters on the face of the stone. At home, Fortunato sometimes wrote letters or poems for people. He proved himself an effective carpenter by having built their family house, a nice wood house painted blue, which Samuel, Jose, and Toni had helped Fortunato build and paint. The house at 922 Live Oak street had been sold to Don Suarez when the Vega family left the United States on the Repatriation train. Santos was the last one of their family to be born there.

Antonia hated the year of 1932 when they left Arizona to journey to Mexico. She hated the Great Depression. Fortunato had had no opportunities in Miami, anymore after the Repatriation policies. The United States, staggering from the economic depression, found a convenient scapegoat in the Mexican immigrants and deprived them of jobs in the private and public sectors. Politicians wasted no time in enacting deportation laws. The mass deportation roundups of Mexicans occurred in various places without bothering to exclude Mexican American United States citizens. The Repatriation drives began underlined with intimidation and violence and motivated by the repeated yelling of "get rid of the Mexicans" crossed the country. Antonia's thoughts in her mind were like the dust devils blowing up and down in the dry dirt fields. Only the dog Chocolate came near her and licked her hand to comfort her in her lonely incoherent anguish.

Antonia returned into the house and looked for Lorena to help her arrange some small pieces of furniture and store other larger parts. Antonia and Lorena carefully arranged what ever parts of their family furniture they could fit in their rooms; their rooms looked nice. Antonia felt a pang of sadness, however, because in reality their temporary residence in these rooms was not their home. Now, Antonia thought she knew what the saying: 'no place like home' meant and it rang true in her heart: the "Big House" was just not their personal home.

In the following days, Antonia spent her time taking care of her baby, Santos. She thought that Santos must enjoy being a baby, for he was taking his sweet time to grow up. Santos did crawl everywhere about the house, and she knew he would start walking very soon. It seemed that the baby had missed his baby bed. Now that it was here, Santos determined to stay in it; he liked nothing better than to lie in his baby bed and guzzle the warm foamy milk from One Eye.

Fortunato left early each morning, and Antonia did not expect him to return until late in the afternoon, but he usually missed the two o'clock main meal of the day. Antonia supposed he ate with Chapo and the Chinese field workers, at the far side of the field, where they took a short rest under the *huizache* trees. Antonia's heart ached for her husband because he worked so hard, for so many hours, in the hot fields: all in Antonia's family waited for a harvest time that would liberate them from being a burden to Tila. She felt they should not overstay their welcome in her sister-in-law's house. She prayed everyday for God to help Fortunato have a good harvest. As it was, Antonia's family lived in cramped conditions, and she feared Samuel and Jose, who already spent too much time outside the house, may find other places to stay with new friends they had made. Both boys had taken to hike all over the valley, up and down the El Fuerte River, and across the desert, to visit other villages. Antonia feared for their safety, what were they learning, what were they doing, and with whom were they actually. But who could take care of them, she wondered. She had to learn to let go of Samuel and Jose, and simply pray for them. Worry and fear plagued Antonia's mind; she feared Fortunato, if he failed to have a good harvest, would find out where gambling went on, and that his

The Worm in my Tomato

passion for gambling and his need for money would lead him to card games in some secluded ranch house. Samuel and Jose had already told their mother about rooster fights held in the week-ends in some ranches, and horse racing competitions they had discovered that took place in neighboring ranches and small villages in the valley. Antonia really did not think Samuel would interest himself in rooster fights and horse racing, because she knew that his only interests had always been books, study, research and writing. It would surprise her if Samuel did not want to publish a news periodical to inform the local populations of some important public matters. But Jose, jovial in nature, a seeker of fun, would certainly involve himself in dances, parties, horseracing, and other recreational activities available in the valley.

What would happen to her family, Antonia wondered; she experienced anxiety when she thought of how they had left Miami to keep together. They escaped the hunger and joblessness of the Great Depression; they escaped the menace of the Repatriation: her family now struggled in a strange life threatening situation dependent on a harvest at the mercy of rain, the heat, the insects, the weeds, and chance. Antonia thought of how her family lived in a strange environment of desert and a nearby river, mezquite trees, wild vegetation, strange birds, insects, and animals. Worst of all, her family lived in a rural valley without a church, school, main street businesses, doctor's office or clinic, organizations, or theater. All this could be found in the town of San Blas, Tila told Antonia. But San Blas was miles away across the Fuerte River, to the north. It seemed to Antonia that only the rich hacendados had the money to go out of the valley, but Antonia doubted they went to San Blas; further north was Los Mochis, across the border was Tucson in Arizona, and south was Culiacan, the capital of Sinaloa, and of course, all cities had shopping stores.

Antonia lamented her situation, but could think of no solution. She felt the emerging remorse at having left Arizona and the painful sorrow of seeing her family going separate ways. Samuel and Jose, not too long after their arrival to the Big House, had quit inhabiting Aunt Tila's house because their family's half of the house was simply too small for them. Samuel and Jose almost overnight were compelled into becoming grown men: they sought out work to earn their own way and they made friends with other boys they could accompany in job pursuits and with whom they could sometimes live in their homes; Jose searched for odd jobs to care for horses of ranchers who raced horses on festival days; he also hoped to care for fighting roosters and to earn some spending money for himself. Samuel on the other hand sought a job where his education in high school mathematics and his research and writing skills would help him in his work.

Confrontation with the federal government over land titles loomed in the near future for the Vega extended family. Antonia knew from conversations with Julieta that the various Vega farming and ranching families stood to lose thousands of acres; according to Fortunato, it was rumored that his brother Eugenio from Bacori was considered an early target. Fortunato and Antonia feared the loss of El Potrero, as well.

Many of Fortunato's family and friends, who had heard that Samuel was looking for work with the federal government, could not understand how Antonia's son Samuel, recently arrived from the United States, sought to help the state and federal governments make restitution of common lands or Ejidos to the native people pueblos. Jorge said to Fortunato, "It would not surprise me if your son probably seeks work with the Mexican federal government land office that proposed to rob us of our lands." The Vega brothers and cousins complained to Fortunato. Fortunato in turn complained to Antonia.

"Please, Antonia, you must have a talk with Samuel. Ask him to stop searching for work with the federal land office," Fortunato pleaded.

"No, I will not. Samuel is already of age to be independent. Furthermore, he is searching for work to right the wrongs done to the native people for many years, now, you know how he is." Antonia had no sympathy for any one who had taken lands from the poor natives, and worse, for those who did not practice their holy Catholic faith.

Antonia's sister-in-law Tila suffered anxiety in her disagreement with Antonia.

Antonia suspected and worried that much trouble soon would develop and grow into arguments, armed intervention, and blood shed over land, over religious underground issues, and contribute to the growing hunger in villages. Antonia wondered how her family would survive. How could they struggle against government political

The Worm in my Tomato

policies? She kept thinking about these problems. Antonia intended to follow up in seeking advice from Julieta, and she also made it a point to hold serious talks with Fortunato, Samuel, and Jose about these issues and to discuss what to do about them for their own protection.

Fifteen

Samuel
In the context of reality

Well, Samuel found himself in Mexico, there was no *Prensa Mexicana* periodical to write articles for, no Lion of a Mr. Mendoza with whom to hold long discussions on social justice issues; what was he going to do? Samuel kept asking himself. Antonia had a long conversation with Samuel when he came to visit her and Lorena. He listened to his mother tell him of the dangers he might encounter by working with the federal government to help the natives. She informed him of the displeasure of the Vega families with him, "Eugenio said," Antonia explained, "Especially, don't let him get a job surveying lands that are in question for lack of proper titles."

Samuel's plan in life was to promote social change for the good of society, how to be useful here in Mexico, how to make a contribution towards building a better Mexico, but how to do it was his urgent question.

The first day or so, after his arrival at El Aliso, Samuel walked about getting acquainted with the grounds, the sheds, and the water well, the ranch store, and the huge barn like cheese room. He even played a stick game with Chocolate, the large chocolate colored hound dog. Chocolate was that kind of dog which loves humans and was always around them and played games with them. Chocolate always waited for one of the Vega children to play with him. Whenever Santos, out to get some sunlight and fresh air, toddled about the front yard, Chocolate followed the baby around protecting him and helping the child keep his balance.

One morning, Samuel visited his Aunt Tila in the cheese room. He thought that perhaps they could talk and get to know each other. She was covering some round cheeses with thin gauze like cloth; Tila asked Samuel about his mother, "Do you think your mother will have a hard time adjusting to El Aliso?" She motioned Samuel to sit down on a chair beside a small table.

"My mother has always been an active type of woman with an outgoing personality. She participated in church activities in Miami."

"Too bad, but here there are neither churches nor church activities in which she can participate," Tila said.

"Nevertheless, in Miami, my mother attended Blessed Sacrament Catholic Church, where she, along with us children, regularly attended the Holy Mass on Sunday and days of obligation." Samuel said, "In our hometown, many of the non-Mexican residents were prejudiced against the Mexican American people." Samuel hoped something of their life in Miami would interest his Aunt Tila.

"That is too bad," she responded as she put a large round cheese on top of a wooden plank that served as a shelf for holding up cheeses to dry. "But give me some examples of how people treated your family," she inquired.

"Well, for example, we always sat in the pews for the Mexican faithful, situated in the left side of the central aisle, the women with bowed covered heads with their *tapalos* and the men with quiet endurance, all with brown pious faces," Samuel said, "Sheep obedient to their Shepherd."

"What? Even in the Church, you got treated like that?" Tila said, her face showing an expression of unbelief "can't be true, prejudice is so evil."

"Yes, in the theater, at the Young Man's Christian Association or "YMCA," as it is commonly called, and even at work in the copper mines where Mexican mine workers got less pay for their work than the Anglo or European Americans," Samuel said.

"What a shame," she wrapped another cheese, "Imagine, here in Mexico, President Obregon brought in Protestants to teach school and supported the Young Man's Christian Association."

"How ironic, guess, Mr. Obregon did not know about how the Young Man's Christian Association treated Mexican Americans in the United States," Samuel said.

Tila offered Samuel a piece of cheese, "Didn't Fortunato and Antonia do something about it?"

Samuel glanced to the side, feeling slightly irritated, and looked out the large east window. Outside, the air in contrast to Samuel's

191

feelings, was calm. The dusty green trees did not move except when twittering birds landed on some branch and then flew away. The pale blue sky would later in the day heat up to a blue white color.

Inside the cheese room, the dim light and corner shades provided a cool environment for the fermenting cheese in large wood tubs. The aroma like spoiled cottage cheese seemed pungent to Samuel. "There is no record or knowledge among our family that mother strongly opposed this discriminatory practice by the church authorities, but she did join the non-profit organization, the Alianza Hispano Americana, to help promote improved conditions for Mexican Americans." Samuel informed his Aunt Tila.

"There are no organizations, here," Tila sat down on a chair by the table. "Do you want another piece of cheese?" She handed Samuel a cut slice of white cheese as he nodded 'yes.' "What good did this Alianza do?" asked Tila.

"Well, the Alianza Hispano Americana confronted prejudice and discrimination practices in Arizona society that in time had developed after the new increase of immigrations from the other states in the United States, especially from those states accustomed to prejudice and hatred of others, based on differences of skin color or race," Samuel munched on a piece of white cheese. "Mexican Americans organized non-profit civic, financial, and social organizations. One such organization was the Alianza Hispano Americana, founded in Tucson, Arizona in 1894," Samuel said.

"How do you know these things, Samuel, being that you are so young?"

"Oh, Aunt Tila, I am eighteen years old, going on nineteen, and I completed four years of high school in Miami, I would have graduated this May but we left on the Repatriation train in March," Samuel chewed his piece of white cheese. "Also, I have read many books, but what really helped me know and understand many things were the research and writing I did in helping Mr. Mendoza publish *La Prensa Mexicana* newspaper." Samuel finished his last piece of cheese and wondered if he should ask for another. Samuel liked the taste of cottage cheese and the pliable firmness of Mexican white cheese.

"Have another piece of cheese, Samuel," Tila offered, as if reading

The Worm in my Tomato

Samuel's mind, and she handed him a slice of white cheese. "Very interesting, Samuel," and she looked at him directly, holding the sharp knife on the edge of the round cheese, in the act of helping herself to another slice, "What can you tell me about the history of Mexico in Arizona?"

"From my research for *La Prensa Mexicana* articles and in my discussions with Mr. Mendoza, my study of Arizona's Mexican roots revealed that Arizona formed part of a vast land area first called the *Provincias Internas* under Spain's sovereignty, 1541-1821," Samuel said, and from that point, he told Tila the story about Mexico in Arizona.

> The *Provincias* became Mexico's northern frontier after Mexico's independence from Spain in 1821. Twenty-seven years later, after its independence from Spain, when Mexico was yet not politically stabilized, had a small population, and lacked an appropriate Armed Force; the United States invaded Mexico and acquired the northern provincias through war. Mexico's northern frontier passed to the United States through *The Treaty of Guadalupe Hidalgo* in 1848, which ended the U.S.-Mexico War of 1846-1848. In addition, the United States added a large portion of land from Mexico to southern Arizona through the *Gadsden Purchase*, 1853.

"Well, in addition to economic, social, and political endeavors, in conformance with Spain's colonizing policies," Samuel continued speaking, "Roman Catholic missionaries brought Christianity into Arizona and served the native Indian populations through mission work. Jesuit priest Eusebio Francisco Kino in 1700 established missions at the Pima Indian settlements of Guevavi and Bac," Samuel said, between bites of his piece of cheese. He knew all this history by heart. He stood up, stretched out and looked out the window.

Outside the wind had started to sway tree limbs and on the ground to sweep grass and bushes. Samuel continued talking, "Construction on the present mission building of San Xavier del Bac began in the 1780s and completed by 1797. This was the historical Spanish and Mexican religious heritage in Arizona that our family inherited, worshiped God in the Holy Catholic and Apostolic Church and in which we sought our spirituality as an individual and as a group."

The Worm in my Tomato

"There is no Church presence here in El Aliso, we don't talk about the church here, the federal soldiers may shoot first and ask questions later, Samuel, do you understand," she seemed stern and anxious to make a point. "I hope Antonia does not try to bring the church or organized religion here or to El Mezquitalito, it is too dangerous, it would be asking for trouble," she said in a low voice. She looked from side to side as if afraid of being overheard, "The federal government might even want to take our lands away, you just don't know Samuel," Tila leaned forward and whispered, "In January of this year, barely three months ago, the federales encircled my brother Oton's house with wire and when he rushed out with his rifle in hand to protest and defend his property, the soldiers shot him dead." Tila looked at Samuel directly, "You met some of his children at our welcoming dinner when you first came from the United States, remember?"

"Yes, I did and I am sorry about Uncle Oton, Aunt Tila."

"The federal government wants to return lands to the pueblos so they can cultivate in *ejidos*, to help them, but you can't," Tila chewed her piece of cheese, "You have to let them be who they are; *they* are happy the way *they* live."

"I want to help them through education and creating economic enterprises in their pueblos."

"No, and furthermore, Samuel, you better get those ideas out of your head. The Hacienda system is the only way of life that our family believed in; your Uncle Jorge will tell you the same thing."

"Don't you think we need to develop the pueblos and continue where the encomienda left off?"

"No, we can only go so far, and this is as far as we will go with the pueblos," Tila persisted in her point of view.

"I understand, Aunt Tila," Samuel decided to change the direction of his topic, and he decided to discuss the way of life in his hometown.

"In Arizona, the Mexican cultural heritage has been established and promoted through family life over two centuries. In modern times its cultural expressions in language, music, dance, food, and the arts have been joined in celebration of life, a life integrated in a fiesta of joy, occasions to be celebrated with cultural foods, customs, fashions, work,

The Worm in my Tomato

games, songs, and music; expressed in an evolved stream of traditions stretching over thousands of years to Spain and to Mexico." Samuel said. He chewed on a piece of white cheese, and he added, "But there are those who are enemies of our culture of diversity, they want to make all other people like themselves, they desire nothing but assimilation of others into their own culture but in a subordinate status."

Samuel saw that his Aunt Tila seemed more relaxed with these topics. So, he continued to talk, "Family celebrations like a wedding, baptism, quinceanera, and piñata centered birthday parties are popular in Arizona."

"Our native Indians here in El Mezquitalito have their fiestas, you will see," Tila smiled.

"Oh, Aunt Tila, every town in Arizona with a representative Mexican American population has music dance bands which perform at Saturday night dances; our people love dancing, I don't so much, but my brother Jose does."

"Wait until you see the Indian dances here during their fiestas," Tila said.

"I can hardly wait to learn all I can about the natives here," Samuel responded.

"Only appreciate them and their dances and culture in general, Samuel, but don't get emotionally or intellectually involved. You will hear stories about how badly they have been treated, how they lost their pueblo lands, how underpaid and overworked they are," she waved the cheese knife in the air back and forth in front of her like fanning herself, "but don't believe the stories. We have done more for them than you will ever know. Yet, there are religious fanatics, communists, and other radicals who want to change Mexico according to some crazy vision; there are misguided government revolutionaries who have not given up in changing Mexico according to the revolution of 1910 and the Constitution of 1917," she cut herself a slice of cheese, "*Ejidos* are not the way to go."

"Yes, Aunt Tila," Samuel could think of nothing else to say. But he was impressed with her knowledge and grasp of Mexican history. Samuel made up his mind to study about Mexico as much and as hard as he had studied about the United States. Mr. Mendoza had always impressed upon Samuel to study, to reflect, and make up his own mind, "Always control your own life," Mr. Mendoza had been fond of saying to Samuel, "or you will lose it to others," Samuel smiled in appreciation of Mr. Mendoza's considerate advice.

"Yes, Aunt Tila, I enjoyed our conversation." Samuel made his way out of the cheese room. "Good -bye, and thank you for talking with me, and for the tasty cheese."

Julieta

On Sunday afternoon, two days later, Samuel accompanied his mother to Julieta's ranch house. Lorena and Eligia also went with them for the walk and the visit. Samuel personally wanted to continue to explore his desire to find a positive way to help Mexico in this area where his family lived; he felt discouraged to seek ways to help the native pueblos, from what Tila had said to him. Samuel was anxious to find out what Julieta would say on the subject. Samuel still needed to find what he could do to make some contribution to society.

Samuel had previously met Julieta when he had accompanied his mother to Sunday prayer service at Julieta's house. He remembered that Julieta had turned out to be a pleasant woman about his mother's age, maybe thirty-five to forty years old. Julieta was robust, tied her long brown hair in braids, and sported women's riding pants and boots. Her ruddy face was all smiles as she greeted her visitors.

"Come in, come in, please, sit on this sofa. I will bring you some lemonade."

"Thank you, Julieta, this is my son Samuel and my daughter Lorena, whom you met, the first time we visited you after prayers, some weeks ago; you know Luisa's daughter, Eligia." Antonia said.

"Yes, yes, how are you Samuel and you girls doing," Julieta smiled, while she set on the table some cups and a pitcher of lemonade, "Luisa and Eligia come regular to our church services on early Sunday mornings, and it was Luisa who told me of your desire, Samuel, to come meet with me. She told me last Sunday," Julieta turned to

The Worm in my Tomato

Antonia, Samuel and Lorena, "glad to see you and your children, again, Antonia, please come visit me when you like, I am here for Sunday prayers."

Lorena and Eligia served glasses of lemonade to everyone around and served themselves a glass.

They held an enjoyable conversation and exchanged concerns about the problems the Church faced with the federal government. Julieta wanted to know about how the United States granted asylum to Mexican priests and religious sisters who escaped from the federal government during the Cristero war. Antonia asked Samuel to explain what he knew about the situation. Samuel talked to Julieta and the others of what he had learned about Mexico. Lorena and Eligia listened with interest while they drank their lemonade.

Outside the open door, could be seen the road leading down along the irrigation ditch, the sunlight shone bright on two pale green palm trees standing on a corner of the yard. A flock of blackbirds could be heard twittering in the branches of the yard mezquite tree.

Samuel became encouraged to ask for some advice from Julieta, "Julieta, how can I help improve our local society, here, you know, in our own agricultural valley, you know, with my education and writing skills, maybe help the native Indian people?"

"Well, Samuel, these are difficult times when the federal government threatens to take lands away from Hacendados and return them to Indian pueblos," Julieta took a sip of lemonade, " but for me, the worst is that the federal government continues to provoke the Church and limit its educational and other services to its faithful. I do what I can through providing religious instruction, here, the sacrament of baptism, and preparation for holy marriage for when a visiting priest comes to visit."

"Is that a safe way or thing to do?" Samuel asked.

"No, a person involved in helping the church can find persecution and even death," Julieta answered, "but we do what has to be done, safe or not."

"Well, I want to help make a contribution, but not place myself or my family in any possible trouble."

"I see, so, why not find a position with a government agency,"

Julieta sipped her lemonade.

"Is that work safe?" Samuel asked.

"Yes, but only if you don't mix politics with it or if it is not too political."

"I see, thank you," Samuel felt somewhat dejected and he took a swallow of lemonade from his glass.

Samuel thought about the time when he had visited the Miami library, and he had checked out a number of books about Mexico. Mr. Mendoza had advised him, 'If you are going to live in Mexico, you should study the country and its people,' Samuel remembered.

Samuel had done exactly that. He addressed Miss Julieta, "I have learned," Samuel took a swallow of lemonade, "that Mexico, in the late 1920s and early 1930, had its own contending social, economic, and political forces. Mexico is a country threatened for its own survival by its own uncontrollable poverty, its constitutional laws governing the ownership and distribution of lands, and the religious laws that attempted to strip the Church of its legal jurisdictions, isn't that so?"

"Oh, yes, I know," exclaimed Julieta, "The government incredibly prohibited priests to wear clerical dress by law in the 1917 Constitution, as I told Antonia and you before, remember?"

Antonia told of how she couldn't believe about the war between the Church and the government and said, "I still just can't believe that such a war could happen in Mexico, a war that thrust federal troops against men and women warriors defending the Church." She drank from her glass, "These Cristeros fought hard and many died for the rights of the Catholic Church."

Nevertheless, the war resulted in curtailed religious services; the federal troops threatened priests with loss of life, can you imagine." Julieta energetically raised her right hand up in the air. "Religious services went underground and held services in secluded private homes," Julieta nodded at Antonia, "Periodically, I help smuggle a priest into our own area, to assist in celebrating a Holy Mass right here in my home; you are invited the next time we have a Mass."

"Oh, I would love to attend Mass; I can't wait when that day comes," Antonia smiled and raised her arms and hands up above her head, "Alleluia," She swayed her uplifted arms side to side in pure joy,

The Worm in my Tomato

and prayed "Alleluia." She wiped away tears from her eyes.

"Numerous priests and religious sisters escaped during the Christian wars into the United States in 1929 and 1930," Samuel said, and added "My mother and father provided a place to live for two religious sisters, in a one-room guest house in our backyard," Samuel looked pensive and said, "I will do what I can here in Mexico, but I have to overcome my fear of hurting my father, my Aunt Tila, and others of the Vega families."

"Only you can follow where your heart leads you, Samuel," Julieta said.

"My children and I joined my husband Fortunato on the Repatriation train and escaped the policies of the United States against Mexican non-citizens," Antonia informed Julieta, "These are trying times, with our struggle against government policies, and we escaped the hunger and lack of work of the Great Depression, and suffered our own Repatriation to Mexico."

"Back home in Miami, sometimes I lived with good friends and mentors of mine, Mr. and Mrs. Mendoza, at the *Imprenta*, a small printing press in their house located high up at the end of a long flight of cement stairs from a street below named Forest Street. There I worked to help print the paper, *La Prensa Mexicana*," Samuel said.

"Was the paper written in Spanish?" asked Julieta.

"Yes, it was in Spanish to serve the needs of immigrants not yet fluent in English. But I did all my reading and research in English and then translated all into Spanish." Samuel drank some lemonade from his glass; he noticed that Julieta seemed interested in his research. "What I learned about Mexico, I think will be of much help to me."

"Like what?" Julieta asked.

"When I looked at El Aliso, Sinaloa at the time of our arrival," Samuel continued, "I wondered how we would survive at all. The poverty of the Great Depression, terrible as it is in the United States, appeared to me to amount to no more than an annoying hard time in comparison to Mexico's destitution."

"You are correct in your observation; there is much poverty or destitution as you said," Julieta agreed. "Mexico has not yet come to terms in helping our indigenous populations or knows how to help

The Worm in my Tomato

our native peoples." She stopped, looked at Antonia and the girls, "Want some more lemonade? She smiled, "In a minute, I will make something for us to eat."

"No, I am fine," Antonia said. The girls helped themselves to more lemonade.

The wind outside rattled the front door. The western sun began to lengthen the shadows toward the east.

"When in my conversations with Mr. Mendoza, with whom I had worked for two years in his home press prior to leaving Miami, we had discussed Mexico. I learned from him that Mexico had a history of hunger. "Prior to the economic deprivation in the United States, Mexico had been a poor country, at least according to my readings," Samuel said.

"Yes, you are correct, unfortunately." Julieta nodded her head in agreement.

Antonia listened to Samuel's conversation with Julieta and made a point, "The poverty of the Great Depression and the Repatriation law pushed us out on the railroad, like the thousands of hobos riding the tracks looking for work, a place to sleep under a bridge, and a food hand-out at the end of a long line and tiresome wait." Antonia continued, "When our train brought us into Mexico, it seemed we traveled, as well, back into time, a hundred years," Antonia leaned toward Julieta, as if ready to emphasize a point, "standing in food hand-out lines can never compare to where there are no food lines; a waiting line gives those who wait some hope; in Mexico there were no waiting lines to be seen anywhere. We are fortunate that Fortunato's sister Tila took us in to stay in her home, otherwise we would have been homeless, jobless, and hungry."

"Nothing can compare with the destitution of Mexico's rural areas, people have no food and people go hungry everyday in Mexico's own economic depression, according to reports about Mexico that Mr. Mendoza gave me to read," Samuel said. "I carefully observed the animals, some goats and some dogs around the train station at San Blas, and saw how they were bone thin, not unlike many people, mostly indigenous Indians, who I suspect lived imprisoned in Mexico's oppressive society. I remembered what Mr. Mendoza, who in past years had been a newspaper reporter in Mexico, had said, that Mexico's problems were rooted in the country's social and political laws governing religious practice, dress and church jurisdiction; land laws that dictated land use; long overdue laws and practical action promoting education and rural school construction: He told me that the poverty of Mexico was rooted in its culture and historical experience because it had been a colony of Spain for three hundred years. Mexico's people had allowed Spain to develop the country only according to Spain's benefit," Samuel studied Julieta's face to see if she showed any signs of anger. After all, she appeared in her physical features and her white complexion to be Spanish. But there were no signs of anger, but instead she smiled her agreement. There was no doubt in Samuel's mind that she was a true Mexican citizen and patriot and a true faithful practicing Christian.

Julieta stood up and made her way to the kitchen, "Excuse me, let me see what I can do about our late afternoon lunch," She motioned her guests to follow.

Antonia, Samuel and the girls promptly followed her.

"Perhaps you would be interested in meeting Mr. Isabel Garcia," Julieta volunteered. "He is not a Catholic and may even be Communist, but he works at the federal government land office set up in San Blas; he is an intelligent man, who wants to help the indigenous pueblos get their lands returned, the lands some rich hacendados and army generals took illegally by encroachment." Julieta took out some corn tortillas from a round basket. "In that way you could be promoting justice for the native pueblos." She started a fire in her wood stove, and she said, "Good people with a conscience promoting justice and helping the poor may not always be Catholic or capitalist, you know what I mean?"

"That may be the man I can learn from and work with," Samuel answered, hopefully. "Mr. Mendoza was like that, a committed man for helping anyone who suffered from some injustice. Once he learned that I would be leaving for Mexico, he considered it his responsibility to teach me all about Mexico. He said that the people in Mexico had learned to be told what to do and how to live and to work for someone else under the colonialism of Spain. It was a poor used up nation after it won its independence from Spain in 1821. Then only twenty-five years later, the United States, its northern neighbor, a free nation for more than three-quarters of a century, which had had covetous intentions of land grabbing from Mexico since 1823, and with four times more population and with more modernized and powerful armed forces than Mexico, fabricated reasons for justifying an attack on Mexico in 1846. With the end of the war and the United States – Mexico's Guadalupe Hidalgo's Treaty of 1848, Mexico lost its northern territories to the United States." Samuel said, and he added, "The loss of land placed Mexico in the path of poverty and all its modern national problems."

"Yes, many years ago, I studied about Mexico's war with the United States in defense of Mexico's rights to Texas and the northern frontier," Julieta said. Then she and Antonia skillfully heated red chile meat and beans, which Julieta had previously cooked, and now served on five plates, for all to enjoy their late afternoon lunch.

"Come, all of you, sit down at my table," Julieta sat down at the head of the table and folded her hands and prayed thanksgiving for their meal. She smiled her happiness at having Antonia and her children along with Eligia as her guests, "Usually, I eat alone, and today, thanks to God, I have such delightful company. Why don't you continue your story Samuel while we eat, if you don't mind," Julieta said.

"Mr. Mendoza published history stories of Mexico every year in his magazine, La *Aguila Mexicana* in which I wrote the English version of some articles." Samuel scooped up red chili beans with his corn tortilla, "Mr. Mendoza thought it important that United States citizens understood that the Treaty of Guadalupe Hidalgo of 1848, backed by the United States armed forces, attempted to make legal the take over of Mexico's land. Mexicans living in the Southwest, however, at the time were granted citizenship and were protected under the United States Constitution; this was on paper; in reality, Mexican American land owners lost their lands in California, New Mexico, Texas and other states by devious means on the part of the government and land companies."

"What a tragedy for Mexico," Julieta said, "Yes, the newly created border stranded families on both sides of the border, to this day, Mexican people and families reside on both sides of the border."

Antonia agreed, "Yes, it is a shame," she said.

"Mr. Mendoza said that after the long Spanish colonial experience and the land loss of 1848 to the United States, Mexico's government and people never recovered from both experiences," Samuel said, while serving himself red chile with meat cut up in small squares. He added, "Mexico's political leaders went crazy trying to fix everything wrong with their country's political and social life, thereafter, through oppressive laws and revolutions led by warring generals on horseback for land, liberty, and bread. General Emiliano Zapata led a most popular struggle, since 1908, to recover the common lands for native pueblos."

"There is no end in sight, yet, Samuel, you may have your own experience in the country's efforts to transform itself, at anytime soon, but let's hope you and all of us, for that matter, will be spared our lives," Julieta said.

"Just what will happen, only God knows," Antonia said, "We will help you wash the dishes, Julieta, and then we better return home before sunset, it's been a lovely day."

On the way home to Tila's house, Samuel was pensive, thinking about meeting this man, Mr. Isabel Garcia, who Julieta knew about. Samuel's description of Mr. Mendoza had prompted Julieta to remember Mr. Garcia; she suggested that Samuel should meet him. Samuel thought about how Mr. Garcia worked for the land office and how his work had the objective of helping the indigenous pueblo people legally retrieve their lands lost to unscrupulous rich land owners. He was ready to help those who suffered from injustice. Samuel knew that the native Indians were the underdogs, but Samuel was ready to help the underdog.

When they arrived home, Samuel was so excited that he stayed outside Tila's house for a while; he played the stick game with Chocolate. He thought the stick game with Chocolate was more fun than playing washers with Jose. Also, Samuel was excited about the possible opportunity to work in the land office helping the indigenous get their land back. Samuel, however, was troubled about the possible dangers from rancheros shooting their firearms at surveyors. These dangers Julieta alluded to may await him, he thought, in his life experience, soon. Samuel hoped that his life would be spared. A cold chill ran down his spine as he threw the

The Worm in my Tomato

stick for Chocolate to fetch it for him.

After playing the stick game for awhile with Chocolate, who never seemed to tire, Samuel felt a need to sit down and think about his situation. Samuel spent time reflecting on his past life in Miami, Arizona. He wanted to get some bearing on himself before he looked up Mr. Isabel Garcia. Samuel recalled his days when he had lived in the *Imprenta,* Mr. Mendoza's small printing house, located high on top of the hill after climbing the long flight of steps up from Forest Avenue. Samuel worked there to help print the newspaper entitled *La Prensa Mexicana.* Samuel was given room and board and a bed to sleep when they worked late at night. Mr. and Mrs. Mendoza were kind to him and had offered to take him in as their own son, if he wished not to accompany his family to Mexico. Nevertheless, Samuel decided to support his mother and join her on her family's journey to Mexico.

At the time of Samuel's departure aboard the Repatriation train in 1932, he was almost nineteen years of age, and he had no idea of his future role in Mexico. But now, it seemed that he had come to a crossroads, sooner then he had hoped for; he planned not to lose this opportunity. It remained to be seen how Samuel would carry out his work. He knew about the enforcement of Reform Laws in this rural area of Sinaloa, Mexico. Conflicts were prone to flare up, settled with the gun, and later discussed. Samuel's fear of violence and death at the hands of those who disagreed with what he was doing, for the moment, overwhelmed him. Then he worried about how his father Fortunato, his Aunt Tila, and Uncle Jorge would react. 'No,' Samuel thought and determined that he would not do work for the land office that directly influenced the land ownership issue, like surveying, but rather, he thought, perhaps he could get a typing or a writing job assignment. Furthermore, Samuel planned to insist on an indoors desk work assignment.

However, when he met with Mr. Garcia, Samuel learned the Land Office had need of active work surveying lands. As it turned out, Samuel found Mr. Isabel Garcia quite engaging, and after a lengthy conversation with him, Mr. Garcia, knowing that Samuel had the

The Worm in my Tomato

qualifications for office work, title research, and surveying, offered him employment. Samuel overjoyed at having found work did not object to the assignment in assisting in the surveying of lands as well. Mr. Garcia also happened to have an extra room in his own home which Samuel could rent.

Sooner than Samuel had expected, he was out in the field helping to survey Agricultural land property in the valley, including the lands of his father's extended Vega family, his Uncle Eugenio's lands and Fortunato's El Potrero.

Samuel (right) and a friend rested on the bank of El Fuerte River.

Samuel found employment with the Land Office; he went to live in the home of Isabel F. Garcia. Shown here are Mr. and Mrs. Garcia.

The Worm in my Tomato

Sixteen

Fortunato
Desperation in Disguise

The Vega family's effort in opposing the federal takeover of their lands caused Fortunato's brothers and sisters to fear great personal loss of land, and in some cases loss of their lives. Yet, to Fortunato's anguish, his older son, Samuel, having had high school education and being an intelligent young man, found employment as a surveyor with the local rural federal land office. He assisted in the surveying of the Vega families' land holdings. This led to bad feelings between Fortunato's family and the other Vega families. Samuel had told Fortunato that Mr. Isabel Garcia, with whom he worked, surveyed lands in the valley for the federal government, had informed him that no landholder need fear losing his land, if he held proper title to it.

Fortunato, while inspecting the weeding, done by workers hoeing along the rows of his tomatoes, thought to himself that after one hundred and fifty years, where were the land titles; with the change of governments after various revolutions, the *diseños* of the lands were lost. For his part, Fortunato, in his thinking about the context in which he would farm and harvest his crops, found himself in a desperate situation disguised by his vision based on faith and hope that obscured realities out of his control. It was the *place*: In *El Aliso* there was a lack of water, an utter dependency on natural rain for crops to grow; a lack of economic development in a rural dry desert area. The place lacked roads, housing, and large cities nearby to provide markets for agricultural crops. Produce for sale had to be transported on mule-drawn wagons to markets in small villages and transported in railroad cars from San Blas, a small town, to larger cities near railroad facilities. It was a place of isolated desolation.

The *El Fuerte* River sliced through the northern boundary of El Aliso and El Mezquitalito, but lacked the depth and breadth to offer river transportation. The river only separated the El Aliso southern area from the more populous north and the roads that led to *Los Mochis*, a large city, and to *Culiacán*, the capital city of Sinaloa, Mexico.

The meager *place* had for centuries formed the interior character of its people for survival: by being frugal, reticent in speech and manifestation; cautious in helping others with goods, but yet remaining personally willing to provide services, and willing to help generously once they knew and trusted someone. They, the natives, accepted from each other what little they needed, and they shared what little they could give; they had found a way to survive in poverty and sometimes in destitution, but yet maintained respect for one another as persons and for each other's goods, while living in and promoting community.

Fortunato felt as if he and his family had ushered in changes when they arrived in the *El Aliso* valley. Fortunato knew that it was purely a coincidence that compulsory political activities engendered and promoted by four Mexican federal laws, now in belated enforcement, had arrived with him and his family. These laws promoted political, social, educational, and land use changes that confronted Fortunato's extended family. This was not the best time for Fortunato and his family to be in Mexico. Twenty years after Mexico's revolution of 1910, the impetus of social change was just then impacting the *El Aliso* valley part of Sinaloa.

Mexico's land reform laws threatened, as in the recent past, Fortunato's extended Family land holdings. In Fortunato's family's perception, the federal government Secretary of Agriculture had a communal like concept to convert large land holdings into small parcels called *ejidos* or small plots of land. These ejidos would be allocated to indigenous pueblos to be owned by the native community in common. In this way, individuals could not sell their individual agricultural parcels under their cultivation.

The great revolutionary leader Emiliano Zapata had led his native indigenous army from southern Mexico and fought for land and liberty, during the revolution of 1910. His cause championed the return of lands to indigenous pueblos and advised Indian pueblos not to sell the land. These parcels of acreage consisted of a few acres for farming, distributed to the local heads of families.

Samuel's work with the federal land title office, however, led to the real problems with Fortunato and others of the Vega clan. The government intended to take lands that lacked legal title from the rich ranchers and agricultural land owners; to parcel them out to the native pueblo tribes who many years earlier had lost them to hacendado intruders, mainly through forced encroachment. These Indian Ejidos would be parceled out lands for farming, but the present landholders were convinced that the lands would remain uncultivated and create more poverty in Mexico, because the natives lacked funds to pay for seed, water, and labor. The hacendados who cultivated the lands also were certain that the state and federal governments would not provide the necessary seed, equipment, or funds.

When Fortunato, Jorge, and Tila were inspecting sacks of seed that Chapo had purchased in San Blas, and storing the sacks in the store for safekeeping, Jorge spoke to Fortunato. "Fortunato," Jorge pleaded with him, "ask Samuel to quit his work and return to your household and work with you in the fields, as a son should."

"Samuel has his own mind, he is already past eighteen years of age and he has left our home," Fortunato told Jorge and Tila, too, and added, "Furthermore, my wife supports her son," Fortunato piled another sack of seed on top of the stack.

"Well, I warn you, brother, and forget I told you, Samuel might get shot," Jorge persisted, and he slammed down another sack of seed, " if he persists helping the federal government in its intent on taking our lands."

Fortunato personally suffered demands from other family members, placed on him, urging him to dissuade Samuel from working for the federal land office. Antonia was maligned as well. Fortunato and Antonia had heard from other people that Samuel was doing well and keeping busy surveying lands. Vega families feared some of their lands were destined to be lost to the indigenous pueblos which had valid claims to lands because of precedence in land occupation prior to the Vegas' take over of lands for farming. Eventually, Fortunato and Antonia heard from reputable persons, that Samuel was dating Mr. Garcia's oldest daughter, Julia: Fortunato and Antonia rarely saw Samuel again.

Fortunato did not dispute the strong possibility that his brothers and sisters had enlarged their land acreage in past years through the practice of encroachment, when they had fenced in pueblo land as their own. He thought that perhaps El Potrero may have had a similar history, for all he knew. But if his brothers and sisters had not taken in more land, Fortunato reasoned, the lands would have remained fallow, vacant and unproductive desert. Such similar situations had occurred in other parts of Mexico. However, throughout Mexico the land laws enforced by the federal government aimed to correct this state of affairs, in keeping with the social revolution of 1910 and the Constitution of 1917.

Antonia, in contrast to Fortunato, because of her Christian faith and practice, defended the native Indian people. "It is not right to steal land from the native peoples," she exclaimed.

"Woman," Fortunato's own brother, Eugenio, one day, said to Antonia, "If the Indians owe us money for food and household items, well, we take some land in payment." Eugenio felt that his lands in particular were targeted and he said often, "For hundreds of years, my grandfather and his fathers before him were deeded land from the King of Spain himself, because of their helping the natives first through the Encomienda system and later through the congregaciónes that forced natives into communities by law of 1856." Eugenio had no doubts. "We are entitled to land because we established the European civilization in Mexico and Christianized the native people."

Fortunato's brothers and sisters would always defend their position in similar ways, in justification of their actions, and Eugenio added, "If we had not cultivated the desert, the lands would still be wasteland."

Of more concern with Antonia was her bone of contention that had to do with Mexico's laws governing religion. The government laws called *La Reforma*, according to Fortunato's brother Jorge, go back to the time of the administration of Benito Juárez and the

Constitution of 1857. These Reform Laws included Ley Juárez, an effort to secure equality before the law; Ley Iglesias, an effort to provide church sacraments to the very poor who could not afford high fees; and Ley Lerdo, which prohibited ecclesiastical and civil institutions from owning or administering real property not directly used in day-to-day operations. In actuality, Ley Lerdo caused the great amount of land forced to be sold, to end in the hands of the rich and wealthy hacendados, to the detriment of the native Indian pueblos. These Reform Laws caused much determined opposition from the conservative and monarchist political side. More recent the efforts to enforce the religious laws had caused the Cristero Movement warfare. But much of the Catholic Church's aftermath, the struggle to preserve the Church and its practices reached El Aliso and Mezquitalito, before and up to 1932. Fortunato's own brother Jorge had told him all this history. Fortunato's son, Samuel, knew it, too, and that is why he supported the efforts of the federal government to right itself in regards to land reform and make amends based on the Revolution of 1910 and the Constitution of 1917.

Fortunato knew that his wife, Antonia, had always been a devout Catholic woman. In contrast, he knew that for all his brothers and sisters, religion had been a personal affair, more spiritual, and they shied away from organized religion. Perhaps they had their hands full with the land challenges they faced, and they did not want to bait more government armed intrusion.

Fortunato worried that Antonia frequented Julieta's home to attend prayer services in her house. Antonia told Fortunato, based on what Julieta had told her: "Next week, for certain, a priest will secretly, in an unobserved way, sneak in here to our area, and we will have a celebration of the Holy Mass."

Fortunato only shook his head and said to his wife, "Antonia, you will not let things alone, why don't you accept things as they are. You may yet get me, my sister, and my brothers in trouble with the federal government. Armed soldiers may descend on us, yet."

If federal troops caught them, the priests would be executed on the spot. Nevertheless, Julieta and her faithful indigenous neighbors in El Mezquitalito lived each day in hope a priest would arrive. No one knew when or how. Antonia was above and beyond herself in joyous expectation because she had not attended a Mass since arriving in Sinaloa months ago.

Fortunato's wife had for some time been attending prayer service at Julieta's house. Fortunato's sister Tila had told him, while he helped her and Jorge to store the sacks of seed in a back room of the store, "Nato, it would be best for me and for you and all the Vega families, if Antonia did not attend prayer meetings with Julieta."

"Tila," Fortunato answered, "I want my wife Antonia to attend at least prayer service at Julieta's, given the fact that there is no place around here to attend church and the holy Mass."

"No, Nato, there are many anti-religious in this valley. There are also anticlericals that do not care for anything Catholic in the valley and throughout Mexico," Tila emphasized, "your wife and your son Samuel risk danger and perhaps even death."

Fortunato, as he labored to stack sacks of seed, reasoned that Tila expressed sincerity in her concern for Antonia and Samuel. He believed that deep down his sister was good hearted and meant well; she was survival driven, he thought.

"You yourself, Fortunato," Tila said, "will not be trusted by our family and others. I regret to say this but it is the truth, and I myself may lose credibility. Therefore, I doubt that you should be working for me, and furthermore, if you continue here, you should send your wife back to her country, back to the United States."

Field workers cultivating tomatillo, the green tomato.

The Worm in my Tomato

Fortunato, deeply perturbed by what Tila had said, welcomed the good news about the possibility of the opening of a school in the native village. Mexico's education laws promoted rural local one-room school houses in the native pueblos. Fortunato took an interest on rumors; he had heard, that a government-paid teacher would be assigned to the Mayo Indian village, El Mezquitalito. At long last, he enjoyed having some good news to share with Antonia and Lorena. A government paid teacher would provide an opportunity for his daughter Lorena to attend school, along with her friends Eligia, Carmen and other village native children. There in the native school, the students, thought Fortunato, probably would not learn about Mexico's social revolution, Mexico's land laws, the education laws, religious laws, and the immigration laws, but they at least would learn basic education consisting of arithmetic, geography, reading, writing, and ancient history of Mexico. Fortunato thought this would be good for Lorena.

Antonia, although happy with the news of the possibility of a school in the village, continued to be very critical about the religious laws. Fortunato sympathized with her and he could understand his wife's perspectives as well as understand his daughter's desire for education, but Fortunato's own critical urgency concerned the land laws.

Fortunato's immediate desire was for a good harvest. That is why he criticized the immigration laws with intensity because the government had in mind to repatriate the Chinese immigrant workers back to China. This would in time impact the eighteen Chinese field-hands working on his sister Tila's agricultural lands. Fortunato supervised a few Chinese workers, loaned to him by his sister, on his own El Potrero fields of corn, tomato, vegetable, and cotton. Fortunato was anxious for the harvest of his fields that would provide him with the money he needed to pay his debts to his sister. Fortunato often thought that he needed to purchase a piece of land upon which to build a house for his family. Equally important he hoped to have money to place Lorena in a good school in Los Mochis or Culiacan. It was long overdue, he knew. Lorena desperately hoped to attend a school or have a private tutor.

Fortunato felt that this boiling kettle of change would certainly cause political and social conflicts usually settled with bullets. It was within this pot full of trials and danger in which Fortunato and his family survived in a most uncivil and unsafe situation threatening at any moment to push the family into a deteriorating dysfunction. Fortunato wondered how he could keep his family from breaking apart. How could he provide Antonia and his family with their own home? How could he give them enough food and protection? How could he provide a good school education for Lorena?

These were the pressing questions in his mind that worried him constantly. But many of these problems became less important to him when he compared them to the threat upon his marriage based on what Tila had said. Tila's statements continued to ring in his head: "You yourself, Fortunato, will not be trusted; therefore, I doubt that you should be working for me, and furthermore, if you continue here, you should send your wife back to her country, back to the United States."

Fortunato's solution in escaping the Great Depression and the Repatriation in the United States had been to return to Sinaloa and to farm. It was a risk that he gambled on, he knew, but the gamble was not over, he thought. Fortunato intended to win by having a great harvest. All the signs were there, his hard work showed the results: cleared fields, erected new fences, plowed fields, seeded rows of fertile land, hoed weeds. Indeed, his planted fields had set in motion a promise. The possibility of some rain, the help of field laborers, and the control of insects gave Fortunato hope and fed his faith. But at times, Fortunato felt impatient, a feeling of doubt threatened his resolve and he felt the urge to find a good card game in the valley and win some quick money to help solve some of his immediate problems. Fortunato knew, of course, that he gave up gambling for life, as he had promised Antonia, and to depend only on his agriculture, but if there ever came a time when it seemed to him that the situation and the time when gains from gambling at cards would save his family, he felt strongly that he would not overcome the temptation. Fortunato felt strongly that with money won from gambling, he could provide a house for his wife and his children.

But for his immediate problem concerning his sister Tila and his

The Worm in my Tomato

wife, Fortunato determined to find a solution to the conflict brewing between them. Fortunato also worried about the possible conflict between Samuel and Fortunato's brothers. Fortunato knew that he had definitely been told to send his wife away and furthermore to discourage her participation in religious activities with Julieta.

Seventeen

Jose
Family: If there was a choice, Jose did not see one.

Jose did not like to live in the cramped area of his Aunt Tila's house. Jose hated that he had no job that paid him some money. His father and mother had no money, nobody had any money. Jose felt like the caged rooster down in the chicken coop, who had no where to go and yet had to crow each morning. Jose could work for Aunt Tila, but it would be for no pay, for his room and board, and he could work in the fields with Fortunato and the Chinese and Indian field hands. Not for me, he thought. Jose needed to find work that paid, and he wondered where he could find work and a place to sleep.

El Aliso, in daylight hours, neither interested Jose nor did anything positive for him. The vast desert behind Aunt Tila's house, stretched south for miles. The desert offered an opportunity for hiking, but that was not for Samuel; there were no books in that direction, and so Jose had to hike by himself. As for Jose, he had already walked for miles west and explored the indigenous village El Mezquitalito. On another occasion he had hiked north across the El Fuerte River, passed small ranching villages. To the east were vast agricultural fields; some irrigation ditches led into the fields from a canal supplied with water from the El Fuerte River.

Everywhere Jose went, local residents wanted to know who he was and why his family had come to live in the valley of El Aliso, Mezquital, Bacori, and several other villages. Jose would always explain that his family, all born in the United States, came here to escape the Great Depression on the Repatriation train to San Blas.

"Oh, yes, I know the Vega families. Jorge has been one of our local political leaders for years, but I don't know Fortunato, you say he's Jorge's brother?" One rancher named Francisco Graxiola quizzed Jose.

"You don't know my father Fortunato because he lived in Arizona for years."

The Worm in my Tomato

"Well, if you ask me," said another man, who identified himself as Ricardo Rodriguez, "Fortunato should have stayed in Arizona, it's worse here. There are no jobs here, only hunger, even babies are dying for lack of food."

"My father is working the fields and should have a harvest, real soon, and that should provide garbanzo beans, peas, and other foods for the area," Jose responded.

"Oh, no," said the man named Ricardo, "All vegetables, tomatoes, and corn are for sale," Ricardo spat on the ground, "There is no money here." His look at Jose was as if his eyes were asking if Jose was that naïve, "We don't even get one slice of cheese, or not even one pork skin, nothing, from your Aunt Tila's ranch store," Ricardo said.

"You know, I lived in California for some time, working there as a migrant field worker," A man called Martin, said, "In the United States there are many organizations with the sole purpose of volunteers helping people in need," he took a swig of water from a canvas *talega*, tipping the water bag higher than his head. "In Mexico, nothing like that exists to a significant degree, it's everyone for himself, '*chingar*' the other, all *pendejos* take advantage of each other." Martin spoke in bitterness.

"But, I am searching for a job and a place to stay," Jose studied the men's faces and asked, "Do you have a job and a place for me to stay?"

"No," said Martin, "As he spat on the ground, "and what's more, I don't think you will find any work, not with how the economy is today in Mexico."

"You are yet very young, Jose, how old, about seventeen?" asked the man who introduced himself as Francisco Graxiola, "But you will see, soon enough, that Fortunato jumped from the frying pan into the fire, as the saying goes."

"I am sixteen, but I must leave now," Jose shook hands all around and excused himself to complete his sight seeing and return to his Aunt Tila's big house.

Jose walked on, engrossed in his thoughts. He thought about what the men had said that it was a mistake that Fortunato had brought himself and his family to his birthplace, Sinaloa.

Jose became inclined to blame his father, although Jose understood that in some ways his father could not help it, for placing his family in a strange place, with a people who did not share their United States culture, heritage, and language. Like with those men Jose had been conversing with an hour ago, Jose had trouble communicating with them in his broken Spanish and in their fractured English. Samuel and he were lucky, he guessed, along with Lorena and Catalina, in that his parents always had spoken to them in Spanish in their home in Arizona.

But in some ways Jose blamed the United States government for what happened to his family. His mother had to leave her pious religious activities at the Blessed Sacrament Church of Miami where he, his brother Samuel and his sisters were all baptized and come to a place without a church. Jose remembered how his brother Samuel was up-rooted from his fourth year of high school and from his job at *La Prensa Mexicana*, Miami's Spanish language newspaper. Heck, Jose thought how he had left school when he was barely a second year student in Miami High School. Jose thought about how his sister Lorena, a precocious bundle of curiosity, was almost ten years old when the train swept them out of the country. She had always been in pursuit of learning and loved her school, Bullion Plaza. But what could she learn here, he wondered, unless she learned from the very rocks, plants, and the ants. Jose thought about his sister Catalina, and about how she was her brother Santos' baby-sitter, and now she had been sent away from the family to live in El Bacori with Uncle Eugenio. Jose especially felt sorry for his sister Lorena because she had always been so prim, proper, and particular. How is she to survive now, what with milking a one-eyed cow with a slapping tail, throwing buckets of water for stupid hogs, and chasing after chickens to wring their necks? Lorena had cried out her heart to him so as not to worry mother.

Jose remembered that when he had expressed similar thoughts to Samuel, that Samuel had responded, "My poor sister, all she wanted was to go to school. It's just too bad, but there are no schools in this area for her grade level. I overheard my father and mother talking, but it seems, as they said, that even Catalina had to go live in the nearby village of Bacori, with Uncle Eugenio and his wife, Sara, where there is a primary grade school."

The Worm in my Tomato

Soon enough, Jose came upon the big house. The dogs were jumping about, wagging their tails, and appeared eager to greet him. All three dogs came at Jose to hug him and lick his hot, sweaty face. Especially, the large chocolate brown hound dog with his black snout; Chocolate, licked Jose's arms and hands and pranced about and bayed up to the sky. Jose appreciated the dog's caresses, but still felt empty inside, dried up like a purple prune, but he knew that he had no choice but to continue to search for work.

~~~

Jose had decided for some time now to leave El Aliso and live on his own with a ranch family and help with horses. Jose liked horses; the ranchers in the valley held horse racing on festival days, and Jose liked to be around horses and watch the races. Jose hated to leave his parents, and he reflected a lot on why his father and mother decided last March to take this journey to Sinaloa. He knew that his father wanted to work the lands that Eudoro, Fortunato's father, who had died, had left to Fortunato. His parents' decision, Jose knew, was caused in part by the deprivations of the Great Depression and by the promptings of the Repatriation for Mexican citizens to depart from the United States. "But what did all this have to do with me, except that I wanted to support my mother on her journey," Jose had told Samuel.

Now, Jose knew it had not worked out. His family was breaking apart like seeds in the wind, scooped up, scattered about, and what would come of it all, who knew? Jose had to find a job; aim and throw his iron washer into the hole, so to speak, or forever remain a peon in his Aunt Tila's hacienda.

Well, all that was in the past for Jose. Now, he planned to find a job, save his money, and return to his hometown, and he made up his mind to move out of Aunt Tila's house; no, he would not stay: Jose believed that he could not really help in any way to keep the family together. Moreover, he believed he would actually help make things worse if he stayed. If there was a choice, Jose did not see one, except to move on.

The Worm in my Tomato

Jose found work

In another day, Jose left the Big House to seek work for pay. Jose hiked along the roads and visited the nearby villages. In time Jose found a family who befriended him. Mr. Manuel Martinez needed someone to help care for his horses. Manuel was fond of his large mustang named Colorado, who competed in local races; Colorado had won his good share of races. Mr. Martinez's other passion was rooster fights, these rooster fight competitions were held periodically in various nearby ranches.

In their first meeting, Jose asked, "Do you have work I can do?" He asked the rancher Mr. Martinez because Jose had heard from Graxiola that he might need some help.

"Yes, if you want to, you can work here with us," Mr. Martinez said.

"Is there a place where I can stay?"

"There is room in the worker's bunk house. Your main job is to help me take care of the horses, you know, feed them, water them, and exercise them, you know, don't worry, I will show you," Mr. Martinez stretched out his hand and shook hands with Jose, "My name is Manuel Martinez."

"I am Jose Gutierrez," Jose smiled, "Heck, I like horses, roosters, and dogs, no problem, gosh heck, I accept the job," Jose tried not to appear too eager, "But does the job include meals?"

"Absolutely, my wife Consuelo makes the best meals in the valley."

"What about spending money?"

"I will pay you in Mexican money the equivalent of a dollar each day, provide a place in the bunk house for you to stay, and the job includes your meals, what do you think?"

"Sounds good to me, I can start today." Jose had independence, and the terms were agreeable. Jose felt confident that he could learn all about horses, he was sure. "What about the fighting dogs?" Jose asked.

"Oh, no, I don't fight dogs, and I don't often fight my roosters; I do race my horses on festival days," he started to move toward the corals, "Come on, lets start exercising the horses, I have six; I trade, sell, and buy them, but not my own favorite, Colorado."

The Worm in my Tomato

Rabies

Next day, early in the morning, as Jose exercised a gentle white mare by leading her with a rope tied to her bit, around and around the coral, he heard Mr. Martinez calling him from the kitchen door of his house, "Hey, Jose, I got a rifle for you."

"I found out from my neighbors, Manuel said, "that there is a rabies alert throughout the valley." He handed Jose a small rifle, "Take this 22 caliber rifle and shoot any skunk or stray dog that comes around our ranch."

"How can you tell if a skunk or a stray dog has rabies?" Jose asked.

"Most often, you can't, so shoot first, and then we'll see," he held a larger rifle made for a higher number caliber, "a dog will froth at the snout and animals with rabies will act crazy." Manuel sounded a bit worried, "We have to protect Colorado, if you hear the horses or the roosters make a nervous loud fuss or act crazy, there is a skunk in the area, look around, and shoot if you see one, but don't get close."

"What about your dogs?"

"We only have two, and I will keep Sargento and Patron in the house for a day or two, until the police posse decides what to do; usually to avoid the spread of rabies, they go from ranch to ranch and hang the dogs in the premise, elimination of potential sick dogs is the solution; the police consider the dogs contaminated, you can't take a chance with rabies."

That Sunday of the first week on his job, Jose walked over to pay his mother and Lorena a visit at the big house. Mother and Lorena were preparing to walk over to Julieta to attend Sunday prayer service. It was late in the morning but the bright warm sun of earlier in the day already was threatened by encircling dark clouds in the sierras.

"Hold on Mother, there is a threat of rabies in the area," Jose said.

"We know; your Aunt Tila already has Chapo and the Chinese workers on the alert. Fortunato is riding about on his horse looking for any signs of crazy skunks or dogs; he has a rifle to shoot any suspicious

The Worm in my Tomato

animal," Antonia said.

"I have this rifle, too, that Mr. Martinez gave me to shoot skunks or stray dogs; I will walk with you to Julieta's and walk you back after services, mother."

Just then, before Antonia, Jose, and Lorena, who carried Santos, walked out of the yard, a 1928 Ford pickup truck drove up into the front yard; in the back of the truck were four men and they all had rifles; the driver got out and sauntered toward Antonia, Jose and Lorena. "Where is Miss Tila?" he looked about the patio, and he looked at Chocolate, the always friendly greeter hound; he carefully studied Dia, the white mongrel female dog, and he stared at Noche, the dark black Labrador mix dog. Both dogs pranced about in circles around the armed deputies.

Jose looked at the four lawmen holding their rifles at the ready, "The dogs are friendly," he said.

The deputy on the passenger side of the truck got out, carrying some long ropes.

"What do you want, Captain Jasmin?" the booming voice of Tila was heard as she came out the kitchen door.

"We are at your service, Miss Tila; it's about the possible rabies epidemic." He walked toward her and extended his right hand. "You know what happened two years ago, and we don't want any person bitten and come down sick." He withdrew his unshaken right hand.

"What are you doing?" asked Tila.

"We visit the ranches and see how their dogs look," he scratched his right ear, "Of course you can't really tell, until it's too late, and then we are not around to shoot the dogs," he carefully studied Chocolate who in a friendly manner tried to lick the police captain's right hand, but he jerked it up and out of Chocolate's reach, and he quickly stepped back and away from the dog.

Dia and Noche, not interested in human talk, only curled around three times in a circle and reclined into their dirt nest on the ground. Chocolate, the large chocolate colored hound, friendly as always, wagged his tail, and milled about the nervous police deputies, who stood still, and looked at Chocolate with suspicion.

"Any possibility, Miss Tila, that these here, your dogs, could have been contaminated?" the captain asked.

"Well, who knows, for sure?" Tila looked at Chocolate; the dog wagged his tail, and Chocolate studied Tila and Jasmin and paid attention to every word that was spoken, like if he was part of the conversation. "The last two nights, Chapo told me, that the chickens were restless, the dogs were barking and chasing something into the desert," Tila said.

"Well, who knows, the incubation period is a week or so before real signs appear indicating rabies contamination, then it is too late, want us to hang them, now?" the captain said, and the deputy holding the ropes tight with his two hands moved up and stood beside the captain.

"Jasmin," Tila said, impatiently, "I am a busy woman, with many other problems in my mind, and I can't stand here and talk, don't have the time, you do what you think is best," she walked away across the front yard and went into the large cheese room.

The police captain waved his hand to the other policemen; the man with the ropes wasted no time, and helped by the other four men, they put a noose around the neck of each dog, Dia, Noche, and Chocolate, tightened each noose, and swung the other end of each long rope over the large mezquite limbs. They yanked hard and the dogs lifted up and dangled in the air, anxiously exhausting whimpers and low squeals, shivering and pawing at the air, they expired and hung quiet with their bodies turning slowly back and forth in half circles.

All of a sudden, Santos let out a loud cry. "Wah, Wah," Santos screamed in shock, his little body shaking.

"The baby," Antonia cried out, "Lorena, the baby."
Lorena turned around and picked up Santos in her arms, "I am taking him inside the house, mother."

"Yes, hurry." Antonia said, as she and Lorena hurried into the house.

Luisa brought a glass of water; she mixed up the contents with a small spoon, "Here, give him some water; I put a tea spoon of sugar in it." Antonia took the glass and gave Santos some sips.

"That is good, Antonia, give the baby Santos some sweetened water. It is good for freight, and it should calm him down," Tila affirmed after she had stepped into the kitchen and saw what was happening. She had run out of the cheese room in alarm after hearing Santos cry out.

The Worm in my Tomato

Antonia and Lorena took Santos to place him in bed and calm him down. That had been quite an ugly thing to see. Chocolate and Santos had a special relationship; the large hound dog had always followed Santos about, often protecting the baby, when he tottered all over the front yard. Now, that Santos started to walk, at nine months old, he walked inside and outside the house. Chocolate had been in the habit of following Santos everywhere he walked, like giving the baby support, if he tended to lose his balance. It was such a cute sight. The baby could pull Chocolate's ears, hold on to his tail, lean against him, hug him, push him, anything, and Chocolate would calmly give support, wag his tail, and lick Santos' face. The dog and the baby were best buddies. There was a love connection between the baby and Chocolate. Jose hoped Santos would not have a nightmare tonight and remember this episode all his life.

Antonia decided to stay home and not go see Julieta this Sunday. Jose returned to the Martinez ranch in the late afternoon before the sun went down. On his way out, Jose saw the dogs stacked one on top of another on the ground. He assumed that the deputies had hurried away after they hung the dogs, took them down to retrieve their stained ropes; dragged them to form a pile of shrunk dogs, each with its tongue sticking out their open jaws.

Down the road south around the desert, clouds of dust billowed and swirled around the black truck, and flew high into the gray sky. Jose thought about how the police captain and his deputies had promptly driven away in their Ford truck in quest for family pets. He waited for Chapo to come by with a wagon to cart the dogs away to dispose of them. The place looked odd to Jose, without the dogs keeping guard over the premises. Jose could not help, but think how unfair life was for a dog. So what! Jose thought, if last night, there had been some commotion in the chicken coop, and the dogs had chased something into the desert brush? It could have been a thief after eggs, anything. Jose shook his head and lamented for the dogs, especially for Chocolate; he thought that the whole event was tragic for them. The dogs, Jose thought, did not have a forewarning, not a simple presumption, nothing, and then before they could say "bark," whack, they are up a tree, stretched out by a heavy rope. Jose felt angry at the policemen and he felt that they should not have been so anxious, so quick to hang the dogs. Also, Jose could not understand why Aunt Tila allowed the hanging of such wonderful dogs. To Jose, it was like letting down one's own family. But Jose was impressed and considered the fear of the unknown that every one involved showed: the policemen, Aunt Tila, his mother, Lorena and himself. Jose thought: all of us did not know for sure if the dogs were contaminated, and fearful that they might be, hung them; those who did it were not less guilty than those who just stood by and did nothing to prevent it.

Indeed, the police and Tila, who had the authority to prevent the hanging, acted in a pre-emptive manner and hung the dogs. The only ones who did not have any fear of the unknown were the dogs and Santos. The dogs got hung; Santos suffered shock; Tila, so uncharacteristic of herself, let the police decide what to do. Jose could not believe what had happened. He walked along the road, by now the shadows lengthened and the sun gasped its pink tongues over the sierras to paint white clouds with bloody stains. But soon blackness would overtake the valley and it would be another ended day.

Jose walked in fear of what was yet to come tonight, tomorrow, and tomorrow? Jose continued on his way to his work at the ranch; he thought about what plans to make, or what should he do to prepare: to avoid the fate of the unknown. Only yesterday the dogs were alive; today they are dead forever; who would have guessed the destiny of Dia, Noche, and Chocolate from one day to the next. Jose shuddered as he remembered the suddenness of the Repatriation, how the train took them away to change their life for ever. He held on tight to his rifle.

A house near the cemetery (Panteon)

The Worm in my Tomato

Eighteen

Catalina
A Death in El Pueblo

In contrast to Jose, Catalina, Antonia's youngest daughter, only seven years old, could not provide for herself. Catalina's father had sent her to live with his brother Eugenio in El Bacori where she could attend primary school.

On this particular day, Eugenio came to visit with Fortunato at Tila's house, and he brought Catalina and Sara with him to visit Antonia and Lorena. Tila, Luisa, and Eligia were not at home at the time, having gone to visit Jorge and his family, a short distance away in the next ranch in El Aliso. Chapo had taken them in a wagon pulled by mules.

Catalina was bubbling with enthusiasm, anticipation and happiness for visiting her mother and her sister Lorena. That evening, Catalina accompanied her mother to a local wake in the village. When Antonia returned home with Catalina and Lorena, Catalina talked non-stop with Fortunato, who had stayed in the big house having coffee and talking with his brother Eugenio.

"Mother took us to a service for a dead woman at "L meskitalito." Catalina took pleasure in telling her story, "Julieta said the prayer rosary, and momma said," and Catalina quoted her mother Antonia: "Hurry, we must go to the wake of Maria Teresa in the 'L Meskitalito' pueblo."

Antonia prepared fresh coffee and sat down to visit with Fortunato, Eugenio and Sara; Fortunato and Lorena sat opposite her mother in a wooden bench. Catalina hopped about, happy and talking to her father and uncle. Then, she sat next to Fortunato.

"When I went to this wake and there was Maria Teresa, as mother had said, lying down on the table and she had flowers around her, decorating the table," Catalina stood up and turned toward her mother, "Can I have a piece of tortilla with cheese?" she asked Antonia, and continued her story on the wake to Fortunato. "She had been a sister of *Tell- is- foro*, and wife of some man called *Pam- fee- lo*," Catalina said.

Antonia heated a tortilla on the stove, and she cut slices of cheese on it and folded it in half. The heat melted the cheese in the envelope shaped tortilla.

Catalina took the cheese tart in her hand and gave it a big bite, "Thanks momma, I really like these, what do you call them I forgot?" Catalina said, and continued with her story, "And she died from a fever in the head cus momma said Maria Teresa had a bad head," Catalina said, and took another bite of her tortilla with cheese.

"*Quesadilla*," Antonia said.

The whole family was all ears listening to Catalina and finding her enjoyable. The evening outside, shone like day illumined by a huge low hanging moon with a backdrop of blinking stars. Catalina continued her story, "Then all of a sudden Maria Teresa, I saw it all, she sat up for awhile. Pam- fee- lo and Tell- is- foro, and two more other crying people ran up and pushed her back and held her down."

Catalina hopped to Lorena and pressed down at the shoulder, "Cuss they said that she did not want to die at this time. But they said that she had to die off to do what the great God who made her wanted, cus it was her time." Catalina grasped her half of the tortilla with cheese in both her hands to keep from dropping it. Lorena laughed out loud, and Antonia did all she could do to keep herself from laughing.

"But I am sure that Maria Teresa did not want to go anywhere if her baby was not there," continued Catalina.

"Catalina, sit down daughter and finish your tortilla," Fortunato said.

Eugenio smiled all around; he looked outside the big house and studied the stars to get an idea of the time of evening.

"Maria Teresa, she had just given birth to her baby boy, but mother said, was dead, but I don't know how it was born," Catalina chewed her last bit of her tortilla.

Lorena decided to help Catalina understand and said, "I will explain it for you," she opened her mouth wide forming the words: "The baby is born and is still born dead, see?"

"I don't hear you, Lorena," Catalina cupped each of her ears with the palm of each of her hands, "I only asked momma: momma, how was the baby born dead and is still born?" and she added, "But mother said that the baby was an unnamed baby. The baby was next to Maria Teresa, his momma, on another table, and was to be buried beside her in her arms, the next day," Catalina said and continued, "The wake was tonight. I fell asleep in my mother's lap because baby Santos slept in Lorena's arms," Catalina said.

Fortunato's eyes brushed her tenderly as he softly said, "Catalina, you were tired during the long day."

"They had lots of food and music, *ak-cordions*, drums and flowers and they had the crying ladies there," Catalina said and added, "Mother told us that is the custom here to pay some ladies to cry because there has to be tears, they call them "*las lloronas.*" I did not cry cus no one paid me," Catalina said.

Lorena patted her little sister on the shoulder and asked her to tell father about Maria Teresa being asleep, "Tell father about Maria Teresa being asleep."

"Momma, can I understand death?" Catalina asked her mother, "I asked momma when I woke up one time and the big people were drinking *tea- kill- ah* and some eating *me- nu-doh.*"

Antonia smiled at Catalina, "Tell your father, what I said," Antonia asked.

"No, it's a *mis- too- ree*, momma said to me," Catalina answered. She continued her conversation, "We thought Maria Teresa was alive but she never sat up again. Maybe she was alive but her time was up and she had to be dead. She never sat up again. Tell- is- foro, her big brother, guarded over her to keep her from sitting up again and show that she was not in agreeing that her time was up. One should not do that but accept one's time of death and leaving this world of tears," Catalina said.

"The baby was still born and had no name," Lorena said.

"No, no, let me tell the story, Lorena," Catalina spoke up and said, "The baby had no name. Miss Julieta hurried to baptize him even after he was dead. Lorena said that Tell- is- foro left his sister's baby unnamed because there were no more months in the year, he and his wife Marta had used them all up to name their kids. Of which I know Maya, Junis, and Julia. But they were asleep on the floor. Only Julieta said the prayers, and momma, too, but she always prayed cus she knew God her father. I fell asleep again but thinking all about that," Catalina spoke rapidly.

Eugenio sipped the last of his coffee and said, "That is a good report on the wake you attended, today, Catalina, now let us go to our house," Eugenio said.

"Yes, Catalina, let's go home, now," Sara said.

Catalina began to whimper, "Can I stay with you, momma, like Lorena does?"

Fortunato also stood up and said, "No, Catalina you can't just yet, don't you want to go to school? You must go with your uncle and Aunt Sara," he put his cup down.

"Yes, we must leave now; Fortunato has the fields to tend to early in the morning, goodnight," Eugenio said.

Fortunato kissed Catalina on the cheek, hugged Eugenio and Sara, "Say goodbye to your mother," Fortunato told Catalina.

Antonia embraced Catalina and kissed her on the forehead, and blessed her, "You be good, behave yourself, and we will try to visit you, soon."

Catalina, obedient to her parents, walked away, holding unto her Uncle Eugenio's hand.

The evening, well lighted by the silver moon, appeared like clear water but it was dry. Lorena with tears in her eyes waved goodbye to Catalina; she thought about her brothers Samuel and Jose now gone somewhere. The fact that her brothers were gone, now, their absence punctuated each one of her thoughts about them with finality. Also, Catalina's short visit had ended so soon, too, she thought, and Lorena shed more tears to wet the evening.

Nineteen

Lorena
By the sweat of my brow I earned my education.

Lorena kept asking herself in her mind, how am I doing? She had lost sight of her personal goals of escaping from her Aunt Tila's house and run away north. Lorena jogged down to the river's edge. She picked up some stones and one after another she hurled them into the river. She screamed with all her might up to the sky in frustration. Tears ran down her cheeks. She said over and over again, "Why did Samuel and Jose leave before I could run away, now mother is all by herself; how horrible, and just as bad, Catalina is in El Bacori, staying in the house of Uncle Eugenio and Aunt Sara. I really can not leave mother alone, not now."

Lorena wept as she slowly walked back to her Aunt Tila's house. But how, am I doing, getting adjusted in this place and in this way of life, she wondered. Eligia gave no report cards like Miss Yoakum did, and Lorena felt like being in a yesterday time and not being able to see a tomorrow. She lived a day by day time: doing her chores, keeping company with the chickens, the hogs, carrying water, and helping make white cheese. We all wait in a standstill time, just waiting for father's harvest, she thought to herself.

Antonia's American made furniture made Lorena's place look nice but unfortunately her home became a sad place. Lorena thought that her mother spent too much of her time cleaning, washing, taking care of Santos. Lorena and Antonia talked only when both had time. Fortunato left early in the morning; he worked in the fields all day, and came late at night. As for herself, Lorena adjusted to do all her chores in the order she wanted.

Several months had passed snail-like into the past of time, punctuated by hardship and pain, 'associated', as Miss Yoakum's vocabulary drill had taught, Lorena mumbled to herself, *associated* with her chores. For example, when Lorena went to the well, she never could get the hang of it, that is, in manipulating, another of Miss Yoakum's taught words, she thought: *manipulating* the well rope and pulleys without banging the bucket and spilling water.

When Lorena fed the hogs, she neither comfortably *maneuvered*, thank you Miss Yoakum, she thought, the palanca with the two buckets, nor avoided spilling pig food. Then to make her problems worse, One Eye learned to hide from Lorena, One Eye hid behind her shed, and she put up an *obstinate*, thank you Miss Yoakum, Lorena thought, effort to keep her from squeezing her udders. But Lorena persisted, at least, for the sake of Santos who still sucked on his bottle day and night, but more so, for fear of Aunt Tila, she thought.

One day, Eligia met Lorena at the well and said to her, "How are you doing?" Lorena replied that she was doing the best she could.

"What do you think?" Lorena asked her, "I want to do my work, well. What do you think?"

"What I think really is not that important, it's what Aunt Tila thinks," Eligia said. Eligia hesitated somewhat, cleared her throat, threw her head backward as she rolled her large brown eyes up and blurted to Lorena what Aunt Tila had said, "That girl will never learn, she is like a mule," Eligia mimicked Aunt Tila by lifting her head up high and shaking it from side to side.

"No, you are not doing well, and also, Aunt Tila thinks that you don't want to learn," Eligia said.

Lorena was speechless. She just stared at Eligia and did not know what to say. Eligia, with a friendly grin on her face, said, "If you want, I will teach you again and again until you can prove Aunt Tila wrong."

Lorena heartily accepted that proposal, not so much as to prove her Aunt Tila wrong, but to give poor One Eye some relieve, to help fatten the skinny hogs, and to fill the water jars in the kitchen with more water than Luisa needed for cooking. So Lorena became Eligia's pupil, again, for another round of it all.

Sometimes Lorena heard her mother crying softly at night.

Lorena knew she missed Samuel, Jose, and Catalina. Antonia would at times remark to Lorena, "We came together to keep the family together, and look what has happened," she would say, expressing her misery turned into tears; tears that glistened in her eyes like stars; inner suffering that turned into large drops of liquid-pain that burned her cheeks. Lorena resolved not to run away just yet because she determined to keep her mother company for the time being, and not to leave her alone.

But, what should I do, except pray to God at night, Lorena thought. Other times, Lorena had poured out her aching heart to Julieta; Lorena worried about her mother.

As for Lorena's own schooling, her mother had heard from conversations with Julieta, that the home teacher that had been promised to Lorena by her father and that had been expected to come to their place and tutor her, never arrived because the federal army had kidnapped him. "It was the *Leva*," Julieta had explained to Antonia, "The federal government's draft is carried out by kidnapping suitable looking men and forcing them into service with the federal army."

For the time being, Lorena was trapped into a seemingly never ending routine. Each morning she woke up when it was still dark, but she was excited; Eligia showed her what Lorena had to do, and how to do it, all over again and again. It was the practice that helped Lorena; she became almost an expert, just like Elegia, in drawing water from the well, filling the clay pots in the kitchen to the three quarters line in each pot to avoid spillage and waste of water. Also, Lorena never failed to fill the two clay pots in the dining area.

Lorena wasted no time, as each morning, she hurried to milk the one eyed cow, feed the chickens, feed the pigs, and later put water in the mud hole so the pigs could muddy themselves. More important, the chickens were not overfed. Most satisfying to Lorena: One Eye let Lorena milk her and not once did the cow ever whack Lorena with her long cow's tail. Lorena was so excited, she had learned from what life had to teach, to learn from her environment; to learn from nature, the animals, and to learn from people around her; this learning experience gave Lorena a peaceful joy that filled her whole self. To Lorena it all was an insight about a new type of learning.

The Worm in my Tomato

Eligia rejoiced with Lorena, and she celebrated her learning. "Lorena, you learned so fast and so well, that you lessened my responsibility from your assigned chores and freed me to concentrate on helping Tila make cheese and serve customers in the store," Eligia said as she skipped around the mezquite tree in the front yard. "Tila is also happy about your work, now," Eligia said.

One day, while Eligia and Lorena ate their lunch, Luisa told them that she had heard that the village school would be opened this year, soon. Eligia and Lorena, both were immediately overcome with joy. The two girls just swooned and let the wonderful news immerse into them. Lorena assimilated the school opening news along with her rice and beans. Both became part of her, the good news in her mind and heart and the rice and beans in her stomach. Luisa's words were absorbed into Lorena's mind, and she turned them there, over again and again. Both her stomach and her mind ate well that day, for sure, Lorena thought and smiled.

Lorena was elated and decided to plan on how she would attend school this year, but her heart still desired a beautiful real school like those in Mexico City. Lorena had to try again in convincing her father to help her to go away to school. Lorena noticed she was having more time to herself during her chores; so one day she went and sat under the big mezquite tree and waited to see if her father would come to talk with her. Lorena could see him off in the distance in the field, riding his horse and supervising Chinese field workers. Finally, he came over and sat next to her.

"Father, I still want to go to school in Mexico City; what do you think?"

"Yes, you can attend school, but after I get a good harvest of my crops and when I sell my crops at a good price in the market." Fortunato looked at Lorena with his kind brown eyes.

"But can't you borrow money from Aunt Tila or Uncle Jorge?" Lorena decided, in her mind and heart, it was now or never, "You could pay them later when you sell your harvest, please," she pleaded.

"My daughter, at the rate that cotton in the fields is developing,

232   *The Worm in my Tomato*

that cotton is going to make us rich and then you will be going to the best schools in Mexico."

Lorena was truly impressed with how pretty the green cotton plants looked up and down hundreds of rows. However, her wanting to get some education, now, preoccupied her mind. "That tutor never came, father," she muttered, but her Father ignored her for a moment.

"That fellow must have left the state to avoid religious persecution, I heard he was a devout Catholic; I also heard that he was kidnapped by the federal government and forced into the federal army, I will look for another," Fortunato said.

Then he changed the subject, "Come, I will show you the tomatoes." Across the road from the cotton fields were several fields of tomatoes. Along side the fields ran irrigation ditches. "Although, I depend on natural rain for my crops at *El Potrero*, some of these fields here are watered by irrigation. The Fuerte River supplies the main canals and these irrigation ditches with water."

Lorena was proud of her father at that moment. "The tomatoes are so pretty and green, growing in those beautiful bushes," she said. Lorena shielded her eyes from the sun and grinned. For a gambler with smooth hands, at the start, he was succeeding as a farmer with rough hands, she thought.

"Here, Lorena, this is your tomato plant. This here is your tomato, watch it grow and when it ripens large and red you can cut it free and eat it, you'll see how delicious these tomatoes will be," Fortunato pointed to a small green marble-size tomato on the green tomato plant.

Lorena was thrilled with her very own tomato plant and her own for now imagined juicy big red tomato to bite into someday when it would grow large like an orange. "Thank you, father, for giving me my very own tomato," she said.

Fortunato smiled overjoyed that Lorena was happy with her tomato, although now it only carried with it its potential and a promise of fulfillment. But Lorena was distracted by someone waving at her from across the dirt road. It was Eligia. Lorena saw her waving at her to come to her. Lorena departed from her father with a big hug, "Thanks poppy for my very own tomato." She ran down the road to meet with Eligia.

The Worm in my Tomato

Eligia smiled and joyfully informed her: "Lorena, I have good news," she beamed; her hazel-nut colored skin blazed into cinnamon colored cheeks, "Our school is open, yes our school is open today."

"What, where, calm down and tell me slowly, Eligia," Lorena yelled.

"Our Indian village school opens whenever the local municipio government has enough money to pay a teacher. I heard from Chapo that the government has the money and that a teacher has been contracted. A teacher will come teach in our village school, Lorena, you can go to school, now," she laughed in delight, "Well this year it happened, they had the money and found a teacher and our school opened yesterday. It's open today. Every day from three each afternoon until six evening, we can go to school. Right after our afternoon chores, we can leave." Eligia jumped up and down and twirled around.

Lorena, so overtaken with emotion, laughed and cried at the same time, and both girls hugged each other, and held hands as they hurried to the big house to share the good news with Luisa and Antonia, and of course, be there on time to eat their main meal in the kitchen. Lorena informed her mother; Antonia was overjoyed, although Lorena would not be able to help take care of Santos during the late afternoons. Luisa was happy for Eligia and Lorena, both.

Lorena did not know how her Aunt Tila would feel about Eligia and her attending the village school, at last; would Aunt Tila give us permission, what with us not being available for extra work in the afternoons, Lorena wondered. Tila was in the cheese room or in her store; Lorena planned on how best to ask permission from Aunt Tila. Lorena decided to simply be herself and ask directly for what she wanted with all of her heart. Lorena only remembered about Mary Cota, school, and Miss Yoakum, books, and the fun of learning. But Lorena found herself shaking all over with nerves and decided to wait for the next day.

Next day, with her desire burning in her heart to attend the village school, Lorena planned to ask Tila for permission. Early in the afternoon, after her dumping of two buckets of water in the hog holes, Lorena hurried to the big house to search for Tila. Luisa told her that Tila was in the Cheese House. Lorena hurried to the Cheese House, and she went in through the large side-door of the Cheese

The Worm in my Tomato

House. Lorena found Aunt Tila busy supervising Lepo and Telesforo, two Indian workers from the village, packing cheese into boxes.

"Aunt Tila," Lorena stammered, "May I attend the village school with Eligia each afternoon at the village?" She held her breath.

Tila stared at Lorena for some moments before answering. "How much time will you be gone?" Tila finally responded.

"The class is from three in the afternoon until six, only three hours and then I can come home and light the Cachimbas." Lorena did not know what Tila would say.

"Well, I will have to think about it because I want Chapo to help look after the Chinese camp. He also needs to help your father in the tomato fields." She returned to her work and left Lorena standing there, shifting her weight from one foot to the other. "I don't want Chapo doing any of your assigned work." Lorena heard her say.

Lorena hated these days when she lived with the humiliation of lacking control of her own time; time that she needed for her personal interests. Lorena had talked with Julieta about this situation. Julieta had said, "Will these days ever end? I know, is the question that concerns you at this time, Lorena," Julieta had looked at Lorena with tenderness, "But don't let this time become for you an illusion of being a forever, based on a mistaken false impression that life here in El Aliso has no recognizable potential for redemption from its painful environment. It does, Lorena, for all life stories that must be lived, are authored by God," Julieta said. Lorena wrote down what Julieta had said in her notebook and memorized it word for word, just like she memorized Miss Yoakum's vocabulary drill words.

Discussions with her mother about what Julieta had said to Lorena, and what it meant, helped her realize that she depended totally on the unknown, the invisible powers of future time, hoping for the time in which her father would harvest his fields of cotton, corn, and tomatoes; for the time of marketing the crops at a good price; for the time of sending her away to the best schools in Mexico. "Why not," Antonia told Lorena, "Live the present as best you can, without being so anxious about the future?"

Lorena for her part thought that type of advice was all right, if and when she had the future in hand, but not for someone like herself who

The Worm in my Tomato

had no control over anything; Lorena was convinced that she needed something she could control, to give her some piece of the future to hold in her hand, not something she imagined but rather something she supposed to exist.

Anxiety gripped her inner being when Lorena faced the reality of all *this*; her life being a bad dream tortured into a nightmare. Lorena knew all *this* so well, especially after discussions with Samuel and Jose, when they had come by to visit mother and her. She remembered now, and read Samuel's words from her notebook, "You know, Lorena, how our family escaped the Repatriation and the Great Depression? We were railroaded out of the country, and you were first on the train," Samuel had smacked a huge green grasshopper off his sleeve, "But do you know why our father chose to leave?" Lorena had shrugged her shoulders. "Because," Samuel said, "Father represented a challenge against the injustice of the United States political policies which took control of his choices in caring for his family."

Lorena admitted to herself that she had to think about all what Samuel had said. But, more pressing for her at that moment was her Aunt Tila's final response to Lorena's request for permission to attend the village school.

Later at the main meal, Tila joined Antonia, Eligia, and Lorena at the kitchen table. Tila looked at Antonia, "Did you give Lorena permission to attend the Indian village school?"

"Yes," Antonia cut a piece of meat for her plate, "Lorena can attend school since the Tutor, Fortunato contracted, never showed up." She glanced sideways at Tila.

"Please, Aunt Tila, can I go to school, it won't interfere with my chores," Lorena saw an opening in the discussion and pressed her interest.

"Well, it's dangerous along the road, but if your mother has agreed, I suppose you can go, but only after you do your afternoon chores," Tila demanded, "But, I will have to add another task, however, that Chapo was doing. Twice a week on Monday and Friday, Lorena, you must kill a chicken for Luisa to prepare," She looked at Eligia, "Eligia will show you how it's done," Tila served herself some Chile with meat and cut her tortilla in half, and then she added, "You can go, on condition that you kill a chicken, and if you do all your chores first. Do your chores first before you leave," Tila emphasized.

"Yes, I will, thank you Aunt Tila," in her mind, Lorena decided to accept, anything, to go to school, even if it was the local Indian village school.

As far as Lorena was concerned, her cousins can envy her from Mexico City, Tucson, or Paris. Lorena did not mind that, and she did not mind that to add to her problems, her Aunt Tila piled another chore for her to do, that as a chicken killer. The Mexican menu, Lorena knew well by now, after lengthy conversations with Luisa, in Sinaloa, called for chicken broth, chicken with rice, chicken in mole sauce, fried chicken, chicken soup, chicken tacos, and many more dishes created around the main element of chicken, and included some recipes that Luisa had herself invented in Aunt Tila's kitchen.

Later, on the way to the chicken yard, Lorena asked Eligia, "Do we have enough chickens so as not to run out before our school term ends?"

"Yes," Eligia said and she instructed Lorena, "Leave the egg laying hens alone; only kill the young '*pollos*', until this batch of pullets is gone, then we can start on the next group of chicks growing up for our skillet, don't worry," She laughed, and added, "Here is the way you grab a chicken; this is the way you twist." Before Lorena could count to one, two, three, Eligia had wrenched the pullet's neck. "Did you see?" Eligia laughed and hurried off to take the future delicious meal to Luisa.

In the following weeks, Lorena twisted chicken necks, in such a regular basis and in such an efficient manner, that soon when chickens saw her coming, they started running away from her. Only the big red rooster would dare confront Lorena in his futile efforts to protect his domain, but Lorena attacked him with her palanca and the two buckets, and he backed off. For her part, Lorena made sure that Luisa always had chickens, young meaty pullets, to magically turn into a tasty meal.

It became like a game of hide and seek: chickens saw Lorena, and they scampered off to hide. In the morning they ran to Lorena when she scattered their chicken feed. In the afternoons on neck wringing days, they hid under mezquite brush or ran away from her. Lorena really worried for their state of mind. She hated to wring the poor chickens'

The Worm in my Tomato

necks, but on the other hand, she rejoiced in finally going to school.

Nevertheless, from that time on, at least three days a week, when Lorena did not wring chicken necks, she ran over to look at her very own tomato and saw it change from its baby stage and began to grow larger as time went on. Lorena saw it gain color from pale green to a rich green before it began its metamorphosis from a pale pink, then soft red, then into a deeper red juicy tomato. Lorena's mouth watered in anticipation.

As Lorena twisted chicken heads off, she became certain that life in El Aliso was not in her best interest. Lorena's mind resumed planning her escape back to Miami to attend Bullion Plaza. She recalled how the tutor had been kidnapped by the federal army; now she worried about her teacher at the village school. She was sure no other teachers, in all of Sinaloa, would stay around to be found and drafted by the federal Army or worse yet, persecuted for being a Catholic.

In the meantime, when Eligia and Lorena did their chores, they both giggled, acted silly, and laughed as they held hands and twirled around and danced like fairies among the wild field grass. Oh, the wild grass was so high, green, and sweet, Lorena thought. Lorena and Eligia could hardly wait for each day at the village school; the girls hopped and skipped, and kicked at large orange grasshoppers on their way to school. As they walked toward the village El Mezquitalito along the road they passed El Potrero fields. A lone desolate tree stood on the plain beside the fence.

"What is that tree called?" Lorena asked Eligia.

"That is a huizache tree, a tree that grows in the plains and deserts of Sinaloa and other parts of Mexico; do you smell the sweet aroma of its flowers?" Eligia said.

"Yes, um, um, it is so pleasant; I will ask our teacher about the tree." Lorena said.

Lorena anticipated the time her father would harvest and become rich like the other Vega families and most important send her away to school. Lorena lived with that expectation in her mouth and daily chewed on it and swallowed all the hoped for goodness it would bring in the future.

The Worm in my Tomato

The Village School

As Lorena hurried to complete her tasks, her mind raced ahead of her, eager with ideas as well. The thought crossed her mind of making preparations for going on the road again to back home. Lorena planned to ask her teacher for a map of Mexico on which to outline her route on her journey back to Miami.

After 2:00 o'clock in the afternoon, on each day of school, Eligia and Lorena hurried north on the road for about a mile from the big house toward the Fuerte River, and then walked east, about two hundred yards, to a small dusty village of several mud adobe houses. This village, known as El Mezquitalito, surrounded by mezquite and huizache trees, sat on the flat empty dirt space fronting the desert on the south and east sides, and near the El Fuerte River on its north side. Close to the village they passed an empty one room adobe house that, according to Eligia, had been a stable for Lorena's Uncle Jorge's horses. Now it was empty and deserted. Some fifty yards almost in the center of the village was a white plastered one room adobe building. This was the school house.

The girls went in. The inside was dimly lit by outside light streaming through two open windows and the open door. There were rough benches to sit on. Lorena noticed right away that the room lacked student desks, a blackboard, and a teacher's desk. Lorena's lips automatically pursed and curled up to her nose. She wondered if Miss Yoakum would teach in a school like this one.

"Hello," said the teacher, and Lorena saw a pleasant looking man, clean shaven, small green eyes, and wearing a straw hat like the ones some men wore during the summer in Miami. "Welcome, my name is Mr. Luna; please take a seat on the bench."

There were less than twenty students and they were of all ages, five students in the seven to nine year old range, and the rest of them ranging in ages from ten to thirteen years. Lorena had turned ten years old in July, and Eligia was twelve. Students sat quiet and attentive to begin their day in school. Lorena was elated. At last Lorena thought she was in a school and eager to learn all she could. Lorena intended especially to ask questions about the geography of northern Mexico and how best to travel from here to Arizona.

When Lorena talked with Mr. Luna, she asked him for a map. "Mr. Luna, can you give me a map of how to travel from El Aliso to Arizona, United States?"

"Why do you want a map?" He asked.

Lorena was surprised and caught unprepared, so she stammered, "To go to the United States, to the state of Arizona."

He looked at Lorena, quizzically, "No, I have no maps, and moreover, if I were to draw one for you, I would have to discuss your request with your parents, first," Mr. Luna answered.

Lorena felt miserable and disappointed, but she intended to soak up new knowledge like dry frogs soak up rain water and resurrect again from the mother earth. Lorena was sure she would learn as much or more than her cousins attending expensive schools in Mexico City, the United States or Paris. Had not I just successfully finished my schooling from Eligia on how to do my chores and make my Aunt Tila happy, Lorena thought, and had not I proved to Aunt Tila that I was not a mule, Lorena smiled, and thought to herself, and what better testimony that I succeeded than the response from One Eye, who now everyday eagerly comes to me to be milked?

Time, like sand in an hour glass, sifted quickly into the vast eternity. Lorena lived in heaven as she breezed through her work chores and as she attended the small one room lime whitewashed school. Mr. Luna never gave an indication of being in the same level of academic achievement as Miss Yoakum, but he was a teacher and Lorena was attending school. So for now, all was well. Nonetheless, Lorena began to plan how she could get a map from Mr. Luna, a map to follow from El Aliso to Tucson, Arizona and then to Miami.

Lorena's immediate goal was to achieve self-dependency; Lorena intended to learn all she could and become self-sufficient. Lorena thought about her learning every day, and she would say

The Worm in my Tomato

to herself: I do not intend to work for Aunt Tila all my life. So, every day, Lorena attended school along with the village children. Lorena thought that Mr. Luna, by his asking many questions, had singled out Carmen, Eligia, and Lorena as his prize students. The few paper books were meager in content and soon Lorena and the other students were forced to rely only on verbal conversations with Mr. Luna which seemed to Lorena to quickly exhaust his store of knowledge. Soon, Lorena felt he was only giving them the top part of the lard in a spoon but that the bottom part of the spoon was empty. His reservoir of knowledge unlike the pond which had an unending supply of frogs, soon dried up. Mr. Luna began to talk about leaving in a month or so to attend a university in Guadalajara to study for an academic degree. Lorena, to get her map before Mr. Luna went away, once more asked him for a sketch north to the United States. Mr. Luna again said no, and in addition refused to discuss her request. Lorena sincerely believed that Mr. Luna did not know the way to Arizona and that was the reason he had not given her a map. He was going to Guadalajara and that state was in the south of Mexico, she thought. But Lorena thought that even if Mr. Luna did not know his way to Arizona, she still wanted him to stay and keep the school open. "Please, Mr. Luna, can't you stay and keep the school open? We students waited so long and I myself must go to school and get an education."

"No, I can't continue here. What's more, I must leave sooner than I had planned," Mr. Luna said.

Lorena felt cheated again from her desire to go to school. She ran home to her mother and once there in her room, she cried hysterically because her world had ended. Lorena would have continued weeping over her loss of the school, but she had other pressing problems. She was terribly hungry.

⌒

Lorena's attendance in the village school had opened a door to look into a world of village life she had not known existed. Telesforo and Lepo who worked part time in Tila's cheese room and sometimes helped at Tila's store lived in the village. Telesforo and his wife Marta had twelve children. Each had been named after a month of the year. Lorena made friends with three of the younger girls named Maya, Junis, and Julia, who were in school with her, but she called them the girl Three Months for short and to save time. Telesforo, known as the Philosopher in the village spent much time studying and meditating on the life of the ants that crawled on the ground beneath his mezquite tree. Lepo's wife was named Josefa and they had one daughter named Carmen who also attended school with Lorena and Eligia. Lepo owned a well for water in his back yard; for this reason he was considered the village rich man. Lorena had visited the home of the girl Three Months and had joined them in learning from Telesforo, their father, about the life of the ants. By listening to Telesforo, Lorena began to discover the world of nature and how to learn from it.

After Mr. Luna announced to his class that he would leave for Guadalajara, Lorena had been disappointed and had cried. But Lorena, in all reality, was so busy learning from 'Mother Nature' as Telesforo had said to her, that she felt that Mr. Luna's absence would probably not disappoint her that much. Besides, her mother had told her that another teacher would certainly be sent to replace Mr. Luna.

Lorena had discovered through her village friends that a different life existed in the village Mezquitalito from the life she knew at the Hacienda with Aunt Tila. There she and Eligia always had plenty of food to eat. But in the village, the residents did not have as much food. Carmen and the children of Telesforo and his wife Marta, called the "Twelve Months" for brevity, were by necessity as well taken up with keeping themselves from starving. The girl Three Months talked to Lorena about their friend Mr. Hunger. To Lorena's mind there began to appear another world, one full of invisible forces. She wondered about the strong force that had knocked Telesforo down to the ground, in a dizzy spell. Mr. Luna called the force *gravity*, her mother said it was faint from hunger, and her father said that Telesforo may have been stung by too many ants.

Lorena, now more than ever, appreciated her life in Tila's Big House. She rejoiced that her father seemed carried away with happiness over anticipation of harvesting his first year's crops. She felt that her father was already spending the dollars from the sale of his harvest; she worried that there might not be enough left for her education. Lorena's mother attributed Fortunato's behavior to hope; Julieta affirmed that Fortunato had faith; Lorena knew that her father felt joy. Mr. Luna called it a delusion. Josefa, Lepo's wife, brewed *hierbabuena* tea leaves and brought the tea to Luisa's kitchen for Fortunato to drink, and then she studied the bottom of his cup to read his designs of fate.

Lorena, whenever she found time from her work and even for a few minutes after her school class in the village, visited with the girl Three Months and with Carmen in her home. At least one or two Sundays, while on their way to attend prayer service at Julieta's home, Lorena, Antonia, Luisa, and Eligia had stopped for a brief visit with Josefa and Marta in the village.

Lorena noticed that El Mezquitalito's village endeavors continued to evolve in different areas of life. Lorena, ever curious about people, came to realize that Marta, Telesforo's wife, spent most of her time hiding from him. Telesforo, on the other hand, spent most of his time sitting in the shade of his mezquite tree, studying the ants on the ground. Lepo persistently guarded his water in his private well from villagers. The Twelve Months and Carmen had problems with their own personal invisible adversary that they called Mr. *Hunger.*

Mr. Luna did not know the kind of hunger that drove the village children to hunt for frogs, rattle snakes and large orange grasshoppers; he called it a need for nourishment and an appetite for food. Mr. Luna taught about eating well three times a day and the importance of a balanced diet. He showed his students in class pictures from magazines of breakfast, lunch and dinner in the United States to help his students understand basic required foods for proper growth. But Mr. Luna never brought a morsel of such foods for his students to sample.

Eligia alone sometimes smuggled out from Luisa's kitchen a tortilla and some beans for students to divide into ant size crumbs to reluctantly share. Lorena once had asked Teleforo, while he taught the girl Three Months, Carmen and Lorena under the tree, what was his main goal in life. Telesforo had said, after a long time pondering the question, "Someday, to eat a whole empanada by myself, alone." Lorena thought to herself that someday she would give Telesforo one empanada to eat by himself. The problem would be how to keep the Twelve Months from not being around Telesforo to beg their share of a morsel.

Lorena felt that if she were in similar circumstances as Telesforo, Catalina would not be around to beg for her piece of an empanada. Lorena in her thoughts, however, struggled with her feeling of selfishness. But Lorena comforted herself with the knowing this was make belief and that Catalina was still in El Bacori living with Uncle Eugenio and Aunt Sara, but most important, Lorena thought: Catalina is attending primary school and her teacher is not leaving to Guadalajara; her teacher lived in El Bacori. She frowned at her other thought that for sure, Santos would be there to beg his share. Lorena was disappointed that the school would close when Mr. Luna left for Guadalajara, but her resentment of his leaving, caused her to belittle his teaching and his status.

In the meantime, Lorena enjoyed the company of her friends and had much fun with Eligia, Carmen, and the Twelve Months. But Lorena's main thoughts now were about how to convince her Aunt Tila and Julieta to urge the federal government to send another teacher. Julieta and Antonia prayed novenas and rosaries for spiritual consolation and for God to send a clandestine priest to celebrate Mass. So why not pray for a teacher, as well, Lorena concluded. Lorena hoped that she, her mother, Catalina and Santos would have to return to Arizona, soon, because Lorena reflected that her father's harvest money would not be enough for all his plans: she feared that there would not be money left over to include for her education, as well.

The Worm in my Tomato

Twenty

Lorena
Premonitions

Samuel and Jose had left Tila's big house some months before, and Catalina lived in El Bacori with Eugenio and Sara; this situation may have influenced Lorena in a negative way. Lately, Lorena had been having preoccupations when doing her chores or going to school. She had a deep sense of fear that something bad was going to happen. Antonia had told Lorena to pray and not to worry. But Lorena's qualms led her to think about whether she should stay in her Aunt Tila's house or not. But then, Lorena wondered, where she could go?

As Lorena went about filling the kitchen pots with water, she saw through the open kitchen window dark clouds approaching from the west over the sierras. The dark clouds appeared menacing. I hope the storm doesn't break before I milk One Eye, Lorena thought. She hated the uncertainty of the unknown.

Life in El Aliso, day after day, at the big house and at the field, required hard work in all the chores Lorena did with the help of Eligia, but there were moments of laughter, and time for Lorena to attend the school in the native village. Yet, at times, Lorena dreaded this situation as being transient. Lorena smiled, *transient* remembering Miss Yoakum's vocabulary drills. Somehow, Lorena felt tragic times of some sort would come to make life miserable and change life around. First of all, from very early on, Antonia did not fare as well. Antonia's and Aunt Tila's friendship and relationship had deteriorated slowly at first and then accelerated. Antonia discussed this situation with Lorena, and Lorena really thought it was a personality conflict.

Lorena had mentioned the problem to her father, but he had shrugged his shoulders and merely said, "It is only two hard headed women, with their minds made up on seeking different kinds of life and believing in different styles of living." Fortunato had put his coffee cup down on the kitchen table and had stridden out the door and had

The Worm in my Tomato

gone to tend to his tomatoes. For sure, Lorena thought, her mother and Aunt could not live under the same roof. But Fortunato insisted they do, unable to figure out to where else he could move his wife.

As Lorena hurried to finish all her day chores, she thought about her mother. While she milked One Eye, Lorena remembered that her mother had always been a pious and quiet woman. In Miami, Antonia had always liked to care for her family, keep the house clean, cook tasty and hearty meals, wash and iron, and yet find time to pray her rosary or pray her novenas for the departed souls. Lorena, while spreading seed for the chickens, thought about how her mother had always attended Church on Sundays and made certain all her family accompanied her to holy Mass. Lorena thought, while pouring water for the pigs, how her mother had a strong commitment for doing what is just and good. She always helped the poor and down and out. For example, Lorena remembered while she ran after a *"pollo" to* wring off its neck, how Antonia had provided a home for the two religious sisters that had arrived in Miami, after they escaped Mexico's religious persecution. Lorena remembered what Samuel had said about the conflict between the Mexican government and the Catholic Church, known as the Cristero War of 1926 to 1929; how the conflict culminated in a heavily fought armed struggle with tragic results of loss of human lives on both sides.

Indeed, many priests and sisters had taken refuge in the United States. Antonia, while the family yet lived in Miami, had turned a small two room house into a small one-bed room and kitchen apartment, located behind and adjacent to her family house in Live Oak Street. Antonia had provided shelter and food for the two religious nuns for two years until Antonia and her family was railroaded on the Repatriation train to Mexico.

The storm clouds were directly over her head now, and Lorena rushed toward the "Big House" with her *palanca's* buckets flapping in the gusty wind. Large drops of rain began to pelt Lorena as she quickened her gait. While Lorena got wet, she remembered that she had argued vehemently against their leaving Miami, yes *vehemently*, thank you Miss Yoakum, Lorena thought, and yet Lorena remembered with some remorse that she was first on the train, in obedience to her father. *Obedience*, yes, thank you Nanita, Lorena thought; Lorena

The Worm in my Tomato

knew that her mother in obedience to her Catholic faith, and at Nanita's suggestion, had carried her Christian cross, in her marriage, and followed father to Sinaloa. Well, here we are in El Aliso, Lorena thought, cooking ourselves raw in the midday heat and freezing in the desert cold at three a.m. before dawn. And now as Lorena ran soaking wet to reach the Big House, she wondered if Nanita, Antonia, her mother, and the Catholic Church understood that it was the whole family that would be obliged to carry the Christian cross. Who the heck moved the Big House further away while I was busy with my chores, Lorena wondered. Anyway, Lorena thought, she still hoped in some reward from her father's tomato harvest. Oh, for certain, Lorena thought, the sale of those tomatoes will set me free from this misery.

Antonia and her family lived, however, in Tila's house, in a strained situation. The two perceptions of life and work like the North and the South would never agree.

Tila on the other hand, different from Antonia, was a very practical business oriented woman. Tila believed in no nonsense, preoccupied with frugality, faithful in hard work had for years made a profitable enterprise of her agricultural fields and her ranch store. Where many in the valley had given up in desperation and gone to the cities to seek a livelihood, Tila persistently survived and remained in business; she meant to keep her lands bequeathed to her by her father Don Eudoro. Tila endeavored to keep peace with the federal government over religion by keeping it to herself, and she wished Antonia would cease her religious activities with Julieta.

During one of their heated arguments, Antonia asked Tila, "Should we move out?"

"Yes, move out," Tila answered.

"You don't want us in your house?" Antonia asked.

"No, and furthermore, you should leave as soon as possible," Tila responded.

Fortunato, in spite of his desire to stay out of this sister and wife dispute found himself obliged to deal with these bones of contention. Fortunato's question in his mind was what to do about the relationship between his wife, Antonia, and his sister Tila. Fortunato suffered in consternation about what would happen to

The Worm in my Tomato

his own relationship with his wife and his sister.

Fortunato and his family were in El Aliso only three months during the year 1932, when in this short time, they all realized all too soon that they came into the area as outsiders from *El Norte*, from the United States. Perhaps, because for a number of years, Fortunato had resided outside of Mexico, he, too, was considered an outsider. His family's southwestern culture and spoken Spanish dialect caused disapproval of them by local Mexican residents who ridiculed his family members for speaking *pocho*, clipped Spanish. The indigenous who inhabited El Mezquitalito, who themselves spoke Spanish *pocho* with their own peculiar accent, were more tolerant in every way of Fortunato's family members than were his own extended family. But more serious, his nuclear family's problems, based on personality conflict between his wife and his sister Tila and other members of his large extended family, began soon after Fortunato and his family had arrived. Thus, although Fortunato's family had been welcomed into a home with many rooms by his sister Tila, and given space to live in the Big House in El Aliso, it was only for a few months; Antonia's personality and style of life soon clashed with Tila's.

Fortunato's wife, dressed in her dark gray skirt, her long black hair done up in a bun, her large round brown eyes narrowed, and her fists resting on her hips, would speak up in defense of local Indians, "It is not fair to dip a large spoon of *manteca* in the can and smear only the top of the spoon on the wax paper and leave the deep part of the spoon full of lard, and to return it to its cooking fat container; then charge the native for a whole spoon-full," Antonia would indignantly defend the native customer when she helped out in Tila's ranch store.

"Antonia, one has to make a profit, or go out of business," Tila would retort.

Fortunato knew that his wife always had believed in helping the poor and the underdog. Antonia chafed at the treatment given the local Mayos, indigenous inhabitants. Eventually, she and Tila had words. "You must leave this house, Antonia," Tila demanded.

Tila, all five feet five inches of her heavy set body, dressed in a black skirt and white blouse, with Tila's head covered with a *tapalo*, her hazel eyes in her round fair face, stared at Fortunato and from under

The Worm in my Tomato

her head shawl, she scowled: "Your wife is intolerable. You and your family must get out of my house," Tila said.

Fortunato did not feel that he could argue the point with his sister. Clearly, he felt that perhaps he and his family had overstayed their welcome. Fortunato planned to bargain for more time. "We have no place to go, Tila, could we not have more time?" Fortunato asked.

"No, move," Tila said, and in keeping with her nature in being punctual in all things said, "Furthermore, you must leave today."

Fortunato talked with his brother Jorge about what to do. Jorge suggested that Fortunato could move his family into Jorge's old one room adobe house with an outdoor *ramada* located in El Mezquitalito. Fortunato moved his family to the one-room adobe hut at the edge of the native pueblo, El Mezquitalito. Fortunato was grateful that his brother Jorge let him borrow the hut. At one time the hut had served as a stable for Jorge's horses. Later, a family had lived there, but it had been empty for some time. Antonia and her daughter Lorena had a tough job ahead of them in cleaning up the place.

For his part, Fortunato would continue to stay at his sister's house, for the time being at least, to remain close to the fields and finish his work until the harvest. He also felt that in this way he could maintain a brother and sister friendly relationship. Every so often, Fortunato planned to go visit his wife at the hut and spend some time with her. Fortunato knew that life would be doubly hard for them, but he hoped that once he harvested his crops, he would find a better place for his family to live.

When Lorena, wet to the bone and shivering, dried herself in her room and changed to clean clothes, heard from her mother that they were moving out of her Aunt Tila's house, Lorena almost fainted. Lorena felt a rush of emotion and amazement engulfed her and she could not talk. Finally, she said, "What?"

"We have to move out," Antonia said.

"But, why," Lorena stammered, "What happened?"

"Tila wants us out right now. Your father has arranged for us to occupy a hut in the Indian pueblo, El Mezquitalito. Start packing; your father will be here with Chapo and the wagon." Outside, Lorena heard a lightning strike nearby. Santos ran in fear to Antonia, seeking protection in her arms, "Oh, my poor baby, ya, ya, it's all right," Antonia said, and added, "Wonder how Catalina is doing, if she heard that lighting in El Bacori, she is probably under her bed, now."

Lorena was dazed. "But what about my chores, my school," Lorena sat down, "What will we eat," she asked, and she became angry, "Why, this is a second Repatriation, mama," she said dejected. Lorena sat on the bed and covered her head with the bed spread and said, "No kidding, mother, while I did my chores, we were repatriated to El Mezquitalito, a native Indian village, why?" Lorena cringed as another lightning struck close by, "Mama," Lorena said, "We, for sure, are not citizens of the native pueblo; we will be crossing borders illegally this time. We are refugees at the mercy of the villagers." Lorena hoped, nevertheless, they would be accepted as part of the community. She knew that there were no more choices, as Jose had once told her.

Lorena felt, on the good side of things, that she would not have many problems living in the native pueblo because she attended school there and had friends there. Lorena thought to herself about her friends Carmen and the girl Three Months and she smiled. The rain outside had quit pelting the Big House and the storm had moved on to harass other areas.

"Our friends who live in El Mezquitalito, Lorena, will be happy to see us live there." Antonia said.

"The Twelve Months and Carmen along with their parents, I am sure, will welcome us in the village." Lorena answered, "I don't mind being repatriated again, if I must. I like the pueblito, besides, I have gone local anyway," Lorena said and added, "Now, I wear open leather strapped sandles made by the local native leather worker." Lorena's skirts and blouses were made of hand woven cotton cloth. She had become totally native; when Lorena saw her reflection in the bucket of well water in a recent early morning, she did not recognize herself.

But Lorena, even if she was forced to move, did not intend to move without a word or two with her father. "When father comes to Aunt Tila's house to move us, I intend to let him know how I feel and ask him if we can stay," Lorena told herself.

The sky cleared all of a sudden copying the manner in which the storm had approached. Fortunato and Chapo arrived to move Antonia

The Worm in my Tomato

and Lorena's things. Antonia again would have to get rid of much of her furniture that could not possibly fit in a one room hut. Only the bare minimum of bedding, cooking utensils, chairs and tables, and personal clothing would be moved to the hut.

"Please father, let's stay," Lorena pleaded. "I am going to school every day with Eligia in the afternoons." Lorena said to Fortunato.

"No, we must move. You can keep going to the village school from where we will live, in fact, I can't think of any reason why you can't continue going to the school," he said, and again, he impatiently paced the floor, back and forth like a caged tiger. "In fact you will be closer than from here; now I have borrowed the wagon from Chapo," Fortunato stopped and stared at Lorena, "And he is willing to help us move," he spun around and hurried out carrying Antonia's things that she had bundled and placed on top of her bed in what had been Antonia's room.

Lorena turned to face her mother who was already packing additional items including bed sheets, blankets, and kitchen utensils. "Can't you convince him, mother?" Lorena appealed to Antonia, "We have what we need here and I am going to a school, first time since we came from Miami."

"Your Aunt Tila wants us out today," Antonia answered firmly, "Now, pack Santos' pants, shirts, and his sandals," she continued to pack and arrange, and she ignored Lorena. But Antonia, however, like a mother eagle felt compelled to gently insist on her eaglet to fly.

"But I want to stay," Lorena sensed that the move would only sink her family further into poverty and that she would not enjoy Luisa's fine meals. "Besides, finally I have begun to perform my chores as well, if not better than Eligia," Lorena knew that if her family ended up in destitution, the situation would preclude her from making her escape. Living at Aunt Tila's, if I ran away north, at least my mother and Santos would have a place to stay and then move out when father becomes rich with the sale of his cotton and tomatoes, Lorena thought.

"We are moving today, and that is final, don't nag anymore," Antonia said.

Fortunato returned from the village hut with the wagon pulled by two mules for a second load. Chapo, Antonia, and Lorena again helped Fortunato load up the wagon; Fortunato and Chapo drove away with the wagon.

"Well, that was the last load," Antonia said.

"Aunt Tila is no where to be seen," Lorena looked about the house.

"She may be in the Cheese room supervising the cheese making, or she may be in the store selling a large not so full spoon of lard to some poor village client," Antonia answered.

Before Antonia and Lorena walked out of the house, Luisa and Eligia wished them the best. Luisa and Antonia had become good friends like Eligia and Lorena. Luisa worked so hard but she always had a smile for all persons who were in her presence. Eligia, like her mother smiled and laughed at almost anything. Lorena would miss them both. They all hugged. Luisa and Eligia cheek-kissed Santos, who each time wiped away the kisses from his cheeks with his chubby hand.

Antonia and Lorena walked a mile, in no time, to a one room adobe hut that Lorena had seen before. Of course, Lorena remembered. Their new home turned out to be Uncle Jorge's old horse stable. It had been cleaned out after its stable days and there were signs some other human beings had occupied it but who had long departed from it. Lorena prayed to God that she and her mother would soon depart, as well, even before they moved in; if only we could, Lorena thought to herself.

It took Lorena a long while to overcome her temptation to scream to heaven beyond the clouds and complain the injustice of all this, "How can I bring in my new shoes into this old horse stable, mother?" Lorena complained.

"Wrap them up carefully in a towel," Antonia answered.

"Definitely, thank you Miss Yoakum, *definitely*, for sure, mother," Lorena said, and then she thought: I must make plans in a few days to vacate this miserable place.

Antonia inspected in her usual quiet way every corner of the hut, planning how to make their home a nest. Antonia was a nester. She always knew how to change a place into a homey nest for her family. The first thing she did was open the large tin trunk and take out the *bultos* statues of Saints and *retablos* or flat pictures of Saints, a picture of *Our Mother Virgin Mary*, and a wooden crucifix with Jesus Christ nailed to the cross showing his pain and suffering in a grimacing face. She carefully placed her spiritual members of her family on top of a wooden three foot high dresser. She had made her corner small altar where she would say her rosary and her novenas. The pictures of her spiritual family occupied a whole corner of the hut, by themselves. That left three corners for Antonia, Lorena, and Santos.

But Lorena knew it was useless to argue that fact of critical space with her mother. Antonia left many things behind in Miami to make room in her old tin trunk for her spiritual family, riding on the train with her and her flesh and blood family. Spiritual saints and human family, all victims of the United States Repatriation were now repatriated from the Big House. Antonia sympathized with her saints. They had paid no train fare, had illegally crossed the border, they were in fact worse off than legally repatriated Mexicans. Her saints were repatriated as well, and Antonia respected them for their accommodating spirit, something she felt lacking in her own children.

Lorena always wondered when her mother's spiritual family would help *her*, Lorena, escape across the border. Had not the holy family, as her mother called them, been immigrants to Egypt, but they had returned home, thought Lorena. We shared something in common; so why did they not hear or answer my prayers, Lorena wondered. While sweeping out her corner of the hut, Lorena asked her mother, "Why mother, do your saints cross borders without problems?"

"Don't be silly, Lorena, Saints are spiritual," Antonia shook her head sideways like saying 'no', "Saints are universal and go wherever they please; for them all nations are nations without borders," Antonia said, "Haven't you learned that in school," Antonia wanted to know.

"Well," Lorena persisted, "I wish I was spiritual; I'd be back in Miami by now."

⌇⟶

El Mezquitalito

So it finally happened, Antonia's family, what was left of it, went from the frying pan into the fire, as the saying goes. Lorena hated to leave behind her Aunt Tila's large, warm kitchen and well stocked pantry with plenty of food. When Antonia and Lorena moved to El

The Worm in my Tomato

Mezquitalito, Lorena honestly thought that now for sure, her mother, her baby brother Santos and she without a doubt would starve. Lorena, without a doubt, knew that her friends the girl Three Months' and Carmen's *Amigo*, Mr. Hunger would soon welcome her to the village.

Fortunato moved his family to a one-room adobe hut at the edge of the native pueblo in El Mezquitalito. Lorena noticed that her father's former five foot ten inch body now stooped to make him look much shorter. His former muscular body had lost weight over the last few months. The hot sun in the fields, as Fortunato supervised his workers, had tanned his usual potato white skin to a brown cooked potato. His once-upon-a-time black neatly trimmed hair of his former days as a gambler in Miami now hung long, sweaty and string like. Lorena pitied her father. "Oh, how I remember him, in former times in Miami, dressed in his dark blue suit, white starched shirt, and bow tie, as he went to manage the gambling table at Limonada's Pool Hall," Lorena told her mother more than once. "He would always kiss you mother on the cheek and say goodbye to us. He would look at us tenderly and say, "Lorena, let's see what kind of cookies they have out tonight, and I will bring home some two dozen from the Pastry Shop, do you remember mama?" Lorena asked.

Now, in Mezquitalito, a changed man, transformed into a gruff and shabby rancher, spoke to Antonia and Lorena, "Goodbye, Antonia, Lorena," Fortunato waved at them. Fortunato picked up Santos and gave him a peck of a kiss on his cheek. "I will come visit you as often as I can." Fortunato climbed into the wagon and yelled for the mules to move on, "Hyeah, hyeah." Mother and Lorena waved goodbye to Fortunato as he led the mule- pulled wagon back up the road toward

The fields in El Aliso.

A small jacal (house) of the Indigenous in the village.

The Worm in my Tomato

the Big House. Santos wiped the kiss from his cheek with his chubby hand. "Mama," said Lorena, "Why did Chapo say that he would come back to visit us as often as he can."

"Don't be silly, Lorena, that was your father," Antonia said in a dubious voice.

Antonia and Lorena got busy. They cleaned and swept; Lorena hauled a bucket of water from the nearby bovine watering pond. They washed inside the hut with pond water. They set up two cots and covered each with a blanket. The cots for mother and Santos were set in one corner and Lorena's cot was placed in another corner of the shed. The floor was hard packed dirt. There was one window and one door to the hut. Both door and window faced the village plaza. In front of the door was a ramada constructed of mezquite poles and thatched with large palm branches. Under the ramada was a large adobe brick stove. The adobe brick stove was plastered with red clay. Outside the ramada was a large oven for baking bread, made in the same fashion as the stove. The stove had a place to hold up a flat iron for making tortillas and another square space for cooking in a large pan or skillet. The fire space, directly below the top of the stove, had room for lighting a fire with brush and mezquite logs broken to the proper size. The oven simply allowed for a fire of mezquite chips and larger wood pieces to burn directly inside the oven. At the proper time when the oven was hot, the tin cover at the entrance would be pulled aside to allow for bread pans to be placed inside for baking.

Of course, for Antonia and Lorena, the cooking and the baking were at this point only a castle in the sky. They had no flour, no lard, no eggs, no milk, no beans, nothing, not even matches to light a fire. Both Antonia and Lorena would from time to time look expectantly up the road toward the big house, watching and waiting for a miracle. Lorena really expected her father or even Chapo to return with food and other household materials from her Aunt Tila's store. The road was always empty, only the shimmering of heat waves could be seen in the distance. In the shimmering heat waves Lorena made out the gray figures of men on horses. The men wore metal helmets and they sat tall in their saddles. What did they want, why did they come, where were they going? Lorena was quickly bathed in cold sweat. She rubbed her eyes. There was nothing on the steamy dirt road.

Before dark, Fortunato galloped up in his horse to the hut's yard. He apologized for being so late in getting back; he explained that he had had to complete his work in the fields. "Here are a few dry food items, some tin cans for your cots, matches, salt, tortillas, cheese, and some meat burros that Luisa made for you, and a *talega* of water," Fortunato handed them the sack. Antonia and Lorena hurriedly received the gunny sack full with the items in their hands. Fortunato rode off into the night. Lorena wondered if her father would join the phantoms on the road and disappear into nowhere.

In the wagon, Antonia and Lorena had brought a kerosene lamp, some linen, blankets, a small hatchet, and two straight back chairs from Antonia's furniture. The rest of Antonia's furniture, beds, a sofa, and all of her household items, icebox, stove, and much of her clothes had remained at Tila's Big House and in boxes in a shed near the chicken coop. She planned to sell all her furniture and some of her clothes to the Vega families. Fortunato had said that he would help Antonia sell her furniture by informing his extended Vega families and friends. Santos only had a few clothing items like pants, undershirts and underpants, a pair of sandals. Lorena fared no better with a few cotton dresses, underclothing, and a pair of sandals. Antonia had not much more than Lorena did in the way of clothing.

There was not much room in the one room hut and the one ramada. The tin cans numbered only six, old sardine cans that Aunt Tila had for sale in her store. Fortunato had probably bargained for the food items and the cans and consequently got further in debt to his sister. Poor father, Lorena thought. She carefully placed one sardine can under each leg of the cots, and she filled each sardine can with pond water. This was to prevent scorpions crawling about the dirt floor at night from climbing into bed with Antonia or Lorena. Antonia placed a wood board, four feet long, one inch thick and one foot high that was already leaning against the wall inside the hut across along the foot of the outside front door. "This will keep the rattlers out," Antonia said, "I think." But Lorena saw her bless the window and the door to keep out evil and uninvited guests and snakes.

An uninvited guest Antonia and Lorena could not keep out was named *Hunger*. The first three days they ate the food, but any left over pieces and crumbs would spoil in a day with the heat. But too soon there were fewer items they could eat, by themselves, alone; they lacked enough food items in a variety to combine into edible meals.

After the first week, Antonia and Lorena began to scavenge the desert behind on the south side of their hut. They knocked down *pitahayas* from the high saguaros to eat. Antonia and Lorena knocked down the red pulpy round fruit from the top of saguaros with a long thin mezquite pole they had cut and stripped with the small hatchet. Antonia and Lorena ate *tunas*, the purple red pulpy small pickle shaped fruit, they gathered from prickly cactus plants. They cleaned off the fuzz and stickers by rubbing the *tunas* on the ground. They also harvested wild spinach that grew along water ditches. The natives called this delicious wild spinach, *quelite*. Antonia boiled the broad green leaves in a pot until done, and she and Lorena ate it with beans, salt, and a slice of hard cheese.

Hunger returned each morning and stayed for breakfast. *Hunger* kept them company throughout the day; kept them awake at night, and slept with them until the next morning. But since Antonia and Lorena lacked food, hunger persisted in obnoxious ways and would not leave. Lorena hated the uninvited guest that persisted in staying until fed. *Hunger* was never fed, thus from the beginning *Hunger* became a family member: closer to each one of us than each one of us to each other, Lorena thought.

Santos became pale, thin, and sickly, with droopy sleepy eyes. He ate everything Antonia and Lorena ate but there was not enough food. Antonia and Lorena would at times eat less in order to share food with the baby. "What else can we do, mama?" Lorena asked Antonia the question. How long before they starved into a slow oblivion and join the phantoms on the road to nowhere, Lorena wondered, and she often looked up the dirt road and waited for her phantom to gallop up on his horse and bring them another sack of food. To encourage the return of the phantoms, Lorena would walk up the road from the village to as far as the corner of El Potrero field and stand underneath the huizache tree. There under its shade, Lorena felt a serenity followed by comfort she knew not from where it came, but she was moved to pray.

The Worm in my Tomato

Twenty One

Antonia
El Mezquitalito and Antonia's neighbors

A lot of open ground lay between Antonia's *adobe* horse-stable-hut and the desert thickets behind it. The desert, from miles around the village, crept up to their backyard. The deep blue unending sky had its horizons in the four spiritual directions: east, west, north, and south, pinned down by mountain ranges. Yet, the village could not escape the hot sun by day and the stars and moon by night.

It was into this small one room hut in this tiny village that the universe came to Antonia. She felt like being isolated, completely in the dark. She only knew what was in her memory; the outside world was hidden from her. She felt captive in time and space.

"I do not know how to control my unknown existence," she said to Lorena. She knew that her present time and circumstances called for urgent decisions on her part and that her space demanded a change. She knew that the new environment demanded learning for survival. She knew they were refugees in a poor native village.

Antonia started to think of asking Julieta's opinion on serious matters troubling her, thoughts about continuing to stay here in El Mezquitalito or finally return to Arizona; she questioned how long she must carry her Christian cross in supporting her husband. But what actions could she take within her responsibilities to her family and to Fortunato within their marriage, she wondered?

The village consisted of about two dozen adobe houses all spaced away from each other about fifty yards. The indigenous people here, Antonia noticed, kept their houses well separated from others. In the center of the village was a large flat dirt plaza used for religious dances and other cultural fiestas. Their adobe house, Antonia noticed, resembled all other houses in that each had a *ramada*. "All the other houses in the village," Antonia remarked to Lorena, "are larger than our mud hut."

"All the houses are constructed of brown sun-dried adobe brick," Lorena offered, "But their houses were meant to be a house, while ours was meant to be a stable for Uncle Jorge's horses," Lorena said.

Each house had a *ramada* or outside thatch roofed addition where inside the ramada the *estufa* was located for cooking. Outside and away from the ramada was located the *horno* for baking bread. Guests and neighbors paid their respects to each other by making friendly visits among themselves. They would sit on the ground, on old tree cut stumps, or on some old wooden bench, if available, to visit outdoors under the ramada shade, to avoid the hot sun, and hold long conversations, especially in the early evenings when stories were told, toasted the occasion with *mezcal*, and sang and laughed into the night.

Antonia's closest neighbors across the road from her house were friendly. One of the neighbors across the road named Lepo worked at Tila's place and Antonia and Lorena had previously seen him and his wife Josefa working in the cheese room. Lepo and Josefa helped make the cheese. Lepo made periodical scheduled trips to San Blas or other neighboring *municipios* and larger towns to market the cheese and other products from Tila's store. Lepo and Josefa had a *noria*, the only water well in the village. Consequently, Lepo was the village rich man. They had dug the water well themselves, and according to Carmen, their daughter, who was about Lorena's age, and befriended Lorena, her father Lepo guarded the water like if it was gold. Lepo's family drank cool, fresh, and clean gold. On the other-hand, Antonia and Lorena, on their side of the road, had to get water from the *laguna*, a small

The Worm in my Tomato

pond that was more like a watering hole located down the road from their house. Cows waded into the *laguna* to drink their fill. Thousands of frogs populated the small pond and the frogs had nothing better to do than to serenade the moon with constant croaking in the evenings and into the night.

Carmen talked to Lorena and Antonia outside their house in the yard space between the two homes. Carmen told them many things about the area. Antonia and Lorena for the moment were mainly interested in what wild plants were edible.

The first night in El Mezquitalito was black. Antonia and Lorena were struck by the uncountable multitude of stars in the black sky that they saw when sitting outside and gazing into the unending bejeweled universe. Antonia remembered that in Miami the town lights and their reflection blurred out the stars. At Tila's big house, Antonia had not had the impression of the stars outside. She wondered why. It dawned on her that Tila's house was surrounded by tall large mezquite trees, and that the *cachimbas* kept the inside of the rooms illumined with some degree of light. In contrast, Antonia's hut and the village were dark at night time; the night depended on the stars and the moon for light.

Yet, before long, Antonia and Lorena could find their way in the dark in their little one room adobe house with one window and one door leading to the outside ramada or lean-to- kitchen with its adobe plastered wood stove, with a flat iron on top for making tortillas. That was it, the inside and outside of their nest. So Antonia and Lorena spent much of their time looking at the stars at night. The village had a few mezquite and *huizache* trees that provided shade in the day time. The land was flat, hard dirt, sun baked, dusty and empty. Carmen said the open plaza was the place for the village fiesta celebrations and dances. Each house outside had its *horno* for baking bread, and beside the horno there was a pile of mezquite wood. Wood choppers brought cut wood on donkeys, from the desert, to sell or trade. This reminded Antonia of Mr. Galvan, who sold firewood throughout Miami's neighborhoods. Here Lorena and sometimes Antonia, carrying Santos along on her hip, went out to cut their own wood from the desert behind their hut.

Antonia said to Lorena, "I have noticed that there are no clothes lines on which to hang the washing."

"No, mama, because according to Carmen, the women and young girls wash their dirty clothes down in the river along the shoreline, banging the clothes on flat rocks and using home-made lye soap or soap purchased at Aunt Tila's store, hand-squeezing out the water, and spreading the clothes to dry on top of bushes under the hot sun during the day," explained Lorena. Thereafter, Antonia and Lorena took Santos with them under one arm and a gunny sack full of their dirty clothes to wash along the river shore. There, they discovered that village men and women used areas of the river where they could bathe in privacy. Thereafter, Antonia and Lorena with Santos in tow frequented the river to bathe. Santos loved to splash in the water and became a regular skinny tadpole.

The days were hot, the evenings cool, late nights were cold, and at dawn the desert village was teeth- shattering cold. There was season when clouds passed by and rained elsewhere. This rural area was arid with little rainfall. There were at times pleasant breezy nights, depending on the seasonal climate.

Outside the hut, in the desolate but abundant vegetation desert tract of land, giant saguaros stretched up thick green thorny arms to hold up the sky. Desert night owls perched on top of tall saguaros from where they pounced on field rats and other small game.

All three inhabitants in Antonia's hut always knew when it was dawn because Mr. Hunger in their stomach would wake them up to the dark silent reality that it was cold and that they were hungry. Antonia felt abandoned, alone, isolated from the world she had known. Now, her grocery store stretched for miles outside her home, but she had to find and gather what was edible. She and Lorena had no alternative but to learn what were the edible vegetation and animals available in their grocery store. Time had run out and the forbidding space held the promise of life; the relationship between the possibility of that life or its twin, death, rested in their heart's courage and in their mind's reasonable determination. Baby Santos was instantly weaned from babyhood and milk and changed to a reality of escaping the dangers of poverty.

Antonia in desperation prayed to her saints in heaven, not the statues and the retablos on top of her altar, whose icons were images which reminded her of the real saints in heaven. She prayed with all her heart for food for Lorena and Santos. Not long after, before noon, there were visitors from Mezquitalito. Carmen and her mother Josefa came with a cup of beans, a pinch of salt, a table spoon full of lard, four eggs, six comal made tortillas, some stick matches, and a canvas bag, large like a leather purse, called a *talega*, filled with water from their well. Josefa hung the talega from a mezquite cross pole in the ceiling of the ramada.

"The air when it blows will help keep your water cool, Mrs. Vega," She said, and both she and Carmen departed, saying, "We will come again when moved in our heart."

Josefa did not know how to address Antonia because Josefa knew that Antonia somehow was related to the rich Vega clan in the valley and both Josefa and her husband Lepo worked for Tila, the very rich lady owner of much land and the ranch store.

Other village residents did not know how to react to their neighbors from the north, the rich United States; they saw Antonia and Lorena daily gathering food from the desert, try to fish in the river, chase frogs and fail to catch them, and other very odd things that they did. Some villagers considered their strange neighbors pretended to be poor but perhaps were crazy, rich Americanos. Everybody in the village had always considered anyone from the United States either crazy or close to it.

Antonia's immediate plans were to make friends with her neighbors from El Mezquitalito. Fortunately, her daughter Lorena knew the boys and girls who attended the village school with her. Of these students, Carmen lived across the road from their hut. Also across the road on the opposite side lived Mr. Telesforo, his wife Marta, and their twelve children ranging in age from two years old to twenty-four. The seven girls were older than the boys. The oldest boy was ten. The parents had named each one of their twelve children after the names of the calendar months. Thus their names were Enera, Febrera, Marsis and Abrilis, these were the four oldest girls; Maya, Junis, and Julia were the youngest of ages sixteen, fourteen, and twelve; these younger girls were Lorena's school buddies. Augosto, Septiembre, Octubre, Noviembre, and Deciembre were the five boys, and they ranged in age from ten to two years. Lorena, Eligia, and Carmen called them the *Twelve Months* for short, or when playing with the girls they called each one of them by their given month name or grouped them into the girl *Seven Months*. But Lorena called her three school friends the girl Three Months. The boys, Lorena combined them into the boy *Five Months*.

Antonia looked out the one window of the hut on the side of the wall facing the road. Antonia saw that the green leaves of the trees were held tight by their stems and not one was dancing with the breeze because, as Josefa had said, "The world somewhere else held the wind captive." Antonia remembered, as she had learned from Josefa, who had said, "When the wind blows, it carries the heavy precious aroma of the huizache tree's flowers."

Josefa returned again when she saw Julieta come over on her horse to visit Antonia. The three women sat outside in the ramada. The day baked in an extremely hot day; nothing stirred, only the sound of a lost bumble bee could be heard. The women, dressed in light cotton skirts, except Julieta who always wore her riding pants and high boots, perspired and fanned themselves, all the while talking and laughing.

The orange glow of the sun high overhead reflected from the bovine pond not far down the road but visible from the hut's ramada. The shimmering vapors could be seen rising up into the airless void of a sand colored afternoon. "What brings you into our village, Mrs. Antonia?" Josefa asked.

"We were forced out from El Aliso, from my sister-in-law Tila's comfortable large home," Antonia told Josefa and Julieta. "We moved here to El Mezquitalito. It was an easy move and light because I had sold much of my American made furniture."

Antonia, while she had owned her American made furniture, entertained hopes of using it, and she had always felt from it a rooted sense of connection with Arizona. But by now, although she had let go of everything American to assist her family's survival, she held to her yearning for being there, anyway, after her five years of helping Fortunato would end. She never forgot that she and Fortunato had agreed to return to Arizona after five years in Sinaloa. But Antonia always had felt some doubt that it would come to pass.

"What does Fortunato say about all this?" asked Julieta.

"He helped us move in a wagon," Antonia answered. "But two

days before the move, at noon, during an escape from his riding on horse back and supervising the field workers, he rode up and told me, in a voice charged with resentment: 'Tila had wanted you out the same day because of your conflict with her over her treatment of village resident customers in her store.'" Antonia said.

"That's like all men," laughed Josefa, "Lepo is the same; they blame their wives for all their problems."

"Yes, he shook with resentment and glared at me, he blamed me for our having to move out," Antonia said, and she poured out warm water from the *talega* in three clay cups, and handed each of her friends a cup. "It is not hot enough for coffee, but the wind has not blown today cool enough for the water in the talega."

Julieta and Josefa sipped from their cup. Antonia chased away the lethargic bumble bee. The trees stood still in the yard. Not a single bird came by to rustle its feathers and shake the tree limbs. "Well, I think there might be other reasons besides me. Lorena and I rushed to pack our bed sheets, blankets, and what little clothes we had. We packed pans and skillets that I had brought with my furniture from Miami," Antonia said, and she shooed away the bumble bee which had returned and bumped into things around the hut.

"Good for you, Antonia," Julieta said and added, "How did your daughter Lorena feel?"

"I was ready to leave, but Lorena hated it. She told me that she hated moving away from her room and bed in the Big House, and she dreaded leaving her meals in Luisa's kitchen," Antonia dried tears from her eyes with her handkerchief. "My brave daughter Lorena carried in both her hands, held tightly, her only precious personal treasure: her new black leather shoes, carefully wrapped and placed in a shoe box, which she brought with her from Miami. She only wore them once, on the train. But when we arrived at San Blas, she removed them from her feet after she saw the rough boards on Chapo's wagon," Antonia smiled, "Imagine that, she did not want to scratch them. She has always been a cultured girl, very demanding on herself."

The women laughed. "Isn't that cute? What a careful girl!" Julieta said.

"Oh, she always protected her shoes and now has them safeguarded under the altar," Antonia pointed to the small wood table with the altar

The Worm in my Tomato

on top, and underneath a carefully wrapped bundle in a small gunny sack. "Now, she keeps them under our home altar, so the saints will protect her shoes," Antonia whispered, her throat almost choked up, "The shoes are her only prized possession from the United States. Lorena told me that she and the shoes were both repatriated in 1932," Antonia said.

"But her feet will grow and she can't wear them again," Josefa stood up to leave, "I must go home now and be there when Lepo returns from working in Tila's store and cheese room. Also, Carmen wanted me to braid her hair. I enjoyed our talk," Josefa said.

Julieta stood up, "I must leave, too," Then paused, "Do you suppose, Antonia, Lorena could help me in teaching catechism to the young children of the village?" Julieta inquired as she approached her horse dozing in the shade of a near-by mezquite.

"I will ask her, Julieta, and she can talk with you," answered Antonia and the women said their goodbyes. Antonia felt happy that she had her own place now, where friends could visit her and Lorena. But Antonia felt apologetic that she had not had even a small piece of sweet bread to offer her visitors. Antonia heard Santos in the hut stir from his afternoon nap. On her way through the ramada, she smacked the bumble bee with a dish towel; how am I going to feed the baby? What do I do?' Antonia thought. She worried about Lorena, and she thought: for all I know she may be looking for honey in a wild-bee hive in the desert, accompanied by some of Telesforo's girls; Lorena is mature for her ten years and determined, Antonia thought, and she wondered where Lorena could be.

Lorena arrived home in mid-afternoon. "Mother, I am so tired. I searched for some red, juicy *tunas* in the prickly pear cactus desert area. But somebody else seemed to have gotten to the *tunas* first, and the girl Three Months, and I could not find any for us, and I am starved. But Antonia had nothing, and thus Mr. *Hunger* remained with them at all times pestering them, and worst of all, made Santos cry in pain. Lorena and Hunger sat at the table with nothing to eat. The sun was hot outside the ramada and lizards crawled into the ramada's shade. Lorena wondered how a grilled lizard would taste, "Naw, they are too thin," Lorena said out loud. Antonia, fanning herself with a towel, asked, "What?"

"Nothing," Lorena reclined on her cot to take her afternoon siesta and stay indoors away from the heat of the hot sun.

Later in the afternoon before sunset, Julieta returned; she came over again to bless Antonia's one room house with holy water. "I saved this holy water, blessed by father Simon, the last time he visited us," Julieta also brought with her a basket of bean burros, meat and cheese tacos, and *empanadas*. Julieta, Lorena, and Antonia with Santos on her lap promptly gave thanks to God for their food and shared the meal.

"Knowing our dire needs, I have no doubt that in this sad place we will say many prayers and rosaries. I hope the blessings, whatever they will be, will come soon for the sake of Lorena and Santos. Santos, especially, now going on two years old had learned to walk with the help of Chocolate, Tila's dog, and now runs outside in our yard. He weaned himself from milk, and demands solid food like we eat," Antonia said.

Lorena asked Julieta, "Doesn't this table in the ramada kitchen outside the hut provide a nice shady place to eat and hope for some fresh air, Julieta."

"Yes, I think so," Julieta said and pointing to the adobe stove added," I like the adobe clay *estufa*, these wood burning adobe block stoves, plastered with clay on the sides not only keeps the areas warm at night but make the best tasting tortillas, ever."

"We have two hornillos, one hornillo serves to hold the pot for cooking beans or the *quelites,* the field spinach that grows wild along the canal walls, and one hornillo for the comal or flat iron on which to make corn tortillas, " Antonia said.

"What I like, too, is your kitchen shelf hanging from the ceiling on one side of the ramada, to keep clay dishes, coffee, salt and sugar for their protection from animals," Julieta said.

The meal was soon ended and they washed it down with tepid warm water from the *talega*. There had been no fresh breezes from the river to cool the water. Lorena showed Julieta where underneath the top of the altar wood box in the hut, she had placed her new shoes in their cardboard box, wrapped in a gunny sack.

"Here my shoes will be safe in a shady dry corner, where the box can not get wet, if it ever rains," Lorena explained. She looked at the

The Worm in my Tomato

saints on the altar and said, "My shoes are in your care, now," Lorena implored the saints.

From outside, the sun's pink fingers reached into the *ramada* as if to hang on to something before plunging down behind the west horizon in the direction of the Gulf of California. Songs of festive frogs, celebrating the approaching night, broke out in a disconnected melody of "urag, urag, ug, urag." The dry rotted wood smells and swooning sounds of a desert coming to life following an afternoon *siesta* filled the village as a warm breeze blew in from the desert.

"Lorena," Julieta looked at her, "I would like you to help me teach catechism to small children. I have too many children and adults this year. We must prepare children for first communion, and I must prepare

A house isolated from the world with the vast desert in the background. The desert served Antonia and Lorena as their grocery store.

the parents for having their babies baptized, and prepare adults for marriage, all this for when a priest comes to visit us," Julieta said.

"Yes, Julieta," Lorena responded and blushed in joy, "My mama had already mentioned to me that you wanted me to help you with the teaching of catechism."

Julieta said, "Thank you, I will give you more information later

The Worm in my Tomato

when you come to my house, now I must leave." Julieta, Antonia and Lorena embraced each other goodbye. Julieta climbed on her horse and rode away.

"You know mother," Lorena said, "The other day, in the shimmering heat waves on the road, I saw the gray human figures on horseback and the figures wore metal helmets. They looked majestic, and I wondered if they were friends or enemies, what they wanted and why they had come?"

"Well, Julieta is a friend and she wears the Christian helmet of charity," Antonia said, "We must be humble and practice humility in receiving from others in charity, but we must do our best to become independent and learn to feed ourselves from the desert."

Twenty Two

Lorena

The worm in my tomato

In El Mezquitalito, Lorena liked her neighbors. She always enjoyed her conversations with Carmen and her parents. Lorena appreciated Julieta's invitation for her to help teach catechism. She began to think how to convince Lepo to allow her to draw water from his well. She did not like to fetch the buckets of water from the bovine pond and then have to boil it before using the water for cooking or drinking. Lorena always remembered the cool, fresh, pure water she and Eligia pulled up from her Aunt Tila's water well in the early mornings.

Lorena missed Eligia and thought of her often, when she did not see her at school. But now, she had new friends in the village, especially the girl Seven Months. Each of the girl Months fascinated Lorena because each acted like their month name-sake; Lorena had noticed, for example: Enera and Febrera were reserved and cold in personality and they kept to themselves most of the time. Maybe because they were older, Lorena thought. Marsis never stopped talking, giving directions, advice, admonishment or praise; Abrilis, naturally sweet, blossomed in colors like desert flowers, and both overshadowed the rest of the children like a chaperon. Lorena's closest friends, Maya, Junis, and Julia were warm, friendly, and liked to study with Lorena on how to do arts and crafts with grass, weeds, and twigs. The boys were just like little boys everywhere: distant, climbing trees, chasing grasshoppers, hunting frogs, field rats or snakes, either alone or with their father, Telesforo.

Fortunato, months ago, had given Lorena her own tomato plant with her own particular tomato. In her eyes, her tomato was the best of all the tomatoes from the hundreds of tomato plants. Lorena had visited her own tomato, from time to time, on a regular basis. She contemplated it and watched it grow. She patted it now and then, sang to it a song Lorena made up to the tune of "Black, black sheep, have you any wool, yes sir, yes sir, three bags full." Lorena would sing:

The Worm in my Tomato

"Father, Father, have you any tomatoes, yes sir, yes sir, three fields full; One for market, one for Tila and one for the little girl, Lorena."

One night Lorena crawled under the light blanket on her cot to sleep. She hoped to dream about eating her tomato, because tomorrow she planned to do just that.

Lorena discovered, after moving into the hut that several unwelcome entities had moved in with her: cold, hunger, and fear of creepy things. Yes, these felt or imagined realities had taken abode with her and her mother; yes, *abode*, as Lorena remembered Miss Yoakum teaching the word *abode*, thank you Miss Yoakum, Lorena thought.

The first unwelcome intruder to invade the hut was *cold*; a feeling of ice moved into Lorena's cramped cot, a numbing coldness would hug her every dawn around three a.m.; there simply were not enough covers for Lorena to keep warm. Lorena named cold Mr. *Cold*. Next, her old adversary Mr. *Hunger*, a rumbling monster in her stomach demanded to be fed. Lorena tried to sleep through her shivering and her hunger. In addition, a *fear* invaded her sleeplessness, Mr. *Fear* , as Lorena named fear, caused her a dread of insects, snakes, spiders and other imagined creatures that she supposed came out at night. Her mother, her baby brother Santos and she were victims of a menacing situation. They had forgotten how *this* unbearable situation all began and they did not know how to end it.

Through all her shivering and shaking and stomach growling, Lorena's hope tonight was tomorrow to eat her ripe sweet tomato. This thought gave her hope to grope for continued survival in this destitution, thank you Miss Yoakum, Lorena thought, and she repeated *destitution*; Lorena remembered learning the word from the vocabulary drills in Miss Yoakum's class in Bullion Plaza. Lorena had brought her vocabulary drill book with her to Sinaloa and had studied it on regular intervals.

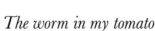

The worm in my tomato

Lorena ran down the lane along the dirt road, chased by *Hunger* who would not leave her alone; for sure my tomato is ripe now, she thought. Lorena anticipated, thank you Miss Yoakum, *anticipated*, her first big bite into her red juicy fruit; her mouth watering and dribbling all over, Lorena scurried and hopped from the shade of one bush to another to prevent burning the underside of her feet.

Lorena reached her plant, there was her tomato. Finally, she thought, my tomato has grown from a small green marble to a large orange sized red tender fruit. On that very special day, with great care, she pulled it off the mother plant, dusted it off by caressing it and washed it with some water from the bovine pond; water which she had carried in a tin can for this special occasion. Lorena with tender care brought her tomato to her drooling mouth, and when she was about to take her first bite of her juicy red tomato, a large green worm poked its beady eyed head through the red pulpy flesh. "Eek, Ahh, Lorena screamed; she flung her tomato across the field.

She ran home crying. During the next two weeks Lorena's world, awake or asleep, day or night, became a nightmare of worms in all her father's tomatoes. Lorena sobbed over her encounter with the worm in her tomato.

In the black pit of nothingness, in the silence and desperation, as far as Lorena was concerned, her family had died in Mexico; no one cared. Mother had not only carried her Christian cross, we were sacrificed on it, Lorena thought. She made up her mind to ask the priest, if and when he came to visit, about the meaning of suffering. Nights, she could hear the baby whimper from hunger. Dawn was the saddest time of the night, it was a stillness that weighted heavy on her; a thick sea of cold air from the El Fuerte River chilled her to the bone. There was no escape; she knew that her father had escaped the Repatriation, but for her there was no escape. She had frightening dreams of worms in her father's fields of tomatoes, but her father did not know: it was the worm of the unknown that she feared the most.

Lorena's hunger for knowledge now included a hunger for food, but she hungered more for food than for knowledge, at this time. *This* hunger pursued Lorena and intimidated her at every moment of her day, when she was awake; *it* haunted her during the night until she fell asleep from exhaustion.

At night, Lorena counted hot bricks spouting out from an imaginary

The Worm in my Tomato

volcano, and she thought of how to elude her merciless pursuer, thank you Miss Yoakum, *pursuer*, the *Cold*, that finally lay down with Lorena, too weak to menace her anymore. Sleep, nevertheless, when it finally came, brought dreams in which Lorena cooked soup from sun dried bones, used over again and again for soup, but the soup, however, turned to white clay, too thick to swallow.

Inside the hut, Antonia and baby Santos slept in one bed made of a wooden frame with crisscrossed leather straps. Lorena slept on another similar cot. Each of the four wooden legs of their beds stood inside wide oblong one inch deep sardine tin cans filled with water to keep scorpions from crawling up into bed with them. When Fortunato came to sleep in their house, he slept in Antonia's cot; at such times the baby was moved to Lorena's bed and he slept in her arms. In this way, two by two entangled in each other's arms they fought off *Cold*.

The family tossed and turned, unable to sleep. Lorena feared bats that could fly into the hut's room at night. As for snakes and field rats, Lorena placed her trust in the front door wooden board that was about one foot or more high and long enough to stretch across from one side to the opposite side of the door. This board was held propped up in place by two boulders placed against the inside of the board facing outwards and leaning against the door frame. This board, because the hut lacked a real door, was the best the family could do. The board had a purpose of keeping out inquisitive field rats, foraging about outside in the dark; the board prevented snakes from slithering into the house. The snakes slinked about at night seeking a field rat that may have ventured into the hut's ramada. No food was ever kept on the ground to prevent tempting desert thicket rats from entering the house because the rats smelled food. Lorena thought that her family was fortunate in that respect, because they had no food. No snakes ever entered their place of rest; Lorena was certain that snakes were busy seeking field rats in the thickets.

In the mornings, Lorena scooped water out from the bovine pond and carried the brown liquid home. The drinking water was boiled by Antonia and after it cooled, the water filled a *talega*. The canvas water bag was then hung out in the ramada from a cross mezquite rafter. The cool river breeze during the early mornings and night time refreshed the water.

On the first night, after Antonia's family exile to the hut, the noisy songs of hundreds of frogs, living in the small pond, croaked: "Ahugged, erred, ahugged" all night; Lorena was sure, or at least she thought, that the frogs welcomed her to El Mezquitalito to share their life, "A life, mama," she said to Antonia, "I would at any time trade for any other life in this world." No, Lorena thought to herself, I will not stay here for long; more important, I will not let mama and Santos stay here, either. "We must leave, mama," Lorena often said to Antonia.

Carmen told Lorena that the mosquitoes, which Lorena had not noticed when she lived at her Aunt Tila's house last June, were not out yet but that during the damp months of July through August they would make life miserable. "Lorena, you will be happy for the frogs out hopping around zapping at mosquitoes for their meal." Carmen said, and she also told Lorena that about every few years or so a plague of locusts would follow a wet season. "But with plenty of rain," Carmen said, "We all will have more food: many green plants, weeds, and the desert flowering into a colorful garden of abundant pitahayas, cactus tunas, quelites, and other edible desert foods will happen." Carmen threw up her arms in a sign of despair, "Somehow this time of plenty, however, will attract the grasshoppers and a grasshopper plague will unexpectedly sweep over us, devouring every green plant on sight." Carmen gave Lorena a frightened look.

Lorena had heard enough from Carmen to scare her into wanting to immediately return to Aunt Tila's house, which had protected her family from all these calamities, *calamities*, thank you Miss Yoakum, she thought, but she knew mother would brave hell itself without the help of her relatives the saints rather than return to Aunt Tila's house.

Lorena felt for sure that she must be helping her mother carry her cross. If only Nanita knew what her advice to mother had gotten them into. Lorena hated the United States mean-spirited Repatriation laws; Lorena hated all laws in China and any country that forced people to leave; she hated any kind of deportation to foreign countries that forced people into a life of suffering like the Chinese field workers in Aunt Tila's fields. Lorena felt sorry for her father who was forced to return to Mexico after living in the United States for thirty-eight years. He had been a successful gambler at Limonada's' pool hall. Now, Antonia and Lorena dreaded that if Fortunato did not harvest and sell his crops, he might be forced to risk his health and very life by gambling here in El Aliso during the dark nights in some unknown ranch. This imagined horror kept Antonia and Lorena worried and Antonia saying her novenas and rosaries.

The first night at Mezquitalito had been a most miserable night. The first day and night in Mezquitalito would be followed by countless more similar days and nights; some more miserable than others. Lorena had nothing to look forward to but more of the same misery. She feared the threat of a wet season full of mosquitoes followed by the plague of grasshoppers. It was not only the incessant croaking and droning song of frogs in the evenings that subjected Lorena to a sense of awakened anxiety, but more so, it was the cold. Antonia and Lorena discovered that the desert became the coldest place on earth at three a.m. before the dawn. Lorena and Antonia lacked the extra required *sarapes* or woolen blankets to throw over them during the cold dawn. The white thin cotton sheets and one woolen blanket would not keep out the numbing cold.

In the morning Lorena discovered that their hut lacked even the warmth from warm embers in the hut's adobe stove. Also there were no surviving coals smoldering among the cold dead ashes in the adobe brick wood stove for fanning into life for cooking in the morning. Lorena discovered that only dead coals remained, amid the pile of cold soft ashes. Antonia and Lorena knew that they had to learn how to keep the embers alive during the night and use them to light a fire in the cold morning.

It was then, in a cold morning, that Antonia, with clattering teeth, begged Lorena, "Please, *mijita*, go beg from Lepo a live coal and find out how to keep coals alive to light the morning fire."

Lorena, with her legs and knees stiff as icicles, and with her teeth babbling against each other, teeter-tottered one frozen foot after another over to their nearest neighbor, Lepo, and whisper his name outside his front door, to wake him up and to beg for a live coal, "Please, Señor Lepo, give us a live coal to start our fire," Lorena clacked.

The Worm in my Tomato

Lorena soon learned that Lepo hated to be wakened by her rattling his hut's ocotillo plant makeshift door. After some elapsed time and the distress of Lorena's clacking teeth, Lepo came out to his ramada adobe brick oven stove and grudgingly and in snail like movements dug in under his earthen stove's ashes and pulled out a live coal. "Here," he gruffed, "Carry it wrapped up in this corn husk," he carefully wrapped the coal up in the corn husk, and gently handed the husk bundle to Lorena, "Now, take and hurry now to your stove; blow on it slowly, deep, and with much love and tenderness."

Lorena asked, innocently, "Why?"

"Because child, you are the spirit that is blowing this coal to life," he impatiently began to nudge Lorena toward her hut, "Hurry, before it gets too cold and dies, and don't come back, learn to keep your embers alive overnight," Lepo grumped.

Lorena double-stepped, as best she could, back to her *estufa*, and there she gently placed the warm husk down above the dead ashes of yesterday, and gently began to blow her spirit with much love and hope and her faith in what she was doing into the pink lump of coal. The coal slowly began to color and increase in heat and turn a reddish hue until the corn husk burst into a flame; the husk provided the initial source of nourishment for a yet to be born fire, and the flame ignited the other leaves and sticks that Lorena gently placed over the flame into a fire. Lorena placed some twigs and dry cow dung over the fire and continued to give it air. Soon the twigs and dung began to burn into a larger fire. Lorena placed heavier mezquite bark over the thriving fire, carefully allowing air from beneath the small pyramid to work its way up and feed the fire its morning breakfast of oxygen. The hut's stove had a fire. Antonia could boil water; Lorena hoped for the day to bring them something to eat.

Lorena was not a fast learner in this new school of experience in life. Nothing was written in books. She was happy and grateful for the time she had spent learning her chores from Eligia. Lorena knew that what Eligia had taught her served as a bridge to whatever else new Lorena had to learn for her survival. Lorena began to understand what Julieta had told her: "All knowledge was contained in an emerging incident from another previous incident, in each integrating event, in any and

The Worm in my Tomato

all particular phenomena." Lorena remembered the words *integrating* and *phenomena*, thank you, Miss Yoakum, and thank you Miss Julieta, Lorena remembered, and then she added outloud, "Thank you Senor Lepo for showing me all this in how to start a fire."

Again when visiting Julieta to learn how to teach catechism, Julieta had said to Lorena, "Life events are like the fluid water in the Fuerte River," when Lorena had asked Julieta why the Great Depression and the Repatriation had happened.

"For sure," Lorena answered Julieta, and she thought about how she felt being carried along by the churning fluid events of her life, with their demands, and she, sometimes, felt almost drowned in life's misery. Lorena had to learn how to swim in a new environment comprised of a different culture, language, and perspectives.

Julieta had even quoted a reading from her prayer book, "We give thanks to God whose power is revealed in nature and whose providence is revealed in history."

"Explain to me the meaning of what you said Julieta," Lorena had asked, "what does that mean?"

"It means we see God's power in attendance in all his creation and his divine intervention in all that happens," Julieta answered.

Julieta had told Lorena that village Indian *curanderas* or healers could interpret these life unfolding relationships between time, space, and participants. Julieta had said, "These events are shoved and pushed by relationships that seem to emerge from eternity into time segments," and she had also said, "It is not the persons or people that we accept or reject but their behaviors and the relationship their behaviors create," Julieta taught Lorena.

In Lorena's concern, she had asked Julieta what would become of their Church, the Vegas' land holdings, and the village school. Lorena had discussed with her mother all Julieta had said, and Antonia had added her own interpretations, but Lorena supported what Julieta had said. Lorena had told her mother that from now on, Nature would be her school. Lorena would learn from all living things and those not living, like stones, but existing things of what they could teach her.

Lorena's native Mayo Indian neighbors had a definite perspective on life and all created things. In observing how they lived, Lorena noticed that the women made round balls from dry bones they called *tizas*, which they used as a dry ointment to rub on their hot skillets or flat irons to keep the food or tortillas from sticking on the hot surface. Lorena now felt confident that she could learn anything her neighbors or nature wanted to teach her. She was grateful for all Eligia had taught her in the school of work. She appreciated the opportunity Julieta had given her in teaching catechism. Also, Carmen, her neighbor and new friend, had helped Lorena learn how to adapt and cope with life in the village. Lorena appreciated how Lepo, Carmen's father, taught her how to keep embers alive. She had managed to keep her hut's stove fire coals alive overnight. It was all in how she covered them for the night, "Keep the coals warm but give them space to breathe," Lepo had said. On the other hand, Lorena determined to find out from Telesforo, her other neighbor, how to keep alive by eating small amounts of food. She already knew that revulsion could overcome hunger, and Lorena intended to find the secret of aversion to food when in the moment of hunger, but yet keep the desire for just enough food. Telesforo had said, "I learn all that from the ants."

Heat and silence prevailed during the day. Clouds passed by and only teased the village with rain that seldom dropped to visit and quench the thirst of dry and cracked dirt.

The Worm in my Tomato

The village residents had to fetch water from the nearby pond or the river; the pond served the cows as a watering hole, depending on a village resident's frame of reference; *Reference*, thank you Miss Yoakum, Lorena thought; to Lorena, the pond was a large watering hole for the cows. It was the home of the frogs. The pond's water somehow seeped underground from the El Fuerte River nearby, like an underground spring that replenished it and kept it fresh. Lorena, however, wondered why she never saw village residents fill their buckets from the pond. She thought to ask Carmen about where were people in the village getting their water, because Lepo certainly did not share his water.

Lorena expressed more interest in poor Telesforo, who had Twelve Months to feed. Telesforo had the habit of studying the ants in his front yard. For this reason his neighbor Lepo nicknamed him the Philosopher.

Telesforo would point out to Lorena the red ants busily digging their underground tunnels and storing what food they could find amidst the grains of sand. Then he would point out the black ants across the trail doing the same tedious labor. "Each side is actually preparing for war." He scratched his left arm pit. Telesforo was tall and thin with dark features accentuating a large hooked nose. "When each feels secure in having built their defense of tunnels and having gathered their food supplies, each ant tribe will seek ways to provoke the other in such a way as to justify their claim to have been provoked, themselves. Then they go to war, each convinced they are defending their ant domain and retaliating in self-defense. Both the red and the black ant tribes are hypocrites," Telesforo explained in a slow droning manner. But Lorena found what he said motivated her to new insights gained from studying ants.

Lorena would spend half a day watching ants and taking in the shade under the large mezquite tree while she and Telesforo listened to each other's intestines growl from hunger. Maya, Junis, and Julia, the summer girl Three Months, would accompany Lorena's growling stomach with their own meows. Soon Lorena marveled at the hunger concerto made by stretched intestines empty and taut, a *Symphony*, thank you Miss Yoakum, Lorena thought.

"What is your main ambition in life, Mr. Telesforo?" Lorena asked again the same question she had asked before, but she sincerely wondered, and asked Telesforo during one afternoon when both were doing research of ants busy in their preparation for war. A sun-beam of light must have escaped through the canopy of tree limbs and leaves above and had cooked my head long enough and evaporated from my head such a question, thought Lorena to herself, but it was too late, she had asked the question.

Telesforo thought about Lorena's question in his mind a long time, sucking at it, like if it was the soup bone of Lorena's dreams. Gray clouds had mercifully placed themselves between the hot sun and the village so that shade blessed Lorena and Telesforo. Finally he said slowly, "To be able to eat one *empanada*, all by myself, one day," He had responded solemnly and made known his life ambition as he deliciously but laboriously worked out the word empanada through his sun-cracked lips. He shook off the red ants that had climbed up his bare feet while he had pondered his life ambition.

"Really, Mr. Telesforo," Lorena feigned surprise, and thought it *incredulous*, thank you Miss Yoakum, Lorena thought. But she had actually seen Mr. Telesforo purchase a fruit turnover, the most delicious looking empanada from the vendor woman who came by periodically calling out, "Empanadas, hot pumpkin empanadas," marketing Aunt Tila's store fruit turnovers. But always, on the rare occasions Telesforo could afford to buy one empanada, just as he caressed the fruit turnover between his right hand thumb and forefinger, and moved his mouth forward to take that delicious bite, all his Twelve Months would appear, as if coming out like frogs from the ground when it rained, or like mice from the trees, or like scorpions from an adobe hut's walls, yes, all the boy and girl Months would approach to beg from their father a piece of that tan and browned tempting turnover. Of course Mr. Telesforo would begin the tortuous task of dividing the hand-sized empanada into thirteen morsels. He was always left with a tiny piece and an unfulfilled desire of someday eating a whole empanada by himself. None of the Twelve Months would ever drop a microscopic crumb for the red or black ants to kill each other over in their on-going economic war.

Lorena remembered Telesforo's predicament in sharing his empanada with his Twelve Months. "If you had asked me the same question Mr. Telesforo," Lorena said, "I may very well have said to

The Worm in my Tomato

eat a ripened red juicy tomato without a green beady eyed ugly worm sticking out of it."

"Ah, yes, I remember your story, Lorena, and I see that you have a fear of the unknown, the fear of the worm," Telesforo said.

"What do you mean? My fear started after my father told us the Repatriation train would take us away to Mexico. What must I do?" Lorena sincerely asked.

At that moment before Telesforo could answer Lorena's question, the girl Three Months arrived and joined Lorena and their father Telesforo. The girls sat next to Lorena on the log under the mezquite tree. All three girls greeted Lorena and Telesforo. "We were washing our clothes on the river bank with our mother, and we are glad to he home, it's so hot, today." Maya said.

"Father, do you know if the boys caught any fish, rabbits, or frogs to cook?" Junis asked. She glanced at Telesforo and said, "Mother wants to talk with you, now."

Telesforo greeted his daughters and continued his answer to Lorena, "It is a Christian fear, the fear of the snake and its hatred between it and mankind; ask Julieta, your teacher of Christian scripture." Telesforo said and he stood up from his log seat and turned to go into his house and said, "Julieta will tell you about the Mother of God, but later remind me to tell you about El Huizache, a tree that incarnates the mother goddess of sustenance."

But in reality, what Lorena wished for, her mother might provide. Lorena wished her mother would confront the Mexican federal government because there was no Catholic Church, no Mass, and no Christian life in El Mezquitalito. Antonia's conflict with Aunt Tila, Lorena reasoned, had gotten us deported from her house. Perhaps her mother's conflict with the federal government over the lack of Church services would get her mother and her and Santos thrown out of Mexico back to Arizona. But nothing of the kind occurred. Lack of sufficient rain negated a harvest for Fortunato the first two years but toward the end of the third year at last he was able to have excellent crops of cotton, corn, tomato, beans, and chile on the ground, and he expected a productive harvest.

Lorena had grown older and at age twelve had matured in

comprehension and understood learning from the natural world and nature with the help of Telesforo, but learned from Julieta and scripture her religious faith. She continued attendance at the village school, first under the academic tutelage of Mr. Luna and then later with Mr. Duran. Lorena also could see how the federal government laws about lands, religion, and education, like the red and black ants preparing for war, caused the conflicts with Aunt Tila, her mother and father, Julieta, the native villages, and the hacienda ranchers, including the Vega families.

Samuel continued to work with the federal land office, helping in surveying lands located in the rural rancherias of El Aliso and Mezquital areas of the municipio El Fuerte. Many of the lands Samuel was assigned to survey included land holdings of the Vega families. Jose worked in the ranch of Mr. Martinez, taking care of horses and at times riding Colorado in horse races during festivals. Catalina attended primary school in El Bacori where she continued to reside with her Uncle Eugenio and Aunt Sara. Catalina was now nine years old, going on ten. Santos, going on age three by now, explored the entire village, swam in the safe areas of the river beach, and he hiked the desert with Lorena in search of edible greens.

Fortunato had of course continued to work the fields and get deeper in debt to his sister Tila. He never lost faith that the next agricultural effort would result in the long hoped for harvest. Antonia prayed for his success as a farmer and for God to bless his work. She attended prayer service on Sundays at Julieta's house where with several other women, including Luisa, Eligia, and Lorena she prayed for the arrival of a priest to celebrate the holy Mass.

Oh, soon enough; Lorena, of course was not aware, but her mother and father, were very much aware and feared the pot would boil over; a future relationship, for certain, emerging from eternity would cause the present events of conflict to flare up in armed struggle. Each side was waiting for provocation that would justify the fight, not unlike the ants.

The Worm in my Tomato

Part Three

Year Two, Three, Four, and Five:
1933 - 1934 - 1935 - 1936 - 1937

Twenty Three

Fortunato
The locusts and life thereafter

Time had slowly emerged from eternity, bringing with it present events from the unknown into present history to be experienced; two years had gone by and at last, after two failed harvests because of lack of sufficient rain, it appeared for certain there would be a plentiful harvest in this third year.

Antonia could hardly wait: at long last Fortunato would afford to pay Tila his debt for seed, water, workers, and yet have enough to build their own home. Fortunato was beside himself in anticipation of having a plentiful harvest. Lorena was overjoyed but at the same time suspicious that something would go wrong. The worm in her tomato experience had transformed for her in her mind a notion of expectation of inherent failure in what was basically good; this transformation in her life had caused her to be dubious and think that all was not as it seemed to be and caused her to fear the yet unknown. Telesforo had concluded that her experience and fear of the unknown beyond the experience with her tomato and the worm, was due to the Christian enmity with the snake.

For now Antonia, Lorena, and Santos, now three years old, lived in destitution in their small hut in Mezquitalito. Lorena, somehow motivated by her internal body clock, arose early in the morning to start the fire in the adobe wood stove.

"Well, mother, we survived another night without getting stung by a scorpion or a centipede," Lorena glanced at her mother kneeling at the side wooden altar, as she prayed, as was her custom each day when she awoke. "Oops, sorry, I thought you had finished praying, you're so quiet," Lorena said.

"Well, I was thinking that after another night wrapped in loneliness, cold, and fears, I am happy to see you start a new fire," Antonia said, "I just hope for something to eat for breakfast and for a better day."

Lorena and Antonia were brought back to the reality of the day by Santos' crying. He awoke like he did each morning and asked for something to eat. But suddenly Lorena and Antonia realized it was not yet morning, although their bodies told them it was morning. They looked out from the ramada, and saw that dawn had not even broken out in the east; no light could be seen entering the ramada. Antonia heard roosters crowing somewhere. Antonia looked out from the ramada, "It is a strange morning because there is no light, you see Lorena, dark outside," Antonia described.

Antonia felt that it was a strange darkness. Her body feelings told her that it was a new day; she remarked about the strangeness of the morning, "It is morning, and morning calls for a new fire, but why are there no streaks of pink light sneaking into our ramada like every morning," Antonia said and again walked into the ramada and searched outside, "There are no signs that the sun wants to come up. There is only a peculiar darkness." She hurried back into the hut's room, "Something is not right and I feel a cold shiver down my spine."

Lorena quickly got up from her cot and ran outside to see. "Mother, I see the village people like shadows running about in the dusk-like darkness; all the dogs are barking," She yelled. Lorena's face puckered and her mouth's under lip quivered as she kept herself from crying, she did not want to frighten Santos.

"But it can't be dusk, already, why we have not lived the day, yet," Antonia said and she picked up Santos, who was whimpering, and she held him tightly in her arms. "Lorena run and ask Lepo if he knows what is wrong with the daylight, where is it," Antonia commanded. She stepped aside to let Lorena run out past the ramada and across the road to Lepo's house; Antonia held Santos in her arms.

There were no birds chirping in the trees this morning, there was no light of the early dawn softly streaming through the trees into the ramada, there was only a strange darkness and a stifling heat. Presently,

The Worm in my Tomato

Lorena returned to the hut; she was out of breath, with wide eyes, and frightened pale. Antonia also saw Lepo run up close to their door.

"The sun is clouded over like a moon eclipse by some dark mass of something," he was panting, "See the mass of dense things that look like black clouds." Lepo said, and he hurried out the ramada with intentions to run back across the road to his house, but before Lepo had even finished speaking, other village men were running from house to house in the village, causing a great commotion. A runner came near Antonia's hut and Lepo's adobe house and shouted out a warning, "It is a swarm of locusts, several large dark clouds of them; cover your doors and windows." He disappeared into the darkened village plaza.

"Oh, no, not again," exclaimed Lepo, and in his mind he remembered how a few years ago, a swarm of migratory grasshoppers stripped all green plants in the area and ruined Miss Tila's and Julieta's harvests. He ran across the road to his house, yelling back at Antonia and Lorena, "Quickly, cover your window and door. Keep them out, they eat everything."

Antonia and Lorena looked up into the space where the sky normally was located and saw instead a low canopy composed of a dark thick mass, which covered the whole valley; hanging down from the invisible sky. "Look, mama, look at the large black mass like huge rain clouds covering the whole village and all the fields," Lorena exclaimed.

The sun was obliterated. Antonia leaped into the hut from the ramada and yelled, "Hurry Lorena, let's cover the door and the window with the white sheets." Antonia and Lorena ran inside and took the sheets from the cots; they stumbled in the dreary hut in their attempts to place sheets, one from the inside of the hut against the door frame and the other sheet against the window frame. They placed the long mesquite poles, brought in from the ramada, against the sheets to hold them up. All through their running and covering the door and window, Santos wailed, cried, and shrieked all the louder.

Lorena sat down holding Santos, against her chest, she kept crying and saying over and over again, "Oh, God, please protect my father's fields, protect my Aunt Tila's fields, protect my father's tomatoes, his bean plants, his cotton, his corn, his garbanzo, Oh, God, have mercy, and protect Julieta's corn fields, too."

The Worm in my Tomato

Antonia quickly put a stub of a candle on top of her altar shelf, but she could not find the box of matches. The blackness of the inside of the hut stifled them. There was no light, there was no air. Silence, nothing stirred, until they heard the sound like large heavy hail; it sounded like pebbles pounding the hut, like large heavy rain drops that bombarded and slammed into the hut's mud roof and walls, the ramada, the trees and the ground outside. The heavy mass of grasshoppers began pelting the sheets at the door and the window. They began to cling.

"Oh, my God, help us; for certain, it is only a matter of time before their weight will pull down the sheets," Antonia yelled out loud so Lorena could hear over the dull buzz of locusts that covered the village. The heavy dark mass of creeping, hopping and flying grasshoppers made a low monotonous chomping dull sound.

Antonia found the matches where they had fallen at the foot of the wooden altar; she lit the candle, she prayed out loud all the while, "God our Father, help us." Then, barely, with the light of the candle, Antonia saw them, "Help, Lorena, look at those things." Antonia pointed at the large, short horned, beady eyed, orange -gray, winged grasshoppers peeking in around the sheet covering of the window. Antonia screamed, "Oh, they are here, take care of Santos, Lorena." Antonia recoiled away from the window and did not know what else to do, so she took off her sandal and begin to swat the ugly creatures with her shoe.

Lorena covered Santos with a pillow, and held him tight, but with one hand she reached into the shelf below the top of the altar and retrieved the box with her new shoes, wrapped in a towel in a gunny sack; she held them tight along with Santos. Antonia hopped about the hut and reached for another match. With another match, she lighted another stub of a wax candle and placed it on the top shelf of the home altar. Somehow, Antonia felt more secure with two candles lighted in the dim, suffocating room. Then, Antonia sat with Lorena and Santos and she huddled them together, embracing them into herself with her arms. Antonia and Lorena prayed an Our Father, "Our Father who art in heaven, hallowed be thy name…,"and a Hail Mary, "Hail Mary full of grace, the Lord is with you…," over and over again. The creatures swarmed all over their hut, inside and outside. Finally, but not soon

The Worm in my Tomato

enough for Antonia, the locusts departed from the hut, going after the green trees outside. The locusts, like the field rats, must have realized there was nothing to eat inside the hut. Outside, the noise increased of pelting bodies slamming into the trees, the bushes, the plants and the ground. Actually, the dull noise heard outside all over the valley was the chomping of the huge flying grasshoppers attacking all living plants, trees, and especially the vegetation and crops in the fields.

After Antonia and Lorena had gotten used to the sounds of the locusts eating away, they thought of their own hunger. Lorena blew life and her spirit into the embers in the wood stove. After some time, the family had a fire. Antonia made coffee and they ate dried tortillas and sipped their coffee. From time to time, Antonia and Lorena kept swatting or kicking at fat grasshoppers, who somewhat disoriented away from the vegetation outside had ended up inside the hut, to knock them off themselves, off Santos, and keep them out of the ramada. Lorena kept busy with the broom sweeping them outside from the hut and the ramada.

Two days later after the locusts had come and gone, when Fortunato visited the family's one room adobe nest, Antonia's and Lorena's daily situation changed; he brought a black night, a deep darkness void of any light: he brought no hope. Antonia could see that a deep depression had gripped him; Antonia knew that he would never again tell them of his forever ripening tomatoes, his almost-ready-for-harvest string beans, and his maturing cotton. Antonia knew that he would never again say that soon he would be ready to harvest in time for sale to a waiting market in the United States. Antonia knew that he would never again talk about how the Chinese field labor and the native migrant field workers were ready to harvest the crops and that upon marketing his crops the silver dollar, like the sun, would rise up golden with the sunrise.

Antonia and Lorena sat quiet, dejected, weeping; Santos, with his head covered with a pillow; clearly exhausted from his crying and shaking in fear, during the long night, slept. Antonia, in hopes of making it easier for Fortunato and Lorena said, "But we had heard

The Worm in my Tomato

something like *this* might happen as in the past, before, many times, in conversation with the villagers. We had lived in hope for months, for three years. We must not let out hope be taken away, but again, we must have new hope, remember, before the Repatriation? We knew we could have survived the economic depression quite well. Thus, this too, we can survive quite well." Antonia tried to smile, be brave and give consolation, courage, hope and new faith to her husband. Like Lorena, Antonia blew her spirit and love upon the ambers of hope to begin a new fire of inspiration and kindle a new beginning.

"Yes, we can survive, but we must yet grieve the end of our dreams, before we make new ones," Fortunato whispered, "Now, all the remembered words, the sayings full of hope, held dreams wrapped in faith within; they were not and are not meaningless, they were ours, their meaning is yet a symbol of hope, faith and love: now the whole undertaking does not prove hollow, but rather our work always had value. Nothing will end our hope." Fortunato hugged Antonia, Lorena, and Santos; he wept silently. There was nothing to say; for the moment there was nothing to do.

Lorena had no doubt it was the worm in the unknown; she could not understand why her mother spoke about hope and faith to her father. Lorena held the baby in her arms and she and Santos were soon asleep; they kept each other warm during the cold night.

Fortunato and Antonia, hand in hand, sat in the ramada, drinking their cup of coffee, enjoying a full moon that in partnership with the stars brightened the village. The moon bathed the hut in purplish-blue light, and in the aroma of lavender as it rose up, pulled the sky's blue dark veil toward the west and over the village. Husband and wife held hands, embraced in love with the blessing of their creator. Life and the creation of new life brought new hope, faith, and love.

During the following weeks, the situation failed to ignite any hope that was based on some real tangible plan of action. Instead, Antonia felt forever mired in this desert black hole collapsing inward unto itself.

A more immediate serious situation, however, had developed for

The Worm in my Tomato

Antonia: she realized that she was pregnant; she experienced a terrible turmoil in her mind and heart about her pregnancy. Antonia found herself in her perceived dreadful circumstances, and she determined to discuss her condition with Fortunato. She also planned to tell Lorena.

Fortunato of course had not realized that when he helped in the moving of his wife to El Mezquitalito, he had also failed to foresee the move of any future progeny yet unborn into a prison of destitution. The Repatriation had a similar comparison with the movement to El Mezquitalito because the moving of Antonia and her children from their rightful home, Arizona, and their family heritage: robbed them of their future; denied them of their pursuit of happiness and development of their God-given gifts and potential.

Antonia felt strongly opposed to bringing a new baby into such a deplorable situation. Her mind was tormented with temptations for aborting her child. She sat depressed outside in the ramada, not feeling like doing anything during the day. At night she tossed and turned with her eyes wide open, worrying and not knowing what to do.

Antonia thought to ask Julieta for needed advice; she knew for certain that beyond worrying each day of what to do about her pregnancy, where their meals would come from: there needed to be time for making decisions that would bring change into their lives. Antonia hated in her heart the idea of bringing a baby into this life and place, and she knew that she could not bring a baby into this environment; no, she could not, and moreover, she and Lorena could not continue living in this misery.

This is when the thought came into her mind and seared her heart. Antonia asked herself, out loud for Lorena to hear, "Lorena, should I continue to carry my cross or seek personal liberty to do what I think is best for my family?" Antonia wrung her hands; wiped her hands on her apron, and stared out the window, "You, know, return home."

Lorena offered no answer but only held Santos tight in her arms, and her heart raced in expectation, and her mind could not believe what it supposed her ears had heard.

Every time Antonia had asked Fortunato to inquire into building a house for her family, Fortunato's response had always been: "After I harvest my crops and market them for a good price." He always explained, "It all depends on the harvest and sale of our crops, Antonia." Also, when Lorena asked her father about helping her to attend school, he always said, "After the harvest and sale of the crops, we will be rich, *mijita*, and you will go to school," Fortunato always had said, but now all seemed hopeless.

The locusts which had not died, bloated in the sun, or ended in the mouths of frogs, continued on their instinctive migration to the north mountain range; finally the locusts were gone. Villagers began to count passage of time from the invasion of the locusts. Antonia and Lorena knew that it was the late fall of 1935. They had been in Sinaloa for three years. Santos, now going on four years of age, romped everywhere in the desert and in the village.

Another year of destitution had waned, forlorn and wasted, into the unknown eternity from Antonia's internal time calendar. For in reality, after her family arrived in El Aliso, they had no calendar; they told time by the sun. They were immersed in a different culture from the one they had known. They drank water from a dry well, from small filtering positos or holes along the river's edge, and from a bovine pond. They washed their clothes beside the shore of the river; they had lived on wild spinach, pinto beans, cactus and other edible plants, wild bee honey, cheese, and corn tortillas.

Lorena and Antonia had cried over the loss of Fortunato's harvest, the end to Antonia's dream for her own home; for Lorena's hope for an academic education. Lorena said to her mother, "The locust plague came and nobody had talked about it, with hope that is, had wanted it to come, or expected it to come, so soon," Lorena lamented, "Then, it came, like death, uninvited and in the disguise of a black cloud, an eclipse, an obscured event," and Lorena thought in her mind: *obscured*, thank you Miss Yoakum, "eating monster that made the crops, the village trees, plants and the desert disappear," Lorena breathed out.

Now, in the village, the hot winds blew free, unobstructed by naked, bare and fragile trees; after the locusts came. Only the frogs had been inundated with food from the sky. They zapped so many hundreds of locusts that now frogs, everywhere around the bovine pond, sat fat and immovable, silent un-croaking bulging frogs. Lorena listened, even at night, for a frog's croak, but not even one could be heard, only faint burps. A day or two later, in the hot sun, hundreds of rotted, stiff and dried up frogs covered the ground, from over-stuffing themselves.

The village looked pale white like sand with bare trees standing alone with skeletal shadows. Villagers had lost their shade, and they cried over their loss and feared the strangeness of their new place: always in the light, always hot and bright.

〜⟩

Teachings of Julieta and Telesforo

Lorena read a catechism book in Julieta's home; she looked out the open window and her eyes searched for the loud chirping birds in the naked trees. The midday sun's heat made heat waves rise, shimmering up into the hot afternoon, from the top of the road extending away from the house. Lorena started a conversation with Julieta. "Telesforo is a great student about ants and he thinks they are like people," Lorena said.

Julieta, while writing information on a report about the faithful of the village, looked up and nodded at Lorena and said, "Heh, yes," she got up from the table and took two pale yellow lemons from a basket, "Let's have some lemonade, Lorena," she took out a sharp knife to cut lemon halves, " Telesforo has many children; he has twelve children named after the months in a year, I just wrote down their names in my record book to show Father Fermin or Father Simon, I am not sure who will come, when he comes here what children need to make first communion." She poured water from a *talega* hanging by the front door of the porch, in the shade, into a pitcher, "Let's see if the breeze has cooled this water a little," she said and added, I am certain Marta, Telesforo's wife, must be happy that there were not thirteen or more months in the year," Julieta squeezed the lemon halves into the pitcher and grimaced up her face, "Telesforo has no idea about what it means to truly love his wife."

Lorena wondered out loud about Telesforo, "The Philosopher," as his neighbor Lepo had nick-named him, and Lorena now also called him; "he knows so much about ants, why doesn't he truly love his wife?" Lorena asked.

Julieta served two glasses of tepid lemonade. "I think that he must know the pain each child month caused his wife," Julieta swallowed her lemonade. The birds stopped chirping, confused at the lack of leaves and flew away from the huizache tree in the front yard.

Marta, Telesforo's wife, was an even tempered, quiet woman of over fifty years old. She was younger than Telesforo, but had aged much faster, and now she was very ill, and she spent most of her days in the house.

Julieta, concerned about Lorena's spirituality, was determined to speak with her about a believer's relationship to God in his or her religion; "Lorena," Julieta said, "spirituality is like having to peel an onion, a layer at a time to get down to the center of it all, the meaningfulness of one's faith in relation to one's life in loving God."

"Yes, Julieta, I wonder why my father did not grow onions in his fields, only cotton, corn, tomatoes, garbanzo beans; that's all." Lorena set aside her catechism book.

"Lorena, if you don't mind, I will talk about religion as in a manner of a lesson,"

Julieta finished her lemonade, placed the glass down on the table, and went over her lips with her tongue, "Oh, how sweet that lemonade, Lorena, did you like it," she asked and looked at Lorena who was dredging her glass and who then smacked her lips, "That was good." Lorena looked out the window and saw that the evaporative heat waves had ceased, and she wondered why.

"Each layer of a large onion represents an aspect of one's religion: the first layer represents simply being cordial, like going to Christmas Mass, celebrating Easter, like in the large cities, or dancing with the *Matachines* here in the village once a year."

"So, what happens, then, Miss Julieta?" Lorena asked.
"Well, a person forgets all about it, faith has not really taken over his or her heart," Julieta said.

"I guess that is different for the ants, the ants are as one; it's what Telesforo means when he says the ants must be together in work," Lorena said.

"That is correct, Lorena, and I think the ants have a sincere unity in what they do; it gives you a good notion of how many can be one;

The Worm in my Tomato

it may help you understand how three divine persons can be one God. Anyway, the second layer is one of interest, as a person at this point wants to know more concerning what the church is all about; the person wants to learn some prayers and say prayers, but this situation lasts only for a short period of time and in a luke- warm condition," Julieta emphasized. Julieta stood up from the table, "Do you want something to eat, Lorena, are you hungry, "Here, have an apple," Julieta handed Lorena a yellow-pink apple. Then she sat down again, "The third layer is one of dependence, where a person asks God for everything."

"That is the point where I am," Lorena said between bites of her apple.

"I don't think so, Lorena, you are more centered in Christ and you have such a strong hope for God's blessings, than that. I can tell; want some more lemonade?"

"Yes, please, Miss Julieta."

"Don't mind if I drink another glass myself, it's so warm today," Julieta handed the pitcher to Lorena, "At this point the faithful look on God as being a giver of favors."

"Yes, that is where I am, Julieta, I keep asking God for favors," Lorena said while serving herself another glass of lemonade.

Julieta continued, "Then the fourth layer is one of acknowledgment as when a faithful person acknowledges that God is the creator of heaven and earth and all living things, and a person realizes that all things depend on God."

"Now, that is Telesforo, Julieta, he is humbled by the ants, really," Lorena said and sipped her lemonade. The birds returned in greater numbers and escaped from the heat into the bare limbed canopy of the trees; the feathered creatures carried on a non-stop commotion with their chatter, no doubt complaining about the nakedness of the huizache tree which got a complete bird shake down.

"All should be humbled by knowing that all depends on God, hear those birds, they praise God just by being themselves and doing what God made them for, now, that is humility." Julieta tried to look through the open window at the birds perched on the bare limbs of the tree branches. A cool breeze swirled about outside the house and kicked up a dust devil down the road where the evaporative heat waves had been, but now, the thin shadows of the trees stretched out toward the east.

"That is where Telesforo is for sure, Julieta, he depends on God for every thing, just like the ants," Lorena munched on her apple, and said, "Telesforo told me to ask you to explain to me about the Christian fear of the snake, you know the unknown, like my worm, or something like that," Lorena informed Julieta.

"What snake?" asked Julieta.

"The one that there is hatred between it and mankind," Lorena munched on her apple.

"That is the story in the Bible in Genesis, here I will show you, Lorena," Julieta opened her Bible and read in Genesis 3: 15, "I will put enmity between you and the woman, and between your seed and her seed; he shall bruise your head, and you shall bruise his heel," Julieta read, and then added, "that's because the serpent tempted Eve to eat from the fruit of the tree of knowledge of good and evil."

"That is why I am scared of the worm, but Telesforo calls it the unknown and says my fear is a Christian fear of the snake," Lorena said and took a bite of her apple.

"Oh, Lorena, don't be afraid, ever; Our Mother Virgin Mary crushed the serpent and that is our Catholic belief of the Immaculate Conception, she is the mother of Jesus, Son of God, who is one with the Father and the Holy Spirit, but you may yet be too young to understand that part of our Christian salvation history," Julieta said.

"Oh, my, Julieta, Father Westhoff in my church in Miami told me that the mother of God lives in Mexico, he said that Our Mother Virgin Mary of Guadalupe, the mother of the true God, lives in Mexico; is there where she crushed the serpent?" Lorena took a drink of her lemonade, "Because if the serpent is in Mexico, I will tell mother, we have to leave tomorrow."

"Well, our Mother Virgin Mary is everywhere, in heaven and earth, but Our Lady of Guadalupe is one of her many titles; she is really: The Immaculate Conception Our Lady of Guadalupe who appeared to Juan Diego on December 9, 1531 near Mexico City, but the serpent is not in Mexico," Julieta explained.

"Where is it, so I won't go there," said Lorena and she drained her glass of lemonade.

"It is evil, but don't be afraid of it, Lorena, just have faith in Jesus and pray to his mother, Hail Mary full of grace…, you know your prayer, and the worm, the unknown, or the serpent can not harm you, promise me," Julieta said.

"I promise Julieta, I won't forget, and another thing I won't forget is that I am an American citizen, Miss Yoakum told me not to forget," Lorena said.

Julieta started her lesson again from where she had left off, "The fifth layer is one of appreciation, you begin to see God and his power in all things of creation and think of God as an artist and how he gives all things shape, form and color; God tells stories by his creation," Julieta continued.

"That is Telesforo, again, Julieta, he tells stories, all right, to the Twelve Months, Carmen and myself, around our bonfire, some nights; he appreciates all creation but especially the ants that crawl back and forth all day and Telesforo studies their every move, Julieta," Lorena said, and filled her glass with more lemonade, "May I have an apple to take home for Santos, Miss Julieta, he likes apples," Lorena said.

"Yes, take two apples home for Santos and for Antonia," Julieta handed to Lorena a small basket containing yellow apples colored with a blush of pink.

"The next layer is one of understanding of the relationship with God; the faithful begin to understand how God has love for them and for all, the faithful understand about unconditional love, and the believer arrives at that aspect of comprehension," Julieta said.

"Oh, my mother has a lot of understanding," Lorena said, "She understands my father very well."

"God is like your father, Lorena," Julieta added, "The believer comprehends that God loves all like a father, a creator, a mother, and that all persons are God's children."

"And all birds are God's birds, Julieta, right," Lorena said.
"Yes, of course, God created all things and keeps all in being; the sixth layer is one of assimilation, where you pray to love God for himself and do all things for the greater glory of God, to love God with your whole heart and love your neighbor as yourself," Julieta said.

The birds quieted down some, the shadows of the trees lengthened,

The Worm in my Tomato

and Lorena thought about going home, "My mother assimilates with God, I know, Julieta, she is so kind to people and really tries to help them like she did the nuns back home," Lorena said, "She is one with God, for sure." Lorena felt a surge of tenderness sweep over her when she thought of her mother and how much she has suffered; Lorena wiped away her involuntary tears from her eyes with the back of her hand.

"But I think your mother is here with the last layer of the onion," Julieta said, "The next layer is one of modification; you begin to find yourself as a child of God with your unique gifts that God has given you for his service and glory," Julieta stood up, "I will have to take you home soon Lorena, before sunset," Julieta hurried on, "Antonia as a faithful person gave of herself to accompany your father here to Sinaloa; she has been one for her family and has lived her life for a greater glory and love of God," Julieta looked out the window. Sleep had silenced the birds that like chickens went to bed early along with the setting sun. The tree shadows lengthened and started to blend with an approaching soft orange tinged dreary evening.

Julieta endeavored to finish her lesson, "Finally the last aspect or core of prayer and faith is being a co-creator; here you create love for God's service, love for you and love for his creation," Julieta stood up, "Let's go Lorena, I will take you home," Julieta kept talking as she and Lorena walked out the door, "The believer gives thanks for all things, and being one with God, participates in all creation and prays for all things," Julieta explained, "Lorena, try and do all for the glory of God and with God."

"Yes, but, Julieta," Lorena answered as both walked down the dirt road; the setting sun behind them began to hide behind the blue mountains for the night, the thin tree shadows already disappeared, "I only wish the early dawn would not be so cold, but as Lepo taught me, I co-create a fire in the morning by breathing life into ash covered embers," Lorena hurried along side of Julieta, and she added, "Telesforo told me that ants don't need fire to keep warm." Lorena said. Then she added a question for Julieta, "Julieta, you know how much I like to learn, well then, will the sin of Eve keep me from seeking knowledge?"

"No, the tree of knowledge of good and evil does not mean all knowledge that we as human beings are encouraged to learn, do keep learning all you can, Lorena; knowledge of good and evil does not mean the unknown. The unknown is known only by God our Father; He alone knows the future, we can only guess at it, but never be afraid, have faith; that is how trust, hope, and love grow through faith in God's love for us."

"Thank you, Julieta; I will not fear the unknown anymore, the worm in my tomato." Lorena thought a moment and then said, "Well, I ask because Telesforo told me that he would teach me about the huizache tree. He said that it incarnates the mother goddess of sustenance or maintenance; I wanted to be sure it was not the tree of knowledge of good and evil."

"Well, Lorena, in time as you grow older and can reflect on God's total creation, you will learn of how God has expressed Sacred Self among all peoples. So all peoples have their own legends of faith or how they encountered God. Jacinta, my house maid is a curandera; you've met her; well, she is a Mechica or Aztec native that lives here in the village, and she can tell you about the huizache tree and its significance in their legend. They had, I am sure, their reasons why their notion of the mother goddess of sustenance is incarnate in the huizache tree. The Mayans believe as a people that they originated from the corn plant. We Christians share the belief in the Old Testament that we are dust and to dust we shall return; you are young Lorena and have a lifetime to learn but you will never learn all there is to know, not even when you die and become a spirit and return to God."

"I know, Julieta, if I were spiritual like my mother's relatives the saints we pray to, I would be back in Miami, my hometown, you know."

Antonia's family continued to survive in the mayo village, *El Mezquitalito*; Lorena continued to either beg for water from Lepo's dry well, or used the bovine pond.

One day Antonia and Lorena sat in the shade of the ramada, "Lorena," Antonia said, "I remember Julieta telling me, "After Mass, the priest will change himself into a blind beggar, again. Lorena will lead him atop his donkey into the cornfields. He and his donkey will disappear, under cover of corn fields. The priest will then journey to another village," Antonia looked at Lorena, "Julieta said this to me many times," Antonia said. Antonia looked pensive and worried at Lorena who remained quiet. Antonia herself remained silent for a moment, then continued speaking, "Lorena, I fear that Julieta will not realize her dream of a harvest of souls in the village; just like Fortunato failed to harvest desired crops, she, too, may fail; it seems that there is not a priest left in all of Mexico to come celebrate the Holy Mass with us," Antonia said again. She hoped to strike up a conversation with Lorena.

"But it never has happened, mama," Lorena said, "Not yet, but if a priest came by, there are no more cornfields in which to hide."

The religious laws forced Antonia to hope for attending an elusive Mass that never happened, at least not yet; the clandestine hoped-for Mass in a hidden room in the home of Julieta, a Cristero, whenever an underground movement priest, in shabby clothes and in danger of losing his life, would arrive incognito, continued to be something in the unknown that may or may not happen. Julieta had said several times during the past two years that a priest would ride his donkey under cover of cornfields. "He carries a cane and pretends to be a blind beggar," Julieta had said.

Antonia hoped that the priest would appear soon, but she worried that the priest would have no corn fields to hide in; with a sudden surprise, she realized what the locust plague had done: Julieta would have to cultivate new cornfields, Antonia thought.

Antonia day-dreamed, based on what Julieta had told her many times, that once hidden in the corn field, near Julieta's house, Lorena, would be sent out into the corn field to lead the blind man atop his donkey across the dirt road and lead him over a trail to the back of Julieta's house. There, a room will have been prepared for the priest to celebrate the Holy Mass. In attendance would be the Mayo native village faithful, Luisa, Eligia, Antonia, Lorena, and Santos.

But it never happened. They waited forever it seemed, but no priest ever showed up, their hope for a priest and for a holy Mass shriveled up like the hope for Fortunato's harvest; the religious laws and the armed soldiers on the roads destroyed the hope of the faithful who had prayed and waited for a holy Mass; they destroyed the hope for a Mass like the locusts had destroyed Fortunato's and Tila's hope for a harvest now gone from the remaining brown barren fields.

The Worm in my Tomato

Twenty Four

Catalina
Visiting my family

At long last, Eugenio found time to bring Catalina to visit with Fortunato and Antonia. Catalina told her Uncle Eugenio, "We came to Mexico with my father to keep our family together," she paused, "that is what my mother said."

In El Bacori, Eugenio, Fortunato's brother, and his wife Sara, had provided a home for Catalina. Catalina told herself, I do not like my Aunt Sara. Somehow Catalina blamed her Aunt Sara for owning Antonia's American furniture, and for keeping her away for so long without a visit home. In Catalina's mind the same thought, swirled about like a dust devil full of something, but of what not always clear. She thought that her Uncle Eugenio did not have to work all the time in the fields. Now, after the grasshoppers came to his fields, he had time to visit Aunt Tila.

The hamlet of El Bacori was a short two miles away from El Aliso where Tila lived, but the terrain was rough and overgrown with brush, cactus, and mezquite trees. The dirt road was impassable during heavy rains of late July and August. But in November, the early morning breeze felt welcome. Catalina rode in the mule drawn wagon and sat between her Uncle Eugenio and her Aunt Sara on the front bench board.

The day shone with a soft light which radiated in slow motion from an indifferent sun that did not care to heat up another November morning. There was not much wind so Catalina would not be bothered with dust-devils along the road. Pale green and brown vegetation contrasted with the beige colored sand and dirt on the ground.

Catalina, anxious and excited, could hardly wait to seek assurance from her mother. She thought to herself: Soon after we arrived, I was sent to live with my Uncle Eugenio and my Aunt Sara; they lived in

El Bacori where there was a primary school. My mother said that I would live in El Bacori and go to school, but now I want to come home and live with my mother. As Catalina was thinking these thoughts to herself, she was surprised to reality when a wild rabbit scampered across the road, bounding ahead of the trotting mules to seek safety in the embracing tall yellow grass of the desert.

Catalina remembered that it was Lorena who wanted to attend school, not her. She thought how she always wanted to stay with her mother who wanted to keep the family together.

Eugenio yelled at the mules "Git up, mules," and he cracked his whip right over their ears and above their bobbing heads. Catalina saw the struggling mules and heard the crack of the whip, and she remembered that Chapo had also cracked the whip over the mules's ears when he drove his wagon from San Blas to the big house. Chapo's mules ran faster and pulled harder, but Uncle Eugnio's mules ignored the crack of the whip and his "Git up," thought Catalina, except when he used cusswords at them. It was that kind of day when the sun ignored to heat up the late morning; the family and the mules took their leisure time in going to Aunt Tila's house. Catalina wriggled one way and then another like as if she was pushing the wagon faster. "Uncle Eugenio, I want to ask my father and my mother if I can stay with them, now," Catalina spoke out loud to make sure that her uncle heard her, "if that is all right with you and Aunt Sara." The easy clippity-clop of the mules only elicited a slow-motion response from Eugenio.

A flock of quail, startled by the approaching wagon, flew out from within the brush in a lazy arch along the right side of the road. The billows of dust waltzed behind the wagon wheels and died on the side of the road.

"We will see, your father must decide," Eugenio answered.

When Eugenio halted the wagon in the front yard of Tila's house, Catalina dismounted with a jump, and she quickly looked about as if searching for something. "Where are Chocolate and the other dogs?" she asked no one in particular.

The Worm in my Tomato

Catalina entered the big house, "Hello, Aunt Tila, I am so glad to see you," Catalina hugged Tila, who had walked up to greet her and Eugenio. "Where is Chocolate?" Catalina asked, again.

"Welcome, daughter, the dogs had to be hung to prevent the spread of rabies, after you left," Tila shook Eugenio's outstretched hand, and then she and Sara embraced.

From the kitchen came the sounds of pans being washed. Luisa and Eligia came out into the dining area to welcome Eugenio, Sara and Catalina. Luisa hugged Catalina; Eligia came over to Catalina and clasped her hand and kissed her on the forehead.

"My, Catalina, you have grown tall," Elegia said.

"I am ten years old, now, on November 22nd," Catalina said.

"Your mother and your sister Lorena must be anxious to see you Catalina," Tila said. "They don't visit me, and your brothers, Samuel and Jose, have not come around for a long time," Tila's voice trailed off as she walked to the kitchen to get a glass of water, "Please, everyone, have a glass of water."

"I feel sad because of all the changes that have happened," Catalina said, wiping her tears from her eyes with her handkerchief.

Catalina cheered up when she saw her father enter the house. He walked right over to her and gave her a hug and a kiss on her cheek. "I am so glad to see you, my daughter," he too wiped his eyes with the back of his right hand. "I will take you to El Mezquitalito to visit your mother, Lorena, and Santos." Fortunato said and he turned around and also hugged Tila and Sara, and he shook hands with Eugenio.

"Yes, let's go," Catalina hopped about excited as she headed toward the door.

Tila, Sara, and Eugenio smiled. Eligia waved goodbye to Catalina, "I will see you again, soon."

Both Fortunato and Catalina walked hand in hand down the road, not far from the river, leading to the village and Antonia's hut.

"Catalina, my daughter, I will ask Tila if I can continue to work her fields and my field at *El Potrero*," Fortunato told Catalina. "I have no compensation until my future crops are harvested and sold." This year, the grasshoppers cleaned me out, but next year, with a good harvest, I can pay my sister Tila, and provide for a home large enough for all of us." He hoped Catalina would understand. She just nodded.

Father and daughter walked hand in hand down the road. Catalina noticed that her father's hands were not smooth anymore. Catalina thought about what her Aunt Tila had said before her father arrived. She had heard her Aunt Tila tell her Uncle Eugenio, "Fortunato's eyesight has begun to give him trouble and he should not gamble, anymore," Her Aunt Tila had said this and Catalina pretended she did not hear a word.

Fortunato and his ten year old daughter walked to El Mezquitalito. Catalina thought of her Uncle Eugenio and her Aunt Sara, who had stayed to visit in the Big House. At El Mezquitalito, Catalina's mother was so happy that she cried and cried while hugging Catalina. Lorena and Santos hugged Catalina and kissed her, and Catalina kissed Santos on his side of the face and held him close to her. Lorena smiled and said, "Look Mama, Santos did not wipe Catalina's kiss off his cheek."

"Oh, no, he knows who always baby sat him," Catalina said.

Catalina saw that her mother and father kissed each other and held each other a long time. Catalina heard her mother tell her father, "I was so worried about you and wondered where you were after you left the hut, since the grasshoppers came." Antonia had a fire going in the stove and made some coffee.

"We always have to boil our water that Lorena brings over in the bucket from the bovine pond to make coffee and use in our cooking," Antonia said to Catalina.

"I do miss seeing you and Lorena and baby Santos," Fortunato said, "But, whew, I never would have guessed the amount of work there is in the preparing the grounds of El Potrero for raising new crops." Fortunato said, as he sat down to join his family in the shade of the ramada.

"I missed you, too, and worried for you, especially when I imagined that you had perhaps stayed out all night." "I remembered how you would hurry to your field work in the early morning to supervise the field hands." "I was concerned about you, that you would fall asleep and tumble off your horse," Antonia said, as she poured coffee into two cups. "But now there are no fields to work and no horse to ride, but you're still gone all night."

Lorena and Catalina laughed, as they imagined their father tumbling off his horse, and the two girls followed their mother and father outside under the ramada. Lorena said, "Some mornings Eligia and I would meet with father coming home as we were going out at five in the morning to fetch the water from Aunt Tila's well, before we did our chores."

Lorena placed a plate with small cup-cakes in front of Catalina, "Happy birthday, Nina, happy birthday to you," and Antonia and Santos joined in the singing.

"*Feliz cumpleanos, mijita*," Fortunato said.

Catalina smiled and cried and laughed all at the same time.

The family sat outside on the stump logs and on a wooden bench. They sipped their coffee; they enjoyed looking at each other. Lorena talked about El Mezquitalito and how wonderful and funny their neighbors were.

In the outside Ramada, that provided a site for the cooking estufa and Antonia's kitchen pots and pans, of their Mezquitalito one room adobe house, the river breeze wafted in to tease them with something less than coolness. It was a Sinaloa's typical November day. The family in a rare moment found time to be together and share a cup of coffee. Lorena had made tea for her and Catalina.

Catalina was thinking about her trip on the train into Sinaloa, Mexico years ago, trying to put her experiences into some kind of comprehension, but she lacked the maturity of her older sister. Catalina thought that perhaps she was having such a problem figuring out her experience because she had not attended Miss Yoakum's class in Bullion Plaza and taken vocabulary drills like her sister Lorena. Catalina hoped that her mother would join her in conversation and talk to her about the train, and help her understand what it had been all about.

Catalina looked at her mother; for a moment she thought she saw an angel. The limpid glow from sunlight escaped through the bare thin huizache trees outside, lit Antonia's pale face into almost a translucent hue. Her white-streaked black wavy hair crowned her face and emphasized her dark brown eyes and pink colored cheeks. Catalina saw her mother smile and sip her coffee; Catalina felt good and warm all over.

The Worm in my Tomato

Catalina began to remember about the time they arrived in El Aliso at the "Big House." She remembered that she was seven years old, her sister Lorena was ten, and Santos was a baby of 6 months, and that her older brothers Samuel and Jose had been in high school back home in Miami.

Catalina paused, unsure if remembering would cause her to cry. She could not yet get over being on the train which she had thought of as a picnic on wheels when her mother had provided food from a basket to her family. But instead, in reality, she and her family had left their hometown to come to Sinaloa. These thoughts in her mind bothered her and she thought: What had happened? She wondered and wished her mother would explain.

"Why are we here, momma," Catalina got up from beside Lorena on the bench and sat on a stump next to her mother and asked her mother what she most wanted to know, "Why did we come here on the train, momma?"

"I believe there is a purpose for all that happens," Antonia said, "But I really don't know." Antonia paused and glanced out from the ramada to look at the village with her round brown eyes, "We came with your father so he would not be alone; to keep our family together, remember." Antonia turned aside to hide her tears from Catalina.

But now in the humid warm and darkening afternoon it seemed Antonia and Catalina were not remembering about a nice experience. Instead, it seemed something horrible had happened and both had suffered some violation of themselves. The leaving of their hometown on the Repatriation train had never been a picnic on wheels but more like a tearing away under duress a family from their home and later a child from her mother.

Lorena, who always liked to explain things said, "The past event of our coming here, that indeed, Lorena paused, as usual, to thank Miss Yoakum in her mind for the word *indeed*, she thought, thank you Miss Yoakum, and Lorena continued, " may well be historical in our lives, but a bad memory, you know, like dry bones in the desert that still glare white when uncovered, and no one knows why they are there." Lorena said, and added, "You know, as Telesforo taught the Twelve Months and me, that some memories carry with them experienced pains yet stare at one's mind's eye when uncovered," Lorena said, and added, "I memorized that from what Telesforo said," and Lorena in her mind thought: thank you Telesforo.

"What are you talking about, Lorena?" Catalina asked.

"What Telesforo taught me, in regards to your question, who knows why we are here, maybe for me to learn the lesson of the worm in my tomato," Lorena said.

Catalina shook her head side to side and her long curly black hair spun around, "Lorena, what you don't know, you just make up, and I don't understand a word of it all," Catalina laughed.

Antonia, with a wave of her hand, quieted Catalina and Lorena's discussion, and she started to talk about what she wanted to say, "Both of you girls know about how I had to sell my American furniture to Julieta and to Vega family members who had money." Antonia sipped her coffee, and continued talking. The afternoon yellow light from the sun had now darkened into a darker tone with dusk approaching somewhere on the near side of the mountain, "Some of my furniture promptly ended up in the spacious houses of my brothers-in-law Jorge in Mezquital, Antonio, and Eugenio from El Bacori."

"I know momma, I saw your oak wood dining room table in my Uncle Eugenio's dining room," Catalina said and added, "It looked so pretty with the four curved and carved legs underneath the round table," and said, "Remember mama, how each one of the legs ended in an eagle claw grasping a glass ball." Catalina looked sad, she remembered in her mind about how she had gone to her room and cried herself to sleep, that night.

"Tell us about your attending the primary school there in El Bacori, Nina," Lorena asked.

Catalina noticed that both Lorena's and her mother's eyes glistened wet, "Well I knew that I had to live in El Bacori to go to school. Later, when I heard that you had moved here, I knew there was no room for me to stay in this hut with you, that I had to stay with my Uncle Eugenio and my Aunt Sara. I went to school and the teacher taught us Spanish, but my friends in class from the pueblo talked their own language."

Catalina continued talking as she saw that her mother and Lorena were interested in listening to her. Catalina turned to face her father, "I knew that father had asked my Uncle Eugenio to let me stay with his family in El Bacori. There, I could attend the primary school. Uncle was good with me, but my Aunt Sara was too strict. One day I saw a sugar bowl on top of mother's table, I reached in to help myself to a cube of brown sugar, but Aunt Sara, when she saw me, screamed at me, bawled me out, and told me not to be getting her sugar cubes." Catalina thought in her mind about how she was refused a cube of sugar. She thought about how since then she refused to eat sugar. Never again, not even at Aunt Tila's big house, Catalina thought to herself. Catalina's self-expression had somehow given her courage to express thoughts and feelings agitating her deeper in her heart and then, finding her courage somewhere in her she asked, "Father, can I please stay and live with mother, Lorena and Santos, here in El Mezquitalito please?" Catalina begged.

"I am so sorry, my daughter," Fortunato said, with a tight low whisper, "But you will have to continue staying in my brother's home until I can afford to find a large home for all of us."

"But, I could sleep with Lorena, in her bed, at her feet," Catalina said, and pleaded again, "Please, let me stay, I can help carry the water and look for wood for the fire."

"No, my daughter, you must go to school in El Bacori; stay in my brother's house, and what's more, if you don't behave yourself and obey your father, I will ask Eugenio not to bring you again to visit, if you are going to act this way," Fortunato whispered. "You must do as you are told." Catalina heard her father say.

The dusk from the western mountain had arrived and covered the village, embracing it in light darkness but in time the dark would increase into the black of night.

"All right, father," Catalina sobbed, as she hugged him and hugged her mother. They both held Catalina in their arms and kissed her cheeks. Santos toddled over to Catalina and hugged her, too.

"This is best for you, at this time, Catalina, but at the next harvest, when I have a large house built, you can live with us, and attend the village school here with Lorena," Fortunato said, "So, tonight, when Eugenio and Sara come for you to take you with them to stay overnight at Tila's house, and leave early in the morning, you go with them, all right, daughter, and put on a smile for them, all right." Fortunato said and cuddled Catalina in his arms and kissed her on top of her head.

The family sat there and looked out into the bare village. The village looked strange and forlorn with the mezquite and huizache trees bare of green leaves. In the late light of a setting angry red sun, the village in its bare vegetation looked like pale yellow pears of adobe dirt, but now in the dark of dusk, the village looked like mounds of gray silhouettes standing in their shadows.

"How do your fields look?" Catalina heard Lorena ask her father.

"There is nothing there, bare, just dirt," Fortunato responded. "What about the tomato crops?" Lorena asked her father, again, trying to dispel the idea in her mind that all had been a nightmare event, but that it never had happened.

"All gone," Fortunato hung his head downward and clasped his right knee with his hands.

"Father," Lorena asked, "Would the plague of grasshoppers, when they chewed on the sweet red tomatoes, would they also eat the worms in the tomatoes too?" Lorena asked.

"Our tomatoes were the best; they had no worms in them." Fortunato answered. Catalina laughed at Lorena's question, and even baby Santos giggled.

From the darkened road in the direction of Tila's house came the sound of squeaking wagon wheels and the snorting of mules. The approaching moving shadows stopped in front of the hut's ramada.

Uncle Eugenio drove his wagon, pulled by two mules, up in front of Antonia's hut. Aunt Sara sat beside him. "Good evening, we came for Catalina," Eugenio said.

"Stay with us a moment and have a cup of coffee," Catalina heard her father, call out.

Catalina saw both her Uncle Eugenio and her Aunt Sara dismount. Antonia served them coffee. The adults sipped their coffee in silence.

Lorena did not say anything anymore. Catalina saw that all her family sat there and just enjoyed the moment of being together, one family moment; she saw that from time to time, the adults, Lorena, and Santos gazed up to the sky to see the most wonderful display of blinking stars beginning to come out in the late dusk.

Catalina quietly sat by; I hope father will let me stay, she thought.

The Worm in my Tomato

She waited nervous and in dread that too soon her Uncle Eugenio would decide to leave, to take her away from her mother, Lorena, and Santos. Fortunato and Eugenio were talking in low tones, but Catalina heard her Uncle Eugenio ask her father if her father thought it was necessary to go out evenings and play cards. "Now, that the locusts have cleaned us out?" Catalina heard her Uncle Eugenio say. Catalina felt embarrassed, and she pretended not to have heard. She remembered that back in Miami, her father was good at playing cards for earning needed money. Father needs money again, she thought.

Catalina could not help but think that like the stars, she was home tonight but gone tomorrow. Her tears flowed freely in the dark.

In search for his future

Fortunato, deep in thought and feeling heart-broken, trudged along the dirt road to Tila's house, oblivious of the heat lifting up from the desert ground. Overhead, the sun blazed in the tenth hour of the morning. The stiff desert breeze brought with it the stench of dead animals and rotten wood, and Fortunato covered his nose with a red bandanna. In the distance, climbing over the top of the horizon crowning the pale, blue mountain, the gray clouds slid down on the near side of the valley. Thoughts about his experience as a rancher thus far and how nothing seemed to have worked out profitably confused Fortunato. He thought for certain that he had not been dealt the lucky cards, a winning hand. He thought to himself, no matter what strikes us down, we must continue to struggle. Life at times is like a card game, a game of chance, but we must play to win. I plan in my heart to continue, what else, can I do. He stopped for a moment under the tall huizache tree in the front yard of Tila's house. He looked about, trying to plan what he would say to Tila, but the only thoughts that formed in his head were memories of Chocolate and the other dogs; always friendly, they would approach him with wagging tails, dancing eyes, and a bark of a happy greeting. He felt sad in remembering the hanging of those fine dogs.

The Worm in my Tomato

Inside the house, Fortunato and Tila sat down to enjoy a cup of coffee and talk. "Tila, as we both know so well and deeply regret, there was no harvest the first two years for lack of rain. That was out of our control, of course," Fortunato blew on his coffee to cool it down. "There was no harvest in the third year, well not for us, anyway, but the locusts had a real good one, unfortunately for us," Fortunato half-smiled, tried for some levity but failed, looked out the open window and noticed the clouds that had been far off near the mountains were fast approaching. The chirping of birds outside in the large mesquite trees could be heard, noisy as ever. "Their greed turned against them though," Fortunato said.

"Who is them, Fortunato?" asked Tila, blinking herself out of her own reverie.

"The locusts," he answered, "They ate so much that they could not fly, and they were so bloated that they died on the spot where they gobbled up our corn, tomatoes, and all our crops." Fortunato took a cautious sip of his coffee. "The locusts were so fat that frogs went about zapping them for their meals," Fortunato looked at Tila, "Isn't it confusing, Tila, how one never knows for certain for whom we work, in the end."

Tila quietly listened to Fortunato while drinking her coffee; she too, made an effort to cool her coffee, "Luisa, why did you make the coffee so hot today?" Tila yelled at Luisa who was busy preparing lunch in the kitchen.

"Do you want Eligia to go pour a little bit of cold water in your cups Tila?" asked Luisa.

"No, it is cooling down some, already," Tila responded, and turned to speak to Fortunato, "In turn, there seemed to be a plague of frogs that cleaned up the plague of locusts, eh, Fortunato," Tila smiled, "It was truly a nightmare for all of the ranchers in the valley."

"Well, shall we try again?" Fortunato asked.

"Farming around here turns out that way, now and then, during some years. The blasted grasshoppers don't come visiting every year, and probably won't for another ten years," Tila said, and added, "Luisa, bring us a small plate of cheese and two tortillas, please." Then she asked Fortunato, "What do you plan to do?"

"I don't know at the moment. I can't think of anything else to do except to continue cultivation for next year." Fortunato looked at Tila for a moment, "Can I work your fields, again, and try for a harvest by next fall, we are sure to get good crops?" Fortunato hesitantly asked.

"Not with my fields. I lost too much on this venture; I will only cattle ranch," Tila helped herself to a piece of cheese, "Here, have a piece of cheese." Tila studied Fortunato. "You are welcome to stay here, long as you want," she said, "Have another cup of coffee, Luisa will have our meal ready by the afternoon," she smiled, and added, "You know, our father left you the El Potrero, a large field of twenty-seven acres for you to farm." She served herself and Fortunato a cup of coffee, "Why not cultivate El Potrero, again if you want," she stirred her coffee. "Why not ask support from Jorge for seed," Tila said.

"I really feel bad, that you lost everything in your fields, as well," Fortunato said.

"I still have the ranch store making a profit, and I have the milk cows, the cheese room, the hogs, and the well water," she offered Fortunato a piece of white cheese and a half of a tortilla. "The ones I feel sorry for are my brothers and other ranchers around the valley who lost all their crops, too, but have no other way of making it," she ate a piece of cheese wrapped up in a half of a tortilla. "Our brothers Jorge and Eugenio in El Bacori also had crops wiped out, but they have no other choice but to continue, that's what they have been doing all their life," she gulped her coffee, "This is not the first time a swarm of locusts came by and cleaned us out."

"What about the Chinese field labor," Fortunato asked, "Could they help me next year, in cultivating El Potrero?" Fortunato wanted to know.

"No Chinese field labor, not even local Indian labor," Tila said and added, "And in addition, you can't use my fields as I have told you," Tila chewed on her tortilla, "I think I will leave them uncultivated for a year, until I save enough money for another try."

Gloomy gray clouds hung over the valley and darkened the day, outside, the birds flew away from the protective trees; a silence before a storm dominated the valley.

"I will ask Jorge for a loan to purchase seed and pay for a few field workers," Fortunato said.

"Remember, El Potrero strictly depends on natural rain water;

The Worm in my Tomato

lack of enough rain during the growing season will prevent your crops from growing," Tila pointed out.

"I know, it is a risk I must take, but what else can I do, and where else can I go," Fortunato said. He sipped his black coffee. Then he added, "Yes, I will talk with Jorge." In his mind began a nagging worry, an anxiety warning him that if Jorge said no, he surely would be doomed with no money, in debt to his sister, and no support to cultivate El Potrero. He felt trapped by a situation beyond his control.

"That is all we do in this valley; we farm and we raise livestock," Tila said.

"I will try again," Fortunato said and added, "But what do you think, if I give you back the two calves that you gave to Lorena and Catalina, it will help ease up your loss," Fortunato suggested.

"No, no, brother, absolutely not, keep the calves," Tila drummed the top of the table with her right hand's forefinger. "I gave the girls each a calf to start them off on their cattle herd; I know it will take a few years, but you have to start sometime," Tila said.

Luisa served the main meal of the day to Tila and Fortunato. A heavy silence permeated around them as they quietly ate their meal, the same silence that now filled every corner of El Aliso and Mezquital Valley. A cold streak of emotion ran down Fortunato's spine; a great sense of guilt overcame him when he thought of how he was sitting to a full meal, while his wife Antonia and his children in El Mezquitalito lacked food to eat. He had no food to take to them. He wondered: what will they eat?

Twenty Five

Lorena
The struggle for water

The locusts had come and gone. Village residents returned to their daily routines. Lorena, although sad for not having her sister Catalina at home, determined to keep busy by helping her mother, by searching for food, and by hauling water to their hut. She thought about asking Lepo, the neighbor across the road, for a bucket of well water.

It seemed that the lack of drinking water shaped the interior motives of the village residents' character. At least, that is the way Lorena felt about herself; she became more competitive to get the water her family needed. One day, Lorena tried her luck with Lepo. With her bucket in hand, she crossed the road between her hut and Lepo's house. She approached Lepo's water well, and asked Lepo, sitting under the shade of his huizache tree, for a bucket of water from his well.

"Lepo," Lorena breathed in deep, "The water in the bovine pond is muddy this day, more so than other days; can I have a bucket of water from your well; we need water for drinking and cooking." Lorena stared at Lepo, as if staring him down would force him to say yes. Silence in the village dominated the moment and the lonely huizache tree in the village; the tree, naked of leaves which were eaten by locusts, stooped to the ground in embarrassment.

Lepo did not say a word, but simply, stood up from his chair and in a hurry, replaced his new hemp rope with a knotted old rope. The knots on the old rope would tilt the bucket as it was pulled up and cause water to spill out back into the well. In this manner, Lepo plotted to keep more water in his well, if anyone attempted to pull out water from his well.

"Don Lepo," Lorena complained, "the knots on the rope when it goes through the pulley will cause my bucket to tilt and spill out my water."

"The well is dry; perhaps you should go fetch your water from the bovine pond."

"It's too muddy and there are still too many fat locusts in the pond."

"No, you can not have water. Go to the river bank and make for yourself a posito and get your water from your posito." Lepo sat down again and ignored Lorena.

"The river is too far, and I need to help mother with breakfast to feed my baby brother, Santos," Lorena begged, "Please, Mr. Lepo."

"No, my well is too low in water, now. Furthermore, I don't think you should come here for water, again," Lepo said. The silence was overbearing and the village became an arena for a debate. Lorena looked at the huizache tree, slim, calm, and serene in bearing; in spite of being solitary and growing on the plain of the desert's edge near the village, and she thought that the huizache tree stood tall in her support.

Lucky for Lorena, Lepo's wife Josefa overheard their talk. Josefa was a tall and slender woman with waist length black braids hanging down her back. She was always kind to Antonia and Lorena. Josefa had come out from the kitchen to see what was going on. "Let little Lorena get her water, Lepo," She said. She looked at Lorena and added, "When you can, child, bring me some dry bones from your Aunt Tila's ranch, after Chapo butchers a beef cow."

"You can have water this time only on condition you bring those dry bones," Lepo said.

With all her strength of her twelve-year-old skinny body, Lorena pulled out her bucket, half full of clear water, and she sat it on the ground; she untied her bucket from the rope and held its metal handle firmly in her right hand. With much difficulty, she pulled on the handle and lifted the bucket off the ground as she took small steps toward her house. The weight of the bucket forced Lorena to bend toward her right side and this posture shaped her body into a "C".

Lorena glanced sideways and saw Lepo's short and stocky muscular body convulsed in restrained laughter, as he watched her struggle to haul her half-filled bucket of water to her house. Josefa waved goodbye, "Don't forget Lorena, please, I need the dry bones to make some *tizas*."

Lorena remembered Catalina's question about why her mother and family were here. Lorena thought of how Telesforo had explained it once when she had asked him why things happened. Lorena was sure that he would know. Everyone considered Telesforo to be the village philosopher. Lorena thought: *philosopher*, thank you Miss Yoakum.

Of course, Telesforo always credited the tribal ants for teaching him what little he knew. "I have learned much of what I know from the red ant tribes and the black ant tribes," he always said.

What Lorena could not understand was that if Telesforo was the village philosopher, why Julieta appeared not to have much respect for Telesforo.

Lorena walked across the road to where Telesforo sat under the leafless un-shady tree, studying the ants and talking with his girl Three Months, Maya, Junis and Julia. She sat beside Maya, near the end of the long tree trunk that served as a bench. "Hello, *Senor* Telesforo, Maya, Junis, and Julia." Lorena began, "Telesforo, my little sister Catalina asked my mother this question: "Why did we come here on the train?" Then Lorena asked Telesforo, "Can you help me understand this better and give me some more answers so that I can tell my little sister, next time I see her, please?"

Telesforo remained calm and silent for a minute or two, looking down at the ants crisscrossing back and forth, as usual, carrying heavy loads twice their physical size, "Well, it's like these ants," he said, looking at Lorena and the girl Three Months, "We share something in common with them," Telesforo said.

"What?" Lorena and the girl Three Months asked.

"Hunger," Telesforo said, and added, "We are all hungry, so each day we get up to search for food."

"Is that all?" The girls asked in unison.

"No, hunger drives us to seek food in hope that we will find it," Telesforo pointed to the ants, "I have never seen an ant return home empty handed, in all the years I have watched them, they have hope." A string of red ants scurried along on hair thin legs, carrying large loads over their heads.

"Julieta says we must have faith, hope and charity," Lorena said, "And I learned that from my catechism book."

"No, Lorena, you have to learn the spiritual from a physical way of life," Telesforo said, "Look at the ants, see how they work to care for one another, for their family and for their tribe, and it is because they are driven by hunger and the hope to find food each day; see how their hope is caused by a need and given life in an actual way?"

"Well, what about the hope, faith, and charity in my book?" asked Lorena.

"After many years, in fact all their life, of finding their food, a fulfillment of their hope, they expect to find food each day, without a doubt, and that expectation based on their hope is faith, and that they do it together for helping each other is charity," Telesforo looked down at the ants.

"Now, I understand what I memorized from the book," Lorena exclaimed, standing up and hopping about. The girl Three Months laughed out loud, and Maya said, "That's Lorena."

Lorena ran across the road to her hut to tell her mother what she had learned from Telesforo, "Mama, I know now what Julieta taught me from the catechism book and from her talks on religion; I know what hope, faith, and charity mean." Lorena skipped about the ramada and tickled Santos under his chin.

"I know now what to tell Catalina; why we came here on the train," Lorena said.

"Why?" Antonia asked.

"Because we share hunger in common with the ants, and we came here in hope to find the food; we have found food and not died yet, so we have faith in finding more; because we love each other as a family, we have charity; that is what Telesforo said," Lorena pointed out. "But I don't know why Telesforo is so poor like us," Lorena added, "He knows so much like Julieta and he is the village philosopher, too, why is that, mama?"

Antonia said to Lorena, "Telesforo is poor like us because we live in a poor farming area, and the world of ideas and the markets and banks of money are controlled outside the village and faraway in the rich countries." Ask your brother Samuel about it; he will explain it all to you, like he showed me," Antonia stirred some rice in the hot skillet.

"But mother, Telesforo is so poor that he has as his life ambition

The Worm in my Tomato

someday to eat a whole *empanada*, all of it by himself," Lorena said. "As for myself, mama, after really taking a good look at Telesforo, studying Telesforo like he studies the ants, and *seeing* Telesforo, I have determined not to be like him, hungry and thin." Lorena sat down on the log bench in the ramada, bathed in the sunlight streaming down past the bare limbs of the trees, "No, mother, for me, my ideas must lead to something practical, useful, that will make my life better, you know like make something to sell or trade, like Aunt Tila does; maybe make tizas to earn for us water, food, and wood."

Another thing Lorena pondered about was that her friend Carmen told her that Telesforo always sends his boy Five Months to fetch water from his many positos. His girl Seven Months wash clothes on the river's edge, beating the fabrics on the rocks and after rinsing the clothes in the river and squeezing the water out, laying the garments on top of bushes to dry by the sun. Telesforo worked part time in Aunt Tila's cheese room, but he spent a great deal of his time observing and studying the ants in his front yard. Lorena planned to find ways to acquire food, clean water, and purchase enough mezquite wood from the wood cutters to live comfortable in their small hut. She felt empowered now that she understood hope, faith, and charity. She planned to work hard like the ants.

When Lorena first arrived to the Big House, she recalled how Eligia had sat with her in the kitchen table at Aunt Tila's house. Eligia had told Lorena that she was her cousin. At first, Lorena thought it odd that a cinnamon, reddish-hued skin colored girl with straight black hair was sitting among the pale skinned, blond, green eyed Vega cousins. But Lorena had noticed how Eligia was well mannered and beautiful; Lorena had no trouble claiming her as her cousin. That same day, Lorena had seen Gonzalo, sitting quietly, almost in the shadows, in Aunt Tila's kitchen, when family and guests had supper. "He is a cousin," Eligia had told Lorena. He was a young man, darker than Eligia, with his long straight black hair tied together behind his back. He was agile and quick of movement. When Antonia and Lorena later had talked with him, he claimed to be a cousin of all the Vegas because he said that he had been fathered at the El Fuerte River beach under the spell of the river god of love. Upon Antonia's query for a specific father and as to who was his mother, he named Luisa as his mother and he may have known the name of his father, but he simply said that it was one of the Vega men from El Mezquital. Once when Antonia in conversation with Luisa asked about Gonzalo's father, his mother Luisa would not reveal Gonzalo's father's identity. But if Luisa was his mother, then Eligia was his sister and indeed the Vega clan children were his cousins, including Lorena.

After Antonia, Lorena, and Santos were repatriated to El Mezquitalito from Tila's house in El Aliso, Gonzalo would appear periodically at Lorena's front yard. He always introduced himself to Lorena as being her cousin named Gonzalo. He appeared at her adobe's hut door carrying something for them to eat: a rabbit, *tunas*, the fruit of the prickly pear cactus, or desert *pitahaya*, the fruit of the *saguaro* giant cactus, in season, or fruit of the Guamúchil tree.

Gonzalo claimed to live among the thickets in the desert, surviving on desert plants and wild bee honey. Antonia referred to him as John the Baptist. Each time Gonzalo visited, he would bring the family food, including wild honey. The large waxed slab saturated with golden honey would be placed in a small tin tub. Antonia would share honey with the neighbors; afterwards she, Lorena, and Santos feasted for days on wild honey. Antonia would never, however, accept the large furry squirrels that Gonzalo offered for the family's meat diet. He said he would bring Antonia snake meat sometime, if she wished. Antonia had said "Thanks, but no thanks." Just as John the Baptist had suddenly appeared, like an unexpected breeze, he would leave and disappear into the desert.

Lorena had, however, asked from Gonzalo for dead cow bones, even if bleached by the sun, if he ever ran across bones where ranchers had slaughtered a beef cow. She told Gonzalo that she planned to use the bones to make *tizas*. "Tizas," she informed Gonzalo what they were and for what they were used, just as Eligia's mother Luisa had informed Lorena, "are prized by the native Indian women to use on their skillets and flat irons so as to prevent tortillas from sticking on the

The Worm in my Tomato

hot surface and burn to a crisp." Lorena remembered how Luisa had showed her some *tizas* and taught her how they were made.

Gonzalo remembered Lorena's request and upon his most recent visit had brought Lorena some leg bones from a huge beef cow, recently butchered.

Lorena dried the bones in the sun, pounded and grounded them into fine powder in the *metate* with a lava rock pestle, a *metlapil*, mixed the bone powder with water in a bowl and made dough, and rolled it into white bone dough balls, and shaped them like pears. She carefully placed the tizas by rows on a clean washed board outside to dry and harden by the hot sun. Then she placed her pear shaped tizas inside the outdoor adobe *horno* to make the tizas porous brittle by fire heat and at the same time harden in the hot oven. The pear shaped tizas were easy to hold firmly in one's hand from the top of the pear. The tiza was hard and durable enough to bang on top of the hot cooking flat iron and brittle enough to leave the thin bone dust to prevent the tortillas from sticking on its hot surface. "That is my secret, mother; harden my tizas just enough by the heat of fire, to get that hardened brittleness." Lorena said to Antonia.

Lorena, however, did not have enough bones for the number of *tizas* she wanted to make, so she decided to search for more bones herself.

After lunch, Lorena skirted from mezquite shade to bush shade to avoid burning her feet on the hot sand, as she scurried from tree to bush toward her Aunt Tila's Big House. Lorena remembered seeing the dry bones that Chapo discarded, after he butchered a steer. The bones now glistened in the sun. Lorena thought to herself: I will not give Josefa the dry bones. I will make the *tizas* for her. I know how to make *tizas*. I have already made *tizas*. My tizas are not round. I have trouble making nice round ones, but mine, being pear shaped, are easier to grasp and work with, mama uses them; she finds them easier to grasp, much easier than the round ones. Lorena reasoned and convinced herself that she should make the *tizas*.

"How did you figure that out, Lorena, I really don't think other women in the village make tizas in the same way?" Antonia asked.

"No, they don't, mama; they stop after the sun dries and hardens the tizas, but I learned my way from what I remember doing in Miss

The Worm in my Tomato

Yoakum's arts and crafts class."

Lorena had remembered how she had learned to structure her papier-mâché figurines in Miss Yoakum's arts and crafts class in Bullion Plaza Elementary School. Lorena shaped her *tizas* in such a way that Josefa would find it easy to hold and easy to rub the dry bone on her skillet. Oil and lard were luxuries the villagers could not afford. But, when they had lard they only used lard in their direct cooking of beans, tamales, or other dishes that required lard.

Lorena placed more pear shaped bone *tizas* in the hot adobe outdoor oven, which had been stoked in fire with mezquite logs, to bake and harden the *tizas*. Lorena felt empowered at having put her training in arts and crafts class to good use. Lorena thought to herself: not only do I use the vocabulary words Miss Yoakum taught us in our class vocabulary drills, but I use other skills I learned as well. Hooray, the *Tiza* Maker danced.

Tizas for water

Lorena glided about the hut's ramada dirt floor in joy. Lorena's goal was to make *tizas* to trade to local village women for food items. She planned to trade with Josefa for water from Lepo's well. She planned to trade for a hemp rope from Lepo, to use for drawing water from his well. Outside the ramada, birds dared to swing in the bare green limbs of trees. The locust plague had forced its influence even as high as the sun, and the sun now yearned for the challenge of forcing its light through the thick foliage of leaves.

The following day, Lorena skipped across the road to Lepo's house and she took her bucket to fill at Lepo's water well. She carried Josefa's *tizas* in it. Lepo promptly came out from the Ramada shade and hurried toward the well to protect his water. Josefa came out to inquire about her request she had made to Lorena for dry bones. Lorena knew that Josefa would be delighted to learn that Lorena had already made the *tizas*. This would save Josefa much hard work, and Lorena eagerly anticipated Josefa's joyful surprise at the ease in handling pear-shaped *tizas*. The birds chirped in the bare huizasche. Lorena thought she saw the sun stop momentarily to witness Josefa's anticipated joy.

Lepo carried in his left hand the old knotted rope. Lorena knew that he intended to change his good rope with the old knotted one. "Back so soon for more of my water, I see," Lepo half smiled half sneered.

"Leave the rope on, Lepo," Lorena squared her thin shoulders, "I will trade you and Josefa my especially made *tizas* for your hemp rope." Lorena showed Josefa the pear-shaped dry bone tizas from her bucket. Josefa's black eyes sparkled with interest and appreciation of the pear-shaped bone cooking tool for rubbing on her flat iron. Josefa carefully inspected the *tizas* and she smiled and her face glowed with pleasure. Lorena smiled in delight and she thought she saw the sun now move on about its day journey.

Lepo stood his ground, standing between his water well and Lorena; he held tight to his new hemp rope, "You can't have any water, Lorena, go to the pond."

"I want these *tizas*," Josefa stared at Lepo.

Lepo hesitated, "But this is *Ixtle* rope," he pleaded with Josefa, "I would have to go cut some maguey plant fronds and tease out the *Ixtle* threads to weave into a rope. It's a lot of work." His dark acorn-colored face reddened.

"Lepo," Josefa said sternly, "Do you want some fresh corn tortillas or not?" She looked him in the eye, "Because, if you do, I need *tizas* to keep my tortillas from sticking on my *comal*," Josefa said, and she took the bone *tizas*.

"All right, Lorena, it's your rope, use it," said Lepo, and then said in a measured tone, "But only this once, and furthermore, go to the pond from now on."

Lorena tied her new rope to her bucket. She carefully pulled up her brim-filled bucket of clean fresh water. She swayed from side to side as she, in a slow and laborious snail-like body movements, inched her "C" shaped self to her home with a full bucket of water. In her other hand she carried her own new *Ixtle* hemp rope. Lorena intended to make more of her specialty *tizas* and use them to barter with the pueblo women for other goods. She intended to figure out a way to get Lepo's permission for her to help herself to the fresh well water

The Worm in my Tomato

whenever she needed. Lorena hummed a song she had learned in Bullion Plaza about bones connected to other bones.

⌒⟶

Early next morning, Carmen came to visit Lorena.

"Lorena, I have come to learn from you how to make pear shaped bone *tizas*." Carmen said in her sweet charming voice, and Carmen smiled her dimpled cinnamon colored cheeks, "Please, Lorena, my mother wants me to learn," her naturally curly hair bounced from side to side. Carmen's hair was unlike the long straight hair of the Seven Girls Months or like Eligia's.

Lorena was glad to see her, and she thought in her mind, as she greeted Carmen, that Carmen was the most natural beautiful girl she had ever known; not even Maria Cota, her school chum from Miami, whose hair was black and curly, too, was as naturally beautiful.

Carmen was tall, on the thin side, but strong, and she reminded Lorena of a long-legged Flamingo; Lorena suppressed a laugh and said, "All right, Carmen."

"Thank you, Lorena," and Carmen asked, "What do I do, to make *tizas* like the kind you make, because my mother likes them better than any other kind?"

"The first thing is to wash the bones clean and then dry the bones in the hot sun," Lorena said. "I really have to run over to the pond and get another bucket of water for later use since I used up the water for these bones," Lorena grabbed her tin bucket and walked toward the pond.

Carmen hurried beside Lorena, and both girls made out straight to the pond, "Lorena, why do you get water from the pond?" Carmen asked, "Why don't you get water from the Fuerte River?" She hurried to keep up with Lorena.

"Let's hurry before the sun heats up the sand on the road, Lorena said, "The water is too dirty, the current is swift, and it's farther away than the pond from my house."

"It's not that far, and many girls from the village, like the Seven Girl Months, fetch water from the river, because as you know, my father, Lepo, does not like people from the village to use his well." Carmen said.

The Worm in my Tomato

The sun began to hurry, too, and rise up the high slant of the eastern side of the pale blue sky. The naked trees tried to sway with the wind but still lacked their leaves with which to dance. The frogs around the pond stayed buried under the wet mud to escape from the heat.

"What about the dirty water? Where does it come from? Now and then dead drowned dogs are fished out, right?" Lorena asked, as she kicked at a mound of dirt.

"Well, yes, but you don't get the water from the river directly, you take it from a *posito*," the Flamingo's long legs swiftly stretched out in a fast pace to keep up with Lorena who scooted along the road like a road-runner plume headed bird.

"A *posito*? What's that, for real?" Lorena thought for a moment, "Gonzalo used that word the other day when he said that Lepo's water well was a giant *posito*," she remembered.

"Lorena, you have not learned from us what a *posito* is, so I will show you all about a *posito* and you can show me how you make your pear *tizas*?" Carmen negotiated to confirm her petition.

"All right, but let's hurry now to the pond."

"No, let me show you my *posito*. You can have a bucket of water from my *posito* and I will show you how to make your own *posito* and you will always have cool clear pure water, and no more boiling your water, either," Carmen insisted.

"Really, this I have to see; let's go to the river." Lorena was quick to get an insight into how to decrease her tedious work of boiling the water. The girls hurried past the pond and presently they stood on the village side of the shore, opposite the bank covered with dense growth of brush and trees. They looked at the middle of the river with its churning swift flow cascading in undulating ups and downs with the sparkling glints of light gliding on the tops of waves.

"We have to find the friendly side of the river and follow it to its quiet places behind the huge boulders along the beach," Carmen said and led the way. She took her leather sandals off and wiggled her bare feet and toes in the cool mud. She smiled and squished cool wet mud up between her toes, and then continued on wading in the low water, like a flamingo with her long legs striding along the shore.

"The hole dug in the earth along side the beach will fill with

The Worm in my Tomato

deposited water that seeps into the hole after being filtered by the sand. The water collection takes time to fill, but you'll see how overnight your *posito* becomes full with pure, sweet clear water that filtered up through the bottom sand along the river beach and up though the sand." Carmen explained as she led Lorena to where Carmen's water hole was dug behind two large boulders.

Lorena, after seeing Carmen enjoy the cool mud with her bare feet, also took off her sandals, as well, and twisted her feet around in the mud. She stood still for awhile and squished and squashed the mud under her feet and said, "This is fun, Carmen, but we must make my *posito*." She kicked at the mud, "I can understand how the water will seep through the sand into the hole. Water flows underground all the way to the pond, and also goes underground to fill your father Lepo's water well, too." Lorena remembered Miss Yoakum explaining in her science class how water would seep up, seeking its own level.

Lorena could see that all along the shore of the River on the sand, the young village girls dug holes in the sand. Carmen and Lorena arrived at Carmen's *positos*. She had three large bucket sized positos. The water in them was clear and cool. Lorena saw how the water had filtered through the sand.

"Carmen, I remember when Miss Yoakum had covered this *phenomenon*," Lorena thought aside to herself, thank you Miss Yoakum, and continued speaking to Carmen, " Miss Yoakum, my teacher, covered this *phenomenon* in our science lessons, and I remember this word from our word drills," Lorena said.

"I have no idea, Lorena, about what your teacher taught you, but all I know is that this happens, fill your bucket, Lorena," Carmen half shouted and laughed at the same time. Lorena filled her bucket with the clear cool water. Then Carmen and Lorena sauntered barefooted along the shore searching for an ideal location to dig Lorena's very own respective *posito*. Along the way, Lorena picked up a round shiny slick blue stone.

"My own water collection hole in the sand," Lorena said, half-sliding along with her feet enjoying the cool mud, "Wow, Carmen, this is great. I will have my own small well." The girls searched for a proper location for Lorena's water hole in a secluded place, protected by large boulders with sand at a level with the river.

323   *The Worm in my Tomato*

"The location for the hole must be at a level with the river so that whatever it is that allows the water to seep upward into the posito, can do its work," Carmen stopped and pointed to a sandy spot, "Right here on the shore side of the river between these two large boulders." Carmen stood in the cool slow moving water close to the shore.

Lorena began to dig with both her hands; she dug a large *posito* and decorated the outside with small rocks and marked it with her initials, LV. Then she tightened her jaws and puckered her lips and declared: "Nobody mess with my *posito*." Lorena stood up, and grabbed her bucket of water. "Carmen," Lorena became pensive, and asked, "why do you have three *positos*, when your father has the village well?"

"Oh, Lorena, if you only knew, the well goes dry most of the time, and my father has to wait until it fills up again," She laughed, "I come to the river with Maya, Junis and Julia for water early in the mornings, you know, those Three Girl Months have dug many positos along the shore."

"Carmen, something else, I have seen some blankets placed on the dry sand between the huge boulders away from the shore, why is that?" Lorena asked, as she struggled with her bucket full of water.

"That is where lovers come in the evenings to see the bright moon touching the trees along the far shore, hear the murmuring sounds of the water, and perhaps bathe in the dark of night and touch the silver light that rides the waves," Carmen said.

"Who are the lovers?" Lorena wanted to know.

"Lorena, don't you know, well, the older girls and boys in our village and sometimes from the ranches around the valley." Carmen took the lead and hurried along, her long Flamingo legs gaining ground, with Lorena gasping and out of breath following after, being left behind, carrying her bucket full of cool water.

"Carmen," Lorena said, trying to catch her breath, "What do the lovers do?" she panted, "I mean, look at the moon, swim in the dark, and what else now, I want to know," Lorena asked.

"I don't know; why don't you come down to the river beach with the girl Three Months, Eligia, and me sometime at night and find out. I have only seen the shadows walking along the beach; on the sand they danced in the rhythm of the river's waves cascading in the moonlight; then the shadows together blended into one." Carmen explained,

The Worm in my Tomato

"But you have to spy on them in secret or you'll scare the river god of love away; my mother told me that there and then the river god was creating children for the people of the village." Carmen rushed along and yelled back in exasperation, "Gosh, Lorena, you should know; Miss Julieta baptizes them and you teach them catechism."

Carmen hurried back to Lorena's hut for she was anxious for Lorena to continue her lesson on how to make pear shaped *tizas*.

Lorena finally placed her bucket down in the ramada. "What do the lovers do, Carmen?" Lorena persisted, gasping for air.

"Well," Carmen said, her hands on her waist and her elbows sticking out, impatient to learn to make *tizas*, "My mother says that there is where river babies are made, you know, by the river god of love," Carmen said, sitting down on a chair, "Oh my, my feet are packed in mud," she looked at Lorena, "My mother says that most of our village babies are river babies, and Julieta baptizes them and you have been teaching them catechism at Julieta's house, as I've told you before Lorena, that's all I know, ask the kids you teach, now let's get to work on our *tizas*," Carmen stood up and moved out in the yard.

Lorena explained to Carmen about the use of the bone *tizas*. Lorena was certain Carmen knew about *tizas* for many years. But she thought that like Miss Yoakum, a good teacher can not assume what students already know or don't know. Yet, Carmen did not know how to make *tizas*. "It's like knowing about tortillas and not knowing how to make them," Lorena said out loud, like if talking to herself.

Carmen listened and Lorena continued to explain, "The bone meal ball is a pear shaped ball, Carmen, because I choose to shape it like a pear, it's easier to grab and use than when it is shaped round like a rubber ball."

Lorena's *tizas* were as large as a small coffee cup, and she showed Carmen a *tiza*.

"It's like making a dough round ball for making a tortilla, right," Carmen exclaimed, excited.

"Uh huh, the dough is rolled up into the size of a rubber ball and then squeezed to form a neck and shaped like a pear and then left out in the hot sun to dry and bake."

"I know all that," cried out Carmen, "You have told me before,

The Worm in my Tomato

Lorena, but *how* do you make your pear design *tiza*."

"Just shape the ball of bone dough into a pear," Lorena said, and demonstrated with some dough.

"Oh, that is all, nothing mysterious about that, now I see how that is done." Carmen prepared to leave for her house across the road. Carmen laughed in delight and said, "All right, I am going home now to make *tizas* from some old dry bones my mother got from Chapo and has been saving for my project." Carmen hurried across the road to her house.

"Carmen, tell your father Lepo I am coming over tomorrow for some nice cool water from his well," Lorena yelled at Carmen, "I will barter some *tizas* for the water."

"No, my father said he will not trade water for *tizas* with you, and furthermore he wanted me to learn how to make pear shaped *tizas* for my mother so he does not have to give you water, anymore," Carmen yelled back, "You have your own posito, now."

Lorena watched Carmen go into her adobe house; she felt smug; she smiled, fingering her dry small smooth stone that was now black in the light. Lorena thought how glad she was that she had kept her secret about how she hardened her tizas in the adobe oven by fire to make them hard yet brittle when rubbed for easier smearing the skillets with *tiza* residue. Lorena was certain she still had something to barter with Lepo for water and food from Josefa and other women in the village. "I'm smart like my Aunt Tila," she said out loud to herself.

A hut is near a large mezquite tree; under the shade of the tree is a wooden bench on which Telesforo can sit and study the ants.

The Worm in my Tomato

Twenty Six

Antonia
Feast of reality

The trees outside the hut's ramada stood stooped and bare. Their natural heritage of green leaves was slow in becoming visible, although the promise was in progress within the trees. The birds seldom bothered to visit the sad trees anymore; where they had gone to nest, no one knew.

In the morning, Fortunato surprised Antonia by bringing her a letter from her cousin Josephina in Florence, Arizona, that had been delivered to Tila's house. Josephina in a few sentences informed her about Nanita's death during a cold February of 1935. She apologized for writing her letter a few weeks late, but she said that Nanita, going on ninety-six years of age, had passed away in her sleep during the night. "She had a burial Mass with lots of friends praying for her. We buried her in the Florence cemetery," wrote Josephina.

Antonia grieved all day and she prayed a rosary for her Nanita. Somehow Lorena and Santos managed without her help on that day.

Next day Antonia felt miserable and she had her usual problem about finding food for breakfast and supper; she took a short excursion with Santos on hand, to search for edible desert plants. She returned to the ramada and searched the cupboard. Lunch had gone out of her's and Lorena's life style. For some unknown reason, all of a sudden, Antonia remembered Catalina's question, "Mama, why are we here," and her eyes misted over with pent up tears. Lately, however, she had begun to spend more time thinking about her personal and family situation. Her thoughts for some time had been preoccupied with memories about Nanita. She appreciated Josephina's letter informing her that Nanita had died. This is what Antonia had always feared: that Nanita would die when she was yet in Mexico. Like Catalina, she asked herself why she was here, after all, and what should she do. "I think I will talk to Julieta on Sunday," she said. She wanted to begin a *novenario*, the nine days of rosaries for the recent deceased, with Julieta.

There usually was a lack of food: they ate what was available; there was no problem with what to eat. A month ago, Jorge had ridden his horse to the edge of their yard, and dropped a twenty-five pound sack of pinto beans on the ground. Then he galloped away. Antonia carefully measured out the beans for herself, Lorena, and Santos; the beans would last for a month. Antonia's bean supply would be augmented, when at least twice a month, Fortunato would bring what food he could obtain from Luisa or purchase on credit from Tila's small ranch store.

"I can understand why Telesforo's great goal is to eat a whole *empanada* by himself," Antonia said to Lorena busy cleaning the last cup of beans. "It would be wonderful to have a full stomach."

"Yes, mother," Lorena got up to pour water into a pan in which to wash the beans. "Julieta says that the longer a people stay with each other, the more they become like each other. I am beginning to want to learn from Telesforo how to stay alive while eating very little," Lorena said.

"Well," Antonia said as she poured a cup of white flour into a small tin hand basin, "that is impossible," she began to mold the flour into dough.

"Yes, mother, Telesforo has helped the girl Three Months and me to think more of how the things we eat somehow become part of us," Lorena placed the beans into a pan with water to cook the beans, " like the ants, the animals, the frogs, and the fruit from the trees," she said.

"Thank you Lorena, we'll let the beans stand in the water for awhile to soften them up before cooking them."

"Sometimes I think the skin on my back and on my stomach is only separated by an empty place for food," Lorena said.

Antonia formed small balls of dough to later stretch into tortillas. Antonia thought of how often she found herself always being hungry, and she felt sorry that her children went hungry as well.

Lorena somehow always thought of how she wanted to learn anything she could learn from anyone. "Mother, I wish Samuel would come visit us more often." "I want to ask him so many questions, and the last time he came, he brought me my pair of leather shoes so I

The Worm in my Tomato

would not get my feet burned when I walked on the hot dirt road," Lorena said.

"That was nice of Samuel," Antonia said, "I wish he would come visit us; he must be very busy surveying land."

"I also miss Jose, so much, I can sometimes hear him laughing the way he always laughed, and I turn around to see him and no one is there from where the laughter came," Lorena said, "But the one I miss so much and sometimes cry over it is my little sister Catalina."

"Well, I pray every day for our family to come together again," Antonia said.

"Mama," Lorena took the pan with the beans in her hand, "Do you want me to start the fire, mother, and start cooking the beans?" Upon seeing her mother indicate 'yes' with a movement of her head, Lorena placed the pan of beans on the stove and she worked on getting the fire going in the stove. "But, mother, we will all be together when we return to our home in Miami, don't you think so?" Lorena asked.

"Yes, I do think that way myself, but how your father will resolve his work in agriculture and how we will return home is the problem," Antonia answered.

"I sure hope it is soon, mother, I want to return to school," Lorena said, "My main obsession," Lorena smiled and she thought the word in her mind, *obsession*, and in her mind she thanked Miss Yoakum; she remembered the morning vocabulary word drills; these memories still remained with Lorena and inspired her continued desire to learn, "is wanting to learn, mother, as you well know; since this year began and we started living in El Mezquitalito, I went into a period of asking "Why" and expecting an answer from all creation around me, you know, the ants, birds, frogs, cows, sky, and stars." Lorena looked at her mother, "I think Julieta and Telesforo really helped me." Lorena had the fire burning strong and the beans were set to cook. "My need to know and to understand are a hunger never satisfied." She stepped aside from the stove so her mother could place her comal on which to cook the tortillas. "I think it started with my studying the ants with Telesforo. So, when Carmen asked me one evening to go hunt frogs for supper, I readily accepted, I have learned to hunt for food from what is available in our surroundings."

The Worm in my Tomato

Antonia had made it clear to Lorena to give whatever frogs she caught to Carmen's family. Antonia would not even consider the idea of eating frogs for keeping herself from starving.

"Not me," Lorena had said; "I fully intend to boil every skinny and fat frog I can catch."

Lorena felt confident that she could catch enough frogs to give to Carmen's family, Lepo and Josefa. Lorena was sure that she could trade one or two of her fat frogs with Lepo for some of his well water, too.

〜〜

Feast of frogs under a moonlit night

Carmen, Maya, Junis, Julia, and Lorena spent many moonlit evenings around the pond catching frogs and dumping them into their tin buckets covered over with a gunny sack. The girls would return home triumphant and ready to create a common fire, pour pond water into their buckets and boil their feast. They kept the frogs from leaping out by covering the buckets with twisted wire lids. In no time the frogs were boiled. They then peeled the skin, chopped off the head, fished out the entrails, and dumped their torsos and legs into a sauce pan with red chili sauce. The girls were soon joined by Telesforo, Marta, and the rest of the Twelve Months and by Lepo and Josefa. They feasted into the night under the moon, during many evenings with the moon sometimes full, some times new, and some times a half-moon. Blackness filled the village, stars overhead sparkled, and the large yellow bulb in the black sky was so close it seemed they could touch it with their finger-tips. "I won't touch the moon," laughed Lorena, "I don't want to smear it with red chili sauce."

Telesforo and Marta and their boy and girl Months joined in singing local favorite Mexican songs. Maya, Junis, Julia joined Lepo, Josefa, and Carmen in singing *Cuatro Milpas*. Lorena hummed along. At first, when Antonia and Lorena moved into the neighborhood, Antonia stayed by herself under the Ramada and sipped her coffee in solitude with only her growling stomach for company. However, after a week of hunger pain, and when her own back skin said good evening to her stomach tripe, Antonia joined Lorena and the neighbors around the bonfire. Antonia's hunger won over her inhibitions and she discovered the delicacy of frog legs. The village rich man Lepo no doubt urged and convinced by Josefa donated the red chile sauce and some corn on the cob roasted on the fire which added to their feast. Even Santos joined in by sucking on frog legs. Lorena and the Twelve Months joked and laughed, while the adults enjoyed their coffee, spiced with *pulque*, donated by Lepo; they told ghost stories, jokes, and conversed into the night.

The mezquite logs in the fire crackled and spat sparks into the cool desert air. In intervals of the laughter and loud conversation could be heard the chirping and other noises of night life and the croaking of young frogs that had lived through the plague of locusts; even an owl's hoot could be heard now and then coming from the top of a tall saguaro. Rats awaited the dawn to forage the area for food scraps; snakes slithered in the sand and followed after the rats. Coyotes howled at the moon, now and then, and circled about but kept their distance in the darkness of the desert; they did not wish to challenge the wrath of village dogs.

Some evenings Telesforo joined his Girl Months and Lorena to hunt for rattler snakes that preyed on the frogs. In those times when Telesforo caught a fat rattler, their fare at the bonfire outdoors kitchen included roasted snake meat. Occasionally, Lepo would add one or two tasty field rabbits. Night provided the time when life fed on life: frogs zapped bugs and mosquitoes; snakes squeezed frogs down their snakes' wide gullets; rabbits scoured for seeds and desert greens; Lorena, Carmen, and the girl Months boiled and fried and sautéed them all with red chile and transformed the bounty of nature into their night bonfire dinner.

"In this way," Telesforo said, "What each creature eats becomes them and what we eat becomes us," and he pointed with his index finger to his skinny forearm and said, "Here is the snake meat I ate two years ago become part of my arm." The Twelve Months thought this so funny that they started pointing at each other and saying "There are the frogs we ate last year," and they hopped about like a frog.

Lorena looked at Santos busily chomping on frog legs and she hoped he would not get frog-eyes.

The pale yellow new moon with its crescent crowned the tops of surrounding shivering bare trees in the coolness of the night; the sparkling ornaments glinted all over the black sky; the river breeze caressed the feasters' faces as they all became one with creation. "The sun by day, the moon and stars by night, the water we drink, the air we breathe, the food we eat, the songs we sing, the prayers we pray, indeed all creation becomes us and we become them, we are all one with all and one with our Creator of all," Telesforo said and burped from eating too many frog legs and too many roasted corn on the cob, and he soon swooned from drinking too much of Lepo's *pulque*. Marta and the Twelve Months helped him inside his adobe house and put him to sleep.

⌒

Julieta

Two or three mornings a week Antonia, Lorena and Santos would make their way down the dirt road across the village to Julieta's house. When Antonia and Lorena visited Julieta to pray a novena or a rosary, in her house, Julieta would invite them to sit and enjoy something to eat. They would sometimes eat a potato, a fruit in season, or some green vegetable that Julieta shared with them. Antonia always made sure Santos was given a portion of fruit and vegetables to help his small frail body to grow. When Santos was busy chomping away like the locusts, Lorena carefully studied him and marveled at his tomato red cheeks, his large round shaped moon eyes, his silky corn hair, his corn stem legs, his potato knees and his frog leg fingers. She was certain that Telesforo was correct in his belief that people became what they ate, and that we were all one with all. She made up her mind to learn all she could from nature and carefully listen to what Telesforo said, even when he talked with the red ants in his front yard under the shade of the mezquite tree.

During their visits to Julieta's house, Julieta taught Lorena a catechism lesson. Julieta always lamented the lack of a local priest and she and Antonia would pray that God bless them with an itinerant priest, and Julieta said, "So we can celebrate Mass and enjoy the body and blood of our Lord and savior." Julieta, Antonia and Lorena would plead their case for their deeply felt spiritual hunger.

"I have a hunger of another sort, too, Julieta," Antonia said, looking tentatively at Julieta, "I keep asking myself what am I doing here at this time, after all we have been through, and I ask you what do you think I should do?"

"Well, Antonia, what do you mean?" asked Julieta.

"My heart aches for home," Antonia hesitated a moment, "I feel strongly a physical, spiritual and cultural hunger that only my hometown in Arizona can satisfy."

Julieta handed Lorena her catechism book; she started to make some coffee, "Go on Antonia, keep talking." "The coffee will be done, shortly," Julieta said. A cool breeze blew in through an open window in the kitchen. Lorena read her book.

"Well, I am wondering now, more and more each day, just how long must a Christian wife carry her cross and remain joined together as one with her husband? Ever since the locust plague, Fortunato continued to work very hard on his fields El Potrero," Antonia dabbed at her eyes with her handkerchief, "but I always missed him so terribly and yet resented him for being absent." "He always visited periodically when he did not stay at his sister Tila's house, but still visited with us at the hut on a regular basis, but not too often," Antonia said. She hesitated and waited some time before continuing. "Over these past weeks, I have discovered that I am with child," She said and quickly added, "Lorena knows all about this," Antonia glanced at Lorena, busy with her catechism lesson. Antonia looked disappointed and with a quick jerk wiped her eyes and forehead.

"Oh, how wonderful Antonia; God has blessed you and Fortunato with a child," Julieta embraced Antonia, "Congratulations," Julieta said. "But what do you mean about what you should do?" Julieta walked over to the stove and served a cup of coffee for Antonia, "Here Antonia, there is sugar and a cup of fresh milk on the table."

"I do not want to bring a child into this place of destitution," Antonia reached for the sugar and fresh milk for her coffee, "I have carried my cross as a responsible wife to Fortunato before humanity and God in bringing myself and my family to Mexico," She stirred her coffee; "So that Fortunato would not have to come alone." Antonia sipped her coffee after blowing over it to cool it somewhat, "I wanted to keep my family together, but you know, Samuel and Jose found work elsewhere soon after we came, and they also found somewhere else to stay." Antonia continued talking, "Catalina, my little daughter, lives with Eugenio and Sara in El Bacori. Fortunato comes and goes. Why has God forsaken my family?" She sobbed softly.

"God has not forsaken your family, Antonia," Julieta comforted her; she gave Lorena and Santos each a glass of milk; she sat down on a chair next to Antonia, "You and Fortunato have a holy matrimony, you and he gave yourselves to each other freely, before God and mankind; you united with each other because of love." Julieta drank coffee, and glanced at Lorena and said, "Lorena, after you read that chapter, let's reflect on it and share your thoughts on it, all right." She looked at Antonia, "Your children are all taken care of, one way or another, in some place or another," Julieta reached out and held Antonia's hand. "Fortunato comes and goes because of his work responsibilities, but they are all alive and have survived in this life full of trials, but your family is in many ways together and blessed by God. Be thankful for that, Antonia." Julieta got up to serve herself a second cup of coffee, "Later, we'll make something to eat."

"But yet, it is so cruel to bring a baby into life in this place, a baby to face hunger, thirst, cold and isolation away from a doctor's care," Antonia said. She hesitated a moment but continued talking, "Josefa told me about a curandera who can prescribe an herb to cause the baby to abort," Antonia wiped her tears from her eyes with her handkerchief. The cool breeze that earlier had come through the open window ceased, and a gust of hot air burst in, carrying the wailing sounds of screeching winds blowing around the back of the house. "But I do not believe in abortion. My own mother and my Nanita were good and holy curanderas; they only healed and preserved life," Antonia sipped her coffee, and she watched Lorena turn a page in her book. "Nanita delivered many babies in Arizona," Antonia stopped momentarily, wiped her eyes, "I only wish Nanita were here," She cried for a moment, her face in her hands, and then she continued, "I don't believe abortion is an option for a solution to my problem, my other alternative is to leave right away to Arizona and have my baby at home, there are doctors there who can deliver my baby." She spoke her last sentences in a rush.

The wailing wind had stopped and the sunlight streamed through the open window. There was silence in the kitchen and only Santos could be heard playing on the floor.

"No, Antonia," Julieta said, "Your leaving suddenly would disrupt Fortunato's efforts to make a life for you and his family here. You would have to abandon Samuel and Jose here, as they may not be ready to leave because of their employment. What about your little girl Catalina staying in El Bacori?" Julieta asked.

"What else can I do, then?" Antonia asked Julieta.
"No, you should not leave and furthermore you should tell Fortunato right away and make plans to have your baby here. Your husband will understand and help you, Antonia, remember St. Paul said for husbands to honor, love, respect, and protect their wives," Julieta said and added, "It is not only the wife that carries her Christian cross, the husband must carry his cross, too." Julieta tenderly held Antonia's hand and said, "Jacinta, my housemaid, is a curandera, a good holy person who can help you deliver your baby safely."

Antonia arose from her chair and walked to the stove and served herself another cup of coffee, and sat at the table to think about all Julieta had said.

"All right, Julieta," Lorena stood up, "I finished studying the chapter on the Holy Trinity." Lorena drank milk from her glass and then said, "Well, you know Julieta, our neighbors Telesforo and his wife Marta had twelve children," Lorena said, looking up from her work, "The girls and I are friends and I am sure that we can hunt lots of frogs for the new baby to eat."

"Telesforo," Julieta said, "I don't think he has any idea about true love of his wife; to him, his wife seems to be an object for his own satisfaction," Julieta was in the kitchen placing four eggs in a pan to boil, and she added, "Like a rabbit, she kept on having babies over the years."

"I wonder about Telesforo," Antonia said, she went into the kitchen space and washed her hands in a pan of water, "I will help you, Julieta, would you like me to peel the potatoes?" Antonia continued speaking,

The Worm in my Tomato

"The village philosopher, knows so much about ants, and he holds discussions about ants now and then with Lorena, under the shade of his mezquite tree in his front yard."

"Yes, Antonia, peel these potatoes, so we can make potato salad," Julieta said.

"It troubles me, Julieta, to hear what you think about Telesforo, you know, as you said, that he does not truly love his wife Marta; perhaps, Julieta, Telesforo did not really intend beforehand the pain that each child caused his wife, don't you think?" Antonia asked, "The girl Months tell Lorena that Telesforo worries about Marta, who is now very ill," Antonia said, while she peeled a potato, "and Julieta, Telesforo is such a delightful man when he tells jokes around the bonfire, and Marta and the Twelve Months like to sing, why not join us some evening, Julieta," Antonia said. "Besides, you could help cheer up Marta; Lorena's friend, Maya, told her that Marta is worried about her oldest two boys who want to leave; go north to seek employment in the United States, because, as you know, there is no work here."

"Yes, oh, yes, Julieta, please join us some evening around the outdoor fire," Lorena said.

"Well, perhaps, Antonia," Julieta answered, and she turned to Lorena, "We'll continue our conversation about Telesforo and Marta some other time, Lorena, now we have to see what you have learned about the Holy Trinity," Julieta said, "while the eggs hard boil and Antonia peels the potatoes.

"Oh, Julieta," Lorena interrupted, "Telesforo described the Holy Trinity very well; he knows all about ants and he appreciates all creation and tells wonderful stories to the Twelve Months and myself as we sit around the bonfire eating frog legs," Lorena finished her milk in a last gulp.

"No, Lorena, I don't think Telesforo knows about the Holy Trinity," Julieta said, and added, "It is a very difficult theological subject, and besides Telesforo has never read the catechism book," Julieta approached the wood stove, "These eggs are ready, Antonia, and the potatoes are, too."

Antonia cracked the hard boiled eggs and removed aside the boiled potatoes, and cut both up into pieces, while Julieta mixed in

The Worm in my Tomato

some spices with the eggs and potatoes.

"It's not like mixing eggs, potatoes and spices to make one salad, Lorena," Antonia said, "If that is what you were thinking."

"No, I don't know, I was not thinking that, but only what I read in my catechism book, that the Catholic Church, reads the book, teaches the mystery of the Most Holy Trinity; who alone made it known by revealing himself as being God as Father, Son, and Holy Spirit," Lorena held up her catechism book.

"That is wonderful, Lorena, you have learned your lesson well, come now, let's eat." Julieta hugged Lorena.

All four sat down to share a meal of egg and potato salad, white cheese, tortillas, and lemonade. "Let us say grace," Julieta said, and all blessed themselves and all bowed their heads, "Bless us Most Holy Trinity, one God, and thank you for this food and all blessings, Amen."

"Julieta," Lorena said, while serving herself egg salad, "When the priest comes and we have a holy Mass, do we eat the body of Jesus, alone, or with Jesus, do we receive God the Father and God the Holy Spirit?"

"Jesus, in his last supper with the apostles, took and blessed the bread and the wine and gave thanks to God, his father, and said to the apostles, take and eat, take and drink, this is my body and this is my blood, yes, we receive in Holy Communion the body, blood, soul and divinity of Christ Jesus, whole and entire, received under the form of bread and wine alone or together, consumed by the faithful receiving Holy Communion." Julieta said, "Memorize that part from your Catechism book, Lorena, like I did. Julieta added, "Yes, we receive God the Father and God the Holy Spirit when we receive the divinity of Christ, as divinity cannot be separated, it is one in God Father, Son, and Holy Spirit, and Jesus divinity is in his body, blood, and soul, as well."

"Thank you, Julieta," Lorena said.

"Julieta, I can hardly wait for a priest to come here and consecrate the bread and wine, into the body and blood of Christ, just like we celebrated Mass in Miami." Antonia said.

"Antonia, let us keep praying that soon Father Fermin will sneak himself into our area to celebrate the Holy Mass and minister other sacraments to the faithful of our village. I hope you feel much better Antonia," Julieta chewed on a piece of tortilla, "and I am looking

The Worm in my Tomato

forward to baptizing your baby in the name of the Father, the Son, and the Holy Spirit," then she smiled, "if Father Fermin does not get here by the time your baby is born."

"Thank you Julieta," Antonia said. "I will do all things for God and with God; I will stay with my family and have my baby here." Antonia still, however, felt a strong sense of doubt about her decision to have her baby here in the village, and she decided to talk with Fortunato as soon as she could.

Lorena, never missed an opportunity for Julieta to pray for her, and she asked Julieta to pray for her next, "Let us pray, now, Julieta, for the education I want here in Mexico."

"Be patient Lorena; I am sure that God will see to it that you receive your education," Julieta said.

The daylight had moved from the open window on the east side of the house around to an open door on the west side of the house. Lorena noticed that the trees outside were bare like the village trees. There were no birds to be seen or heard, and Lorena wondered where the birds had gone.

After lunch, Antonia and Lorena helped Julieta clean the kitchen and then said their goodbyes. Antonia, Lorena, and Santos walked in silence on their return home to the hut. Lorena was deep in thought, thinking about what Telesforo had said, "Mother, did Telesforo say that we become what we eat or was it that what we eat becomes us?" Lorena asked.

"Why, Lorena?"

"I was just worried about the new baby," Lorena said, "You know, how much Julieta and you pray, the new baby might become the priest we are all waiting for to come."

"No, Lorena, it takes years and years to become a priest, the baby would have to grow up and study somewhere where priests are made, it is not that easy," Antonia said.

"Well, I was just wondering." Lorena looked at Santos, skipping and hopping ahead at times, and she said, "I was just worried about the new baby."

"What about the baby?"

"Well, you have been eating a lot of frog legs at our night bonfire, perhaps you shouldn't."

The Worm in my Tomato

A Rancheria located in the vicinity of El Aliso.

A rural area of El Aliso: bypassed and forgotten by state and federal governments for economic development.

Village residents make bread in large outdoor ovens made of clay brick.

The Worm in my Tomato

Twenty Seven

Lorena:
The blind man and the fiesta

Finally, another spring season had arrived, the huizache trees had new green leaves; the birds once more enjoyed their cool shade, and they sang all day. The desert bloomed, and from it wafted in the breeze the pleasant aroma of wild flowers. The blue sky shone with brightness: the sun warmed and made the adobe walls gleam like gold.

Fortunato again tried his luck in growing crops in El Potrero and hoped for a harvest for market. The corn stalks stood tall, small green pale tomatoes adorned tomato plants in the fields, and vegetables grew up and down the rows. This year, 1935, looked for certain that Fortunato would reap the rewards of his hard work during the past three years.

One day, Julieta rode up on her bay horse to Antonia's adobe hut. Julieta called out Lorena's name. Antonia emerged from the shade inside the hut with Santos in tow. Lorena was outside spreading some cow bones, given her by her cousin Gonzalo, in the hot sun to dry. She hoped the bones would dry soon so she could make *tizas* to barter with the village women. "Lorena, my child, please listen carefully. You are to walk to the edge of my corn field near my house and search for a blind man with a gray donkey hiding in among the stocks of corn. When you find him, lead him on his donkey to my house, show him through the back door where beggars come to beg their meals." Julieta looked at Antonia who nodded assent, and then Julieta rode off.

"Go, daughter, do as Julieta asks," Antonia said.

"Take care of my bones, let the hot sun dry them well, please mother," Lorena hurried off to do as Julieta wanted. She skipped from shade to shade to avoid the burning sand that trickled though the open straps of her leather sandals. In a short while Lorena had circled the village and hurried along the canal to Julieta's corn field, and after some time she arrived at the edge of the field of tall corn stalks. The hot wind blew against her face. She began to search for a man and his donkey. But there was no one to be seen. She could only see row upon row of corn stalks, tall and green, taller than her Uncle Jorge, she thought. The husks with their long silky yellow hair were ready to be harvested.

Suddenly, a soft voice from among the stalks beckoned her, "Come child, take the donkey's bridal and lead us to Julieta's house."

Lorena stared in the direction of the voice and there well hidden among the long leaves was an unkempt old man wearing dark glasses and sitting cross-legged on a small gray donkey. Lorena cautiously approached the donkey and held the end of the bridal offered by the man, and she noticed the man's thin delicate hands, so smooth looking that Lorena thought his hands were like her father's hands when he dealt cards at Limonada's in Miami. But of course, she reasoned, this blind man could not possibly be a gambler like my father, of whom she had heard from her mother who had heard from Julieta, who knew everybody in the valley, that her father had taken to gambling again in night-long card games. Lorena hoped that this was not true because gambling now would be at a high risk for her father because he had considerably lost his eyesight. With her mind full of thoughts, Lorena led the donkey with the old blind man sitting on top of the donkey out of the field, across the road and followed along beside the irrigation canal for some distance to Julieta's house. Lorena knocked on the back door. Jacinta, a curandera who had no husband and who lived in the village all by herself, opened the door slowly and peered at the blind man. "Yes, oh, it's you child and the blind man. She quickly threw open the door and assisted the old man to dismount from his donkey. The donkey promptly shook his back, sprinkling Lorena with some droplets of his sweat. Jacinta, with demonstrated respect, led the blind man into the kitchen. Pepe the manservant of the place took the donkey away, saying "Come King of the hills." The donkey followed with alacrity, no doubt expecting some food, and pranced away to the stable.

Lorena followed Jacinta and the blind man inside the house. Lorena saw the old man being shown into Julieta's large bedroom. Julieta followed. Jacinta opened the front door and some villagers shuffled in, the men with their hats in hand and the women with covered heads. To Lorena's surprise her mother trooped in, leading Santos by the hand. After awhile, Julieta appeared and motioned all those waiting into her

The Worm in my Tomato

bedroom. To Lorena's amazement the room had been converted into a chapel and a large altar stood at the front of the room. The men as if by practice ambled into the room and stood in a half-circle at the rear of the home-made chapel. The women sat on chairs at the front. Before the altar stood a priest dressed in proper vestments. Julieta introduced the priest by the name of Father Simon. He welcomed all those present and said, "In today's Mass, we will pray for Father Fermin who intended to visit you last year, but he was captured crossing the El Fuerte River and shot to death by federal soldiers." He began to celebrate the Holy Mass, "In the name of the Father, the Son, and the Holy Spirit." Julieta, Antonia, Josefa and Carmen, Marta and her girl Seven Months, Luisa and Eligia, Jacinta the curandera, and other women and their girls standing up front like prayer veterans responded with prayers on cue. In the rear, Lepo, Telesforo and his boy Five Months, and other village men and young boys knelt and stood at the right times. Julieta's catechism classes and her teaching the village faithful was aptly demonstrated today. At the Holy Communion those that wished came forward to receive the body and the blood of the Lord. Antonia received communion and motioned Lorena forward to receive. The teachings of Julieta flowed through Lorena's mind: The Lord's body in the form of a small round thin piece of bread, called the *hostia*, was consumed; the Lord's blood in the form of grape wine was sipped and swallowed; God in this way became his essence in the *hostia*, the *hostia* became God through his own consecrated body and blood, and God became one with us, she thought.

Lorena could not help but wonder where the priest had come from, she imagined that the priest had dropped straight from heaven, no doubt, and she wondered if God had accompanied the priest from heaven, but how could God fit in the tiny pieces of bread, she wanted to know.

After Mass, Julieta treated all in attendance to refreshments and corn bread with honey. All the faithful were invited to return in the evening for instruction from the priest, Father Simon. Everyone seemed to know him, except Antonia and Lorena. Santos, at first cried from fright at seeing the bearded priest. After being assured by Antonia that it was all right, he had slept along with other children on the floor through the whole heavenly event. The adults did not mind as they considered the children to be innocent angels and that God was always in them anyway, as Antonia would always say. Father Simon throughout the afternoon heard confessions, blessed marriages, and the following day he performed baptisms, confirmations, and married those couples instructed by Julieta. Lorena wondered at the many couples the priest had confessed and married who had children, no doubt, under the spell of the love inspired by the river god along the beach and among the large boulders of El Fuerte River. In her mind, Lorena thought to be sure and ask Carmen about the river god of love, again, and go see where the river babies were made, and whom Carmen had said Lorena taught catechism. That evening and the next day were such a busy time that Lorena never got a chance to ask Father Simon about her burning question: would God ever eat her and the girl Seven Months like they ate God?

Julieta's hired help roasted goat meat and barbecued pork, spiced and carefully wrapped in large banana leaves, over hot coals during the night in a large hole dug in the ground. All the faithful in attendance were fed in the afternoon. The priest celebrated the Holy Mass in the morning, and all the village, it seemed, attended. The affair was done in Julieta's secluded back yard, around which guards had posted themselves. They feared for federal intervention; Antonia and Julieta had been discussing the problem of having Father Simon present in the vicinity and of possible danger from soldiers and those who hated Catholics. Julieta said to Antonia, "Soldiers will shoot any recognized priest on sight. Religious sisters in Mexico encounter the same dangers of being shot but in addition might be abducted and raped and then be shot." Lorena had heard all Julieta had said to her mother, but for her part, Lorena made it a point to ask Carmen later what Julieta meant by the word "Raptar", but she doubted Miss Yoakum's vocabulary drills provided adequate words with which to translate into some meaningful understanding, but she intended to look in her drill word book.

Lorena remembered the hungry and sad faces of the two nuns that had arrived in Miami, for whom her mother had provided a place for them to live in and food to eat for months before Antonia and her family were repatriated from the United States.

The Worm in my Tomato

On the third day Julieta asked Lorena to come early in the morning to her house. After Lorena knocked, Jacinta motioned her to go around behind the huge white painted adobe hacienda type house. Lorena went to the back kitchen door and to her astonishment the old blind man emerged dressed in his unkempt clothes. Pepe brought him his donkey and helped the old blind man climb on the donkey's back. Lorena was handed the bridle and told to lead them across the road and down the path along the irrigation canal and into the corn fields, among the tall corn stalks. Lorena left the old blind man and his donkey, King of the Hills, in the field of corn. She walked away and crossed the road from which side she had led the old blind man and his donkey away from Julieta's house. Then from across the road, she watched the blind man on top of his donkey, as both made their way deep into the corn fields. They headed out toward the other end along the wide row of corn stalks. Lorena remained silent and watched the old blind man finally disappear. She wondered where the old blind man had been during the Mass and all the wonderful religious instructions they had. Lorena made it a point to ask her mother and Julieta about where the old blind man had been, as she felt they knew something she did not.

⌒⟶

Fiesta in El Pueblo

It was not a usual day; it was the day before the fiesta in El Mezquitalito. Over the eastern mountain rim the sun climbed over and carried with it a new day. The sun gave light for the day and spread it over the valley. The eastern horizon spread its morning freshness for the clear, bright, new day. The fiesta held on the day before the Feast Day of John the Baptist on June 24th honored his birth. Tomorrow would be John's Feast Day, and the village always celebrated the Feast Day of this one of their several ancillary saints. On this day, however, it always rained. John's Feast Day's promise of rain, therefore, provided an occasion and the reason the fiesta took place the day before. It really did not matter because many of the villagers celebrated all week long. Villagers hoped tomorrow would bring much needed rain. Celebrants

The Worm in my Tomato

from time to time scanned the sky for some sign of at least a small cloud approaching over the horizon.

Days before, visitor vendors and purchasers from surrounding ranches throughout the valley approached the village to participate in the Fiesta.

On the day of the Fiesta, Lepo and Josefa had left their adobe house early before sun-up to work in Tila's cheese room. They were busily packing white round large and small cheeses into wooden boxes on top of a long plank table. "We must hurry now," Tila said, "the morning will pass us up and we need to have our cheese at the village to sell, before noon."

The sunlight peered though the open window of the sky, already threatening the dawn and transforming it into morning. The roosters were crowing their customary announcement of five in the morning call. "We will have all packed and delivered, Miss Tila," Josefa said. "Oh, yes, Miss Tila, I will begin to take these boxes in Chapo's wagon within an hour," Lepo added.

"Good," Tila walked out on her way to open the door to her ranch store, "I must leave now and prepare to serve the road travelers on their way to the village."

Indeed, from every direction, following the dirt roads could be seen wagons, piled high with produce of one kind or another, pulled by mules or oxen; the fiesta participants hurried to the village to set up their stalls for marketing their goods. Some cattle ambled along and circled around mezquite brush, trees, and cactus and greasewood bushes, on their way to the village to be sold or traded. The absence or lack of sufficient coin and paper money encouraged much of the selling and buying of goods by a trade or bartering mode. Bartering had always been a preferred way for acquiring the goods needed for survival in this destitute arid region environment.

Behind the groups of cattle, several groups of donkeys, laden with fire wood for sale at the village, rambled at given distances along the roads. Guiding the donkeys, along side of them, jogged short stocky Indian men with large mustaches, dressed in their best white cotton trousers with white shirts trimmed with red and green embroidery, flailing the air with long sticks to keep the donkeys moving in the desired direction.

The Worm in my Tomato

The cows, donkeys, and the Indian *vaqueros*, and wood cutters strode toward their assigned places in the village marketplace inside temporary corrals constructed for that purpose. "Whoa donkeys, hold up," called the *vaqueros* as the donkeys loaded with mezquite firewood bolted into their respective corrals, anxiously anticipating being free of their heavy loads. Behind the donkeys' rear legs some village scrawny brown and black mongrel dogs barked and frolicked about, snapping at the donkeys' heels.

The sun, now asserted its point of early morning heat; the wind swirled dust, and cows mooed, donkeys brayed, dogs barked, and men yelled, and indeed all the commotion of the motley horde, were enveloped in a whirlwind of sound, movement, and a mysterious urgency. The presence of blue, yellow, red, and white men shirts and women's skirts created a panorama of color that with the movement of people made an ever changing kaleidoscopic design of colors, in the village scene.

Lepo and Josefa left early from Tila's cheese room and by early morning had set up shop at the village to sell wrapped white Mexican cheese, tamales, tortillas and other foods. Back at her ranch store, Tila quickly dispatched Indian customers who shuffled about nervously while purchasing food provisions. Many of the Indian customers had sacks of acorns to trade for hemp ropes, salt, lard, beans, coffee, and sugar. Many visiting Indians eyed the different types of food to eat such as pickled pigs' feet, *chicharones* delicate pigs' skins fried crisp, *empanadas*, delicious fruit turnovers, corn on the cob, white flour tortillas, slabs of ribs and steaks from freshly slaughtered beef, oranges, bananas, corn on the husk, tomatoes, and other fruits. The potential barterers fingered the work tools, blankets, and felt the *serapes*, the bright -colored woolen ponchos to wear in style and keep warm during the chilly nights, especially when sleeping under a tree in the cold of night.

Lorena had made for herself a small space, on Julieta's counter, for her booth to show her hand-made bone *tizas*. Julieta rejoiced at seeing Lorena bargain and haggle over bartering her *tizas* for other objects that later she could trade for what she really wanted. "Julieta," Lorena said, "I am aiming to get some real beef steaks to take to mother for her to cook supper tonight, and oh, yes, I plan to barter for an empanada for Telesforo, the largest fruit empanada I can find." Julieta smiled,

"Good luck, the day is young, yet."

Everyone celebrated, worked, sold, and bought, and all the movement of colored shirts, skirts, hats, and the sound of voices in talk, music and song, combined at the same time to create a collective living symphony. The aroma of frying meat, sweet breads, fresh flowers, mixed with the smell of animal dung of goats, sheep, cattle, donkeys, mules, and horses in the stalls at the far end of the village. By mid-afternoon, Lorena had bartered two tin pails, one knife, and one hemp rope for six steaks, a slice of Mexican cheese, and eight empanadas from Josefa at Tila's market space. Lorena had gotten rid of over three dozen *tizas*. Indian women from other villages commented favorably about her *tizas*.

Lorena hurried home with her groceries. Antonia cared for Santos asleep in his bed near the hut's ramada. Antonia planned to join the festivities in the village in the cool of the evening and spend time visiting with Samuel, Jose, Catalina, and Fortunato who all were expected for dinner. After Lorena arrived home with the food items, Antonia promptly started making supper with the steaks, Mexican cheese, chili sauce, tortillas and black coffee with empanadas.

Antonia was overjoyed to have her family together and eating supper under the ramada. They all talked, laughed, and enjoyed each other's company. Fortunato had marketed early ripened vegetables from a fast developing harvest of his crops. "This is the year at last," he shouted. Jose told of caring for horses his employer had for sale. Samuel introduced his girlfriend Julia, a beautiful young lady. Catalina attended the fiesta with Eugenio and Sara. Antonia could only weep and praise God for allowing her family to spend some time together.

Fortunato felt proud of his young sons who had thrived in a hostile political environment. From the safe classrooms in a high school in the United States, they had found themselves in a struggle in the demanding circumstances of survival by making the right choice in the turmoil of the social conflicts in rural Mexico. Samuel now worked for the Federal Land Office and he was busy surveying the Vega land holdings for the federal adjudication and determination of what Vega land holdings would be returned to the indigenous pueblos for common held ejidos, according to Mexico's ejidos system. In contrast, Jose had stayed away from political land and religious questions and devoted his time to general life in the valley. Jose worked in a ranch as a ranch hand helping to care for race horses. At times, Jose would ride in horse races held in the local village festivals around the valley.

As evening approached, a huge flaming orange ball slowly descended behind the fan of pink light tinted horizon that crowned the dark blue colored mountains. At sunset the stalls, booths, and marketing spaces closed for the day. Livestock was fed and watered. Local villagers and all visitors from neighboring ranches turned their attention to making dinner over countless small fires scattered throughout the village. The visitors also prepared their sleeping places on top of wagons, by the night fires, or used backyards of relatives and friends in the village. Toilets, lavatories, and latrines secluded behind tents had been constructed for public use in several separate areas for men and women, hidden behind desert brush and bushes.

The glitter of village cooking fires in the dark outdoors challenged the multitude of stars in the black sky. Lepo and Josefa at home with Carmen sat near the fire outside in their yard and shared its warmth. Telesforo, Marta, and the Twelve Months attended to their front yard bon fire and cooked their supper. Everywhere people laughed, talked loud and sang popular *corridos*: enjoying themselves. The air was warm, but El Fuerte River provided a steady cool breeze. The overarching high black sky over head glittered in countless stars, which engulfed the village in a canopy composed of jewels.

Antonia looked up into the depth of the sky and said, "Thank you God, you have unfolded your blessings one by one all in good time, even after our Repatriation." She sipped her night cup of coffee, "Tomorrow, another day." Antonia found herself meditating in the quiet stillness of the night. Lorena held Santos in her arms to help him go to sleep. Santos, who in spite of going on four years old, yet liked to be rocked.

Later in the dark night, Antonia awoke in her bunk bed, feeling chilled and she threw a log of mezquite wood in the *estufa* fire in the ramada. She heard the rumble of thunder as it rolled into the far side

The Worm in my Tomato

of the valley near the western *Sierra Madre Occidental* mountain range. She saw faraway repeated flashes of lightning in the sierras. It will surely rain, she thought, and then whispered: "Thank you Saint John the Baptist.

With the first light of dawn, as was the custom in El Mezquitalito for the feast of John the Baptist, a bell rang loudly from Julieta's house, firecrackers exploded, and the Indian faithful began to pour into the village square from all corners of the village. Music flowed from guitar and violin instruments, which sound filled the village air and mixed with the aroma of fresh coffee and roasted meat over numerous outdoor fires. Singers in bright red, white, and green shirts and blouses led other revelers in the festivities, as they gathered into a huge circle around the village square. All sang the *mañanitas* in honor of Saint John the Baptist for his birthday.

Julieta and several village elders took center stage in the village square and led all who stood in a huge circle in prayers as they faced in turn each of the four directional points: east, south, west, and north. Then the religious Pascola appeared and led prayers, and the dancers performed spiritual dances, beginning with the Deer Dance. Both men and women performed the round dances in the large circle. Men played the flute, rattles, drums, guitars, and violins.

The air filled with the aroma of roasting hams and barbecued goat meat that had been left in the ground ovens over night. All would gravitate into the village square to sing, dance, eat; the men toasted each other with *pulque*.

Lorena saw Marta and her children Twelve Months leave for the village square while Telesforo stood outside in his front yard observing the multitude of boisterous participants in the village revelry. Lorena thought that this would be the opportune time to give Telesforo his empanada. I am certain that he has not had breakfast yet, she thought, I must hurry before Marta and the girl Three Months return with food from the village square; Lorena picked up the paper wrapped empanada, and she ran over to Telesforo. "Telesforo, here is what you said your life long ambition was," Lorena smiled, handing Telesforo his fruit empanada, and said, "Happy feast day, eat it all to yourself, and you don't even have to share the crumbs with the ants crawling at your feet."

Telesforo smiled broadly, his eyes sparkled, as he tenderly took the empanada with both hands, held it up close to savor the sweet aroma, "Pumpkin," he said, "my favorite fruit empanada." He took a small bite and slowly chewed the morsel; he tasted, enjoyed the firmness of the bread crust, his mouth drooled from the taste of the soft yellow fruit pulp within the tart. "Umm," Telesforo carefully took his time and ate his pastry like if he wanted to eat it and preserve it forever. "At last, I have eaten a whole empanada to myself." Telesforo finished his last morsel, careful not to lose a single bit to the ants already beseeching at his bare feet. "Thank you, ever so much, my daughter Lorena; may you be blessed for your generosity and may our Father Creator give you more," Telesforo said.

Lorena noticed some tears glistened in Telesforo's eyes and she did not want to linger anymore to watch Telesforo fulfill his life ambition. She ran home to Antonia who had been observing the event from her hut as she prepared herself and Santos to attend the festivities in the village square. "How did it go, Lorena?" Antonia asked.

"Oh, he was so happy, mother," Lorena glanced at her mother and then looked toward Telesforo's house. She saw Marta and the girl Three Months already approaching their home and Lorena thought no doubt carrying roasted goat meat for Telesforo to eat. "Let's go mother to the village square and get in line for that roasted meat and a glass of fruit juice," Lorena smiled, and she added, "Now, I know, mother, what Telesforo meant when he told me that we learn the spiritual from the physical."

"Lorena, you carry our plates and cups, and I will lead Santos," Antonia said while walking toward the village square.

The village had become overcast with low flat base layered cumulus clouds piled up high like White Mountains which had a prismatic effect on the sunlight. The sunlight cast rainbow-like diffused colors that crowned the village. The air felt cool but not yet carried a smell of rain. That would have to wait until the dark nimbus rain clouds arrived over the village from the southwest. Trees, the cactus and wild flowers in the desert had about them an expectation of and hope for rain. Indeed, some dark bank of rain clouds barely could be made out over the high sierras. The festivities rocked on with music, dancing,

The Worm in my Tomato

eating, and visiting. By mid-afternoon the weather conditions began to change. The cool air became a steady quick breeze and now storm clouds could be seen approaching from the southwest horizon. The visitors gathered their wagons, their oxen, mules, and what cattle they had been unable to rid of in barter. They soon loaded their wagons with their goods and began to leave the area. Visitors and villagers exchanged goodbyes, handshakes, hugs, and assurances of seeing each other again at the next fiesta and for certain at the next Saint John's Feast Day.

Jose ran up to Antonia and Lorena to hug them goodbye and promptly left to care for his horses. Samuel found Antonia and Lorena enjoying their fruit juice and a lunch of roasted goat meat. He and his girlfriend Julia said their goodbyes and departed from the village square before the rain came. Later, Eugenio and Sara with Catalina, who all had stayed overnight at Tila's big house, said goodbye to Antonia, Lorena, and Santos; All embraced each other.

The wagons rode away, and donkeys brayed in joy at their heading home, mules kicked up dirt, dogs pranced about barking and nipping at the heels of the donkeys. The multitude headed out in all directions and followed dirt roads and trails to their nearby ranches where they would arrive ahead of the rain.

The fast breeze became a steady high wind. The mountainous cumulus departed; the gray nimbus filled the sky and changed into a dark billowy mass of rain clouds; the wild flowers in their bright yellow and orange colors danced with the wind and reached for the rain drops that begin to fall softly at first and then increased in momentum. The desert life welcomed the rain, the trees moved their limbs from side to side; the frogs croaked their drum beats melody in accompaniment with the patter of raindrops on top of the bovine pond. The El Fuerte River roared furiously. All the villagers rejoiced that it had rained for Saint John's Feast Day, like it always did.

The Worm in my Tomato

Twenty Eight

Samuel

Land laws and federal soldiers at Eugenio's ranch

The land-reform laws were in position to deprive some of Jorge's family of countless acres of land and place in government control for distribution to indigenous pueblos in the Ejidos system. Samuel continued to survey lands of his aunts and uncles who had farmed their lands for generations but now saw their land holdings disappear like the peanut in a carnival shell game. Mexico had launched the world's first large-scale social revolution in 1910, ahead of Russia's 1917 communist revolution. Sinaloa in 1932 through 1935 was feeling the effects of political waves of change from the laws set in motion in prior years. The changes were brought home to Fortunato's family. When the force of the land Reform Laws finally came to El Aliso and the Mezquital Valley, it was like an overnight tornado. Soldiers everywhere enclosed homes with barbed wire and limited farmers' entrance only to their legal titled land holdings. An era of many decades of cultivating vast tracts of idle untilled but not legally owned land had ended.

The federal government's education law, like hard task masters in the fields, pushed political and social ideology as a way of life. Nationally, Mexico exerted efforts to build schools in rural areas and Indian villages. Social education came to the Mayo village rancheria El Mezquitalito in the form of part time school when Antonia's family lived there. Antonia's daughter Lorena embraced learning like her very life. Lorena attended the school but was disappointed at the lack of school books and supplies, in contrast to what she had been accustomed to in her school in Miami, Arizona. Lorena had left behind a memorable school and a learning experience; she never stopped remembering it; she thought of it often and never stopped hoping for the day that she might have an opportunity again to attend such a school.

Mexico had its own Great Depression like the United States, but it was a hungrier and meaner monster. Yet the social and economic realities in China were probably worse, and an uncertain number of Chinese had illegally entered Mexico and Sinaloa to work in agriculture; many Chinese had left an economically depressed situation in China and sneaked into Sinaloa just ahead of the immigration laws. The Immigration laws, however, forced Chinese field workers, that labored on Tila's fields and who Fortunato had supervised, to flee.

Samuel came by to visit his mother Antonia at her hut in the Indian village. His step-father Fortunato was there visiting, too.

"Here, both of you sit on these chairs in the ramada, and I will serve you coffee; Samuel, it is so good to see you, and we are so happy you came to visit us," Antonia said. She prepared the coffee and cups. Antonia had a fire going in the adobe wood stove and from the large soup pot on the stove escaped the delicious aroma of lentil soup.

Fortunato had been braiding a torn leather bridle and he sat down and continued braiding it. Samuel sat opposite him and said, "Here, father, let me hold it from this end and you can better weave the leather strands along its side."

"Thank you, son, this horse equipment and rope need constant looking after," Fortunato said.

Samuel informed Fortunato, "By the way, father, the federal government land office has almost completed the survey of the land holdings in the valley, including the Vega lands as part of the procedure

The Worm in my Tomato

to check the documented titles, recorded for each tract."

"Yes, so I have heard from Jorge and Tila, and it appears the government means to take away some lands from Jorge, but especially from Eugenio at El Bacori, right?" Fortunato said, placing the repaired horse bridle down on top of the bench. Antonia served each one a cup of steaming hot coffee. "Of course the federal land office has been in this area since before we came," Fortunato said. Outside the ramada, the sky looked overcast, rain clouds approached from the southwest, dimming the brightness of a morning sun.

Fortunato blew on his coffee, attempting to cool it down, "I am glad for you, Samuel, that you have a job with the surveying crew," Fortunato looked outside, "Looks like rain; but usually the clouds go by and take their water to south Sinaloa; it used to rain when I didn't have crops planted in seed, and it didn't rain when it would help my crops, Samuel, how about that, but now, I have crops growing good in El Potrero. Soon, I will have a harvest and be able to pay Tila and Jorge for my debts.

Samuel looked out, too, from inside the ramada, "Yes, it looks like rain, but it will pass our valley, for sure, and the clouds will fly over the coast and dump their water into the Gulf of California." Samuel sipped his coffee, and said, "I am happy for you, father, that at last you have crops ready for a harvest."

"Thanks Samuel, but getting back to the land laws, I know that you have been helping to survey and to record land and have begun to do paperwork for the right titles," Fortunato said.

"That is correct father, and I am disappointed to hear that the Vega families have not liked my employment with the federal land office." Samuel took the tortilla and white cheese that Antonia handed him. "I am sorry to hear that Aunt Tila had arguments with you about my work and cooperation with the government," Samuel said and took a bite of his tortilla and cheese.

Fortunato rolled up the cheese in his tortilla, "I had no way to control you, Samuel; although I was not happy with your decision to go work for the federal government's land office, I respected your decision and did not take it personal, myself, and did not oppose your decision to do what you wanted." Fortunato chewed on his food, and

The Worm in my Tomato

took a drink of coffee, "I simply told Tila and Jorge that you were eighteen years old and free to do what you thought best for yourself, and now you are a young adult of twenty-two," Fortunato said.

Fortunato and Samuel, after both drank their coffee and ate their food, walked outside the ramada, and they began to check the ropes and to tie the crossbeams together. "I want to make sure these ropes have not rotted and are in no danger of breaking and weakening the crossbeams," said Fortunato.

"Let me help you," Samuel said and he started to check the ropes of some of the crossbeams, and he added, "I was glad to move out of Aunt Tila's house for the reason that she, and my Uncle Jorge, might be offended."

"You were fortunate to have found a place to work, a place to stay, and I am proud of you," Fortunato said.

"Yes, I was very lucky in that Mr. Isabel Garcia, a supervisor and head of the local land office with the government, has allowed me to live in his house with his family," Samuel stopped his work for a moment and looked at Fortunato, "My mother knows, and now I am telling you, father, in case you have not heard, that I and Mr. Garcia's daughter, Julia," Samuel looked at the darkening clouds above in the sky through the limbs of the trees, " are in love," Samuel said, "and we plan to marry in the near future."

"You have mine and I am certain your mother's blessing as well, Samuel," Fortunato smiled.

Fortunato saw Telesforo sitting under his mezquite tree in his front yard, looking down at the ground and talking with Lorena and three of his girls, and Fortunato and Samuel waved hello to him.

"He seems to be a good neighbor, father," Samuel said.

"Yes, Lorena really likes him; she tells Antonia about how much he teaches his children and Lorena," Fortunato smiled and waved his hand at Telesforo, "He is a good man, called the 'Philosopher' by the villagers."

"You know, father, I personally hope these new land laws will help the pueblos so that they can have common owned lands to plant and harvest," Samuel said, and he sat down on the log bench outside the ramada. "These land problems have deep roots in Mexico. The *Ley Lerdo* prohibited ecclesiastical and civil institutions from owning or administering real property not directly used in day-to-day operations. Unfortunately, the Ejido system of the pueblos was also included as a civil institution that was forced to sell uncultivated lands at auction. The rich hacendados and other capable individuals ended up purchasing large tracts at bargain prices. Later, many of these pueblo common lands added to their land holdings by encroachment and cultivating land not legally theirs. Father, I am sorry to tell you that not only Eugenio stands to lose lands but that El Potrero, your land, is subject to restitution to the native pueblo, here.

"Yes, so I understand, from what Jorge has told me," Fortunato said.

"These land issues go back to 1856. The vast land holdings of the Church, acquired through the centuries were put up for sale at public auction, as I said before." Samuel looked in the direction of the hut's room where Antonia was putting Santos in his cot to take his afternoon nap, "Mama, is there more coffee, please?" He continued speaking to Fortunato, "But unfortunately, however, one of the civil corporations forced to sell its property was the communal landholding, the *ejidos* of the Indian village, as I have said before. Many Indian communities lost their traditional lands when forced to turn over their properties for sale at the various auctions," Samuel said, "because the properties were not in cultivation and could not contribute to the government public resources."

Antonia brought two cups of coffee for Samuel and Fortunato, "Thank you, mother," Samuel said and continued speaking, "This land law, *the Ley Lerdo*, was incorporated into Mexico's Constitution of 1857, and the law for land restitution continues in force in the Constitution of 1917, as well."

"Yes, Jorge has told me all this past history of the land laws," Fortunato drank from his cup of coffee, and continued speaking, "You, Samuel, know, of course you do, that the rich and hacendados with good credit, were the ones who bought up the land, the Vega families here in this Mezquital valley of Sinaloa did the same," Fortunato said.

"Yes, I know, and I and the surveyors' crew are going about surveying the vast Vega landholdings," Samuel blew over his cup, "They have nothing to fear of losing lands unless they lack title to the lands or have lands acquired through encroachment," Samuel studied Fortunato, "The natives are very confident in getting their lands returned to them by the government according to the Federal Land Laws of the Federal land reform," Samuel said.

"I understand, Samuel, but like Jorge said, after 200 years and several revolutions, land titles and records can not be found," Fortunato said, and he asked, "Is it possible to purchase untitled or trespassed parcels of lands from the federal government, at this time?"

"No, and furthermore, these lands can not be sold by the Indian pueblos. The land will legally belong to the native pueblos in common, with parcels or *ejidos* given out to individual native families for cultivation," Samuel sipped his coffee.

"I see," Fortunato said, "but failure of the Ejidos system is probable because it takes large areas of agricultural land, many *hectares*, you know, to make a profitable venture to pay for seed, labor, and hopefully government supported water irrigation, and marketing, and there must exist an external market that pays well," Fortunato said, and added, "Federal and state governments have not been very helpful in the past."

"I know, father, but the government is trying now to help the native pueblos, especially in undeveloped rural areas like this valley." Samuel drank his coffee. "I venture to guess father that the federal and state governments will invest in all manner of industry, mining, fishing, but especially agriculture within the next five to ten years."

"One grave problem," according to valley hacendados and Vega landholders, is that the common ejidos land policy is too much like communism; land held in common, and not based on individual investments of money and time, of course with government help, some subsidies," Fortunato said, and he drank his coffee.

"Well, there may be some truth in that, father, but the lands in the past were held in common by the native pueblos, who believed in having lands in common ownership by the pueblo. Pueblos planted and harvested their fields; they worked their lands enough to have food to eat and cotton to obtain fiber to make their own shirts and pants. They raised beef for their meat, after the Spanish introduced cattle, sheep, and horses, of course, and used leather hides to make for themselves leather shoes, belts, and other items. The goal is again to help the native pueblos support themselves, develop their own economy; in this way the state and federal governments will at last invest in rural areas,

The Worm in my Tomato

in agriculture, roads, water dams for irrigation and electric power, and education. I have learned so much in working for the government, father; Mexico will be different very soon." Samuel said.

"I hope some good comes from it all, Samuel, but if the government does not help the natives with seed, water, irrigation systems, you know, and marketing, nothing will come of all these ideas," Fortunato said.

Antonia, who had been cooking a late afternoon lunch now called out, "Come sit at the table."

Fortunato and Samuel walked into the ramada and sat at the table to eat.

Fortunato continued speaking on what he had been saying outside, "That is too bad, for Mexico, and I seriously doubt the natives will cultivate their lands because I really don't think the federal government will extend credit or financial help for purchasing seed, water, and proper equipment." Fortunato cut himself a slice of white cheese to break up into small pieces and sprinkle over his plate of lentils; he continued talking, "Then the world market will limit profits on their sales, the native peoples will return to cultivating only enough for local consumption." Fortunato began to scoop up a spoonful of lentils, and he said, "Their total ejido properties will not be part of Mexico's agricultural economic development in the world markets; banks will not supply needed moneyed capital investments."

Samuel, chewing on a piece of tortilla, swallowed and then said, "You are probably predicting correctly, but at this moment," he held another piece of tortilla in the air with his hand, "the federal government plan calls for recording legal titles and returning lands to native pueblos." Samuel looked at Fortunato and asked him, "What do you plan to do if your lands El Potrero are lost?"

"My sister Tila refused for me to work her lands last year and this year. She refused for me to use some of her Chinese workers, before they left, to help me cultivate my lands El Potrero." Fortunato waved his spoon in the air as he gestured with his hand, "my lands I inherited from my father, you know. But I will leave it up to my brother Jorge to extend to me some credit for seed and for using a few local native farm workers to cultivate El Potrero, but if the government takes my lands, I will have to go elsewhere to seek a living for my family; who knows?" Fortunato said.

The Worm in my Tomato

Samuel looked at Antonia, "This lentil soup with onions, mama, is the best I've had since I was here last, um, um," Samuel gave his deep plate to Antonia for more.

"Come more often, Samuel," Antonia handed him another plate full of lentils.

"I will, mama," and he looked at Fortunato, "I have talked with my Uncle Jorge, too, father, and he informed me that Aunt Tila will leave her lands uncultivated this year and maybe the following year as well," Samuel waited a moment, then added, " Did you know she went bankrupt?" Samuel asked.

"No, I did not, she did not tell me, or rather, we did not talk about that," Fortunato answered.

"Yes, and although Aunt Tila could have refused, she decided to pay all her workers, including the Chinese migrant workers," Samuel said.

Fortunato thought for a long moment, "Well, I don't know what to say," Fortunato said, "She is a smart business person, hard worker, and deep down, a woman with a generous heart, although she hides all that I've said of her very well."

"I agree with you, father, but what else are you thinking about, father?" Samuel asked.

In Bacori, Eugenio faced the dangers created by federal troops.

The Worm in my Tomato

"I was remembering how brusque, at least in my mind, Tila was in telling me, that she would not let me work her fields the third year and how she refused to advance me financial support for seed and labor to work El Potrero," Fortunato paused, and added, "she even told me to ask Jorge for help."

"The locust storm bankrupted not only Aunt Tila but Uncle Jorge as well." Samuel said, as he looked at his father, "Uncle Jorge also told me that he would leave, he said that he thought the other Vegas would also leave to live in Culiacan, San Blas, Los Mochis, and other cities to seek government posts." Samuel finished his lentil soup with cheese and tortillas.

"That is true, he told me the same thing, but I understood it would be years, after the fight with the federal government over the lands," Fortunato said.

Samuel listened to Fortunato with intent and then he said seriously, "Father, think about leaving for the good of yourself and family. The government, I am sure won't fight the large Hacendados who own millions of acres; the government will come after smaller land holders like the Vegas, those with lost titles, like Uncle Eugenio, I think. The days of gun battles and revolutions and strong man generals on horseback leading armies opposing the government are in the past, father, since President Alvaro Obregon. You should also leave, do the same like Uncle Jorge, talk with him about where to go."

"No, I will wait for Jorge to bring up this moving situation. Furthermore, we must fight the federal government for every inch of our land that they want to take from us."

"Father, before we were repatriated from the United States in 1932, the distribution of land had already started under President Plutarco Elías Calles who served from 1924 to 1928. Three presidents of the republic followed Calles but were much influenced by Mr. Calles, even from out of official office, but these presidents, Emilio Portes Gill, Pascual Ortiz Rubio, Abelardo Rodriguez, from 1928 through 1934 have endeavored to carry out the mandates of the Revolution of 1910. We have been here since 1932, father, and now Lázaro Cárdenas elected in 1934 is president; many have the feeling that during his six year tenure until 1940, there will be more land distribution than ever before." Samuel said, and he stood up intending to depart.

The Worm in my Tomato

Outdoors the rain clouds became darker and more menacing and some thunder could be heard in the distance.

Antonia stepped outside the ramada and called out to Lorena to come home, now. Samuel finished eating, and excused himself and said, "I must hurry home, now, mama, thank you." He hugged Antonia and shook hands with Fortunato. Samuel hurried off ahead of the approaching storm.

Fortunato, silent and pensive, sat at the table; he intended to have a talk with Jorge, Tila, and Eugenio.

⟜⟝

Federal soldiers at Eugenio's ranch home

Early in the morning at El Bacori, Sinaloa, 1935, several platoons of Mexican federal government soldiers encircled Eugenio Vega's house. Workers began to build a fence of barbed wire to enclose his property. Soldiers with rifles at the ready formed a perimeter around Eugenio's house, while protecting some indigenous workers erecting the fence around Eugenio's house. Eugenio came out the front door yelling, "Get out, sons of bitches, you have no right to take my property!"

A Mexican army captain, with a square jaw and an angry dark face, dressed in a dark green uniform, yelled in reply, "Halt, or you will be shot and your house burned to the ground, unless you act in a peaceful manner!" The captain gave an order for the soldiers to aim at Eugenio, but he did not call "fire," as yet.

From inside the house Sara and Catalina hurried out, like quail darting out from under the brush when scared by hunters, "Eugenio!" Sara cried out, "don't yell or threaten them; they will shoot you like the soldiers who shot Oton." She was weeping and held on to Eugenio's arm, pulling him back into the house, "Let it be, please, none of it is worth your life." Catalina stood beside Eugenio and Sara, trembling in fear, she clasped Sara's right arm with both hands.

"Don't move, all three of you, until we complete the work of putting this fence up, don't enter the house where you have your rifle, or we will shoot," the captain commanded. He glanced at his soldiers at the ready waiting for his order to fire, and he glanced at Eugenio frozen on the spot in his porch, with his wife pulling him by his shirt sleeve, urging him into the house. Both Sara and Catalina were white sheets hung out to dry, flapping in the wind, pinned down and helpless, with their cries vanishing in a whirlwind that seemed endless. Eugenio stared at the captain and the soldiers, and they at the ready stared back, daring Eugenio. The workers quickly continued to build the wire fence around his house.

At the same time, while the soldiers surrounded Eugenio's house, Antonia, in her hut at the Mayo village, heard loud yelling near her hut and she looked outside and saw Fortunato waving his arms at her. He rushed in, "Hurry, we must go to Eugenio's house," he gasped, "Chapo is hitching the wagon, Tila told me that federal troops are at Eugenio's, and we don't know what may happen; we must go get Catalina." Fortunato shouted, "I rushed here for you."

Chapo hurried up in the wagon pulled by the two mules. Fortunato, Antonia and Lorena, holding Santos in her arms, hopped up into the wagon. "Heyah, heyah," Chapo yelled; the mules galloped up the dirt road toward El Bacori. Billows of dust swirled back toward the village and the hut. Fortunato, now holding Santos, Antonia, and Lorena hung on tight to the inside of the wagon, their hands turned white from the tightness of their grip on the wagon to keep from falling out. The languid desert air around them became a stiff wind against their face because of the speed of the wagon, pulled by straining, hard galloping mules. Antonia's long black wavy hair streamed backward in the wind, and her face was distorted in fear from her suffering and pain over concern for Catalina's safety. Lorena sat beside her mother, and she held on to the wagon's bench board for her dear life, and all the while worried about Catalina, while she howled in despair, but her crying went unheard, drowned out by the racket of the swaying wagon, the clamor of Chapo's "heyah, heyah", the crack of the whip zipping out over and above the mules's heads, and the pounding hoofs of mules, galloping in terror.

In the meantime, at Eugenio's house, the fence went up, completed, and the government would now legalize it with official documentation. Three black Ford sedans drove up to Eugenio's house and ten well dressed government officials in dark suits, dismounted and cautiously walked up to within hearing distance of Eugenio. The army captain stiffly marched up to the official delegation and smartly saluted. The government dignitary in charge casually retuned the salute; he proceeded to take off his eye glasses, wipe them clean with his white handkerchief, replace his glasses over his large nose, and he commenced reading a document that he had removed from the inside pocket of his dark coat. The document in effect informed Eugenio, that by order of Mexico's federal government, he was to vacate his house and all his properties within ninety days, or be forced off by army troops. That was the official contents of the government document in so many words, and delivered by an overdressed government official in an informal manner. The government delegation then promptly turned around, climbed into their cars, slammed the doors and drove away. The captain yelled out some orders and the troops surrounding Eugenio's home lowered their weapons, marched to the road, and scrambled into army troop carriers that took them away. The native workers who had completed their task of fencing in Eugenio's house, also left without a word; they went away and disappeared into the desert.

Chapo's wagon sped up around the corner of the dirt road, with mules out of breath, the wagon enveloped in a cloud of dust, with Fortunato and his family holding themselves inside the wagon; Chapo halted his mules and his wagon in front of Eugenio's house. The wind blew the dust away; Fortunato and his family got down out of the wagon and ran toward the house, all crying and yelling at the same time, "Are you all right?"

Catalina ran out from the house porch and sought safety in the waiting arms of her mother, all gathered around her; Eugenio and Sara followed close behind, all embraced one another, "Thanks to God that you are all safe," Antonia exclaimed.

"I feared for your life," Fortunato cried out and embraced his brother.

"No, Fortunato," Eugenio said, "I left my rifle in the house, so the sons-of-bitches wouldn't have an excuse to shoot me like they did our brother Oton." Eugenio continued speaking, "Oton rushed out from his house, fired a warning shot up in the air, and yelling, ordered the soldiers off his property, but of course the soldiers responded with rifle fire at him to kill, right in front of his wife and children. Oton's wife Candida embraced him in her arms and held his head up from the ground, while she cried bitterly, and his blood spilled out into the ground, in his own front yard, while his children stood around him, sobbing." Eugenio wept, "No, my brother, I have our brother's story engraved in my mind and heart, and I was not about to give those federal bastards an excuse to shoot me, too," Eugenio said.

Twenty Nine

Lorena

Lorena learned her spiritual faith from nature in a rural area without a church: for her, God expressed his love in all his creation. She learned from teacher nature, desert, and river.

Over the last three years, Lorena had tried one way or another to have her father help her to obtain an education in school. The only opportunity she had during this time consisted of attending the village school provided by the federal government education department that paid the wages of an itinerant teacher.

Lorena's primary alternative to an academic booklearning opportunity was her neighbors and the village. Telesforo especially taught his children Twelve Months and Lorena how to learn from nature and see all creation as a teacher. Lorena slowly became aware, without her realizing it at first that she had been educated here in El Aliso nevertheless, in its own way, first by the place comprised of the desert, river, climate, vegetation and animals, and second by the mayo people who inhabited the village. Her education in El Aliso almost like by osmosis had been one of learning from Nature. She had also noted in her mind how she had been influenced by Julieta, the village residents and others in the valley and the long talks with Telesforo and the girl Months.

Reflecting upon her experience, she came to an understanding that helped her form some judgment or conclusion from which she drew some insights within the context of her environment. Lorena thought about some things she had learned. For example, she knew how to keep a *brasa* alive from one day to the next over the cold night so she could start a fire from a live coal by breathing it into a red-hot coal in the wood stove in the morning. She knew how to use a mezquite wooden *palanca* with its two buckets, one tied to each end of the cross pole, to carry water; she learned to read the weather changes in nature by the sun during the day and by the moon during the night. She learned how to create her specialty: pear shaped tizas. Lorena enjoyed her encounters with nature and all creation around her: how to hear the desert speak, discern the birds' song, delight in the bees' buzz, the insects hum, the night life chirping, and take pleasure in frogs croaking. Lorena realized she had learned how to see the leaves and trees and plants change in color and the foliage underneath change in texture. She enjoyed cleaning the fuzz off the red plump pitaya or long pickle-size cactus tunas and best of all biting into the sweet pulp.

Lorena came to understand that much of what Julieta taught her in catechism about the Christian religion and God became evident through some specific relationship with nature. Lorena had related her book learning with all of creation that she came into contact with in nature as a book written by God in God's own language.

Telesforo had taught himself how to read much of what God said in the book of Nature language, and he in turn had taught Lorena and the Twelve Months many things about what the book said. In learning how to read the book of God, Lorena had to draw out bits of information from each type of creation. The insights Lorena drew out from this language were all about love, respect, honor, and how all created things lived in faith and hope and love.

Lorena without realizing it, at first, had learned from Telesforo *cataphatic* theology in which she applied to God images and thoughts drawn from her experience with creation, but in which creation God remained a mystery. Lorena also learned from Telesforo's conversations with her and the girl Months about *natural* theology in which she came to know about God through her own reason. In this way, with Telesforo's help, Lorena had learned about faith, hope, and love from the ants at work.

To her question about why was she here in the village, again with Telesforo's conversations, Lorena had learned about how the event of the Repatriation, as an effect, had showed something of God's truth and beauty as lived by her mother and family in faith, hope, and love. However, from Julieta, Lorena learned from the theology of revelation about God through the Holy Bible and Church teachings, what God revealed beyond creation through words and historical events.

The Worm in my Tomato

Lorena felt an intelligence of spirituality, to her it had become a facile common sense in how all creation had an inherent wisdom. To Lorena all nature vibrated with love and goodness and ecstasy; to her all the community of nature danced and sang and recited poetry in their natural being and living continually during the night and day: "God is everywhere and in all things." Lorena sang out loud to herself, and repeated it again. Thank you Telesforo, she thought.

On the other hand she learned from Julieta, unknown to Lorena at first, through pastoral and positive theology about God from her study in her catechism class. Julieta said, "We know God, Lorena," and she held up the catechism book, "based on the revelations in Jesus Christ and known to the faithful through the Holy Spirit, in the teachings of our Church based on Scripture and Tradition. Julieta was a catechist teaching the village children about God and God's church composed of living souls on earth. Lorena helped Julieta to teach small children from the village.

Lorena felt blessed that she learned her catechism from Julieta. She also learned in school as much as she could from Mr. Duran. Although, Mr. Duran was not like her teacher Miss Yoakum in Bullion Plaza, he tried to teach the village students all he knew when he came to class. When he was absent because of his travels, Lorena had taught English lessons to the village students in the class.

The Twelve Months could say to Lorena in English, "Uoodmorneeng teeshur." The girl Months could say their names in English, too, "Yanuari," "Fahbuari." "Marche." "Abril," "Mai," "Unis," "and "Uli." The Months loved to speak in English, "Allo, teeshur, owh ahr uoo?" "I am fine, thank you," Lorena would smile and answer courteously. The Twelve Months would smile and others in the class would giggle.

One day Mr. Duran decided to practice his English and said, "Yeer is a panceel." He handed out one half used pencils for class members to use. Lorena said, "Mr. Duran, the word is "Pencil.""

No, it is "Panceel.""

Lorena said, "No, Miss Yoakum pronounced the word "Pencil," and Lorena pronounced the word *pencil* and carefully enunciated each syllable slowly and emphatically.

"No, here in Sinaloa we say "Panceel," and he pronounced slowly the word "Panceel." He looked at Lorena, "When I am not in class,

The Worm in my Tomato

however, and you teach English to the students, you may pronounce the words as you know them."

Lorena agreed and shook her head "yes" and that's how she became an English teacher. Students did not usually have more than one pencil in class anyway for shared use. It was an instrument foreign to them; thus, they did not appreciate totally its potential to write sentences about important thoughts. But they, conversely, had names for and knowledge about their own home and village tools or instruments they used for survival in the desert.

The village students knew many names for the tools their parents and they used at home. Their tools were tools for the survival of their village and for survival in the desert. They learned important things like how to keep the water fresh, how to keep foods from spoiling, how to make the best pigskins Lorena ever tasted, and how to dance the spiritual dances like the deer dance, and how to enjoy communal life. The village knew how to celebrate life with fiesta; the people knew how to celebrate their village saints day: how to live the moment so they would not lose it. They knew they could not live in the past for it was gone, they could not live in the future because it was yet to come and although the future did not exist in the present moment, in reality it existed at each instance it reached its present time, but like tomorrow morning, it was always on its way from all eternity and returning to all eternity. The village people lived the moment and relished the moment. They knew that when they ate a meal it was gone but its life and goodness stayed with them. The present time was to be lived and celebrated.

The villagers were happy in spite of hunger; like Telesforo, he was hungry but serene and happy. Lorena thought to herself about how fortunate she was to have come here to El Mezquitalito and to have had this different type of learning. Learning from the context of her reality that God had created, learning from her life experience. She was beginning to read God, to understand God from God's own hand.

Julieta explained to Lorena so much about God and people. Julieta said that all things rest in God, and Lorena enjoyed all she learned from Julieta's books, from her religious traditions and from what she taught orally in her lessons, as well as in her prayers. Lorena, as well, learned some important concepts from Telesforo, the old village

The Worm in my Tomato

philosopher; when Lorena somehow found relationships between what she learned from Julieta and what she learned from Telesforo and Nature Teacher.

Lorena had noticed a profound change in her father. Now, Fortunato started talking about leaving. Where to? When? Lorena did not know. But she was already in her hut pulling out her box containing her shiny black leather shoes. Lorena was beginning to pack. She looked at her tiny black shoes and realized with sadness that her feet had grown larger. She felt a minor anger at the frogs and realized she should not have eaten so many. Her leather patented shoes would remain a sentimental memento. Lorena admired her shoes and she thought they were so beautiful. Lorena undusted them and wrapped them again in their towel and packed them in her gunny sack with the rest of her things and her small amount of clothes.

Lorena recalled the first time when her family arrived in El Aliso to the big house. "Remember mother," Lorena engaged Antonia in conversation as both of them sat outdoors in the ramada, "All of father's family was there, his brothers, nephews, nieces, and everyone else. They had a big table and we sat down to eat. To me, who was so curious about everything, I assumed that we would all be sitting at the big table, instead my aunt said, 'All of you children go into the kitchen'; so we went to the kitchen and Luisa served our plates and I noticed they were not like the plates that the adults had at the big table."

"Really, Lorena, what kind of plates did the children use?"

"Our plates were made of red clay, whereas the adults used plates made of blue and white china with flower decorations. I got up to see who was sitting at the big table and there were all the aunts and uncles, and of course the head of the household who was my Aunt Tila sat at the head of the table. I heard her say to my father, "You will take those three rooms to the other side." Lorena looked at her mother and said,

"I knew that I was not going to be a part of the big house."

"Well, we were for about nine months," Antonia said.

"I was thinking that I was going to be a rich little girl in the house. During the time we were there, they had no servants, so you mother and I had to do all the work; I worked with Eligia to feed the chickens, feed the pigs, milk One Eye the cow, and went to get vegetables we needed in the *huerta*. After a time, things got worse in the house with Aunt Tila and we ended in this one room hut in El Mezquitalito. Then, it was the time when father visited us from time to time, and my two brothers left to work and live someplace on their own."

"That was the most trying time for me," Antonia said and wiped the tears from her eyes.

"We were left alone, you mother, Santos and I," Lorena unhitched the talega from the mezquite pole and took a few drinks of water. "Then I, as the big sister, started mingling with the people next door. I learned to make straw baskets, to carry the water jar on top of my head, to do whatever I could do because there was no school to go to at the time. I had chores from morning till night and even at night we had to scrape the corn from the cob." Lorena cleaned ashes out of the stove and said, "We would make a game out of scraping kernels from the corncobs. The next door neighbor's children, the girl Three Months, and Carmen would come over; we would find the first row of the corn to begin to peel it and to become faster at it. We would play games with the corn and the squash, and all the time we were doing the work. It was a way to do the work with a method and did not find it so difficult."

"Life here has been enjoyable in many ways, but we were not used to hunger, thirst, and heat or cold so intimate and so intense in our personal lives." Antonia said.

"Remember mother how you did the squash?" Lorena remembered how her mother would split it in half and then she and Lorena would pull out the insides and separate the seeds to wash them and then to dry them. The game was to count the seeds to see who had the most seeds and then Antonia would wash them and put them on a board to dry. "All our chores turned out to be games," Lorena said.

Antonia began to make a fire in the wood stove. Lorena continued speaking, "To this day I still find ways to play games with what I'm doing. There is no time to play with dolls or to dress them; I never had dolls, here. I don't remember just playing by myself, but even our games with the girl Three Months were to get food from the desert, the river, or the pond."

"I know that here in Mexico children learn to work at an early age," Antonia said.

"Well, since I was the oldest, I knew mother that you mostly depended on me. At night sometimes I played games with the girl Three Months and Carmen. Each hut had a fire and that was each family's light and warmth," Lorena said.

Lent Time

Neighbors sat around and waited for the runners during the day in the Lent season. That was when the *Fariseos* from other villages ran into the village dressed with tunics and masks; they represented the Pharisees and went to village separate house fires and danced. It was customary to give them food. Villagers considered it an honor to have them dance at their fires. Villagers would then feed them fire roasted corn or whatever they had to give them. Throughout all this the make-believe Pharisees never spoke and their faces were covered or painted so that no one knew who they were. Then the family members who wished to do so would follow the Pharisees from their hut and fire to the next fire they ran to which sometimes was half a mile away. The procession ran all the way acting like mean and wild Pharisees seeking Christians to threaten. After Pharisees danced around the neighboring hut's fire, food was always offered to the runners and dancers. Then those who joined the Pharisees from the prior hut turned and ran back to their own hut. Antonia and Lorena discussed Lent time, a religious practice of forty days when Christians commemorate the suffering, passion, and crucifixion of Jesus Christ for the salvation of the souls of mankind.

Antonia said, "The Pharisees continued to run to the next hut, acting wild and prancing about, and they menaced any Christian they encounter."

"Oh, yes, mother, I plan to run, too," Lorena told Antonia, "since I am the only runner in my hut I plan to accompany the Pharisees." Lorena that day ran with her neighbors Carmen and the girl Three Months to the next village and danced and ate with them and then returned with Carmen and the girl Three Months back to their house."

During the following weeks, other people from each new hut visited would continue to walk or jog with the Pharisees for one mile or two and so on. This festive activity occurred only during Lent. Villagers had only corn to offer and no squash but other homes had squash and even beans and tortillas. In this way Carmen, the girl Three Months and Lorena ate their dinner two or three times during the run and dance. Lorena would carefully bring food home to her mother and to Santos, their share of whatever was given to Lorena. In this way Antonia and Santos ate their supper.

"Lorena," Antonia said, "I liked to see the native villagers pretend to be the Jewish Pharisees, all painted and with their heads covered with bright colored cloth and how they ran, danced, and pranced about barefooted and at the same time made music with tambourines," Antonia laughed.

"One of those times that you, mother, let me go along with the Pharisees, we went to the cemetery to dance and make music," Lorena said, "but the villagers were not allowed in my Aunt Tila's big house, however. At the house of a wealthy relative we were allowed to rest in the barn after dancing about and around the fire in the outdoors yard. The reason we went to the wealthy relative's house was because the cemetery was located near their big house in its spacious grounds," Lorena smiled.

"The graveyards" Antonia pointed out, "usually are found in the haciendas or big houses because this is where they buried their dead."

"My own father's family does not seem to practice any form of religion, mother," Lorena said.

"I know, it is mysterious, but in this part of Mexico, in our valley, Luisa told me that there are no churches, and Fortunato's family seems not to be Catholic like the majority of residents in Mexico," Antonia said, and added "I suspected that Fortunato's family probably, although spiritual people at heart, kept their religious practices private because of the religious laws in Mexico," Antonia served herself a cup of coffee and said, "My own grandfather is thought to have come from a family of Sephardi Jews."

"I know," Lorena said, "I can remember that with my Aunt Tila there was nothing about religion; there was commercial with her store and cheese room, but where the money was buried, who knows, because no banks existed nearby, either," Lorena stepped outside to the ramada and took a drink of water from the talega. "I asked Julieta about Uncle Jorge's family baptism records, but she did not know. They never go to Julieta's prayer services; I don't even know if his children are baptized?" Lorena said.

Antonia took out a small pan of pinto beans to clean and wash in preparation for cooking and she said, "Julieta never mentions the Vegas in her intentions to involve in religious services or in preparation for baptism."

"On the other hand, mother, you are very different from my father and his family, in this regard. You learned from Nanita and my grandmother Manuela to be very religious, a pious Catholic. I can remember how you quickly constructed an altar in Aunt Tila's big house when we lived there, and now you have your small altar in this our little adobe hut," Lorena said as she helped her mother in washing three potatoes.

"I think that the problem with the lack of church buildings and the people's wariness in talking about religion is due to Mexico's religious laws persecuting Catholics during now and before the time we have lived in Sinaloa," Antonia said. Antonia sliced the potatoes, "You know, Lorena, what Julieta told me last Sunday at her house was that this year in 1935 in the whole republic of Mexico there were only 308 priests and that there were hundreds of churches closed." Antonia poured the diced potatoes into a skillet to fry. "No wonder, Lorena that no priest had come here to celebrate Mass, perhaps both priests father Simon and father Fermin have been shot dead by now."

"But, mother, remember that time during All Souls day, what is known here as *El dia de los muertos*, in praying for their dead family members, I went with the girl Five Months and Carmen to the cemetery where villagers served the food that the deceased had liked when alive," Lorena said. "The table the women set up with food in the cemetery remained like that until the next day, when all shared in eating it, and in the big house, my Aunt Tila did the same thing, she had Luisa set the dining room large table with plates and food her family liked to eat, and then next day the people of the big house would give the food to the indigenous, that's what my Aunt Tila did," Lorena said.

"Your Aunt Tila, like your father, may be a person of great personal faith and may pray to God in her own private way, but she especially does not pursue public worship or talk about the Church, I think, to avoid being targeted by the federal government or anti-Catholic Church fanatics," Antonia said.

Tila never married and she was a large woman and always wore her black shawl that covered her head. At the time of the religious persecution the people did not openly speak of religion and could not attend church services for three years because the Catholic Church was closed.

"Mother, I also think that perhaps my aunt and my father and their families did not discuss religion to avoid problems with the government. They had to protect their lands." Lorena said.

"Perhaps," Antonia placed the pot of beans to cook on the stove, "Samuel told me in a conversation about the history of Mexico, that at that time there was a great deal of Protestantism and Freemasonry in Mexico, as well," Antonia said.

⟋

Desert and River

Gonzalo came to visit Lorena and Antonia. According to Gonzalo, he had only one name. "I know myself more simply," he said, "with one name." The morning sun climbed with some effort over the bare trees, but village residents already had been at work. Lorena asked Gonzalo where he lived, the first time he came to visit, "I have my *jacal*,"he answered, "that I built myself using mezquite tree limbs and bunches of brush for roof and walls, in the middle of the desert."

"Don't you get lonely?" asked Lorena, "Having no one to speak to."

"Oh, no, Lorena, I have the whole desert around me," Gonzalo's eyes sparkled, and he smiled, "Birds sing to me every morning and owls converse every evening," he said; " Rabbits, snakes, lizards, wild cats, and even javalinas come by and visit."

Gonzalo always called Antonia, "Aunt Antonia" and he brought

The Worm in my Tomato

her and Lorena gifts from the natural bounty of the desert. Through his stories about the desert, Lorena imagined the desert as being a dry ocean of sand, where sand dunes with outstretched arms swam around the cactus, saguaros, brush thickets and mezquite trees, rising and falling, coming and going; where yellow flowers danced with soft hot winds and where many kinds of animals roamed, ran and slithered: an ocean of sand, plants, and animals which provided Gonzalo with everything he needed.

The sun laboriously crawled on all fours across the blue ceiling of the pale blue sky and shared its light over all below. The cool breeze blew in from the river. The aroma of the huizache tree yellow flowers visited the village huts. Gonzalo uncovered a white linen sack, "Look, Lorena, what I brought for you," and he showed her the white gleaming bones. Gonzalo brought Lorena some large cow bones he found in the desert. "I remember that you make *tizas* with the bones, and you asked me to bring you some, next time I came to visit."

"Thank you, Gonzalo," Lorena took the sack," she smiled and felt like dancing about the ramada, "Look mama, the bones Gonzalo brought me." Antonia inspected the bones, "That is wonderful, Lorena, now you can make more *tizas*."

Lorena laughed out loud, and said, "This is what I needed, now I can barter with my *tizas* for water from Lepo's water well and for matches and food items from other women in the village," she said, and added, "Lepo only lent me his rope, once or twice, to draw water from his well, even if I bartered for water with my *tizas*," Lorena told her story to Gonzalo, "but now, I have bones to make many *tizas*."

"Where do you get water from?" Gonzalo asked, "When Lepo refused you water?"

"Every morning I walk to the pond with my hand tin bucket and take water from the pond before the cattle come," Lorena said.

"With more *tizas*, will you be able to convince Lepo again to give you water?" Gonzalo asked.

"Yes, I bartered some *tizas* with Josefa, Lepo's wife, for one of Lepo's new *Ixtle* hemp ropes to use for drawing water and I bartered some more *tizas* for water. I now have a rope for drawing water from Lepo's well once I can barter again with Lepo for some more water,

The Worm in my Tomato

but He told me not to come back," Lorena said.

Antonia who had been busy cooking some potato soup for Gonzalo and Lorena to eat invited them to sit at the table, "Sit down, now, Gonzalo," Antonia said, "I hope you like this potato soup."

Gonzalo and Lorena sat at the table to eat some soup, "That is too bad; that is right down mean," said Gonzalo between spoonfuls of soup. "That water from his well just sips through the underground from the river," Gonzalo cut a piece of tortilla. "It is only a giant *posito*," Gonzalo said.

"Well, we will see," Lorena chewed a piece of white cheese, "For now, I spend a lot of time making *tizas*," she said while taking a spoon full of soup, " Women of the village, who make round ball shaped *tizas*, call their *tizas bolas de hueso*," she made a gesture with her hand drawing a round circle in the air, " But I call mine *peras* because I make them pear-shaped," Lorena shooed away a fly by fanning the air in front of her face with her right hand, "In this way, women will be better able to grasp at the top of the *tiza* and use either the larger end or the smaller end." Lorena showed how to grasp a pear shaped tiza in the air with her hands, "They call my *tizas* "*Peras de hueso*, and really prefer them to round ones," Lorena laughed, "It's just fantastic, my mother says."

Gonzalo smiled at Lorena and agreed with her by nodding his head up and down, "That is wonderful, Lorena, just think that for thousands of years the indigenous mayo women made them round ball shaped, and you came from the north and made them pear shaped bone *tizas*, it amazes me," Gonzalo said.

The sun stood still for an instant straight up in the pale blue sky and showed it was twelve noon, straight up and down.

"It was really an accident, Gonzalo; I could not shape my *tizas* round for the same reason that I never could shape the round balls of flour dough for my tortillas into round tortillas." Lorena laughed, "but to my surprise, my pear shaped *tizas* quickly won over women in the village because they were easier to grasp, hold, and rub with. Soon my pear *tizas* were in demand."

The wind blew a dust-devil round and round outside the ramada, "I searched the surrounding areas for cow bones to use in the process," Lorena finished her soup, "not any other kind of bone from any other kind of animal," and she wrinkled her nose, "For sure not dog bones," She pointed at Gonzalo with her right index finger, and moved it up and down. "These tizas are used in the cooking of meals and have to be made from pure bones of edible animals like the cow," Lorena emphasized.

"The newer the bone is, the better the *tiza*," Lorena arose from the table. Antonia sat to the side of the table, feeding Santos soup with a small spoon. "Bones that are too old are easily broken, when in use," Lorena said, "My *tiza* bones are durable yet allow their surface powder to anoint the surface of a *comal*."

"I will bring you some more bones, Lorena," Gonzalo said as he got up from the table, "if I find some, after the ranchers butcher a beef cow." The sun moved to the right of center in the pale blue sky, and Lorena waved to Gonzalo as he departed. Winds picked up and swirled Gonzalo away into the desert. The sun lost its grip and rolled down the right slope of the pale blue sky and all too soon tumbled behind the western sea.

Thirty
Antonia: Reminisces about the Repatriation
Dry Well

One day, Telesforo spoke with Antonia and Lorena outside their hut, under the tall huizache tree and said, "Although one can never know the event that will happen until it emerges from somewhere in the dimension of time, and then we experience the event for however long it accompanies us and then, of course, we would have had a historical experience."

Later, Antonia recalled what her brother Tomas had said to her, once. He had told Antonia and Fortunato about poor and disoriented people who were crossing back and forth on the railroads, seeking a way of life and finding none. They were called hobos. Now, Antonia felt that the Repatriation had forced them to cross borders and that now she and her family were hobos; they crossed borders, seeking a way of life and finding none. This was their family's historical experience.

She remembered the two religious sisters she had helped with a room to live in and had given them food to eat, when they, with many immigrant Mexican people, escaped Mexico's poverty. Poverty made worse by the Mexican government, and which also had crossed borders with them. In the religious sisters' case, their poverty was made worse, along with numerous priests and nuns, because they had been expelled by the Cristero war. The priests and nuns had desperately sought asylum in the United States. They had not only faced destitution but also lost a homeland. The religious sisters had had a spiritual experience in their historical event as well. For them and for others like Antonia who were spiritual people, the question that needed to be answered for themselves was: Where was God in their life at the time; was this God's Will then and there and what was the meaning of their suffering? Antonia in particular wondered about the relationship between the Repatriation of her family to Mexico and Holy Scripture: the meaning of her family's exile to Mexico. Antonia and Julieta had discussed this very issue, and Julieta had urged Antonia to read and reflect upon Exodus and to read Psalm 137: 1 - 6 in The Old Testament. Antonia and Julieta had reflected on both readings. Antonia said, "My people have suffered inequities in work and living conditions; the majority of citizens that ruled and made the laws forced us out from our homes."

"What does the Repatriation now mean to you, Antonia?" Julieta asked. She looked at Antonia who sobbed quietly.

"We were forced into our type of spiritual captivity where we find no solace for our spiritual needs. By this El Fuerte River in this desert village, I have wept when I remembered Miami, my home in Arizona, when I remembered my Nanita Isabel, my brother Tomas, my cousin Josephina, and my church. How can I ever be happy, again?"

Antonia remembered how her family too, rode the train, but they came to Mexico as a family. But Antonia thought to herself: the Repatriation was an incongruous event because I am a third generation American citizen and my children are all American citizens. Those Mexicans that were non-citizens had been enticed to cross over the border by the need for their labor. Antonia knew that the same historical experience which bothered her also bothered her children. That is why Lorena had sought answers from Telesforo during their study of the ants, when Telesforo talked about the ants to his children the Twelve Months and to Lorena.

The days for Lorena were worn flat as the stones in the river, like the stone she had picked up and kept in her pocket and admired from time to time, and like her stone the days changed colors with the dark of night or the light of day; Lorena matured with the pain of hunger and cold of night and the struggles for food and water of the day.

Lorena and Antonia had gone to the river to wash their garments, they used the lard and lye that Antonia had boiled hard the day before and made into soap. They rinsed their wash and hung it to dry on top of brush and boulders. They had enjoyed the social activity with other village women during their work along the shore. The hot sun had

The Worm in my Tomato

promptly dried their clothes. Antonia and Lorena and returned home, contented that they had completed their washing; they had enjoyed visiting with other village women.

Lorena folded sheets, and became pensive, "Mama," Lorena asked, "why did we come on the Repatriation train when we are all American citizens?"

"The Repatriation program offered us and other Mexican families an opportunity to seek a new life in their homeland and with their family, like your father." Antonia heated her flat iron on top of the stove in preparation to iron some shirts for Fortunato, who came by at the end of each week for clean clothes.

"Miss Yoakum told us in class about how state governments would not have to help with costs and needs of Mexican citizens, if thousands were removed from state and federal welfare roles," Lorena said.

Antonia thought of how Fortunato, the only Mexican citizen in her family, had convinced her that in Sinaloa he would have lands to cultivate; that they would have no lack of food and money. Antonia remembered all these events and reflected seriously about the reality of her family's experience and knew that she had to make a drastic change. Antonia knew that she had brought her family in a journey into the land of perceived plenty, her imagined Egypt, and now she felt that she must lead her family out.

Lorena must have sensed sadness in her mother's demeanor; she tried to bring levity into their conversation, and she said, "For my part, I envisioned myself living in an hacienda and going to a local school; more than anything, I wanted an education," Lorena laughed, "Besides, father bought me a new dress and a new pair of shoes for the trip," Lorena felt her face blush in a momentary bliss. "My shoes, shiny black leather with silver buckles and ankle leather straps," Lorena exclaimed to her mother, "I now keep them safeguarded in their box carefully wrapped in a towel and placed in a corner of the hut to keep them safe from rats and rain, until that one day when I will take them back home, I will keep them forever." She thought for a moment, and said, "As my personal memento." Lorena remembered to herself: *memento*, and thought thank you Miss Yoakum. Lorena folded the clothes and put them away in a box on a wall shelf.

The Worm in my Tomato

"I suppose," Antonia, busy ironing the shirts, began to speak softly, "Your black patent leather shoes will always hold a special place in your heart."

Antonia, in her mind, holding a perspective from a vantage point into the future, thought that after years had gone by, Lorena would somehow return to Miami, and she would be able, perhaps, to afford a self-satisfied pretense of triumph over a moment of time and of this journey's experience. Antonia, determined to show Lorena that she, too, could philosophize like Telesforo, blew drops of water, sipped from a glass of rice water, like a sprinkled mist, on a shirt, and looked outside the ramada and sensed the afternoon river breeze bathing the landscape with coolness, said "You may then see a bit of self-interest in each member of our family who escaped our famine burdened land and undertook a journey into the unknown, like Joseph's family fleeing into Egypt, hoping for the promises of golden wheat of plenty," Antonia paused, "I too saw myself living in a large hacienda, in a large land empire, to hear your father tell it." Antonia ironed Fortunato's shirts with renewed energy that originated in a deep held anger with herself. "But I hope, Lorena, that someday in the future, when you are older, much older, your supposed triumph over this moment of time and of this journey's experience, when you return home from your exile will be one of humility."

Evening approached quickly and claimed the scene of a stillness smothered in humid heat and the desert dusk. All the plants and animals nestled or twisted into a sleeping posture. The insects ceased their buzzing and only the pond frogs croaked a guttural serenade. Pale orange light from the golden moon glanced off the silvery surface of the pond and vanished into the tall trees along the far shore of the river.

Antonia thought that Lorena had not responded to her last comments because she sought time to reflect on what she had said, but Antonia knew Lorena so well that she was certain Lorena, for her part, dreamed of her education opportunity yet to come.

Antonia saw Lorena go to the second shelf of the altar stand and pick up her shoes, wrapped in a towel. Lorena took her shoes and gently wiped them from dust and caressed them. Antonia watched Lorena as she relished holding her black shoes like if they were a pet; Lorena wiped her treasure clean and carefully wrapped it up again in the towel.

Antonia felt a rush of tenderness for Lorena and in an instant hoped for Lorena's return home. Antonia thought of planning an escape for her family back home to Miami, from Aliso, Sinaloa, Mexico, even this late in time. Antonia convinced herself in her heart that Lorena could not leave her alone to cope with all the problems of living here and taking care of Santos.

For once, since their arrival in the valley, Antonia felt anchored in Christian hope to be free from the situation she perceived bound her and her family here in this valley. Antonia also thought about her Fortunato, she marveled at how Fortunato, who had been a fair complexioned Spaniard, was now dark tan, haggard, with dark long hair cascading over his neck, with his hands made rough by outdoors labor. Antonia knew for certain that Fortunato worked harder than any other man in the village, and she felt a surge of love for her husband. She hoped to find a way to get him away from the valley, she had faith in her prayers and she would think of a plan to lead her family out of Mexico.

Antonia was startled back to reality by Lorena's voice, "Tell me about how you came to know father from years ago, mother," Lorena asked. The ironing long completed, and both Antonia and Lorena now sitting quietly in the ramada kitchen, looking out at the dusk colors of the village houses, Antonia responded, "Your father, it seems always had sought protection from outdoor labor and the weathering sun for most of his adult life." Antonia thought for a moment and continued, "Fortunato had instead pursued his trade as a gambler in gambling halls, his hands always had been soft and smooth with quick fingers for shuffling cards. He had escaped the agricultural fields and work of his home here in Sinaloa when a youth and the demanding labor his father was sure to impose. At age nineteen he had left home, El Aliso, and crossed into the United States." Antonia prepared supper for Lorena and Santos, as she talked, and they ate left over noodles, beans, and tortillas.

"Mother, but you met him when he was much older then when he came to the United States, right?" Lorena wondered.

"Oh, yes, he had for many years roamed about the southwest, but when gambling failed to provide for his needs, he had not hesitated to use his strong body to work in various construction projects. He had

The Worm in my Tomato

worked as a cement worker during the building of the Roosevelt Dam in Arizona. But for most of his time, he had been a reputed gambler and card player at the Limonada Pool Hall in Miami. Why he left California and Nevada, he never said, but I think he simply wanted to live in a small town, you know, get away from the big city life. Finally at age forty-six, he settled down, somewhat, after we married; I was at the time of our marriage a young widow."

Antonia remembered about when she was a young widow from her first husband Samuel Gutierrez, and how also she had three children, two boys and a girl. Antonia thought about how Samuel and Jose lived to make the journey to Sinaloa, but her little daughter named Toni died when a teenage girl, at age sixteen, during the typhoid fever plague of 1931, in the Globe hospital. Antonia recalled, her eyes misty with tears. She averted looking at Lorena and sipped her hot coffee. Antonia thought about how she and Fortunato had been married eleven years by 1932, when they with their family departed on the Repatriation train; Lorena, our first child, Antonia thought, was almost ten years old; Lorena was born in 1922 in Miami, Arizona; Antonia felt a sense of remorse when she recalled that Fortunato had made Lorena be the first to climb aboard the train, and she was so young, and Catalina was only seven years old, and Antonia exclaimed out loud, "This, I will always remember."

"What mama, what will you always remember?" Lorena asked. Antonia regained her composure, "As for our journey to Sinaloa, your father looked forward to seeing his family again," Antonia said, and served herself another cup of coffee, "a large family of brothers and sisters awaited his return. Here in El Aliso, were family lands he planned to cultivate into cotton, tomatoes and legumes such as peas, pinto beans, and garbanzo," Antonia stirred her coffee, outside the ramada, they heard noises like horses running through the desert brush, and Lorena covered Santos sleeping in his cot. Antonia continued speaking, "I had heard Fortunato and his brothers talking about how Sinaloa was considered by government bureaucrats, who made agricultural projections, that in a few years Sinaloa would export a great volume of tomatoes throughout Mexico and to the United States," Antonia finished in a whisper.

The Worm in my Tomato

"My father expected to make money in growing tomatoes," Lorena said, "Father, I am sure, mama, as Telesforo told me and I memorized it, my father must have had hopes of finding his tamale wrapped in cornhusks and his treasure in tomatoes," Lorena said, "But, all I found mama, was a green worm with beady eyes in my tomato," Lorena shuddered," and she added, " as Telesforo told me, we are limited as human beings in our ability to see the future, and I can see now, mama, that what father found was not what he hoped for; the unexpected locusts changed his dreams into nightmares," Lorena said.

"Yes, Lorena, that is a profound notion that Telesforo helped you to understand," Antonia answered.

Indeed, no one knows the future one second away from one's own nose. If Luisa had read the tea leaves for Antonia, it may have been revealed that before their stay in Mexico ended, Fortunato would embark, motivated by frenzied desperation, on a return path into gambling. He would try to gain what farming had denied him and his family. Now, in Sinaloa, he had labored hard to succeed as a farmer at this late time of his life when he was sixty years of age. Now, stooped by hard field labor, plagued by failing eye-sight, he gathered his remaining dignity of a defeated man and sought to recapture what once he had been. But Fortunato sought a solution in wrong places and in a wrong way: in card games with deceitful gamblers.

Antonia recognized in a burst of insight, like in the reality of a bright sunlit morning without a shadow, that there were no doubts in her mind, her family was now stranded in Sinaloa and that something had to be done. She thought why not: with all of her family in tow, she determined to strike out again on another journey to their homeland. Antonia sensed without a doubt and felt relief, for once she knew for certain what she must do. Antonia peered at the stars outside the ramada; she listened for the familiar sounds of night, and the frogs crooned to the moon as usual; so what was it, then, she thought, that twice in the same night she had known and felt with certainty that she must leave, return home with her family; furthermore, she thought it must be soon.

"Lorena, I must rethink my belief, as Nanita taught me, you know, the idea of carrying my Christian cross by being a dutiful wife and supporting my husband." Antonia looked into Lorena's eyes, "I think I

The Worm in my Tomato

should do that for as long as it is just and fair to all of us; then something else must be done. When other family members suffer unjustly, when they are made to carry their parents' cross, too, it is time for a change, and now, Fortunato must carry his cross by listening to us, in loving, honoring, and respecting us, his wife and his family."

Lorena could not believe what she was hearing. "Well, yes, mother, I have been thinking that way all along," Lorena said, "I also planned that if my father and mother and the rest of my family would not return home, then I would leave by myself, alone if I had to, I always felt determined to make plans for my exodus," *Exodus,* thank you Miss Yoakum, she thought, and Lorena smiled happily, and continued, "Samuel and Jose had hated coming on the Repatriation train, but probably not as much as I did. We hated to leave our schools behind. We missed our friends." Lorena said, hopping about the cots, but careful not to wake Santos.

"But for Samuel, Jose, Catalina, Santos, and for you, especially, there should be a new beginning," Antonia said, "Soon."

"Oh, yes, mother, in the distance of time and space, as Telesforo says," Lorena remembered Telesforo, and also thought of Miss Yoakum,

House and field in El Aliso, looking east is surrounded by desert enclosed ranching and farming area, bounded on one side by a river and on the other side by a desert; with no schools, no church.

The Worm in my Tomato

her teacher in Arizona, Lorena said, "Our new utopia, *utopia*, thank you Miss Yoakum," Lorena jumped up, laughing and crying, " Waits for us, hooray, a place where we can get an education and go to church."

Young people always have dreams of excellence in a new life wrapped up by the husks of a new place, opportunities and future adventures. As limited human beings, though, people never know what events will emerge from time ever flowing on from the dimension of eternity and returning to eternity leaving behind the memories of historical events experienced in time, some good and some bad. Lorena had heard something of the sort from Telesforo and had memorized something similar to these notions from Telesforo from what he said to Lorena and the girl Seven Months, while they studied the ants in his front yard.

Antonia thought equally similar thoughts about Fortunato, she thought about how the unknown, the unexpected, surprised Fortunato and his family, for certain, as they found out here in Sinaloa, like the locusts and those unwanted events that later became like a dry well with nothing to give. She thought about how Lorena at least had taken the dry bones in her life journey in Sinaloa and had changed these dry bones of events into worthy tizas of opportunity.

For their own particular uncertainties, Samuel and Jose, as young men, searched for their opportunities in Sinaloa and made the best of them. Antonia often wondered, though, if her sons Samuel and Jose would return with her, as a family.

Antonia's Affirmation

Antonia, of course, always had put together the family nest. She kept her family together through the early phases of the hunger of the Great Depression that shadowed her family into Mexico and had become for them the Mexican Great Destitution. She struggled to keep her family together against the forces of government laws, like the land-reform laws, that threatened to strip Fortunato's family from long-held lands in cultivation. The Constitution of Mexico had religious laws that kept clergy from wearing identifying clerical garb. These religious laws forced priests and religious sisters to flee the country. Churches were closed for some time. The faithful who opposed the Federal government and even fought armed battles against the federal troops were known as Cristeros, who as Catholics championed Christ the King.

Antonia, all five foot two inches of her, stout like her mining ancestors of Morenci, Arizona, had a strong prominent jaw, large brown eyes, long wavy black hair. She had not panicked when these government laws threatened her family and their way of life. Like a mother hen, she protected her children; she scratched the ground, literally, to feed them. Lorena had been a quick learner and searched the desert areas, the bovine pond, the beaches of the El Fuerte River; she bartered her *tizas* with the pueblo Mayo natives for water and food.

"How has it been for you mama, all we've been through?" Lorena asked her mother.

Antonia did not respond. Lorena added, "I remember that I was excited," with her right hand Lorena smoothed back her dark brown hair from her forehead, "I was almost ten years old." she paused, "You see, I saw myself living in an hacienda like the rich members of my father's family." Lorena glanced over at her mother to see if she was ready to respond. Antonia seemed lost in a daydream.

Lorena continued speaking, "I thought it was going to be fun, with my new shiny black shoes and my new dress that father bought for me at Miami's Commercial Company Store. But when the train arrived at San Blas there was Chapo, my Aunt Tila's vaquero, waiting with a wooden wagon drawn by two mules. I looked at the wagon's rough wooden planks, and I promptly removed my shoes; until later I thought."

Antonia, momentarily, lost in a trance did not yet respond. "Did you think about Miami, later?" Lorena asked her mother. She wanted to know if her mother had been homesick like she had been. "Did you anticipate with joy about living in a hacienda, like my own hopes, and did you, mother, look forward to living in a hacienda, have your thoughts changed and why?"

Antonia recollected herself, and replied, "After being tossed side to side and front to back and back to front in the wagon and all along the way Chapo cracking the whip over the mules' ears and the dust swirling all about us, the heat and the moisture, and all, made our trip to your Aunt Tila's big house unbearable," She laughed out loud.

Lorena was happy her mother had joined her in conversation. "How can you laugh at being tossed like clothes in a washing machine, mother?"

"I can laugh now, but at that time, all I thought about was how could I leave this place and return to Miami, even if I had to walk," Antonia said.

Lorena jumped in joy and rushed to her mother and hugged her, "You, too?" Lorena was overjoyed at discovering her mother had felt like she had, all along. Lorena felt a bond with her mother that she had not known before; she, too, like me had thought of returning to Miami, Lorena thought. Now, Lorena knew they shared their wanting to escape in common. Lorena knew for certain that they would survive and make it out of Sinaloa, and return home safely, for they had been on the way home all the time.

"The ride with Chapo was no roller-coaster ride at the Bullion Plaza Carnival," Lorena laughed. "I saw Samuel and Jose holding on tight with their hands on the wagon sides. Catalina and Santos were being held by you and me. All of us were being thrown around. I felt sorry for little Catalina, she had a horrified look in her face like a person's expression of certainty of death by swirling in a tornado. I recalled how you, mama, held Santos, for dear life, and Santos screamed all the way, but I knew for sure, he yelled from fright and not from excitement. Father, of course, rode up front on the buckboard, talking to Chapo; "I surmised that dad pretended not to be afraid," *surmised*, thank you Miss Yoakum, Lorena thought. "Who could have guessed that we, all of us, were in for a ride we dreaded but could not jump off, not from the Repatriation train and not from the wagon?" Lorena said, and she and Antonia laughed and laughed.

El Aliso, Sinaloa, gleamed in the sun. Dirt roads, dry irrigation canals, an outlying desert close enough to hike to it on the edge of the village. There trees grew that looked like Arizona mezquite trees, but were called huizache. Tall saguaro giant cactus trees, with fruit at the very top, called *pitayas,* grew among large tall green cactus we called prickly pear cactus in Arizona but here were called *tuna* because of the small pickle-size, pear-shaped red fruit covered with sticker fuzz. Antonia cleaned the fuzz away from the tunas and ate the red fruit in bites or made tuna jelly from it.

When Antonia and her family were forced out from the big house to live in El Mezquitalito, Antonia had observed the cattle, foraging about for food, because she was certain that anything they ate would be safe for humans. The cattle were here and there munching on cholla and prickly pear cactus. The cows would wrap their huge pink tongues around green cactus leaves, one inch thick and the size of a ping-pong paddle, and chewed its juicy pulp, stickers and all.

Antonia remembered now, that at the time, when she saw the desert, she had not realized that she was looking out at the family's source of food supply. "Remember, Lorena, when we first moved here to the hut, and we wondered where we would get our food to eat," Antonia said.

Lorena told her mother: "At that time, I never thought that as I looked into the desert, I was looking at my future grocery store, and that in time I would compete with those cows for prickly cactus pears; consider the saguaros' *pitayas* one of our staple foods, along with the *nopalitos*; the day would soon enough arrive when those cows and I would compete over what brown muddy water filled the bovine pond."

"But I thought we would always have a water well," Antonia added sadly.

"Well, the first chore Eligia taught me was how to draw water from Aunt Tila's well. I sadly remember now that we did have the best water well in the world when we lived with Aunt Tila; a deep well with clear sweet water from where my friend Eligia and I would draw water with a wooden bucket and hauling rope, for the kitchen, house, and drinking use," Lorena said.

"I became angry at the way the indigenous customers were cheated at the store. But after the first year, when all our arguments and fighting happened, we ended up refugees in this your Uncle Jorge's one room, one door, one window square adobe house with a side kitchen ramada," Antonia said.

Lorena glanced at her mother and said, "Now, we barter for clean fresh water from our neighbor's well, always half-dry or dry, depending on how much water seeps underground from the El Fuerte River," Lorena lamented.

Antonia began to search about for wood to start the evening fire

The Worm in my Tomato

and make some coffee.

"Mother, do you think about Miami?" Lorena asked.

"Always, and funny, when I thought about Miami, I craved peanut butter and I knew that if I lived in Miami I could have containers of peanut butter, at a small price, sold by the food store. I find myself craving peanut butter now and then," Antonia said.

"I think about Miami, about my school, Bullion Plaza, and my teachers, especially about Miss Yoakum. I knew that in Miami, even the poorest of the poor could attend school. But here I am in this desert enclosed ranching and farming area, bounded on one side by a river and on the other side by a desert, with no schools, no church, no Miami Commercial store; already thirteen years old, that's when I started to resent my father for bringing us to Sinaloa," Lorena said.

Antonia, while fanning the fragile fire in the wood stove said, "No churches, no stores, no theaters, no Alianza Hispano Americana, no meetings; if it was not for our neighbors and Julieta, I would have lost my mind a long time ago, and we didn't even have a dry well like Lepo."

Lorena, sensing an opportunity said, "No, we can not stay here any longer, and furthermore, we must not wait too long: talk to father, please, mother."

Thirty One

Antonia's Baby

Two months after Saint John's Feast Day on a hot airless August dark night Lorena awoke at the urgent grasp of her mother's hand. "Lorena, go daughter; run across the village square and get Jacinta, the *partera*. It is time for my delivery." Lorena heard her mother's voice halting, dragging itself in bits of sound past the throat, emitting its petition in suffering and supplication.

Lorena slipped on her brown leather sandals and she hurried out the hut, past the ramada and plunged into the darkness of a sleeping village. In less than half of an hour Lorena and the old worn out lady, Jacinta, the *partera*, arrived at Antonia's hut.

"Hurry, Lorena, boil some water in a large pan." Jacinta said and she limped about the hut and placed her hand on Antonia's forehead. Lorena approached the oven with trepidation, uncertain that last night's coals now buried under the warm ashes could be coaxed into flame. The hut became full with the moaning of Antonia, her tossing, and turning, "Oh, Nanita, oh, Dios padre, ayudame, por favor, Ah, ah."

The Worm in my Tomato

Santos, all four years of him, trembled and whimpered, wondering what was happening. Lorena uncovered the coals sleeping under the ashes. She slowly removed the ashes from on top of the coals and caressingly began to blow on the coals with her breath of life. She remembered what Lepo had said, 'Blow on them with love.' Why, she had asked. 'Because child you must give them your breath of life, your spirit of love, for them to burst into flame.' Lorena knew that she had done just this many times before: brought the morning flames to being on which to start the morning fire for her mother to cook breakfast. But now, it was a different occasion; the time was not just right. It was too early, almost dawn, she thought, the coals have not rested long enough.

"Hurry *muchacha*." Jacinta urged. Lorena, startled out of her thoughts, responded by blowing harder and faster on the coals. Antonia was huffing and puffing and pushing harder and harder, heaving and breathing with love and her spirit of life. Would they start, Lorena wondered. Yes, I must have faith, they will start, they must start, she thought, her eyes misty with tears. Slowly, ever so slowly the coals began to awake, turn pink, began to darken into the red color of life. The coals changed from dark red to white and burst into light.

At the same time, Lorena heard the cry of a new born baby: "Whah, whah," the baby burst into light. Antonia gave the light of day to a new member of the human race. Lorena covered the red-hot white alive coals with thin yellow straw that burst into flames. Lorena fed the burning life some thin bark and mezquite twigs. Then she built the pyramid of sticks to feed the fire of life. At the same time, Lorena heard Jacinta exclaim, "It's a boy." Lorena hurried and put the large pan on the stove, poured water from the bucket that she had filled to the brim the evening before from her posito by the edge of the river. The water would be hot soon enough for Jacinta to sterilize white cloths for use with Antonia.

"Here, Lorena, go outside behind the hut somewhere and bury the afterbirth and umbilical cord." Jacinta said.

Lorena took the red bloody towels wrapped around all the afterbirth, the placenta and fetal membranes flesh, and she hurried out, past the stove where the water now boiled up its hot vapors. She hurried out into the outside cold early dawn stillness; her body felt the dawn fresh and inviting; but Lorena shivered in the coldness of the cold air from the river. She took the hatchet and hacked out a square hole in the back of the hut near the large huizache tree. She scooped up the coarse cool dirt out of the hole and dropped in the bloody afterbirth and covered the hole and stomped over it with her leather *guaraches*, her favorite sandals Samuel had given to her one day. The trees were strangely calm; the wind stopped blowing at this time. It seemed the whole world was yet sleeping. A rooster crowed somewhere in the distance, all the world slept except for the roosters, Lorena thought as she hurried back into the hut where she found Jacinta waiting to be escorted back to her house.

"I will return sometime during the day," Jacinta said. She and Lorena made their way across the plaza toward Jacinta's house. Lorena could hear Santos wailing for her in the hut. A breeze began to stir up from the north along the river and west from the Sierra. A faint hint of red blush crested the eastern horizon, barely visible, and reflected for now, by a white cloud lost in the vastness of a blue sky. Stupid rooster, thought Lorena, see what he did, he woke up the day. Lorena stroked the palm of her left hand with the fist of her right hand; I know for sure the new baby boy will wake up the night, she thought.

Julieta came to visit Antonia the very same day she gave birth to her baby boy. "Antonia, how are you, let me see the little angel from heaven; Jacinta told me this morning at my house that it was a darling little boy."

"Yes, come in Julieta," Antonia answered from her cot where she had slept, no doubt exhausted over the ordeal of having a baby.

Fortunato sat on a wooden crate near Antonia's bed. He stood up and also welcomed Julieta. Fortunato looked haggard and unkempt beyond his age of sixty years.

Julieta wondered if Fortunato had been up most of the night somewhere engaged in a card game. Jacinta that morning had informed her that Antonia's baby, although a beautiful baby, seemed to her to have a strange pallor about him. She, an experienced mid-wife, who had delivered hundreds of babies during many years, could almost tell at a glance if a baby was right or was suffering from illness. Jacinta thought that Antonia's baby may not live long. She intended to visit Antonia later in the morning and bring with her some herb that she would gather up in the desert, selected and harvested for the occasion. She hoped the baby could be healed from what ever sickness it had.

Julieta noticed that the baby was quite small but markedly beautiful with an aura of light, almost angelic. The baby was strangely restless and moaned from time to time.

Antonia, too, feared that the baby agonized in a struggle against illness. Strangely the baby did not cry out in pain but seemed too weak to complain loudly and only groaned. Antonia, to distract herself momentarily, looked with fatigued eyes at Julieta, and she commenced on a conversation with Julieta, reminiscing about her life.

Lorena had taken Santos for a walk and to visit the Seven Girl Months. The overcast day was gloomy and silent. Today, it seemed that not even the birds flew above into the trees, the insects did not buzz, the frogs were mute, and the cows did not moo while they stopped to drink water at the bovine pond. The day stood imprisoned in time, mired in its pale green desert dress of brush and its brown of weeds, wrapped in its dryness and stench of dead animals slightly covered with a thin sheet of dirt.

Antonia continued her story: "The governments did not seem to care or worse were inept in helping ordinary citizens to cope with the events in their life. However, our family did fairly well without monetary help or political power to survive in the face of these unbearable events that like dark storm clouds threatened to engulf us and drown us into nothingness."

Jacinta entered the hut. "Fortunato, good morning," Jacinta glanced at Antonia and Julieta and said, "Good morning, I went and picked the herbs I needed, and now I will apply some medication on the baby's umbilical area," she turned toward Fortunato, who now had a roaring fire going strong in the oven, "Give me two small pans, Fortunato, to make a tea from this herb and to make a poultice from this other." Fortunato provided the two pans and made room for Jacinta at the stove.

Fortunato sat down on his wooden crate and stayed motionless like a rabbit under a brush before making a dash for escape in fright, yet captured in the conversation of Antonia, he imagined himself in Arizona, caught up in the turmoil of escaping the hunger and homelessness of the poor, imprisoned in a morass of prejudice and hatreds motivated by stereotypes against the politically weak by the ignorant majority of

The Worm in my Tomato

citizens, who controlled social and political laws for their own gain and for the disadvantage of the politically oppressed.

Jacinta came to care for the baby who tossed and turned and groaned. "I will give him a spoonful of this herbal tea, sip by sip," she said. She carefully and very gently picked up the baby and administered the tea with a small spoon and said, "Then after the medicated poultice cools down a little bit more, I will spread it on the cloth now boiling on the stove; after both cool, I will apply over his navel, which is swollen and inflamed."

The baby groaned and whimpered and then let out a loud cry. Jacinta had a hard time feeding him the much needed medical herb tea. Fortunato could not stand the tension of the moment and excused himself and hastened out the hut. Antonia got up trembling, and with difficulty, steadying herself, very slowly made her way to the adobe stove to make coffee for Julieta. Then she shuffled back to her cot, "The coffee will be ready in a few minutes Julieta," Antonia said.

Fortunato excused himself and got up to enter the ramada area of the hut, and said, "Yes, please let me know if you want some coffee, Julieta." But soon, he left the hut and disappeared away from the village.

Julieta sat near Antonia and said, "Antonia, let us pray a decade of the rosary for the baby and ask God to provide healing for whatever is ailing him."

Antonia and Julieta prayed the rosary; the baby stiffened, stretched out his limbs, and cried aloud, and Jacinta placed the poultice on the navel area of the baby's abdomen. Outside, the imprisoned middle of the day was dark, nothing stirred, and silence subdued the village. Only the mournful song of an owl perched on top of the nearby saguaro was heard, but then it flew away and the dusk ushered in a night, black and silent. The women prayed the rosary and the baby writhed in pain. "Father, I would this cup pass me by, but not my will be done, your will be done," the women offered the first sorrowful mystery in prayer and offered the baby to God.

While the women prayed, Fortunato walked down another road and sought his imagined and desired gain in the risk of the unknown. Motivated by desperation, Fortunato sought out his usual card game at a nearby ranch house. The rancher, named Vasquez, reputed in the valley as a shrewd gambler, and others like him, knew Fortunato. One of them saw Fortunato approaching and said to Vasquez, "Here is the *conejo*," and Vasquez responded, "Yeah, my cards are ready; today we'll skin the rabbit for all he's worth in tonight's *jugada de póker*."

The game started late in the afternoon with a few drinks in a smoke filled room. Fortunato, dressed in his faded old blue suit, did not drink or smoke, but he gambled as a man nailed to his addiction. The game of poker progressed; at one point Fortunato thought he could double his winnings in a final card game; however, he lost all his money. Then in order to recuperate his loss, he gambled away his children's ranch stock, the calves that his sister Tila had given to Lorena and Catalina to help them start their own herd of cattle. With the loss of his children's calves, he knew that for certain he would lose the credibility his daughter Lorena had always had for him. Fortunato helplessly realized that the respect his sons Samuel and Jose had for him would slip away, like shadows into the night. He knew that he would increase the further disappointment from his wife, Antonia: he had gambled away the girls' future in a present moment of madness, when in panic he hastened from the brush cover of common sense.

Having lost all the money he had in his pocket; having lost his children's calves, he left the game and walked down the dirt road leading nowhere. He prayed to fight off the demons that persisted in urging him to end his own life: what was he good for? End it now, the demons demanded. "Help me, Lord; even if I am a sinner, help to keep the life you have given me." Fortunato's life problems and troubles, like invisible gravity would in time touch all his family members, each in its own way; each family member would have to respond in his or her own unique and particular way, to keep from falling.

Fortuato walked down the dirt road leading nowhere; the sky was clear and the night was dark but there were no stars tonight; not even a moon shone for Fortunato to light his path. He lamented his failed agricultural pursuits and his having disappointed Lorena, his eldest daughter of the family, who had only sought the realization of her life goal: obtaining her education. Fortunato knew that Lorena, in her mind, had considered that education happened in a school and was read out of books, but Fortunato knew, as hot tears ran down his bearded cheeks, that Lorena had learned more than she ever

The Worm in my Tomato

supposed under the circumstances of her new surroundings, from her experiences, more so than himself, and Fortunato was proud that she had learned through the education that life experience itself offered here in Mexico, and that she had become a scholar of experience through the education of survival in a demanding environment. He regretted that he had not, but stubbornly had tried to succeed over obstacles of lack of rain, insects, and finally the plague of locusts. "Oh, my God, why hast thou forsaken me," Fortunato prayed in anguish. Fortunato's family including Antonia had never known this part of Fortunato who prayed within himself, in silence but with deep faith, "Help me, God our Father, take me where I am supposed to be," Fortunato prayed.

During the night when Fortunato walked on the dirt road, back in the hut, the women had completed the last sorrowful mystery and had quoted Jesus Christ dying on his cross, "Father, to you I commend my spirit."

That same night before the baby died in the hut, Antonia asked Julieta to baptize the dying baby and Julieta baptized the baby with water from the bucket, water from Lorena's posito; Antonia gave the baby the Christian names requested by Antonia. Julieta and Jacinta were the godparents. Julieta said, "Through the authority granted me, a baptized faithful, by the Holy, Apostolic, Roman Catholic Church, I baptize you Fortunato Jose Manuel Humberto in the name of the Father, Son, and Holy Spirit." Julieta poured water with her cupped hand over the baby's forehead and head as she said the words to administer the sacrament of baptism.

The baby had breathed one last gasp and had died. Julieta said, "His soul, freed from original sin, soared into the night; accompanied by angels, the baby ascended into heaven to be with his spiritual Father, the God of all creation." She comforted Antonia, "Jesus Christ was nailed to the cross and died so that salvation come out of great sin."

Jacinta also comforted Antonia and told her, "The baby will be taken care of by *Xochiquetzal* who will nurse and suckle it in the land of water with flowers, *Xochiatlalpan*."

Fortunato, thoughtless and speechless, walked aimlessly on the dark road, on to nowhere into the dark and silent night, but eventually, Fortunato returned to the hut at dawn. Upon finding out that his baby son had died, he broke down and wept.

Fortunato did not depart the hut all day and did not go to work in the fields. When he found his voice, he said to Antonia, "I am sorry; please forgive me for bringing you and our family here; I made a mistake: I love you and my children; we will leave as soon as we can; I will go and talk with Jorge in the morning." Fortunato, exhausted beyond his limit, reclined down into a cot and fell asleep.

In the late evening, the village slept in silence and a large orange full moon lighted its plaza, houses, and surrounding desert. Above the village the sky shone with all the lights of millions of stars in the black void of space. Julieta and Jacinta with sincere faithful prayers accompanied a sorrowful mother who had lost her son, and they consoled her with the certainty that her son lived on with God in heaven. Lorena prayed by herself and Santos dreamed a child's dream.

The baby's funeral and burial

Next day in the late afternoon, Antonia sat alone and disconsolate, her eyes puffy and red; she cried again and held her baby in her arms and kissed his forehead. "Antonia, please let me dress the baby for burial," Julieta implored, "The custom in Mexico requires the burial of the dead within twenty-four hours."

Josefa, Lepo, Marta, Telesforo, and their children, Jacinta and other village men and women gathered outside the hut. Antonia and Julieta dressed the baby boy and placed him in a small wooden box. A procession formed from outside the hut and walked slowly, the women singing, and several men playing musical string instruments, two violins and a guitar; a drummer kept cadence on a drum, and three men with flutes played a haunting sound; along the dirt road, the procession in grief walked to the village burial ground. There had not been enough time to take the baby and bury him in Estacion Vega, a Vega family cemetery in San Blas.

Fortunato carried the small wooden box next to his heart. Antonia walked along his side. Lorena led Santos by the hand, a step or two behind her parents. Samuel and Jose had been informed and they had promptly arrived for the occasion. Eugenio and Sara had made a special trip from El Bacori so that Catalina could be with her parents.

Fortunato had sent word to all his family members, brothers and sisters, but no one else could come because of work commitments. Julieta and Jacinta walked on Antonia's right side. The procession continued along the dirt road slowly in the cadence of the drum and in the mood of the mournful sounds of the flutes. The women sang a sorrowful dirge in tune with the sad musical sounds of the violin and guitars. At the cemetery, Julieta led the funeral entourage in prayers for the dead, "O death, where is your victory? O death, where is your sting? But thanks be to God who has given us the victory through our Lord Jesus Christ." She had read 1Corinthians 15: 55-57 from her black small Christian book of prayers. The small wooden box was placed inside a deep hole in the ground. The mournful circled around the grave and each threw a pinch of dirt into the hole over the small wooden coffin. Then Samuel and Jose covered the hole with shovels of dirt and stamped the dirt firmly. Julieta placed at the head of the grave a wooden cross that she had carried in her hand to the cemetery. She firmly pushed the cross down into the earth and stood it straight up. Samuel placed large rocks around and against the base of the cross to hold it up and keep it secured. Julieta blessed the cross and the grave and turned away; she helped a weeping Antonia turn away and leave. All the mourners had expressed their sympathies to Antonia. After the burial, the village faithful turned away; all walked down the road and returned to their homes and to their daily tasks in the village.

Thirty Two

Family: Going North

With the sunrise, when orange streaks of light filtered through tree leaves and entered the hut by the open window, Fortunato arose and dressed. Antonia sat by the stove in the ramada; she prayed in silence looking out toward the rising sun. "Fortunato," Antonia looked at him directly, "I want you to know that the husband must also carry his Christian cross in matrimony." She stood up and faced Fortunato and said, "We must leave here, and began our journey home, now."

Fortunato, moved toward Antonia and embraced her tenderly, and he said, "Yes, Antonia, I will carry my cross as well, and we will leave here." Both embraced and kissed in love.

Fortunato knew he had learned a valuable lesson: both he and Antonia were one; both made decisions that were best for the family. He left the hut, and he walked slowly up the road to the huizache tree by the corner of El Potrero near the village. He stood there a moment in silence, in prayer; then he prayed out loud: "I need to have a heart felt cry, over all that I've not cried about. There is turmoil in my soul,

The Worm in my Tomato

and my mind fails to understand. What has happened all along? My life is not easy to comprehend. I surrender, Lord, my life to you. Guide me in all things until I die." He then walked to the river and went to his usual secluded area and prepared for a bath. Afterwards, Fortunato walked to his sister's big house to speak with her. He saw Chapo in the yard as he prepared to mount his horse and ride to the fields. Fortunato asked Chapo to go and fetch Jorge from his ranch down the road, and he entered the house.

"Sit down Fortunato," Tila motioned to him a chair at the table, "Luisa will serve us breakfast; how have you been?" asked Tila.

"You know that during the years we have been here at Mezquitalito, my wife has suffered much, and last night we lost our baby boy, who lived only nine days."

"I know and I am sorry all this has happened to you and your family, Fortunato, please accept my sincere sorrow for the baby's death, for Antonia's suffering, and for your pain, Fortunato." Tila hugged him.

"I can only imagine that the baby died because the village *partera* had no sterile instruments. Possibly the cutting instruments, like maybe scissors or the cloths used became infected. The baby died from an infected navel in the abdomen." Fortunato wiped his face with his handkerchief, "My baby had cried much in pain and died. My baby son, after Julieta baptized him, we buried him in the Indian village cemetery; I will inform Jorge about it."

"I am so sorry, Fortunato," Tila offered her sympathy, again. "You intend to measure out a space for your family burial plot, Fortunato, at the village graveyard?" asked Tila.

"No, sister, I am taking my family away; I don't know where; I will ask Jorge for help in this, but I can not stay here any longer and I don't intend my family to continue to live here."

Within a short time, Jorge rode up on his black stallion horse, and he tied his horse to the mezquite tree; he came into Tila's kitchen. "Good morning Tila and Fortunato, it will be another hot day, today, whew," Jorge sat down at the table.

Luisa served breakfast and coffee to all at the table. "Fortunato has something to talk to you about, Jorge," Tila said.

Fortunato, Tila, and Jorge ate breakfast and drank their coffee while Fortunato informed Jorge about the loss of his baby boy and about his intentions to leave right away and he asked Jorge for some ideas of where to go.

"Brother, you are so fortunate, that at times I think you must be God's favorite," Jorge served himself a second helping of fried potatoes. Luisa refilled the cups of hot coffee. From outside the birds chirped, and their songs emerged into the kitchen, mixed with the sunlight. "Fortunately for me, too, through political friends in San Blas and El Fuerte, I have obtained the position of Mayor of El Fuerte," Jorge sipped his coffee. "You know that the plague of locusts, a year ago, bankrupted me, remember?" Jorge said.

Tila looked at Fortunato, "Me, too, Fortunato, that is why I could not help you any more with seed or finances to pay for your irrigation water from the river canal on that one large field of mine, and not even help you with Chinese labor," Tila said.

"Yes, I know, sister, I learned that later from speaking with my son Samuel, and I am sorry for both of you suffering your losses, much greater than mine, I am certain," answered Fortunato.

"Well, like I was saying, Fortunato, you are a blessed man, for one of my political friends in San Blas is at this very moment holding the position of town tax collector for an appointee named by me, to pay me for past political favors, you know, and neither Eugenio nor Antonio care for the post. Eugenio has made arrangements to move to Los Mochis, before the time imposed by the federal government to vacate his land, where he has acquired a post to work there for the state government, and Antonio is not ready to move away from the valley, just yet," said Jorge.

"I will move tomorrow," said Fortunato, "I like San Blas," Fortunato reached for another tortilla and served himself another helping of chorizo with eggs, "The town has a railroad depot with a railroad that heads north to the state of Sonora and south to Culiacan, and from the state capital north again to many other northern cities, even to Nogales, Sonora and the United States border," Fortunato said.

"How well, I know brother, and the San Blas depot has rail spurs to our sister Lupita's and her Russian husband Mr. Frei's citrus orchards; the train provides rail transportation for them to distribute their fruit

The Worm in my Tomato

to the railroad depot and market to the south and north from San Blas," Jorge said.

The sun light began to heat up the kitchen space. The birds took wing from the outside tree. Luisa cleared the dishes from the table. "If you leave tomorrow, Fortunato, who will take care of Lorena's and Catalina's calves, here at the ranch?" asked Tila.

"I have a confession to make, Tila: two nights ago, I felt I could recover some losses, and it looked like I held a winning hand of cards at poker, but it turned out wrong for me and I lost my girls' calves to that rancher Vasquez," Fortunato said, and he felt displeased with himself.

"That is sad, Fortunato, at your age, your eyesight is not the best, and that rancher Vasquez is a crook, I hear, and he probably cheated you at cards," Tila said, her face flushed red in anger.

Jorge stood up and scraped his chair back in under the table. "Brother, perhaps it is best you move to San Blas; I will help you move and have my friend in town find a house for you," Jorge said.

"Yes, I think moving away is best for you, Fortunato," Tila stood up, "As you know, you ran away north when you were nineteen years of age; in so doing you escaped the agricultural and ranching way of life and thus never really learned its demands and skills; it is too bad." Tila drank from her cup of coffee and then said, "Now you returned thirty-eight years later and expected to earn a living from a way of life you had escaped from," Tila said, and added, "It just can't be done." She looked at Fortunato, "I will have Chapo help you with a wagon to move your family across the river, but sooner than that, I will have Chapo instruct my ranch vaqueros to protect the girls' calves from being taken away. The calves are part of my herds, and no cheating gambler can ever take them away from me unless they pay for them full price," Tila said forcefully.

Both Fortunato and Jorge looked at Tila with admiration in their eyes, "As you can see Fortunato, our sister Tila is the only one who inherited our father Eudoro's strength of character to succeed in ranching; he is the one who acquired all our lands and built the Big House, and now Tila is the one to carry on our inheritance," Jorge said. " I myself am leaving to seek a politician's way of life in El Fuerte, my brother Fortunato, and I have been here all my life, so don't feel bad that you could not succeed at ranching, let us blame the swarms of locusts," Jorge said.

⁕

Back at the hut, Fortunato told Antonia about how Jorge had offered him a job. Fortunato was happy and he walked about the hut in and then outside the ramada and back again and paced about like if the weight of a mountain had been taken away from his back. Fortunato even walked outdoors in the heat of the day to inform Telesforo who sat in the shade of his mezquite tree in his front yard. Telesforo intently studied the ants working and scurrying back and forth with loads on their backs.

Fortunato said, "I have been appointed Tax Collector of the town of San Blas."

Telesforo smiled at Fortunato and said, "With all that work every day for years, all that the ants have is tunnels underground they feel obligated to fill up, only with what they need, but I still can't figure out why, no matter how much and how long I observe them at work, how much and how long I reflect on their doings, my knowledge about them does not produce an understanding or an insight as to why." He looked up at Fortunato. "They are just like human beings, these ants, don't you think, Mr. Fortunato?"

"Why, I guess so, never thought much about it," Fortunato answered.

"Well, if you reflect on these ants and for that matter other creatures, Mr. Fortunato, you will observe how each species of God's created creatures all have an inherent desire to fill up their houses, their caves, their dens, their tree trunk holes, whatever, with whatever they consider they must have to live, but not beyond their needs to survive, except humans, I think." Telesforo added, "What did you say, Mr. Fortunato, are you leaving for San Blas?"

Fortunato, Antonia, and Lorena quickly got their things together and packed them in cardboard boxes and gunny sacks that Samuel had brought over to the hut. Catalina had brought all her belongings in one large sack with her from El Bacori. Now, there was neither heavy furniture from America nor many kitchen utensils to worry about or pack to haul in Chapo's wagon.

"We are leaving with almost nothing but only with our clothing we wear and a few more to change, while we wash what we have used," said Fortunato. He added, "In this way, we may resemble the ants."

"What did you say, father?" Lorena skipped about the hut, darting in and out through the ramada and doing nothing but being deliriously happy, dancing and hopping now in the hut and now outside in front of the hut. "Have you been talking with Telesforo?" Lorena asked her father.

"Is everyone ready?" asked Antonia.

"I am ready to go with you, mother," Jose said. Upon being informed about his family leaving the area, he had hurried to the ranch where he worked, informed his employer and returned, all packed with his clothes. Jose stood by, yet not believing this was happening; he rejoiced in being reunited with his family. Catalina stood beside Jose holding on to his arm. She was packed and ready to go. Santos sensed the importance of the occasion and restlessly ran and jumped around like a young pup. Lorena only smiled at Santos, who when he hopped about like a frog, she was certain that he had eaten too many frog legs.

Tila sent Chapo with a wagon pulled by two mules to take Fortunato and his family to San Blas. The family quickly loaded their things on the wagon. Lorena stood first in line to climb up in the wagon, "I don't have to take my shoes off this time because I carry them in the box wrapped in a towel in my gunny sack," she said. Lorena wore her old rough leather sandals. She had several dresses in her gunny sack as well.

Antonia was sad that Samuel was not present to join the family on their trip north to San Blas. Samuel wanted to stay and complete his land surveying work, and he also wanted to stay near his sweetheart, Julia. Samuel indicated, however, that he would later visit Antonia in San Blas.

Julieta, Jacinta, Tila, Luisa, Eligia, Carmen, the Twelve Months, and village friends were present to say good-bye and wish the Vega family God's blessings and a safe trip. Antonia and Lorena especially thanked and hugged the village families that had come to say goodbye and wish them well; some were crying. They stood so straight with tearful eyes. Telesforo said, "Lorena, little daughter, I will always remember the sweet empanada you gave me. You helped me fulfill my life's dream, thank you. God bless you." Marta and all her girl Seven

Months cried and laughed at the same time. Lepo and Josefa, Carmen and Eligia, smiled and cried and waved goodbye. Eligia carried in her arms her first child, a river god baby. Lorena smiled and both she and Eligia hugged and kissed each other. Lorena had learned so much from Eligia in their relationship as workers for Aunt Tila.

The family helped each other aboard the wagon. Chapo smacked the rumps of the horses and they were off. The hot wind warmed their faces. Lorena's hair was flying back. Santos, Antonia, Catalina, and Jose were all in the wagon holding on for fear of falling out. After some distance along the dirt and bumpy road, the wagon crossed the El Fuerte River, at a safe point from west to east, and then bumped its way east along the dusty road to the small town of San Blass.

San Blas 1936

When Fortunato's family arrived in San Blas, they went to a house Jorge's friend had acquired for Fortunato to rent. The family unpacked, and Antonia erected an altar in one corner of the living room. She knelt down and gave thanks to God. The family moved in, and they realized with awe it was the first time they would live together in four years. It was a large house. It had a *Zaguan*, an entry from the sidewalk in front of the house.

Antonia and her girls went outside the house to look at the town. The town was not as large as Miami, Arizona, but it was a town, unlike the Mezquitalito village

In 1937, Jose age twenty and Lorena age fourteen celebrate an occasion in San Blas, Mexico.

The Worm in my Tomato

in the desert. They saw people walking in the streets and thought it strange. They saw cars driving down the streets and Lorena and Catalina stared at them. Lorena wanted to know what made the cars move, since she had not seen a gasoline station in town as yet. She wished Telesforo was here in San Blas to observe and explain. *This* will be our home, San Blass, Lorena thought.

Lorena could not help but realize that they had moved closer to the northern border. She decided to begin to plan her new escape, now that Santos was five years old, Catalina was eleven years old. Now it was Catalina's turn to stay home and help her mother, Lorena thought; it was time to plan her escape north to Arizona. Lorena remembered Mary Cota and thought for sure she must be attending Miami High School. She knew that at age fourteen, she would probably be in high school herself, if the Repatriation had not forced her to live in Mexico. But Lorena decided not to run away just yet, but wait for some time to see what events would unfold.

Lorena thought what Telesforo would say about the mystery of time. New life and new beginnings, Lorena remembered his sayings: the future, Lorena, not seen by the naked eye and unknown to the hearts and minds, but destined to materialize out from eternity, from the somewhere. Well here we are, she thought, the events had taken a long time to arrive; the events had originated and taken a long time to now become part of our journey in life, as Telesforo would say, Lorena thought what she had memorized from Telesforo.

Gosh, Lorena had thought and could not help but think again and wonder about how at last they lived in a town. She repeated again to herself: San Blas 1936, Santos is five years old; Lorena is fourteen and Jose is twenty years of age. Her father is sixty-one years old and her mother is forty-one years old. But why, Lorena wondered, did it seem to her that thirty years had gone by?

Lorena for the first few days in San Blas spent time feeling sad and thinking about her friends in El Mezquitalito. She kept thinking back on the goodbyes with the villagers. Lorena had said goodbye to Carmen, Eligia, the Twelve Months, Lepo and Josefa, Telesforo and Marta, Julieta and Jacinta. Lorena felt sad that Gonzalo had not been there, so she could have said goodbye to him. Lorena had made a hurried run over to pay a quick visit and give a hug to Aunt Tila. Lorena offered sincere thanks to Tila for everything. She sincerely appreciated her Aunt Tila's help in agreeing to let her attend the village school with teacher Mr. Luna. In addition, Lorena thanked her Aunt Tila, in her heart, for the fine hunks of cheese she had taken, after sneaking into the cheese room, in the dark of night, for her mother and little brother to have something to eat, during those hungry times in Mezquitalito. Then, to her surprise and great happiness, her Aunt Tila came to the village to wish them goodbye.

When Lorena rode in the wagon, she carried her shoes in a box in a gunny sack. Lorena had protected her new shoes for four years. She only regretted that her feet had grown beyond squeezing them into her shoes. Antonia and her family moved what little they had to San Blas.

That year 1936, Santos began school in Kindergarten. He liked going to school. He had a teacher that was very pleasant and motherly to her students. He would ask for her permission to go to a vendor outside the school to buy a penny *peruli*, a red hard candy made from strawberry flavored syrup, shaped like an upside-down cone wrapped around a toothpick.

Fortunato bought Santos a tricycle, which he rode everyday in a reckless and boisterous way on the sidewalk in front of the house.

Antonia wasted no time and soon like a mother hen fixed her house up into a comfortable nest. Lorena herself was going to school. A different school now, a real grade school, she thought. Catalina attended a lower grade in the same school. The girls were learning at last. But sadly, Lorena realized that there would never be a Miss Yoakum again. Teachers at Lorena's school worked very hard. Fortunato told Antonia and Lorena that the teachers were underpaid but that they tried very hard to teach the students. One day, a school teacher came to Antonia's house and sat down and talked with her about the school. Santos was playing about. At that time, the style skirt that the teacher wore had a split on one side below the knee. Santos said "Teacher when you get home, you want to sew this up cause it's torn there." Antonia said, "Oh forgive him, he's just a curious child." The teacher just smiled. Santos was so precocious, noticing everything. He liked to work with mud in the back yard and make mud houses. Small adobe

The Worm in my Tomato

houses. He said he would rent them out. One day he put his hand into one of the mud houses, and a scorpion inside the house stung him on the finger. He let out a loud cry. Antonia placed iodine ink on the sting. Eventually the swelling decreased and Santos got well. Antonia said, "You see, you had a renter there that did not pay his rent and did not want to be evicted." Santos laughed out loud, and he knew that he had learned a lesson: to be careful with scorpions.

Even here in San Blas, – although not as much as in the village Mezquitalito, where Antonia and her family had been invaded by all kinds of insects, all kinds of arachnids, poisonous snakes and worse of all, locusts, – Antonia had seen a few scorpions.

Here in San Blas, for the first time in Mexico, Antonia and her family had their own well, and did not have to bargain with Lepo for water. They had their own backyard surrounded by walls, enclosed, and it was theirs. The family enjoyed their own garden with trees, plants, and the well which produced fresh water. Lorena lost no time in connecting her *Ixtle* rope, which she had acquired from Lepo, to a tin bucket, and she passed the rope through the round pulley and drew up fresh sparkling water. Lorena showed Catalina how to draw water from the well. "I only wish I had a *palanca* so I could show you how to carry water using two buckets," Lorena said, "And if we had a cow like One Eye, I would show you how to milk like Eligia taught me. You would love to drink the warm, foamy sweet milk, fresh from the cow."

Some of the people in San Blas had their wells, and others had running piped water. Antonia and Fortunato had both a well and piped running water. Antonia had running water in the kitchen and well water the backyard. Their house's bedrooms faced inward toward the inner walled patio. The patio had a cistern to collect rain water for use for watering the garden flowers. All rooms were blocked off from the street. The family was happy living here in San Blas. Jose went out to search for a job in a store or for work at the train depot.

The first thing Antonia did in San Blas: she searched in town for a Catholic Church. To her great surprise and delight, she found a small whitewashed church dedicated to Our Lady of Guadalupe. Antonia, Lorena, and Catalina went in and were amazed that there were pews, Saints icons on the walls, and at the front of a huge marble altar was hung a crucifix holding up a crucified Jesus Christ nailed to the cross. To the sides of the altar were large icons of the Virgin Mary of Guadalupe on the right side and a large icon of Saint Joseph on the left side. The church was cool and pleasant. Antonia and her two girls knelt in a pew and gave thanks to God. "We suffered in purgatory for four years and finally we have arrived in heaven." Antonia said and she prayed to God an Our Father, out loud.

A priest presently came out from a side door to the left of the altar and introduced himself, "I am father Moises; may I help you with information about our Sunday services?"

"We are new in town and we were looking for an Apostolic Roman Catholic Church," Lorena blurted out. Antonia felt somewhat embarrassed at Lorena's brashness, but she realized that is the way Lorena was and she probably would never change.

Father Moises smiled, "This is the church you are looking for; it is apostolic, founded by the apostles of Jesus Christ, son of God, and it is Roman because its governance of the Church is in Rome, and it is Catholic because it is universal," he said to Lorena who listened attentively to the priest. Then the priest looked at Antonia and explained, "Nogales Catholic diocese Bishop Juan Navarette, in 1929, arranged for the resumption of religious services in northern Mexico cathedrals; Catholic churches were again opened." The priest turned to replace used votive lamps with new ones and asked Antonia, "Where did you come from, your accents are different from how people speak in this town?"

"We came from the United States four years ago and lived until this week in El Aliso in the Mezquital valley in El Mezquitalito," Antonia answered.

"Oh, that is a very anti-Catholic area except for a few stalwart faithful and the native Mayo," the priest said and then he asked, "Did you by any chance know Julieta Santander?"

"Yes, she and I were very good friends, and we would hold prayer services in her house, and my daughter Lorena helped her with the catechism classes," Antonia responded.

"Do you remember the priest that went to celebrate Mass and provide for the sacraments of marriage and confession?" the priest asked.

"Only once in the four years we were there, did a priest go to

The Worm in my Tomato

celebrate the holy Mass." Antonia answered.

"I was scheduled to go serve in that area and stop at Julieta's as well, but I became seriously ill at the time and Father Simon substituted," Father Moises looked pensive and somewhat sad, "Father Simon always disguised himself as an old blind tramp riding a donkey; not me, I always used the circus clown routine and performed a magic show for the children," he laughed.

Upon hearing this last statement from the priest Lorena's eyes opened wide, so that is what happened, the old blind man I led to Julieta's house was the priest all the same," she thought.

"Where is Father Simon now, Father," asked Antonia.

"In heaven with God, he was shot by anticlericals or armed troops, who knows, not far from el Mezquitalito," The priest turned aside and excused himself, "I have an appointment about this time." He walked away.

Antonia and the girls visited the main business part of town, and they window shopped and purchased food items from a small store located on a corner near their home. Antonia could not get the thought out of her mind about the blind priest, no, rather, the old man who pretended to be blind and who was the priest, who was shot dead, executed, in cold blood, by federal troops, because he was a priest. It did not make sense; she determined to pray a rosary for the old blind man, no, the priest, that very night, she thought.

Antonia knew that San Blas was only a temporary home and that soon they would have to leave; she had not forgotten that she and Fortunato had agreed to return to Miami after five years in Mexico. How this would happen, she did not know, but she hoped for the best. She was beginning to feel impatient and determined to talk with Fortunato. She felt that they should leave soon and moreover not stay here another year.

Thirty Three

Antonia
Inevitable changes: the border, alone, forgotten, and hungry

The Circus

Fortunato regularly worked at the town municipal office, but some times he worked at home. He kept his tax collection records in his home desk; during the day he went about town, collecting taxes from various types of businesses.

One time there was a circus that came to town. The circus administrator gave a large number of circus tickets to Fortunato for his family: "For your children," the circus director had said.

Fortunato gave a ticket each to Jose, Lorena, Catalina, and several of the circus tickets to Santos. Santos invited several of his friends, little boys he had met in school and some who lived near his neighborhood. The boys, a very diverse group of kids with none a look-a-like, all went together to the circus. Santos boldly went and told the door keeper and ticket collector: "These are my little brothers and we want to go in and see the circus." The ticket collector merely smiled, he knew Santos was the son of Fortunato, the municipal tax collector. He said, "How do I know these tickets are actually yours?"

"Because I have them," responded Santos.

The ticket agent humored them, "Yes, these are your tickets, you can go." He let Santos and his *brothers* enter to see the circus; they went in and saw the big animal acts. On the other hand, the gate keeper enjoyed their childish ruse, probably made in all sincerity. Later he told Fortunato about the incident with Santos and his many brothers. They both had a good laugh about the episode.

Too Good to Last

Antonia and her family had lived content for several months in San Blas. One day there was a knock at the door of the *Zaguan*. Antonia opened the large heavy wooden door. A gust of wind rushed in and the shadows of an overcast sky darkened the entry room. A young man selling *tamales* stood outside on the sidewalk. Antonia had ironed clothes all morning and had not yet begun to prepare supper. She thought that it would be good to buy an already made lunch, she thought. She bought tamales. Fortunato liked to eat tamales, but at the moment was busy working at his desk. Antonia asked him, "Nato, are you ready to eat, now?"

"I have to complete this tax report for tomorrow morning, bring me three tamales and a cup of black coffee to my desk, please," Fortunato answered.

Antonia took to him the hot tamales and a cup of black coffee. A short time after he ate the tamales at his desk, Fortunato had terrible indigestion. "Antonia," Fortunato said, "I feel terrible."

Antonia feared that he may have had a stroke. She didn't know if it was indigestion, a stroke, or a heart attack. Antonia asked Lorena to run across the street to a doctor's office and tell him to come quickly and help Fortunato. Lorena ran across the street; an alley dog chased her, barking and nipping at her heals. She begged the doctor to come see her father.

The doctor came in and promptly injected Fortunato with morphine, to ease his pain. Fortunato afterward following the injection could not speak. He was speechless with anxiety in his face, and his eyes rolling backward. Lorena thought for certain that her father was dying. She sat on the side of the bed and she held his head in her arms. Antonia, pale and with sweaty palms, froze in shock, and not knowing what to do, wrung her hands and sat on a chair to wait. Fortunato opened his eyes momentarily and just looked at Antonia and Lorena, but he was unable to speak; he gave a last twist of his body and he died in Lorena's arms. She gently closed his eyes shut.

Antonia, distraught and angered, kept asking "Why did the doctor give a morphine injection to Fortunato?" She quickly put on her street dress and ran out the door, yelling back, "I am going after the priest, Father Moises," she ran to the nearby church.

In a few minutes, Father Moises, hurried back with Antonia to her house, and he in a gentle manner anointed Fortunato; the priest then said the prayers for the dead.

Antonia said nothing, and in a mechanical way, she walked out across the street to the small corner grocery store and asked *Don* Pedro the shop owner, who was a friend of Jorge, and had previously befriended Fortunato, to please send someone to inform Jorge, who now lived in El Fuerte, not far from San Blas. *Don* Pedro kept saying, "Oh, I am so sorry *Señora* Vega, I am so sorry," then he called out to one of his workers, "Juan, hurry, ride up to El Fuerte and tell Jorge that his brother Fortunato has died; to come right away to his house." Then he looked at Antonia, "I am so sorry, Señora Vega," he said.

Sometime later in mid-afternoon, Jorge arrived, saw that Fortunato was dead, and he shook his head in disbelief. Jorge and the doctor gave orders to Antonia and her children who stood about. The doctor shouted *"Para afuera, para afuera,* Get out, get out, out of the room," where Fortunato had died.

Jorge said, "We have to bury him within twenty-four hours, in Mexico that is the law," He looked at Antonia, "Get him dressed with the suit that you want him to wear. I will be back with a wagon," Jorge strode out on his urgent errand.

Antonia slowly, as if in great pain, selected his work suit, a blue suit that he normally wore when he went to his downtown office, and she dressed him up. A month later, Antonia would remember that in that particular suit of Fortunato had been, in his pocket, one hundred pesos that she had forgotten about, and Fortunato took that money with him.

Lorena, her eyes full of tears, sat at her father's desk and wrote on a piece of paper: "My father died on June 2, 1937. He had barely succeeded in gathering us together when he died." She placed her forehead on her forearms and cried.

Later in the afternoon, Jorge returned with a wagon pulled by two mules, and with him were two men to help him place Fortunato in a wooden coffin. Jorge and his helpers lifted Fortunato inside the coffin. The workers nailed the coffin shut, and they carried it out of the house and lifted it into the wagon. The workmen climbed on the front buckboard, snapped the reins of the mules, "Heeya," the driver said, the mules trotted away. Jorge followed behind the wagon on his black horse.

Jorge took his brother's dead body to the Estacion Vega cemetery, a cemetery for the Vegas there in the town of San Blas. There had been no wake, rosary or public prayers. "Oh, if only Julieta had been here to say prayers over Fortunato," Antonia said over and over again to herself.

"But, mama, Father Moises said the prayers, here at home," Lorena gently reminded her mother.

Jorge buried Fortunato late in the afternoon. Fortunato's life had come to an end. The sun set down behind the distant mountains, soon darkness of night would claim the town of San Blas, and a new day would begin with the dawn, but for Fortunato, his spiritual life already had a new beginning.

Decisions to Leave Mexico

Antonia as a mother had courageously kept her family together from the very beginning and through every threatening experience. She immediately decided to return her family to the United States where all of them had been born. The family once again would set out to cross borders.

Lorena said to her mother, "Mother we are all alone now, what do we do?"

Antonia dabbed the tears from her eyes and responded, "We must leave." Antonia knew in her heart that she had buried her cross. "I have no reason to stay in Mexico, now, we must leave," she said with a firm voice.

"Yes, mama, we must leave," Lorena said, choking back her tears, "We must go north to Arizona." Then all of a sudden, not intentionally planned, Lorena hopped, skipped, and jumped about the house unable to contain her joy and she cried and laughed at the same time.

Antonia gathered Catalina, Jose, Lorena, and Santos at her side and said to them, "Our journey to Sinaloa has ended; we have come to a new crossroads."

"Now, it is time for us to hurry on our way home!" Lorena exclaimed.

The family began without delay to prepare for their journey home. Antonia sent a message to Samuel in Culiacán, where his work had now taken him, to come to San Blas, and informed him that they planned to leave Mexico. She wrote: "Please return home with us, and please prepare a letter for the United States Consulate to facilitate our return home."

The priest, Father Moises, came to the house to wish them a good and safe trip. He blessed them all together and prayed: "May God accompany all of you on your journey home to your country."

"Thank you, Father Moises," Antonia said.

"I hope you always remember to pray to our own Mexican mother of God, Our Lady of Guadalupe," responded the priest as he made his way out of the house.

Samuel was undecided whether to return to Arizona or stay with his fiancée Julia in Mexico. That same week, after he received the note from his mother, Samuel came to visit her; he said, "Mother, I had no idea father was going to die so unexpectedly." Samuel shook his head from side to side as he walked about the kitchen, "I am sorry he died, and I regret that I did not have a chance to visit with him here in San Blas." Samuel sat down at the table to drink a cup of tea. "I had planned to come visit you and the family for your birthday on June 13th, mother; happy birthday."

"Thank you, son," Antonia said, "Fortunato's death happened quickly and it was so unexpected, Samuel, but I am sure he understood, your job is very demanding." Antonia uncovered the bread basket and said, "Do you want sweet bread with your tea?"

"Well, it's not only that I am busy with my work," Samuel served himself more tea and took a sweet bread from the bread basket, "but I had planned to marry Julia by the end of this month, Julia always wanted a June wedding," Samuel explained.

"But, Samuel, you are going back with us to Arizona, aren't you?" Antonia asked as she stirred her cup of tea.

"I don't know what to do, mother, whether to return with the family

The Worm in my Tomato

and later come back to marry Julia, or help her come to Arizona after I am there," Samuel said, and he ate a piece of bread with his tea, "I want to return; I feel that is what I should do, yes, perhaps, but I will compose and type the letter for the Consulate in Culiacan," Samuel smiled. "You should have no problem, what with all of you having birth certificates to prove you were born in the United States and are citizens." Samuel filled his cup with more tea and stood up from the table and paced about the kitchen, pondering his thoughts in his mind while sipping his tea. "The letter will describe a mother with her five children, including myself, if I decide to go, telling of a mother who now returns to Arizona after living five years in Mexico with her husband who died," Samuel said.

He sat down at the table and drank his tea with Antonia. "Mother, do you remember that night in our kitchen in Miami when we were both sitting down drinking our tea, and we really did not want to leave." Samuel looked at his mother and said, "But you felt obligated to carry your cross and accompany father, and I wanted to support you and go with you. Now, I am twenty-three years old; I am in love with Julia and plan to marry her, and I have a job with the office in Culiácan. Jose and Lorena are old enough now; I just don't know what to do." Both mother and son drank their tea and did not yet know their destiny.

Samuel used his typewriter in the land-surveying office and he composed the letter for his mother and sent it by mail to the Consulate. He returned to San Blas with a copy of the letter for Antonia. "Here is a copy of the letter, mother, we will ride

Samuel, far left in this photo, had surveyed the lands in his office and had also typed the emigration letter for Antonia to present to the Consul in Culiacan.

The Worm in my Tomato

the train south to Culiacan first. I will help you there. Then from there you and the family return north past San Blas to Nogales, Sonora. I plan to take the train from Culiacan on the following day after you do, and I will meet with you all in Nogales at the San Carlos Hotel, near the border station," Samuel said.

The letter stated the fact that Antonia and all her five children were United States citizens who had lived in Mexico for the last five years, after Antonia with her children had accompanied her husband to Sinaloa on the Repatriation train in 1932. Her husband died in San Blas, and now the family desired to return home to Miami, Arizona. Neither her husband nor any of her children had served in the military or voted in Mexico.

Antonia had no alternative, and her children each had their own particular birth certificate, which Antonia had kept safe in her tin trunk amid all her saints' statues and *retablos*. Among the papers, she had Lorena's last school report card, signed by Miss Yoakum.

The family left by the last week in June, 1937. They carried one suitcase each and the old tin trunk where Antonia carefully packed her pictures of her family, a picture of Fortunato, and icons of her saints, all securely wrapped.

Antonia sold whatever household goods and furniture she had, and what she could not sell she gave away to neighbors and even people passing by on the road in front of the house.

Lorena packed her five year old shiny new leather shoes inside the shoebox wrapped in a towel and placed inside a gunny sack, which she carefully placed in a bundle in her leather suitcase. "Mama, I really wanted my new shiny leather shoes to be my traveling shoes, but now they don't fit my feet," Lorena said and tears welled in her eyes.

The family walked to the train station in San Blas, each carrying a suitcase. Lorena helped Jose carry the large tin trunk. Jose carried his suitcase in one hand and with the other held up one side of the trunk by its handle, while Lorena lifted the other side of the trunk.

Jose, scowling, whispered to Lorena, "Heck, these saints are sure heavy; mother should've left them in the ranch village for Julieta."

"Oh, no," Lorena answered, "She always prays to the saints for their help in asking God for help, and now even Santos murmurs his

The Worm in my Tomato

prayers to the Saints everyday."

At the train station, the vendors as usual were everywhere, hawking their food-stuffs. "*Empanadas, Empanadas calientitas,*" and Lorena on seeing the hot turnovers, remembered Telesforo; she smiled as she thought about how he had not even given a crumb to his ant buddies.

With tickets Antonia bought, one for each one of her children, they boarded the train. Only one of Jose's friends was there to wish them good-bye. There were no crowds of repatriated people heading back to the United States. Lorena remembered there had been crowds of repatriated families when they had left Miami five years before. The whole morning was balmy, a slow breeze, a few soft white clouds: not a depressive day, but a day made joyous by Antonia and her children, who were all smiles.

⌒⟶

Culiacan, Sinaloa

Culiacan was the capital of Sinaloa. Antonia had received a message from Samuel telling her that he would meet them at the train station and take the family in a wagon to the United States Consulate's Office. At the station Samuel met Antonia and his brothers Jose and Santos and sisters Lorena and Catalina. They climbed aboard a spacious wooden wagon pulled by two mules. This time, Lorena did not worry about her new shoes getting scuffed. But, she held tightly to her suitcase. Her glossy black leather shoes had sentimental value for Lorena and she knew that she would always keep them as the shoes she wore when she first crossed the border on the Repatriation train into Mexico. "My black shiny leather shoes I will always keep, for always and always, as a memento," she said to her mother.

Antonia went to see the Consul to arrange the passage to the United States as American citizens. The secretary in service reviewed all her family papers such as vital records showing when and where each one of the family members was born. Antonia had even kept her children's school records. Lorena saw her fourth grade report card and proudly read off Miss Yoakum's name, where her teacher had signed. The secretary, a lean pale man with soft blue eyes smiled. He read Samuel's letter about the family returning to Arizona. He studied the Repatriation's records showing of the family's immigration to Mexico five years previous. "All of you retained your United States citizenship because you never applied or received Mexican citizenship and because the boys never served in military duty in Mexico," he smiled again, "All your papers are in order. Now I will type up your new papers that will show Mrs. Vega, widow of Fortunato Vega and now one single adult mother with five children: Samuel, Jose, Lorena, Catalina, and Santos; these papers, officially sealed, will allow you to cross the border and return home to the United States," he stamped the papers. Antonia paid the fees. "You should have no problem at the border in Nogales, Mrs. Vega," the Consul said, his pale blue eyes squinting as he smiled broadly.

Antonia rejoiced that the government requirements were over, and she was happy that she had presented the letter that Samuel had typed. "Oh, I am so happy Samuel that you are returning home with us; thanks to God." Antonia told Samuel. The Consul Secretary stamped the papers. Yes, Antonia was ready to go. The family was ready to go, and the mules seemed happy to pull the wagon with the family to the train depot.

Lorena especially walked fast to climb aboard the waiting train. Again, as in Miami, she was first to climb aboard the train, but this time with a song in her heart.

At the Culiacan train station, Antonia had purchased tortillas with beans from a street vendor and quieted hers and her children's famished stomachs; empty stomachs that had been growling in protest in the Consul's office. Probably that was why the Consul Secretary had been smiling, Lorena thought.

From Culiacan, Antonia led her family in a new journey as they traveled to Nogales, Sonora a city situated across the border from Nogales, Arizona.

Samuel had informed Antonia that he had arranged to meet Julia, the young girl he planned to marry, in Culiacan for dinner, and that he would catch a night train and meet Antonia and the family next day at the San Carlos Hotel in Nogales. He asked Antonia to stay at the San Carlos hotel nearby the border station.

The Border

The day after Antonia had arrived with her family in Nogales, a telegram from Samuel was delivered to Antonia. The telegram notified her that he could not leave Mexico after all. 'I and Julia are in love and we agreed to get married before the end of June,' Samuel wrote. He informed Antonia that he would live with Julia in her father Isabel's home back in Aliso, until he and Julia could get their own home. Samuel said that he still had work to do with the federal government land company, and that he could not leave, not just yet, maybe in the future, and he said goodbye. Antonia wept when she read the telegram; she wept because her son Samuel chose not to return home with them. Jose felt that the family was almost home, and he tried to cheer his mother.

Antonia and her family were not allowed to return home.

Although Nogales, Sonora was located just across the border from Nogales, Arizona, the distance in time and space was a world apart. The following day, Antonia, Jose, Lorena, Catalina, and Santos arose early and went to see the United States border agency to arrange to cross the border into the United States. Once with the proper papers, Antonia planned to return to the hotel for the suitcases and large tin trunk, where the saints were packed. The American agent, a short, plump man with thinning light brown hair and a penciled-in mustache, peered at Antonia from behind horn-rimmed glasses; finally he reviewed Antonia's papers, after the family had waited in the waiting room for what seemed hours. The man looked sternly at all of them. "Well," he said, "I see here four children and you madam, are you the mother?"

"Yes, of course," Antonia replied.

"We have many kinds of frauds here every day, fraudulent papers, or if the papers are not false, the papers have been stolen and do not belong to the person claiming to be the rightful owner."

"These papers are legitimate and signed by the United States

Consulate secretary in Culiacan," Antonia emphatically pointed to her documents.

"Yes, madam, I see that, I can read, but these papers say five children and I count four, where is the other person?"

"Oh, he changed his mind at the last moment, he is my son Samuel, and he typed the letter for me," Antonia quickly answered.

"I am sorry, you may not be the lawful owner of these papers, so I am not granting you permission to cross the border to immigrate into the United States," he handed the papers to Antonia. "These papers are worthless to you unless you prove to me that you are the right person that these papers belong to," he looked intently at Antonia.

"But these papers are mine; these are my children listed on the papers," Antonia responded with a hoarse voice, dry and split.

"Please leave. These papers may not belong to this family or to you; you need to prove you are the family these papers belong to, you don't have the five children, and please don't come back unless you bring some one to vouch for you, someone from the United States, that can vouch for you and prove you are who you say you are," he got up and opened his office door to show Antonia and her children out the door.

"Is there someone else we can see…," Antonia asked.

"No, please leave, and furthermore, don't come back unless you bring a witness from the United States with proof you are who you say you are," the official declared.

Antonia was devastated. She and her children felt low to the ground, and they crawled out from that office, stunned and they felt as though like bugs were brushed away.

They all thought of how they were almost home. They could not understand. They had come to see the official, he had questioned their honesty, "Why, we are not evil people or liars," Antonia said out loud to Jose. The official had refused Antonia to see other American agents, but Antonia and Lorena, however, walked over and asked another American agent to make sure the first official in the office had not made a mistake.

"Well, let's see here, now, you all are American citizens, according to these papers; you were born and raised in the United States, yes, mam, according to these papers, but the question is, now, you hear me, are these papers yours, see?" The agent said, "Your family can not come

The Worm in my Tomato

across legally until the main border office gives you all permission to legally immigrate into the country," the agent said. His badge glinted in the sunlight and sparkled from the sun light as he moved about, kept busy talking with other persons attempting to cross; he stopped others to see their border cards. He looked at Antonia and at Jose, being he was the oldest and a young man, "You have been living in Mexico for five years," he glanced about the border entrance, "You, Mrs. Vega, although you are an American citizen, you married a Mexican citizen, and crossed over and lived in Mexico for five years," he read her papers again, "Your children are citizens," he grabbed his hat threatened by a gust of wind, "But it says here that you have been rejected until you prove these are really your papers, you have to wait until someone comes from the United States and proves that you are the person who is the rightful owner of these papers and then our border office will let you legally cross; then we will let you through into our country, once the main border office agent stamps their seal of approval on your papers," the agent handed back the papers to Antonia, and he turned his attention to a truck carrying a load of tomatoes, the driver was honking for permission to cross. Lorena stared at the tomatoes, and she remembered the worm in her tomato.

Antonia and her children slowly returned to their hotel and Antonia extended the rent of their room. Jose was so disappointed that he withdrew to himself and would not talk to anyone. The family was near the border but prevented to cross over as a family. Antonia had little money left from the household items she had sold in San Blas. Regretfully, she now remembered Fortunato's blue suit in which he was buried and that had a hundred pesos in the inside pocket, that he had intended to give to her for groceries. What can I do? Antonia asked herself; she decided she would look for employment cleaning houses, washing dirty clothes, ironing, anything.

After some efforts in job hunting, Antonia acquired work to clean rooms in the hotel where they were staying: her earnings partially paid for the rent; she used what little money she had left over for their daily meals. Antonia and her children ate very little, sometimes one meal a day. Antonia immediately, after having left the border agency office, the first day, wrote a letter to her brother Tomas in Miami, and she informed him of her situation and urged him to come vouch for her with some documentation and his testimony. She begged him to 'hurry and to come for her family.'

She wrote a letter to Samuel and asked him to come to Nogales and prove she was the right owner of the papers. She realized five years had gone by and they had no pictures of themselves. 'Please, Samuel, hurry, we were refused passage across the border because I did not have you with me to show I have five children and that we are the lawful family,' she implored.

Her brother Tomas did not respond; Antonia hoped that he and Nellie were sober; Antonia had always prayed for her brother and Nellie to overcome their alcohol problem. Samuel did not respond, but Antonia supposed that he and Julia may have left for who knows where on their honeymoon.

Time for Antonia and her children seemed like a snail inching its way across a vast sandy beach. Antonia's money dwindled; the family was hungrier day by day. Jose went out to search for a job but could not find work; Jose thought to himself, what's the use; he went into a solitary depression. The family became desperate to get across.

Hungry, alone, and forgotten in Nogales

Lorena, seeing that Jose could not get a job decided to take matters into her own hands. Unknown to Antonia, while she cleaned the hotel rooms, Lorena sneaked out into the streets to beg; she stood in the plaza by the church and imitated the other beggars. Lorena stood beside the sidewalk, totally submissive, with her hand out. The beggars would say, "For the love of God, something to eat please."

Lorena would copy their cries for help and say, "For the love of God, please a few coins to purchase food for my little brother Santos to eat." Sometimes, total strangers would give Lorena a penny, sometimes a nickel, and rarely a quarter. After some time Lorena would come home and give her mother the few coins for her to buy something to eat.

"But where did you get this money?" Antonia questioned, alarmed and worried.

"I went out into the plaza area in front of the church and stood, not far from other beggars, and also begged for a few coins to buy my little brother food," Lorena explained.

Antonia, with her eyes full of tears, said: "Lorena, that is dangerous, and begging we never do, we work, but no, we don't beg, promise me you won't do it again," Antonia wiped her eyes with her handkerchief.

Street light from outside streamed into their hotel room through the window's open curtains. It was at this time that Lorena remembered Telesforo's ultimate wish in life being to have one empanada all for him, alone. Now Lorena began to wish for a whole tortilla burrito of beef and beans all for herself; she wished for a plate of *menudo* all for herself. But each day the family shared what little they had by dividing it into small pieces or half-cups, and all of them feared that the next day they would have nothing to share with one another except their pain of hunger. Some days Antonia would not eat so that Santos would get a larger share of what little food the family had for that day.

"Promise me, Lorena, not to beg," Antonia repeated to Lorena.

"Mama, you pray to St. Francis of Assisi, don't you?" Lorena asked.

"Well, yes..." Antonia answered.

"He begged, mother, he begged, mother, and he was a saint," Lorena said.

"He is a saint, yes, but you, but we, but...Lorena, promise me you will be careful," Antonia did not know what else to say. The silence in the hotel room was punctuated now and then by the sound of cars outside in the street braking or blowing their horns.

Lorena promised, and they agreed that she would be a careful beggar. Antonia worked each day cleaning the hotel rooms, but early each morning she would leave the hotel room and hurry across the street to pray in the church. Lorena followed her one morning, concerned about her mother, watching after her, when Lorena saw Antonia almost run over by a car because she failed to look left or right when running across the street to the church. Lorena was so distraught that she made up her mind to join her mother at prayer.

Catholic churches in Mexico had been closed with locked doors for three years during the *Cristero* war, but in 1937 the doors of the church in Nogales, Sonora were open. In the church Antonia blessed herself and knelt in a pew, the church was quiet and dark except for the votive candles that dimly burned in the candle holder near a wall on the side of the main altar. Their pale flickering light reminded Lorena of the *cachimbas* in her Aunt Tila's large house. Antonia prayed to God for help.

Lorena wondered why God would let her suffer here in a strange city so close to Arizona but seemingly without a chance to cross over the border soon enough before her family died of hunger. Lorena would watch her mother pray. Lorena asked herself, why mother was suffering so much this way, with her children almost home and yet so far away. Lorena remembered the ants under Telesforo's mezquite tree and how she had learned about faith, hope, and charity from the hard working ants.

Mother and daughter quietly returned home to the hotel. They shared a renewed faith that somehow God would provide for their needs. Antonia had no home to return to in San Blas. She knew that Fortunato's family, now many impoverished because of the loss of their lands, could not help them. Antonia had no way to get across the border legally; each day she hoped and prayed that her brother Tomas out of charity would come to their rescue.

Six weeks had passed since Antonia wrote her first letter asking her brother Tomas to come help her. She had written three more letters. The family lived in a limbo of despair. Antonia had almost lost hope; she could not understand why her brother Tomas had not responded to her three letters she had mailed to him, one every two weeks, and why he did not come to verify that she was his sister, that the papers were indeed hers. Why didn't Tomas come help the family and take them home to Miami? Antonia wondered about all this.

At last one day, at the end of two months in Nogales, Antonia received a letter from Tomas. He wrote: "Dear Sister, I received your letters. Sorry, I have been sick. But I will not forget you and will come soon with papers and a car for all of you, sincerely, your brother Tomas."

Yes, Tomas planned to borrow a car and come and vouch for them and bring some papers from witnesses that knew Antonia and her family. He planned to drive them to Miami. But that day, like the snail that yet crawled across the sandy beach, never arrived. Antonia remembered the priest, Father Simon the blind man; she thought that after four years of waiting for a priest, finally, Julieta's predictions that a priest would come to visit them and offer the Holy Mass, had come true.

For Antonia and her family, stranded on the wrong side of the border, waiting for Tomas to come for them became crucial. The *when* would her brother Tomas come for them, when would that day come, the family did not know, but it was an unknown that required hope, faith, and love. Lorena thought again about what Telesforo had said of why the ants went out every day to gather food. She remembered what Lepo had said about blowing on the overnight coals in the morning to bring new life into them.

They had not eaten a full meal in two days. In the evenings the last few days they had sat outside on the hotel's porch to watch people and cars go by. One evening, Santos, while being held in his mother's arms, said "I am hungry," but his mother rocked him in her arms and said "Go to sleep Santos, go to sleep."

A neighbor woman in her chair sitting out in the porch said, "The little boy says he's hungry."

"No," Antonia said, "He's sleepy," then she rocked Santos and whispered close into his ear, "Go to sleep, my son."

Santos whimpered and said again, "I'm hungry."

Neighbors sitting there on the porch responded, "The child is hungry, he says he's hungry."

Antonia excused herself and returned to her room with her children as if to give Santos something to eat, but she simply gave him some water. Then she hummed "*Roo-aloo- duermete mi hijito*," over and over again, "Roo-aloo-my son, go to sleep." Santos eventually fell asleep in spite of his growling stomach.

Lorena left the room in the scant daylight before dusk and walked down to the main plaza near the church and solicited her usual few coins, hoping for enough money to buy Santos something to eat. She prayed inwardly, but many times she thought of stealing some fruit from the fruit stands or some bread from the nearby little food store. Someday, Lorena, plotted in her heart, she would steal enough food for Santos to eat a full meal. She remembered when she had done that many times before when she robbed her Aunt Tila's cheese room for

The Worm in my Tomato

chunks of cheese to take home to her mother and Santos, when they had lived in the village hut in El Mezquitalito.

Another month went by; Antonia had run out of money. Santos asked his mother one day, "Where are the *santitos*, mother?" He asked where her saints, her *bultos* and *retablos*, statues and pictures, were. Antonia said, "The saints are in the trunk." Santos, already six years old, having learned from Julieta and from what Telesforo said, had great faith and a spiritual sense, went and knelt beside the trunk and prayed: "Father give my mother much money, *muchos tostones* and *pesetas*, give her many twenty-five cent pieces and fifty cent pieces and dollars: she needs money to buy food for us to eat, please help her," Santos blessed himself, full of a child's faith.

Presently, after Santos had prayed, there was a knock on the door, the telegram messenger man handed Antonia a money order. Tomas sent his sister twenty dollars. All in the family were relieved: they could eat. With the money Tomas sent, the family went out to a restaurant and had a full dinner. Antonia carefully had divided the money, a part for food, a part for rent, and saved some for when hopefully they could cross the border. She bought a postage stamp, an envelope, and used some writing paper from the hotel, and she wrote Tomas another letter thanking him and with an urgent message to hurry up and come for them. But days passed and Tomas had not arrived to help Antonia and her family.

"Uncle Tomas is not coming," Lorena said, she wrung her hands, "We have to do something desperate, we have to go," she paced about the room, like a young tiger, "We have to cross over, cross over now, we must sneak over somehow, or we can go again to beg the American border agency."

Antonia agreed with Lorena and they both hurried out of their hotel room and scurried down the street a short block away from the *Aduana*. "Perhaps we can bribe the American agent to re-do our papers and sign off our papers?" Lorena suggested more to herself than to her mother. She waved away a bee that buzzed her ear and threatened to sting her in the head. "But we really have no money," Lorena sobbed, yet she knew that she had to breathe life into the cold embers waiting to come alive.

"His talk through his mouth always differs from what he says

The Worm in my Tomato

through his eyes, like if he wants us to bargain with him," Antonia abruptly said, "Hurry, let us go talk with the American agents on their side and see what they say." Mother and daughter hurried over to the American side agency office and once more they spied for the tall big round red faced American agent they had last talked with. He was standing outside the office. Antonia said, "We want to go home, we are American citizens." He remembered them; he stepped back into his office. Antonia and Lorena followed.

"Woman you can not go home as a family, the papers may not be yours, their description of the family does not fit yours in number, you can not go home, and furthermore, don't come back."

Then suddenly, Lorena blurted out with a fast demanding reply, "But I am an American, I was born in Miami, Arizona, my birth certificate proves it," Lorena handed the agent her certificate and school report cards, "I want to go home and go to Bullion Plaza with Miss Yoakum." Every word sped out like a bullet seeking its target.

The man looked at Lorena directly and he studied her vital statistics in her birth certificate and he looked at her report cards, and then he said firmly, "You can go."

Antonia, in great surprise and disbelief said, "She can go?"
He answered, "Yes, she can go," Then forcefully added, "Not you all as a family, but she can go separate, she has papers that match her age, gender, physical description and she speaks English; she has those grade report cards from a Miss Yoakum, showing the spelling of her name *Lorena*; she is an American citizen."

Antonia's eyes twinkled; Lorena knew she had an idea, and Antonia and Lorena turned around, hurried out of the office. Lorena quickly turned her head and said, "Thank you sir."

The Worm in my Tomato

Thirty Four

Lorena
Self-Confidence in the bargain

Antonia and Lorena returned to their hotel room. Lorena rushed through the door and took her small suitcase from under the bed and she packed her dress, the gunny sack with her shoes, and other clothing items.

"You must go Lorena before the American officer changes his mind," Antonia said, "We are allowed to cross the line to purchase in stores in Nogales, Arizona like tourists, but this time you can get on the bus and leave for Miami."

Lorena led the way out into the street. They went to the Nogales, Arizona Greyhound Bus Lines depot. Antonia inquired about a ticket from Nogales to Miami, Arizona for a fifteen year old; she also inquired about time of departure. The depot ticket clerk asked, "Two ways, go and return, or one way?"

Lorena promptly responded, "One way; one way."

"The ticket costs four dollars and fifty cents one way and the next bus will leave this afternoon at five." The ticket master said.

Antonia asked for one child's ticket.

"If children are not in the parent's arms and occupy a seat, same price for all as adults, four-fifty, please." The ticket master said.

But Antonia searched in her purse and discovered she only had two dollar bills and a dollar in change. She turned aside sadly and quietly said, "I will have to come back later."

Antonia and Lorena returned to their hotel room where Antonia began to think out loud wondering from whom she could borrow two dollars. "Who could lend us two dollars?"

Lorena wondered what she could do; perhaps, she should hurry down to the street plaza and beg, she thought. No, she knew that would only result in a few pennies. Lorena did not know what to do;

The Worm in my Tomato

suddenly, an idea flashed in her mind. In a desperate quick move, Lorena yanked her suitcase from under her bed and took out the shoe box from the gunny sack. "I will be right back, mama," Lorena said, as she hurried out the door.

This time, on her way to the plaza, Lorena carried with her a box marked "Miami Commercial Company Store and the black lettering on the box read: 'Black leather patent shoes'. Lorena's brand new shoes were in the box. Even the receipt was in the box: "Commercial Store, Miami, Arizona." Lorena read out-loud and then said out loud to her shoes, "My father purchased you my shoes for me to wear on our trip to Mexico, my traveling shoes; my pride and joy; I intended to save you forever." They were part of her story, she thought, but yet Lorena knew what she had to do: "You shoes will never fit my feet again," She said. With tears in her eyes, Lorena stood in the plaza square by the church and called out to passers-by "Shoes for sale, new shoes for sale; new shoes for sale."

A well-dressed gentleman stopped in front of Lorena and asked to see the shoes. Lorena noticed that he wore a dark blue suit like her father used to wear. He looked like a kind father of some little girl, Lorena thought. He looked at the shoes. He said, "I have a little girl

"After you get off the bus in Miami, hurry up Sullivan Street to La Paloma Café, it has a blue sign with a white pigeon; run to the dove."

The Worm in my Tomato

and these shoes are just the right size." Lorena's heart leaped up to her throat. "How much do you want for them?" He asked quietly.

Lorena remembered that her father five years before in Miami had paid three dollars and fifty cents for her pair of shoes. Lorena was not sure how much the shoes would cost now. She said, "Could you give me five dollars?"

The man responded, "Five dollars, oh, these are brand new shoes, patent black leather, so beautiful, that I just know my little girl will love them. "*Bueno pues*," he said, and did not bargain with Lorena. "I will give you five dollars." He gave Lorena five dollars American money. Lorena gave him the box with her black leather shiny shoes.

"Thank you, sir," She said.

The man took the shoes and walked into the street and mingled with the crowd. Lorena stood there on the spot, clutching her five dollars, and she looked at the box with her new black shoes, held firmly under the man's arm, as he hurried away. In her heart, Lorena said good-bye to her shoes, purchased for her by her father years ago, from the Miami Commercial store. Now a complete stranger carried them in the shoe box under his arm. Lorena followed her shoes with her eyes until she could no longer see the shoe box.

Lorena ran into the church and knelt in a pew in the cool shaded side of the aisle. Lorena, with tears in her eyes, gave thanks to God, and she thanked her spiritual mother, the Virgin Mary of Guadalupe, who lived in Mexico, and she thanked all the angels and saints.

Lorena ran home wondering if the man who had bought the shoes was for real, or was he an angel? He had not bargained with her nor disagreed. He just simply gave her the five dollars. Lorena was so elated. She skipped, she ran and skipped, like she had done many times with her friend Mary Cota when going to Bullion Plaza School, and later when she ran and skipped with Eligia on their way to the village school. Lorena ran home, into her corner of the room, and she cried softly.

Antonia, who was ironing a basket of clothes for a neighbor, to earn money, asked Lorena, "Why do you cry?"

Lorena whispered, "I sold my shoes." Antonia said nothing, she understood. "Mother," Lorena repeated, "I sold my shoes." She was so happy, yet so sad. Lorena laughed and then she cried, almost at the same time.

The Worm in my Tomato

Antonia looked at Lorena, and said nothing more. Lorena looked up at her mother, and she saw a tear rolling down her mother's cheek, tears welled in Antonia's misty eyes. Antonia knew how much those shoes had meant to Lorena. But now Antonia and Lorena were rich, they had a lot of money. Enough to buy the bus ticket to Miami, enough to purchase back their future, and enough even to buy a cracker for Santos to eat.

That same day at four in the afternoon, Antonia and Lorena rushed to the bus depot in Nogales, Arizona. Lorena purchased a one way ticket to Miami, Arizona. Antonia reminded Lorena: "After you get off the bus in Miami, hurry up Sullivan Street to La Paloma Café, it has a blue sign with a white pigeon; run to the dove."

The bus left at five in the afternoon on the hour. With the fifty cents that Lorena had left over in change, she purchased sugared candy orange slices. The blue bus with a painted greyhound dog on each side of the bus drove away from the station driveway. Antonia had seen Lorena get into the bus. Antonia had told the bus driver that her daughter was on her way to Miami, Arizona. Lorena had left her mother crying in the bus station, and Lorena had waved good-bye to her mother through the glass window.

The Greyhound bus traveled very fast all that late afternoon. Sometime in the early evening the bus arrived at Tucson. Lorena knew because the bus driver had called out, "Tucson." He looked at Lorena and said, "You keep your seat." Many passengers got off the bus and then many others got on and took their seats. Soon the bus drove into the evening. Finally, late at night the bus swept over the highway down from the western Pinal Mountains and drove into a town with lighted streets.

The bus stopped on a side street. The driver opened the door and said, "Miami." Lorena jumped out from her seat and hurried out the bus open door. She waited for the bus driver to retrieve her suit case from the cargo bay. Then the driver hopped back on the bus and drove away with a loud swoosh sound. Lorena was the only passenger that got off the bus; the night was dark and cold. No one was waiting for her. The lamps on the street posts were on; large black bugs swirled about the light bulbs. But where were Augustine and Rumalda? Lorena wondered.

She knew that her mother had sent a telegram from Nogales to Rumalda and asked her to meet Lorena at the bus depot in Miami.

The Worm in my Tomato

But Antonia had told Lorena that if no one was there to meet her, for her to walk up Sullivan street to La Paloma Café, and ask Mr. Mora to help her find Augustine and Rumalda.

Lorena did as her mother had instructed her to do. Lorena walked from the bus depot over the bridge near Sullivan Street; she turned uptown and walked to the Paloma Café. She hoped that the owner, Mr. Mora, would help locate Augustine, Rumalda, and her Uncle Tomas. In the distance Lorena saw the red and blue sign, "La Paloma Café" and she hurried her steps. Lorena rushed into the café. Mr. Mora was there, Lorena remembered him. He seemed to remember Lorena, too, even if she was five years older. "Oh, are you the little girl of Fortunato, Fortunato Vega," he said smiling.

Emotion suddenly overpowered Lorena and she haltingly said, "Augustine and Rumalda were supposed to meet me at the bus depot but no one showed up," Lorena blurted out, almost crying. She was frightened and disappointed.

"Don't worry," Mr. Mora soothed, "I know Augustine and Rumalda, they eat here sometimes; we will help you find them. How are your mother and your father?"

"My mother is in Nogales, Mexico waiting for my Uncle Tomas, but my father died in San Blas; my mother buried her cross that is why we are coming back."

There was that night in the café a man named Jesus, a friend of Mr. Mora, and he said, "Oh, I know Tomas Carbajal," he stepped closer to Mr. Mora, "I've seen him around, sometimes he's not well, but I will see where he is tonight."

"You could take her to Augustine and Rumalda and later inform Tomas about his niece being here," Mr. Mora said, "But first let us feed you young lady."

Lorena suddenly became embarrassed and thought that Mr. Mora perhaps had seen how skinny and dirty she must have looked, half starved. Lorena sat down in a booth and Mr. Mora ordered a plate of *menudo* for her. A woman waiter brought a bowl of steamy, hot tripe broth. "Oh this is so delicious," Lorena had not had Miami's *menudo* in five years, "The broth is thick with the cow tripe cut and diced in large squares." Lorena scooped up a spoon-full of *menudo*, but it proved too

The Worm in my Tomato

hot for her. Lorena filled her plate full with green onions, cilantro, and red chile sauce. Lorena blew on the *menudo* to cool it and she slowly spooned it into her hungry mouth. All the while, Lorena recalled the time when she, Luisa, and Eligia had eaten Luisa's *menudo*.

Later, Mr. Jesus took Lorena to Augustine and Rumalda's house located at the corner of Sullivan and Davis canyon, close to the La Paloma Café. Augustine and Rumalda were so happy to see Lorena. They had not been at the bus depot because their alarm clock had not gone off; they apologized to Lorena. Augustine had worked the Swing Shift at the mine but had gotten off early, came home and decided to take a nap, but at ten o'clock tonight he had planned to be at the bus depot. The clock alarm, however, had failed to ring. They apologized, again and again.

Mr. Jesus left to look for Lorena's Uncle Tomas and inform him that she was home with Augustine, Rumalda, and Rumalda's sister Belen. Belen was paralyzed and sat in a wheel chair, in the living room. Belen, a prayer woman, was already praying for Lorena's family. Rumalda's daughter Leonarda hugged Lorena and gave her a glass of Kool-Aid with chipped ice. Lorena felt safe and comfortable with Rumalda and her husband Augustine. Both were good friends of her family. Rumalda hugged Lorena again, "Welcome child, my I can't get over how you have grown, why you are a teenager, already." Rumalda tried her best to help Lorena feel at home. "Let me show you where you can sleep." Lorena wept from happiness, as she melted into the arms of Rumalda; she felt so tired and she softly cried.

Next day, Mr. Jesus came to Augustine's house early in the morning. Lorena learned that Jesus had found her Uncle Tomas. "Sometimes Tomas gets sick and has his problems, but at times he can stay well for weeks. He is trying to cure himself," Jesus said, and he sat down to drink a cup of coffee. "Alcoholism is not easy to cure, but I think he is much better now. He and his Anglo-American wife, Nellie, are taking part in some kind of program and trying to stay sober, but one thing I can say about Tomas, he is a very intelligent man, can fix radios, anything electrical; he is a good man."

That very morning, Tomas came to see Lorena; she thought to herself about how her uncle had changed from the last time she had seen him. He still was of medium height, his black hair combed straight back, but he was not plump anymore and he had lost his beer belly. He was very happy and hugged Lorena, and tears flowed from his eyes down his freshly shaven face.

Lorena's Uncle Tomas asked her, "How is my sister Antonia doing?" He wanted to know about Catalina, Jose, Samuel, and Santos. He laughed out loud when Lorena told him that they were all well and packed and waiting for him to go with a car. Lorena told him where to find her mother at the hotel San Carlos, and begged him to please hurry and go to help them.

He said, "I have papers and signatures ready. I had been waiting to borrow a car." He stood on his front toes and stretched up his arms in sheer joy, "But now I have borrowed a car; I will go first thing tomorrow morning. I will prove to the authorities that Antonia is indeed my sister." He said out loud as if practicing: "Antonia Carbajal Vega is my sister, she was born in Morenci, Arizona in 1895; I will tell them and show them the papers." Uncle Tomas left amidst the goodbyes and well wishes of Augustine, Rumalda, and Lorena.

Lorena turned to Leonarda and said, "You know Leonarda, five years ago I wanted to stay and live in my Uncle Tomas' house and not go to Mexico, but my father insisted I go, but now my Uncle Tomas will be our saint and answer mother's prayers, and bring our family home." Lorena looked up as if praying, "Yes, Julieta, I have faith; I am never afraid of the snake."

"What did you say, Lorena?" Leonarda asked.

"I said that I am not afraid of the worm in my tomato, anymore." She looked at Leonarda tenderly: I will be waiting."

End

The Worm in my Tomato

Glossary

Spanish word used in the story	English translation
Acequia (s)	Irrigation ditch to water crops in the fields.
Adobe	Sun dried bricks made from clay mixed with straw.
Aguascalientes	Capital city of the state of Aguascalientes, Mexico.
Águila Mexicana, la	The Mexican eagle whose image is on the Mexico's national flag.
Alianza Hispano Americana, La	A mutual help organization started in Tucson, Arizona in 1894; provided insurance benefits and social events.
Aliso, el	The Aliso hamlet.
Atole	Méx. A breakfast drink made from ground, cooked corn; Simmer; sweetened and spiced with cinnamon.
Bacori, el	The Bacori hamlet, village.
Bolas de hueso	Round shaped balls made of ground bone.
Brasa (braza)	Wood or coal ember after fire glowing in the ashes; live coal, red-hot coal.
"Bueno pues"	Well, all right; yes.

The Worm in my Tomato

Bultos	A statue; a statue of a saint on the altar.
Burros, burritos *(small burros)*	(Coll) Méx. In Arizona, food wrapped in a tortilla.
Caballón	(Coll) Describing a large man metaphorically as being as large as a horse.
Caballada, la	The herd of horses.
Cachimba (s)	(Coll) Sinaloa, a small metal or tin holder for oil and wick used for providing light.
Carpas, las	The Tents.
Catre (s)	Folding cot usually made of canvas used as a bed.
Chicharrón (es)	(Coll) residue of hog's fat; pigskins; crackling, fried pork skin.
Chihuahua, Mexico	Capital city of the state of Chihuahua, Mexico.
Chile or Chili	Hot pepper.
Chingar	(Coll) Méx. to take advantage of someone.
Chocolate	In the story the dog's color as chocolate or brownish gray.
Chorizo	Pork or beef sausage seasoned with chile.
Cielito Lindo	Popular Méx song; beautiful sky, heaven.

The Worm in my Tomato

Cinco de Mayo	Mexican celebration of victory against the French Armed Forces in the battle of Puebla, México on May 5, 1862.
Cochitos	(Coll) Mexican sweet bread in form of piglets.
Cocido	(Coll) Mexican vegetable and meat soup.
Cocina	Kitchen.
Comal	A round clay sturdy disk used to cook corn tortillas. A flat cooking iron.
Compadre (s)	Co-father, godfather with respect to each other
Conejo	Rabbit, in the story a rabbit to be ensnared.
Corrido (s)	A ballad, Mexican ballad about a person or place.
Cristero (s)	Christian rebel against Federal troops in Cristero Rebellion of the Catholic Church versus the Federal Mexican Government, 1926-1929.
Cuaresma	Lent.
"Cuatro Milpas"	Four Cornfields; popular Méx. Song of 1920s.
Culiacán	Capital city of the state of Sinaloa, Mexico.
Curandera -ro (s)	Healer, -ra woman healer; -ro man healer.
Día	Day; daylight.

Día de los Muertos, difuntos, el	The Day of the Dead; All Souls Day, Nov. 2nd or Nov. 3rd if the 2nd falls on a Sunday; The commemoration of the souls of all the faithful departed. Prayers are offered for the dead.
"Dios padre, ayudanos por favor"	"God our father, help us please."
Diseño (s)	Sketch, drawing; outline, design; describe land boundaries.
Don *m*; **Doña** *f*	Spanish title used before Christian names.
Don "Chonito"	Mr. "Chonito"; nickname for the name Encarnación
Dulces de bisnaga	Cactus candy made from the pulp of a bisnaga, a round barrel shaped cactus aprox. two feet high.
Ejidos	Communal lands given to Indian pueblos to cultivate, including forests and pastures.
El, la (*pl* los, las)	*definite article*: the. / *Demonstrative pronoun*: that.
Él,	*pronoun personal masculine*: he, it; him, it.
Empanada (s), empanaditas,	Pie, apple or pumkin turnovers; small turnovers.
Empanadas calientitas	Pies, turnovers that are fresh and warm.
Encomienda (s)	A native Mexican Indian population of great number under the care of an Encomendero responsible to promote European (Spanish)

civilization, language, economic skills, and peace during the time of Spain's rule of Mexico, for exchange of free Indian labor, but not land, for personal benefit and gain.

"Es verdad" "It is true; true."

Fariseos Pharisees.

Federales Federal armed forces, federal troops.

Felíz cumpleaños, mi hijita Happy Birthday my little daughter.

Fiesta (s) Celebration (s); holiday; holy day.

Fiestas Patrias Patriotic celebrations like Cinco de Mayo.

Fuerte, el The Fort; the town El Fuerte is seat of government of the municipio El Fuerte located north in state of Sinaloa, between the municipios of Ahome on the west and Choix on the east and adjacent to the south border of the state of Sonora.

Garbanzo Chickpea.

Garita; Aduana Sentry box; customhouse; border immigration office.

"Gente Puente, La" "The Bridge People" build bridges to solutions.

Gloria Paradise; heaven.

Golfo De California Gulf of California.

Gringo (s) repatriados	Foreigner (disapproving name) repatriates.
Guadalajara	Capital city of the state of Jalisco, Mexico.
Guamúchil	Méx. m. a tree that produces a fruit like the mezquite.
Hacendados	Landholder; cattle rancher; plantation owner.
Hacienda	Landed estate; ranch.
Hectare (s)	Unit of surface or land measure equal to 2.471 acres.
Hierbabuena	Mint; mint tea leaves.
Estufa (Hornillo)	Kitchen stove.
Horno	Oven; in the story an outdoor oven.
Hostia	Sacred Host of the Eucharist in the Catholic Mass.
Huerta	Vegetable garden; fruit garden.
Huevo (s)	Egg, eggs.
Huizache, el (Huizache)	Shrub; tree in Sinaloa; several species; its flowers are very aromatic.
Imprenta	Printing press.
Ixtle	Fiber of the pulpy leaf or heart of the maguey plant with which ropes are made.
Jacal	Mexican native Indian hut.

Jalisco	Second state south from Sinaloa bordering the Gulf of California.
José	A given male name spelled with an accent over the letter 'e' but in the story spelled as preferred without an accent.
Jugada de Póker	Game of Poker; card game.
Kilómetros	Kilometer, a unit of length equal 1000 meters; one mile equals 1.609 kilometers.
La, la (s)	fem. of el; *definite article*: the; *Demonstrative pronoun*: that.
Laguna	Pond, lagoon.
Ley Iglesias	Federal government law of January 1857 by a liberal legislature striking at the Church, sought to lower what it called exorbitant charges for administering the sacraments of the Church. Ley Iglesias along with Ley Juárez, and Ley Lerdo formed the legal basis of the Reforma and were included in the Federal Constitution of 1857.
Ley Juárez	Restricted the authority of the military and ecclesiastical code of laws to cases concerning canon or military law, but required matters in civil or criminal law involving clergy or military personnel to stand trial in civil courts.
Ley Lerdo	Ley Lerdo of June 25, 1856 stipulated that land property should be owned by private individuals

The Worm in my Tomato

and not by the church or corporations and a Liberal government legislated disentailment of corporate property that barred ecclesiastical corporations from owning or administering property, to prevent lands from being untilled or unproductive. The law was incorporated as Article 27 in México's Constitution of 1857 which required native Indian pueblos to subdivide their communal lands (ejidos) among pueblo families that tilled them. Church haciendas were sold intact to the rich and created more large haciendas in the agriculture of México.

Leva   Draft; Recruited by force into the Mexican military.

Limonada   Lemonade.

Llorona, la (s) las   The Weeping Woman; the weeping women.

Mañanitas, las   To serenade some one in the morning or at night with a song named "Las Mañanitas" to celebrate one's birthday.

Manteca   Lard.

Manzanita   Little apple.

Mariachi (s)   A music group varied in number but made up of string, and wind instruments such as violins, guitars, trumpets, and vocal singers. Mariachi groups play at weddings, dances, parties, and other types of festivities. The group members wear colorful charro-like outfits with large sombreros (hats).

Matachines	A group of dancers in church services that lead the procession down the church aisle toward the altar.
Mayo (s)	Mexican native Indian tribe of northern Sinaloa.
Menudo	Beef tripe soup.
México	The Republic of México located in North America has 31 states and a Federal District. The spelling of the country's name in its own land uses an accent over the 'e' but in the story in some situations the accent is not used.
Mezcal	A strong alcoholic drink extracted from the agave plant.
Metate	A large rectangular rock supported on three legs of the same rock and hollowed out towards the front that inclines forward in which deep space are placed corn seed, cacao, and other grain to ground into paste by grinding the seed with a circular hand held rock made for thet purpose of pounding the grain.
Mezquital	The name of a Rancheria.
Mezquitalito, el	The Mezquitalito (Rancheria) of Mayo natives.
Mezquite	Large tree whose bark produces a golden colored gum; its fruit consists of long string beans containing large edible seeds within; shade tree.

Mi	Adj. possessive, my.
Mihijo (mi hijo)	My son, m. hijos, children.
Mijita (mi hija)	f. Daughter.
"Mi niña"	f. Child, girl, my child.
mm	Millimeter equals approx. 0.04 inch of rainfall. mm.
"Mocho", el	The stub limbed; man with a missing arm, hand.
Muchacha (s), (o) (s)	f. Girl, maid, servant girl; m. muchacho.
"Muchos tostones and pesetas"	"Many quarters and half-dollars, money."
Municipio (s)	A municipio forms a small part of territory within the state. Sinaloa has eighteen municipios Each municipio has various communities governed by a town or city council (Ayuntamiento).
Nanita	Great grandmother.
"Nato"	Nickname for the name "Fortunato."
Niña (s) f. Niño (s) m.	Child; children; baby girl (s); baby boy (s).
Noche	Night; in the story the name of the dark colored dog.
Nopalitos	Prickly cactus, edible.
Noria (pozo)	Water well; a draw well.

Norte, el	The North; immigrate to "al norte" to the United States.
Novenas	Nine days of prayer in devotion to God or in honor of a saint.
Novenario (s)	Nine days of prayer; usually the rosary is said on behalf of a soul of a deceased person.
Our Lady of Guadalupe	The conquest of the Aztec Empire occurred in 1521. Ten years later on December 9, 1531 the Blessed Virgin appeared to Juan Diego, an Aztec convert to Christianity. She impressed her image on Juan Diego's Tilma (Cloak). Today, the Mother of the Triune God is titled Mother, Queen and Patroness of the Americas. Countless faithful from all over the world have come to visit her Basilica in México City. They can still see her image on the Tilma.
Palanca	A lever; pole to carry a load in the middle of the pole by two persons, one at each end, or by one person with loads at each end of the pole, well balanced.
Pan	Bread.
Pan de huevo (conchas)	Conch round shaped Mexican sweet bread; contains eggs.
Pan dulce	Mexican sweet bread.
"Para afuera, para afuera"	"Get out, get out."
Partera	Midwife.

Patrón (es)	The Boss, bosses, owner of the ranch, hacienda.
Pendejos	Stupid; coward; dumb; a profane word used to cuss.
Peras de hueso	Pear shaped tizas made of bone.
Peruli	A hard small candy made from red syrup and shaped like an upside down cone set on a toothpick size stick.
Pitahaya (s	Any of several types of cacti bearing edible fruit.
"Pocho"	Disapproving term applied by people of Mexico to Mexican Americans because of their manner of speech of the Spanish language judged to be inferior.
Pollos	Chicken, pullet, hen less than one year old.
Posito	Small hole dug along river to collect filtered water.
Potrero, el	Land dedicated for pasture; a place to care for colts and fillies three years or less of age; a pasture.
Prensa Mexicana, La	The Mexican Press or Spanish language newspaper.
Presidente Municipal	Mayor of a town or city.
Provincias Internas	During the rule of Spain, northern Mexico's political entities and the area north of Mexico in what is now the southwest of the United States, comprised the Internal Provinces, administered by Spain's

administrators and Commandant Generals,
1540s to 1821, and then administered
by the Mexican Government until 1848,
when with the end of the United States-Mexican
War of 1846, became United States Southwest
territory and later several states.

Pueblo (s)   Native Mexican communities located in the
                     rural areas, the country side of Mexico.

Pulque   Méx. An alcoholic drink obtained from the
                     fermentation of the sweet natural juice
                     extracted from the agave plant.

Quelites (Espinaca)   Méx.Wild spinach; leaves used as food;
                          various edible green plants.

Quesadilla (s)   A cheese crisp; a tortilla with melted cheese.

Ramada   An outdoor lean-to or hut usually attached
                     to a larger habitat and used for living
                     purposes, usually a kitchen area for
                     cooking outdoors. A ramada has a thatched
                     roof and sometimes covered walls.
                     The whole structure is made of tree poles,
                     branches, and other plants suitable
                     for constructing it.

Raptar   Rape.

Rancho Grande, el   A Mexican song of life on the ranch.

Reforma, la   A Liberal political path for rebuilding Mexico
                     as a nation combining economic capitalism
                     and social conscience, 1856-1860s, termed
                     a middle-class revolution secured by three

main national laws: Ley (Law) Juárez that changed long-standing practices of military and ecclesiastical code of laws; Ley Lerdo that sought privatization and circulation of property, and ended the ejido or native Indian communal lands with the result that Indians became wage laborers on the haciendas; Ley Iglesias forbade the Catholic Church to charge exorbitant fees for granting the sacraments. The national Constitution of 1857 included the three laws of the Reforma.

Repatriación

Repatriation: 1929-39, Department of Labor's Bureau of Immigration with the help of local state, county, and city law enforcement searched for Mexican immigrants and urged them to return to Mexico on trains and in this way removed them from welfare relief during the Great Depression in the United States.

Repatriar

To repatriate; to deport to one's country.

Retablos

Flat pictures of Saints; framed pictures.

Río Fuerte, el

The Fuerte River originates in the Sierra Madre Occidental and traverses the northern most part of the state and empties into the Gulf of California.

"Roo-aloo-duermete mijito"

A lullaby song sang softly or hummed to lull children to sleep. "Roo-aloo-go to sleep my child."

Saguaro	Giant cactus, its edible fruit matures in July.
San Blas	Town in the municipio El Fuerte in the north part of the state of Sinaloa across El Fuerte River on the east side. It has a train depot.
"Santitos"	Diminutive term of endearment used by attaching ito (s) m. or ita (s) f. to names of persons, animals, plants, etc. ex. Lupe, Lupita.
Sarape	Méx. A type of woven blanket made of wool or cotton weaved in a variety of bright colors.
Señor	Mister; sir; a homeowner of property, of a place. Title of respect. Mr., abbreviation of Mister.
Señora	Mistress; Title applied to a married woman; owner of property, homeowner. Mistress, title of respect. Mrs., abbreviation of Mistress.
Sephardi Jews	A Jew of Spanish or Portuguese origin or ancestry; Sephardic, adj.
Sierras; Cordillera de montañas	Mountain range
Sierra Madre Oriental	Eastern Mountain range.
Sierra Madre Occidental	Western Mountain range.
Sinaloa	State of México located south of the state of Sonora, México facing the Gulf of California and Pacific Ocean. Eleven rivers originate from the Sierra Madre

Occidental in the west and flow into
the Gulf of California and the Pacific Ocean.

Sitio (s)   Location; cattle ranch.

Suero   Whey; yellowish sweet liquid separated
from the curd in coagulated milk in the
fermentation process when making cheese
When the whey rises to the top of the vat, it
can be skimmed and may be fed to hogs.

Tacos   A tortilla wrapped around cooked food as
meat, fried potatoes, and beans. In a corn
tortilla taco, the tortilla is fried crisp and folded
in half to hold the fried beef, lettuce, sliced
tomatoes, and ground cheese.

Talega   Méx. (Coll.) A large canvas water bag used for
carrying water or to hold water for drinking.

Tamales   Méx. Corn dough smeared on corn husks
wrapped to hold cooked beef meat and
other added edibles like olives, potatoes, and
chile; the wrapped meat in corn husks are then
placed in a large pan to cook under steam.

Tápalo (s)   A shawl with which a woman covers her head
and parts of her face.

Tardeada (s)   Evening gathering for a social event by
neighbors in a backyard or a public place that
may include music, dancing, and eating.

Tizas   Méx. (Coll.) A white powdery ball shaped
bone- made tool used to smear

the bottom of a frying pan or other cooking utensil, in lieu of lard, to prevent food from sticking to the pan; smear with bone powder to keep tortillas from sticking to the hot iron.

Tortilla (s)
Flat 1/8 inch thick round eight to twelve inch diameter pancake-like bread made of white flour; smaller ones made from maize or corn flour.

Treaty of Guadalupe Hidalgo, the
A peace treaty signed between the United States and Mexico to end the war of 1846. The treaty was signed on February 2, 1848. By this treaty Mexico ceded to the United States its northern territory which today includes several southwestern states.

Tuerta, f, (to), m., (s)
One-eyed. In this story the one-eyed cow.

Tunas (Nopal)
Edible fruit from a variety of cacti. Red pear-shaped prickly pear cactus fruit.

Vamos
"Vamos" Let's go; get out.

Vaquero (s)
Ranch hand who works with cattle and horses.

Xochiquetzal
According to Aztec legend Xochiquetzal the mother goddess of sustenance nurses (suckle) dead cradle aged babies in the land of water and flowers.

Zaguán
Entry way into a home; hall, vestibule.

Zanjero (s)
Field worker who manages the irrigation ditch water flow to irrigate the fields and crops.

The Worm in my Tomato

Epilogue

Time did not erase our remembered pain; we had not known how to grieve it out. By keeping our sorrow buried in the depths of our heart and hidden in the recesses of our mind, we had prolonged it. We needed to bring our lived experience of the Repatriation into the light of our life. So that just as our day to day life emerged out from an unknown eternity and into our present, we lived it, and from that lived experience, our past liberated us to continue in renewed hope, faith, and love and to help heal our wounds and expectations for our future. In this way our fears of the unknown ended.

Antonia with her two daughters Lorena (left) and Catalina (right), when Antonia lived and worked in Florence, Arizona. Later she moved back to Miami, where she lived until she died. Lorena was at her side and closed her mother's eyes.

The Worm in my Tomato

Lorena (above, right) in time married and she and her husband, Arthur Reade, raised their family in Phoenix, Arizona. She taught bilingual catechism at St. Agnes Catholic Church, in Phoenix, for twenty years. She continues to teach Spanish-speaking catechists. She teaches Spanish to English-speaking students. She is Lay Carmelite of many years.

Catalina (above, left) in time married and she and her husband Vicente Valenzuela raised their family in Miami, Arizona. They celebrated their sixty years of marriage.

Catalina and Lorena visited Bullion Plaza School on September 7, 2007.

Jose C. Gutierrez worked in Miami, Arizona. When the United States entered World War II and the government began the military Draft, Jose's name was the first selected from the basket in the Arizona Draft. He served in the U.S. Army. After honorable discharge, he raised his family in Seattle, Washington. He died on March 6, 1982 in Brinnon, Washington.

The Worm in my Tomato

Samuel C. Gutierrez returned to Miami, Arizona in 1944 and brought Julia and their family from Mexico. He worked in the copper mines as an electrician. He died in Douglas, Arizona on June 4, 1987.

Back row standing, L to R: Ernesto Hernandez, Donna (last name unknown), Salvador Portillo, Beatriz Portillo, Ernesto Robles, Antonia C. Vega. Front row seating are: Thomas G. Carbajal and Maria H. Carbajal (newly weds) September 17, 1921 Miami, Arizona. Antonia participated in her brother Tomas Carbajal's wedding in 1921 prior to leaving Miami on the Repatriation train in March, 1932.

The Worm in my Tomato